THE IN-BETWEEN SERIES

THE HOPE

SAGAR CONSTANTIN

Published by BUOY MEDIA LLC

Cover design by Juan Villar Padron,
https://www.juanjpadron.com

Special thanks to my editor Janell Parque
http://janellparque.blogspot.com/

facebook.com/SagarConstantinAuthor
amazon.com/Sagar-Constantin/e/B093NXD4C2
twitter.com/ConstantinSagar
linkedin.com/in/sagarconstantin
instagram.com/sagar.constantin.author
bookbub.com/authors/sagar-constantin

BOOKS IN THE IN-BETWEEN SERIES

- ***The Life***
- ***The Ring***
- ***The Hope***

1
AN UNWANTED DECISION

My heart is pounding as if I had just run from one end of In-Between to the other. I stand in front of the door to the mirror aisle. Seriousness hangs in the air like an embracing enemy. *An urgent task* said the Master, which will be crucial for the Ring to succeed. I take a quick look at my watch; I still have two minutes before I have to meet him. Before I left Thomas, Luke, and the others in the Ring, I asked if they knew any more than I did, but they didn't.

The walls hover on either side of me, and the characteristic stripe on the floor that shows what part of In-Between you are in is blurred. It's with a certain awe that I stand here. I have been here a few times before, each time with a different seriousness. My gaze wanders around to ensure no one else is here, and I hold my breath.

I take a few deep breaths to slow my heartbeat. But that doesn't seem possible. What could possibly be worse than what I have already gone through? I remember Thomas's words, *say only what you know*. Right now, I only know that the Master wants to meet with me. Slowly, I lift my arm and approach the small green, almost invisible circle on the wall. The door slides silently to the side. A cold breeze flows toward me, and I take a step back. Several chills follow and strike me like miniature lightning bolts. The mirror aisle appears in front of me. The air feels as thin as if I were back on top of the mountain in the Himalayas, and I gasp for breath. I did it. I found both Meera and Luke. The rest should be straightforward, but the Master's tone suggested otherwise. I gulp the cold air down in small chunks.

Everywhere, I can see representations of myself in the infinite mirrors. My feet only move forward in small jerks. The whole room is like one big mirror, and if I didn't know better, I would never find the door to the Master. As I stand there, I suddenly see glimpses of my life with Andreas rushing by.

I close my eyes and see it all as if it were yesterday: the day Luke was born, the three of us lying on the bed while the birds began to sing the morning welcome. In the hours afterward, Andreas took off because he claimed he had to pick up some important papers at the office. The vulnerability that arose when I was alone with such a fine and fragile little newborn. Three hours later, he returned with a gold chain with a heart-shaped pendant. The left side was silver and the right side gold, and where they met at the top was a diamond. He looked at me with wet eyes. "Eva, you are the gold, I am the silver, and Luke is our diamond." Work was just a pretext for escaping. I swallow and let the past slip away. How will Andreas cope without Luke? Why should Luke not have a whole life on Earth? The questions hang in the air, so I can almost touch them, but I cannot find the answers.

The cool breeze from the mirrored corridor makes me open my eyes again. The light is intense. It's easier to see everything clearly here in In-Between. Experiences and challenges I have struggled to understand in the past make sense here. When I was actually alive, my thoughts multiplied with explosive power like a virus that grabbed one's interior. The thoughts turned into worries and reproaches of myself, always with a destructive false sound that played so loud that I could not hear my heart: when I was not at home with Luke and got engrossed in work; when I said yes, and, in fact, meant no. It was an eternal source of remorse and noise within me. Now, I can turn down the false tones and see how I ran for my life and never got to prioritize what made me happy. What made me happy was impossible to hear. The thoughts still exist, and not a day goes by that I don't visit the memories and consider whether I could have done something differently concerning Luke.

The difference is that now I can hear the pure tones from my heart and turn off fake and noisy ones—observe them and let them go without giving them any attention. It has undoubtedly taken time to get here and hours of practice with sessions, watching the personal development program, and meditating every day. I look down at my feet and wriggle the tip of my red sneakers up and down a little. Of course, it has helped to be here in In-Between, but… STOP. I am allowed to praise myself. The mirrors around me reveal a smile on my face. Now, my toes are seriously twitching inside the sneakers. The mirrors double my smiles and send joy back as I begin to stroll down the corridor.

The Master has sent for me, and only me. Why the others in the Ring are not invited is puzzling me. Before I can think the thought to the end, there is a quiet hissing sound, and a narrow section of the mirror wall slides aside. Down the hall to the left is the door to the Master's room. I will never forget the first time I stood here. At the time, I knew nothing about the Ring and my mission on Earth. It would not have been so inhumanly challenging to decide had I just known what I know today. But isn't that the case with all the choices in life? If it were possible to look into the future, I would not have learned to listen to myself, learned to stand firm when uncertainty was about to suffocate me, or when the noise drowned out the melody from my heart. Maybe I would have enjoyed it more if I could have seen the road ahead clearly. The same could be said about life. My mind slips into the uncertain, and I walk with slow and almost silent steps toward the door. My heart starts beating faster and reminds me that I don't know why I am here. But what is the worst that can happen? I try to force a little laugh, which turns into a cough instead. I am dead. Luke is dead. What else can happen to me? I stop my thoughts and say to myself that the worst *is* over—it must be.

"Come closer, Eva. You're just in time."

I know the sound of the soft, warm voice with the patient pauses between each word. A smile creeps across my face, and I have to moisten my lips, so they don't crack. The door to the Master is right in front of me. It is ajar, and I gently push it open with my fingertips. The light from the large windows facing the garden flows toward me so that I can only just glimpse a sea of shaggy red flowers on the large bushes next to the mirror-shiny lake with crystal-clear blue water. Several white swans walk around with straight necks and beaks pointing to the sky, like majesties in their own kingdom. My feet move so slowly that I am about to stumble. No doubt my brain had planned a faster movement but had not been able to coordinate it with the rest of my body. Opposite the door is a large bed with a dark wooden frame and white linens. In the corner to the left hangs a crystal chandelier, glittering in all the rainbows colors, sending fine reflections onto the white walls. There is something utterly magical about the Master's part of In-Between—something I have never experienced anywhere else up here. It is as if the air is more transparent with more clarity—like thousands of tiny particles from pollen that light up in the air and increase the intensity, followed by a friendly high tone which at first is alluring, but in the long run, can be both intrusive and annoying like tinnitus. To the left, the Master has an office as minimally furnished as the rest of his area. A table and a chair, at least that's how it was the last time I was here. Along the wall to my right is a bookcase with thousands of books. It is more of a book wall than a bookcase.

The sun's rays stream through the large window and illuminate the chalky white wingback armchair. He sits like a dark shadow leaning back. Pending. A pair of crutches could do wonders. My legs feel like matches that could easily break or be knocked away under me at the slightest impact. The lightness and laughter from before suddenly seem like a strange part of me and are quickly replaced by an insecure breeze that tries to knock me over.

Maybe it can get worse?

Maybe the worst part is not over at all!

I raise my hands and rub my palms hard over my face to wipe my thoughts away and be present. I take one step closer to the Master. It's like walking toward an invisible wall of energy. There are only a few feet between us. He leans forward in the chair and looks at me. Even though I am on my way forward, my body is swaying back. The sun's rays outline his long white beard and slender but muscular body. His dark brown eyes glow and look directly at me.

"You have come a long way, Eva." He gets up slowly and steps, almost floating, toward me. I want to move but cannot. My feet do not obey and feel fused to the dark marble floor. I'm at least a head taller than he is, but that means nothing; the energy around him is so powerful that it could overthrow an army with a light movement. It is not size that matters here.

"I know it has not been easy for you. I also know that it has been a great challenge and that you have been close to giving up." He speaks slowly and with a precise pronunciation of each word as if every word carries the whole sentence. I stand completely still and do not blink. In fact, I doubt I'm breathing at all.

His long beard slightly moves when he speaks. "But for the Ring to return to Earth and spread the insight and awareness necessary, I have one last task for you to carry out." His grave countenance reveals the seriousness of the situation, and he maintains an intense gaze directed at me.

The pause between the words seems even longer. If I could just get out of my shoes, I would move backward, where the intense energy pressure was less invasive. If I did not know better, I would have thought my heart had stopped beating. It is utterly silent inside me. There is not a thought. Not a sound. Nothing.

"Frank," he says.

My lower jaw drops, and I reach out, probing for something to support me. There is no superfluous furniture that can help me. Before I have time to change direction, I've backed into the huge bookshelf, and the books begin to fall out of it like flies. Automatically, I reach out and manage to catch one as it's falling. The others lie scattered around my feet. "The Book of Secrets." The book in my hand has a faded cover, and the spine is tattered.

I had happily forgotten all about Frank. Naively, I believed everything would work itself out as soon as the Ring was assembled —that my part of the mission was over. Higher powers would take care of Frank. My mouth is still hanging open, and I want to protest, but nothing happens. If only I could bury myself under the books and just disappear for a moment.

The Master stands completely still in front of me. His warm dark glow makes his long thin white hair that hangs down to the tip of his beard light up. "I will ask you to find Frank." The words hang in the air like ice crystals refusing to melt. Out of the corner of my eye, I can see two swans strut past; if only I could move so carefree. The large oak trees sway gently from side to side, sending a cool breeze through the open door to the garden.

"But that's not all...." The Master takes a step toward me. I try to take a similar step back, but I am already leaning against the bookshelf. If I move in the slightest, I will be bombarded by an avalanche of the books still in their place.

"I..." my mouth feels like sandpaper and will not voluntarily let the words out. "I thought we were ready to...." My gaze is fixed on the floor. The "Book of Secrets" gets a kick, sliding across the floor. The Master quickly stops it with his foot. My core feels like a centrifuge whirling all my emotions into great chaos. *FRANK.* I'm so tired of Frank. Why can I not be allowed to enjoy In-Between with Luke? Can somebody make Frank go away once and for all, please?

The Master doesn't get a chance to say anything before it slips out of my mouth. "Why are you asking me for all this?" My voice is straightforward and perhaps a little more accusing than it was meant to be. "I chose to stay here in In-Between and left Luke. I went back—I did everything I could. Everything you asked for." I hold back, feeling the heat from a tear making its way down my cheek. It burns against my skin. As I catch my breath, it dawns on me that my inner warrior has taken over. "Courage" lies at my feet too. It also gets a proper kick. It slides across the dark marble floor and only stops when it bumps into the bed. "Why can't we just get ready and take care of Frank later?" Although I would like answers, I don't leave time for him to answer. "How much damage can one man do? No one takes him seriously anyway." I try to force a laugh, but it becomes more of a sigh. "Frank is just a poor soul longing for recognition." Our gaze meets again. "He is an idiot." This time, the power of the Master's gaze is even more intense. He doesn't say anything, and that's an answer in itself.

A cloud glides in front of the sun, and the very intense and powerful light diminishes. I wish I could rewind my life and just be journalist Eva for a moment with an ordinary life and simple tasks like making money and cooking dinner. The Master blinks slowly. There is a spark in his eyes like stars twinkling in the sky. Very subtle and fragile energy embraces me gently and slowly spreads in my body. It holds me and gives me strength.

"Okay, I'll do it." I can hear my own words but am not sure I agree with what comes out of my mouth. Before I have time to think more about it or withdraw it, the Master raises his hand.

"Good. You're leaving in an hour. But remember that you must be ready in ninety days for the final departure with the Ring. Preparing for that is a part of your task. You have to stop Frank so he doesn't spread the word about In-Between, and get yourself ready." He looks at me as if it were the most straightforward task in the world he has just given me. Each word is in strong contrast to the silence between them.

My head feels as heavy as a concrete block, but I manage to keep it up even though I just want to disappear into the pile of books and feel sorry for myself. The Master's gaze is locked against mine, and I am not allowed to escape.

"What about Luke…?" I ask, stammering.

He starts walking back toward his armchair. "Luke is fine. He is in his own process here. Eva, you must concentrate on yourself and the task. Luke did not die; he is in a coma. When his 42 days are over, you have to decide if he is going back to live with his father or if he should continue on the journey of his soul." He turns around and looks directly at me.

I move away from the bookshelf and fight my way toward him. "But I cannot send him back. He is part of the Ring." I strike out with my arms, trying hard to force a response out of him that can make the chaos inside me subside.

"It's your decision, Eva. And only yours."

2

AN ENEMY RETURNS

The door slides shut behind me, and I look at my mirror image, revealing my red, swollen eyes where the spark is off. Stunned, I stare blankly into the endless renderings of myself in the mirrors. Will it ever end? The challenges. Will they disappear or just get smaller? There is a strange mixture of joy and abandonment inside me.

Luke is not dead; he's in a coma. I bite my lip. The pain is nice, like a friend I can count on. When I was with the Master, I could not come up with any questions. Now that I'm out in the mirror aisle, they appear and double up in the mirrors. The Master said I should be ready to leave again in an hour. But why me? I must be the one who hates Frank the most. Why can't Yoge or Shiva go? There is only one thing to do, and that is to find Thomas.

I grab my Skycon and tap on Thomas's picture. My finger leaves a sweaty imprint on the screen. A moment passes, and the image begins to move. Thomas is running around outside. In front of him, Luke is jumping from cloud to cloud. "Hi, Eva." Thomas stops and breathes heavily.

I enlarge the small picture in front of me to see it better but do not say anything. Luke stops a little further ahead and turns to Thomas. "Where are you going? Can't you catch me?" His frail voice resounds in the mirror hall. A lump gets stuck in my throat. Why is it not me who is playing with him now that I have the opportunity? Why should I be sent down to Earth again when I would rather be here?

"Thomas…" I clear my throat and try hard to control my tone of voice. Wherever I look, my image is thrown back at me. I try to focus on the image of Thomas, which effortlessly floats up from the device and projects a picture in front of me.

"Wait a minute, Luke, I'm coming." His clear, almost transparent, blue eyes light up the image where the clouds have settled around him, making it impossible to see Luke.

"I need to talk to you." My tone leaves no doubt. "Now."

He holds the Skycon closer. "What is going on?" Thomas's warmth beams through the image. He stands completely still and looks at me while a drop of sweat runs down his forehead. There are no signs of any worries on his face. For me, the Ring has suddenly become a burden and a challenge I don't want to wrestle with.

"Can we meet?" I look away and start walking back and forth in the mirrored corridor with small quick steps. Wherever I look, my mirror image reveals my clenched teeth and wrinkled eyebrows that highlight the streaks on my forehead. Thomas's image floats with me wherever I turn.

Thomas has half an eye on Luke all the time. It's only possible to see Luke's hands; the rest of him is inside a cloud. "Of course. Do you want to come out here? We are next to the maze."

Suddenly, Luke jumps out of the cloud and runs at high speed directly toward Thomas. He holds a lump of cloud in his hands, which he throws at Thomas's head while he laughs. The laughter abruptly stops when he sees my picture on the Skycon. Thomas has disappeared in the cloud ball. "Hi, Mom, where are you? When are you coming out to play? This is the funniest place." Thomas waves the cloud away and reappears. "You little bandit." He grabs hold of Luke's waist and lifts him with one arm, so he hangs and twitches his legs.

I nod my head up and down in mechanical jerks, "I will, Luke; I'll be there soon." Finally, I manage to breathe all the way down into my stomach, and a bit of the pressure eases.

"Well, see you soon," Thomas has a firm grip on Luke, who is struggling to get free. He succeeds.

"See you, Mom!" He waves and backs into a cloud hanging behind him. He's one big laugh.

The picture disappears, and I'm left alone in the mirrored corridor. The light descends from the ceiling without direction. It's cold here, much cooler than anywhere else in In-Between. It is not an ordinary cold where the heat is lacking. It's like little snowflakes that are almost invisible. They tingle gently on the skin. There is a slight clicking sound. A section of the wall slides to the side. Almost hovering, the Master steps out of the opening and comes toward me. My body is petrified. He has only been outside his room twice before while I have been here. Once was when we said goodbye to Annabel, the other when the Ring was assembled. Now, he is standing right in front of me.

Maybe the worst is not over yet. His long white beard hangs loosely down over his shiny gold coat, where small stones glitter down the sides. There is a very special expression in his eyes, an expression I have never seen before—staring without being empty. In a quick motion, I put the Skycon in my pocket. Calm and effortless, he raises his hand and lays it gently on my head. My body is about to collapse, and I bend forward. I rest my hands on my thighs and try not to fall to my knees. It feels like an iron plate has hit my head, even though I know with my common sense that it is the Master's hand. My legs begin to tremble, and I tighten the grip on my thighs so much that I only have a tight grip on the jeans fabric. My eyelids slide shut, and in front of me appears a picture of the older woman with the wrinkled face and thick braids.

Around her pupils is a luminous clear ring. She helped me while I was on Earth and stood behind my chair when the Ring was gathered in the octagonal room. She is one of my many incarnations that have fed me with glimpses from previous lives. If it had not been for all the glimpses I received from previous lives, I would never have found the last two members of the Ring. The context would have eluded me. It was like being allowed to flip through an old book with stories that had threads connected to each other in the finest way.

"Eva," the Master's voice pulls me back to the mirrored corridor. "You left before I had time to tell you the last thing." He speaks with his usual calm and long pauses between words. I can still feel his warm hand on my head. It sends energy waves through me and down into the floor, which acts as a lightning conductor. The older woman has sat down in front of me in the mirror aisle, but there is no representation of her in the mirrors. She nods and smiles so the wrinkles on her face fold together and radiate infinite love. Then she disappears again, just as fast as she came. The image is almost wiped away. I try to straighten up, but I only manage to raise my head, so I have eye contact with the Master again.

Something tells me he knows the older woman. His words interrupt my thoughts. "In order for you to help bring back the insight and awareness that the world needs, you must go through a development process yourself. Before you can show others the way, you need to know it yourself. Therefore, the next 90 days will be marked by challenges you must solve before the Ring can gather and travel back."

I put my hand on the mirror next to me. The cold from the mirror chases through my body and makes me straighten up. "What challenges?"

"I cannot answer that." He stands completely still in front of me with his hands folded in front of him. His voice is calm and resounds deep in the hallway.

"But what about the others? Do they get challenges too?" My

tone is determined, and the words are thrown around the corridor, so they sound louder than they were meant to.

"You are all at different stages of development. All of you need to be so clear in your consciousness that you can light up and guide others on the path."

"But, but what about Luke…?" I move my hand from the mirror, where it has left a clear imprint. Every little muscle is tensed, and I bite my teeth hard together.

The Master slowly removes his hand from my head and looks me straight in the eyes. His gaze is like a sword cutting through my ego. "Luke is the only one of you who has the opportunity to go back to his present life. Therefore, it is imperative that you do not influence his development. Even though you have to make the final decision for him, he will have a say too." The Master bows slightly in front of me. "Under no circumstances can you tell him about Frank."

"Why?" My question reaches out to the Master, but he turns around and disappears into the opening in the mirror wall. It closes silently behind him.

3
AN OPEN HEART

Luke comes running at full speed toward me, making the clouds swirl up around his small feet, and throws himself into my arms.

"Mom, I have missed you soooo much." The sky is infinitely blue above us, and below there are only swaying treetops to be seen. We are next to the large maze with the many paths. It was in the middle of this maze that Annabel kissed me. For the first time in my life, I experienced true femininity. That moment has a special place inside me and was the start of a far greater understanding of myself.

I hug Luke close. Finally, I can smell his sweetness and take in his gentle energy completely. My heart opens, and heat begins to flow to all the small cells in my body. He opens the holiest space inside me—the most vulnerable place to let another human being into, but also where the rewards are infinite and indescribable. Once the heart is open to another human being, it is too painful to close it again; Thomas said that to me several times. Now, I know what it means. Whether I can keep my heart open, time will tell because it's probably easier said than done. But at this moment, right now, Luke presses his tiny soft nose against my stomach and tightens his grip further. It's because of Annabel that I have opened the door to my feminine side; she helped me find the key and pry open the lock. I did not know that was what I was missing in my life. Before, frustration and fear filled me every time someone came close, not that I was aware of it. Now, Luke's presence means that love expands even further. There is more and more space inside me.

Thomas appears when a cloud loses its grip around him. His face lights up with a smile when he catches sight of me. His long black coat floats slightly out from his body, letting the boots with gold laces stand out. He doesn't seem to be in a hurry to get to us. I close my eyes, so all my attention is on Luke.

How long we stand there is not important. Every little cell in my body expands, and the heat flows through me and out through my hands and onto Luke. He loosens his grip and looks at me.

"Mom, look here." Luke bends down, grabs a piece of cloud, and puts it on his head. "Isn't it cool?" There are many clouds to pick from; they have settled like a soft duvet around our feet.

Suddenly the Master's words pass through me; *Luke is not dead.* Does Thomas know? I cannot inquire about it right now because I don't know how much Luke knows and understands. The wind grabs my hair; I get it in my mouth and spit it out promptly.

"What's going on?" Thomas steps closer and puts his hand on my shoulder. I stand with my arms stiffly down the sides of my body. My whole body is tense again without me even noticing it—like a bow ready to send an arrow toward the target. But there is no target to be seen.

"I'll tell you later." My head jerks toward Luke.

"What is it, Mom? Do you have a little surprise for me?" Luke jumps up and down on the spot and throws his armful of cloud up into the air, where it stays. There is no one other than us and complete silence. Only the rustling of the wind in the leaves of the labyrinth can be heard. The main area is some distance from here, and on the other side of In-Between, there is usually more activity.

I smile at Luke and run my hand over his blond hair that hangs slightly down over his eyes. "Yes, you could say that I have."

He gets excited and starts dancing around the place while making the most adorable expression with his head tilted. "What is it, Mom? Tell me? Is it a delayed birthday present?"

I look over at Thomas and hope he will come to my rescue, but he smiles and shakes his head. Then I will have to create a distraction myself. "Come, let's see who finds the middle of the maze first." I know the way through the maze from before and know that Luke will easily find his way too. He has already sprinted off, and Thomas has followed. They get a head start before I set off. The bushes of the maze are completely dense with small green leaves. Luke's light strands of hair appear at intervals.

"The one who comes last is a rotten banana." Luke's voice is spiced with laughter that hangs in the clear air. I run as fast as I can, and if it were possible to leave all my worries behind me and just enjoy the moment, I would.

The bushes are taller than last time and full of small white flowers with no scent. It's like running through a maze of summer and innocence. Here, there are no problems, no challenges. I run and feel a slightly hovering sensation every time my feet land on the cloud. Silence follows, and every time I set off, it's as if I am getting closer to myself—around the corner and another one. Neither Luke nor Thomas is to be seen anymore. All I can see are bushes and narrow passages in different directions.

A loud shout, followed by Luke and Thomas, who jump out right in front of me from their hiding place behind a bush, tears me out of the silence. Instinctively, I step back and fall onto the bushes, which gently cushion the fall. Luke and Thomas look at each other and laugh aloud as they give each other a high five.

"We got you, Mom!" Luke struts with joy and winks proudly at Thomas.

After recovering for a few seconds, I let out a slightly scratchy laugh. "You got me!" I reach out for Luke, "You cheeky little monkey."

"Help me." Luke chuckles with laughter, sending a pleading look at his savior.

Thomas throws himself on top of us. The bush gives in, and Meera comes into view. She sits at the picnic table in the middle of the maze with her elbows resting on the table, staring blankly into the air, and does not move an inch when she sees us. Her skin is fair, and her hair is cut like Cleopatra's. I try to turn around, but it's impossible since both Luke and Thomas lie firmly on top of me.

"Hi," I stammer, but she doesn't hear me. She looks fragile, almost transparent, as she sits there on the bench. The black color in her long hair has been washed out, and now she looks like the Meera I met at Lucy's place. Although Meera can be frighteningly harsh, as she was after I told her about In-Between, there is a depth to her, something ancient. It seems that harshness is her defense and that she has used it to protect herself.

Thomas rolls down from the bush, lands on the path of clouds, and gets on his feet. He brushes the cloud off his coat and reaches out his hand to me. I take it. Luke grabs his coat and pulls himself up. They both have their backs to Meera and have not seen her sitting on the bench. Once again, we are surrounded by green bushes with small round leaves in the maze, which have risen and provide cover for Meera.

Thomas looks at me. Right now, he doesn't have to say anything. Heat flows from him, and the care on his face shows how much he loves and values me. It's clear that he has missed me while I was away; he keeps looking at me and takes every opportunity to put his arm around me. Although he has been here in In-between for a long time, he also seemed pressured at times. He was not worried about whether I would find the last two in the Ring; he was more concerned for me. That's what Shiva mentioned yesterday. Thomas knew I was facing an inhuman choice. First, to choose between Luke and my development, and then to travel back and find out that my son was the last member of the Ring.

I have never in my life experienced being seen the way Thomas sees me. When I had been working on a story for weeks and got no sleep, the reaction from the editor when I handed in an article was often, "Well, you are finally done." I had to take care of the motivation at work myself. I think I was skilled and delivered good results, but it's not the same as when another human being acknowledges it. I often pondered how little we actually praised each other at the editorial office. No one said anything nice to each other; people got paid to do the work. It was as if something was taken away from people if they recognized others. Today, I get touched, and my energy rises when Thomas sees me or others do. It opens up to love and gratefulness when I see and acknowledge others. Not the same love you feel in a relationship, but between people. I take a deep breath, put my arm around Luke's shoulders, and pull him close. Thomas steps forward and lays his arms around both of us. We stand still without saying anything.

There is a difference between being recognized for something you do and for who you are. The way Thomas looks at me makes me feel seen in a very special way. Deep inside myself, it resonates in the same way as when a tone is hit completely pure, and it hangs in the air and vibrates. Together with Thomas, I no longer experience that someone or something is taken for granted.

The warmth from Thomas's hand flows into mine as our hands meet. We release the embrace, and together we walk around the last row of bushes before reaching the middle of the maze, where Meera sits at the old, slightly worn wooden table with benches on both sides. In a leap, Luke is in front of both of us. The path is narrow, and we have to walk behind each other. He takes a big step and looks triumphantly at me as the bushes stop, and he has reached the middle. "I came first!"

I can't help but laugh. He's exactly like me at the age of five. I also made contests out of everything, and no one knew they were a part of them until I had won. I turn to Luke. "You are so cool," and tousle his hair. "And you won," I wink at him. My hand reaches out for his, "This is Meera."

Meera must have heard us. She gets up and extends her hand toward Luke, who is hiding his face in my blouse. Thomas walks past and embraces Meera gently. Her arms hang limply down her body. When he releases her, she looks over at me and manages to say, "hi," before sitting back down with a blank look.

"Hi, Meera, how are you?" I ask.

She doesn't answer. Everything is still new to her, and I'm not sure if she has come to terms with being here. Her pink jogging suit makes her look even paler. This is the only table in the middle of the circle that the maze has shaped. The many words scratched into the table testify to the souls who have sought this place to find peace. "Help," "Mother," and "Light" are the words I can just read. Elsewhere, there are just dashes that count days. Luke lets go of my blouse and crawls up on the bench at the opposite end of Meera. We sit down at the table. I sit next to Meera, who reluctantly moves, and Thomas sits opposite. When Luke gets bored, he hops down from the bench and disappears back into the maze. At intervals, his light hair protrudes above the tops of the bushes.

"How old is he?" Meera asks without looking at me. She runs a nail back and forth in one of the cracks in the table. Her eyes are marked, and her haircut is dead straight.

"Five," I pull down the sleeves of my blouse and cross my arms.

The dark wood on the table has a warm glow and is silky soft to the touch. The clear veins look like a river running from one end of the table to the other. In front of Meera is a half-full coffee cup.

"Imagine if you had the opportunity to start your development at such an early age." She pauses. Neither Thomas nor I say anything. We sit still and look at her, giving her time to be. No pressure, no agenda.

"I thought it would be easy once I was here," Meera speaks softly. Her fine, silky voice is a bit hesitant. "All my life, I have longed to get beyond, and when I met you, Ang… Sorry, Eva, you suddenly gave me… a… well, I'm not sure. I keep wondering if I wanted my ex to find me. Did I become less careful after I met you?" She frowns so that two deep gaps form between her eyes and takes a sip from the cup. "I was so afraid when he suddenly stood there in my living room with a knife in his hand." She starts to cry.

I don't know what to say and wait for Thomas to say something wise. The clouds above us glide past and shadow the sun. Thomas puts his black coat around her shoulders. She pulls it tight.

"Although it's great that we are gathered in the Ring, I still feel the fear and pain…." Meera looks up at me and then over at Thomas. The index fingernail cuts further into a new groove in the table. She tries to turn her body away from me, but it's hard when we are sitting on the same bench. I somehow remind her of the fear of her ex.

"It's completely normal. When we experience our deep fears, it will create swells internally. It is a natural part of the process. From today, we have 90 days to work on ourselves. We can look at the fear, the doubt, the anxiety, the anger, and all the other emotions that we carry." Thomas breathes calmly. His masculine charisma and calmness spread to Meera. He is like a rock you can lean on. She falls back into her energy and begins to relax. I notice how the rigid shield around her starts to crackle, and powerful feminine energy emerges. I felt precisely that energy the first time I met Meera at Lucy's. It disappeared the moment I told her about In-Between. Now, it's coming back. I cannot help but smile and see in Meera's eyes that she has noticed it herself. Without thinking about it, we start laughing—a heartfelt laugh. Meera turns to me, reaches out, and holds me completely close. "Thank you… thank you for finding me."

I stroke her long silky hair with my hand. I feel her body against mine and her fast heartbeats.

"Unfortunately, I have to go now." Meera loosens her embrace and gently squeezes my hands while she looks me straight in the eye.

"The Master has asked me to come. He'll send someone to pick me up at the cafe in 15 minutes." She looks down. "I'd rather sit here with you."

I know that feeling all too well. I've always had a hard time being in the present. There was always another place I would rather be. When I was traveling, I would rather be at home, and when I was at home, I longed to get away. Quietly, I look at Meera. I found the Master when I came here. Now, he is no longer a stranger to me. In fact, I enjoy being with him. It is always intense and often associated with significant challenges but still alluring.

A ray of sunshine creeps through a crack in the clouds and grazes Meera's cheek. "I would very much like to talk to you some more. Shall we meet in the café for lunch?" She pulls the hood of the pink jogging top over her gray hair.

A rush goes through my stomach; I have completely forgotten that I have to leave soon and that there will be no time for lunch.

"I cannot…." I stop myself. Is Luke listening, and does Thomas know? "You'll find out later, okay?"

Meera squeezes my hand; her hands are ice cold. "See you, maybe later today…." She looks over at Thomas, "Shall we have lunch when Eva is so precious?" She winks at me and gets a "yes" from Thomas.

"It's a deal, so we'll see if Her Majesty has time another day in her busy schedule."

4
AN UNEXPECTED REUNION

"Thomas…" I touch his arm and turn toward the maze's exit, away from Luke, who is engrossed in playing with the clouds on the path. He has built a small castle and a landscape around it. Unnoticed, we walk a short distance away from the table in the opposite direction so that we can talk without him hearing.

"I have to go back…." One word erases the previous one, so I'm unsure if I said it. My gaze wanders aimlessly around, and my foot kicks a loose piece of cloud. I press my tongue hard against the inside of my teeth, grit my teeth, and endure.

Thomas doesn't respond; he just looks at me with his infinite gaze filled with oceans of love.

"But maybe you already knew that?" I tap my fist lightly against my closed mouth. I try hard to hold onto the delicately vulnerable openness that just filled my body while Meera was here. It has evaporated. My inner warrior is back and has put up a shield to ensure I won't get hurt or show weakness.

"Does it matter if I knew about it or not?" Thomas looks at me and lets the question hang in the air until I catch it myself. I shake my head.

"I have the feeling it never stops." I look down, and all I can see are my red sneakers nearly buried in the white clouds.

"What never stops?" He gently puts his finger on my chin and lifts my face so that our eyes meet.

"The challenges… I thought I had reached the goal, and now comes a new unmanageable task worse than the one I just solved. The finish line is constantly moving as I approach."

Thomas picks up my hand and holds it with both hands. "If there were no challenges in life, don't you think you would be bored?" He narrows his eyes and sends me a teasing look—a raindrop lands on my cheek. The cloud above us is pitch-black.

Resigned, I shake my head. "But they seem to be lining up, waiting for me to be ready." I stare at him, trying to make him understand the seriousness.

"Do you remember the record?" One drop becomes more, but we remain standing. Luke has his little party running, and it doesn't seem like the rain is bothering him. The air is warm, and the drops are refreshing.

I run my hand through my hair. "The one where life runs in circles, and every time we learn something, we let go of an old belief or pattern and move a groove closer to the center—closer to ourselves."

"Exactly." Thomas maintains his gaze. "So, what have you learned?" He steps one step closer to me, so we stand completely close with our hands in front of us. The raindrops make a dark mark on his long, freshly-ironed blue silk tunic. A thin gold thread runs from the shoulder, which draws a pattern of a branch with leaves down over the arm. He looks like a prince as he stands there; the only thing missing is a white horse.

My hands are getting a little sweaty. It is not exactly the conversation I was expecting. I start fidgeting and break a branch of the bush next to us. I peel the leaves off in small jerks one by one before my courage has grown enough to look Thomas in the eyes again. "I have learned...." It's like looking for gold in a disused mine. This is how I feel when someone asks me direct questions. It's like I suddenly know nothing or can't grasp it. Since the branch has no more leaves, I break it into smaller pieces. Thomas patiently waits for me to open the door to the answers.

"I think I've learned to listen more to myself." I look up and wait for a reaction, but it doesn't come. "I have at least found out that not everything is as it seems and that I am not as conscious and wise as I thought. Probably not so cold and numb either," my mouth pulls up into a slightly cramped smile. "The greatest lesson I have learned is probably that I need to believe more in myself."

Thomas still says nothing. It would be easier if he just pointed out all the areas where he can see that I have progressed since I came here.

"Thomas, will you take care of Luke while I'm away?" I break the silence and throw the rest of the branch on the sky path. The black cloud has moved on, and the sky is filled with mountains of clouds in various shapes. The pale colors wrap themselves in the slightly darker ones in a chaotic pattern, and as far as I can see, it's cloudy.

He smiles, "There is nothing I would rather do."

Luke is still busy making his castle bigger and is standing inside it with the cloud walls around him.

"Do you think I should tell him...?" I hold back. It's time to check what I feel is right and not just ask Thomas because he's here, and that's the easiest thing. "I would like to take Luke to the dispatch room, so he can see how it works."

"It's up to you," Thomas puts his hand on my shoulder. "We better get going."

"Thomas..."

He lifts his finger to his mouth and moves his gaze. Luke has sneaked up behind the bush and stands right on the other side of us. He starts giggling. Thomas sticks his hand through the bush, grabs hold of Luke, and slowly pulls him toward him. Luke is in stitches, laughing. I wish I could borrow some of that lightness and zest for life. If only I could keep it in a bottle and take it with me. Then I could enjoy it in small doses while I am away.

"Come, let's go…." Thomas grabs my hand and pulls me along. We are heading toward the exit of the maze.

Luke's little hand crawls into mine. "Where are we going, Mom?"

"Luke," I stop and squat down in front of him. The bushes surround us, and Thomas stands behind me like an unshakeable rock.

"Why do you look so serious?" He grabs my cheeks and tries to model them into a smile. He succeeds briefly.

"I have to go back to Earth." I try to seem calm, but my whole inner self shakes.

"How cool, can I come with you? Then I can go and tell Dad about this place." Luke looks around, "Is there a time machine up here or a space capsule we're going with?" He jumps on the spot and looks around. I get up and run my fingers over my forehead. "Unfortunately, that is not the case. I wish it were." My voice is solemn.

Thomas looks at me, and I send an appreciative nod back. He will never break into my conversations or interfere without asking for permission. "Luke, we will have fun together while Mom is away. There are so many things I want to show and teach you. For example, do you know how to climb a cloud mountain?"

"No," Luke shoots his chest forward and crosses his arms. "Well, you're also a lot more fun to be with than my dad's girlfriend. She's really boring. When she looks after me, I'm just supposed to draw pictures."

"It's a deal then, no tedious tasks, just fun things until Mom's back." Thomas reaches out his hand, and Luke grabs it and shakes it with all his power.

"Auch, at least it's not weight training the two of us are going to do." Thomas pulls his hand back and shakes it. His eyes look like two sparklers that have just been lit. Luke brings out Thomas's inner playful child—the part of him which was never allowed when he was a child. Maybe they can learn from each other. Perhaps there is a meaning to it—to everything.

5

LET THE JOURNEY BEGIN

The car rumbles at high speed down the mountainside through the woods on the way to the city. The seats smell musty, and the fabric is a bit damp. I arrived at the exact same place where I said goodbye to my mother less than 24 hours ago. She left the yellow blankets on the back seat, and the empty bottles lay on top of them. I turn on the windshield wipers and press the button for the washer fluid, but the car just produces a hoarse hiss while the windshield is covered with long black streaks from several dead insects. Hoping to find something to remove the insect streaks, I pull over. My hand gropes behind the seat with no luck. I loosen the seat belt, turn toward the back seat, and move the blankets. A small piece of paper falls to the floor, and I grab it before it lands. Something has been written on it with slightly indistinct handwriting. I bring it closer; it's my mother's handwriting.

Dear Eva, I cannot tell you enough how wonderful it was to see you again, even though you did not look like yourself. A mother's love for her child is the greatest, but you know that yourself. I'm happy that you understand more about life and that we must all do what we can to help the world become a better place. Your Mother. PS. Your little thing is in the glove box.

I quickly grab the glove box handle and rip it open. There is my Skycon. It is flashing green, and I promptly click on Thomas's picture. *Searching.* Nothing more happens—the dot flashes and flashes. My hand is clasped tightly around it, and I'm sending off a thought. C*ome on now, work. Let this time be easier than last. Help me.* Although I managed to get in touch with Thomas without the Skycon last time, I would prefer it to work. I can't help but laugh at myself because, with all that I have been through of unthinkable scenarios, one would think that I had surrendered to the inexplicable, but I prefer the things I can touch. They are more tangible and easier to relate to.

Luke wanted to be at my dispatch, but I don't know how he coped when I was gone. It must be surreal to see your mother disappear—and probably also scary. I hope Thomas explains how it's possible to create a copy of the body you leave behind on Earth in In-Between, making it feel more normal, even though it's completely the opposite. And that I have my Angela body down here that was manifested when I went searching for Meera and Luke since I can't go back as Eva—another magical wonder of In-Between and something that I am the first to be allowed to do. No one has ever been allowed to leave In-between and travel back to Earth. Fortunately, children's brains are in every way more adaptable than adults' brains—or maybe just more adaptable than mine.

I drum lightly on the side of the Skycon, but it ignores me and flashes steadily on and off. It is almost weightless and only three millimeters thick. I'm quite comfortable leaving Luke with Thomas. They have their process to work on, and I have mine if we are going to be ready to assemble in 89 days. I hold the Skycon up in front of me while holding the note from my mother in the other hand. I dare not even think about what her words mean. Instead, I focus on the small flashing dot. It stops flashing, and the screen turns black. My eyes briefly slide shut, and I lean my head back. Obviously, nothing is going to be easy. I start the engine and turn up the heat. The air outside is cool, and the sun is about to set. It's a typical spring season—you freeze in the morning and sweat during the day. The fan starts with a deafening noise. I throw the Skycon on the passenger seat and press the accelerator so that the tires make tracks on the edge of the road. I have done without the Skycon before and will probably manage without it again. At least I choose to stick to that. I look back; there is no one else on the narrow gravel road with the mountain wall on one side and the abyss on the other. The car picks up speed and makes a few strange noises as if it's about to fall apart. The windscreen is still streaked with dead insects.

"Mom…"

I sit up with a start and accidentally press hard on the accelerator; it gives a jerk throughout the car.

Mild laughter spreads through the car. I quickly look at the passenger seat, where the Skycon has taken off to the floor. Luke's laughter is clear and distinct. I saw how my mother crashed when she reached for a drink for Luke, and I won't make the same mistake. Without hesitation, I step on the brake. The tires drag on the gravel, and a cloud of dust rolls up behind the car when it stops in the middle of the road. With a snap, I loosen my seatbelt and lean against the passenger seat. There, down between the seat and the door, lies the Skycon. I can only just reach it and pick it up with my fingertips. It flashes green.

The picture of Luke lights up on the small screen. Thomas is standing behind him. "Is that you, Mom?

I tap lightly on the side of the Skycon, so the image enlarges and floats up in front of me. Luke wrinkles his small eyebrows and puts his finger on the picture. "Why do you look like the Nanny from the other night?" He looks puzzled at Thomas.

Tears rise in my eyes and run freely down my cheeks as I laugh. "Luke…" The heat from the tears and the slightly salty taste fills my mouth. "It's me. I just dressed up in a different look like you do at Halloween." Thomas must have warned Luke because he does not look particularly surprised.

"When are you coming back?" He takes a sip of a red drink in a golden glass with a silver straw. They're inside the Ring's control room; I recognize the red table and the mint green egg-shaped chairs in the background.

My sleeve scratches lightly against my cheek as I try to remove my tears. The blouse will have to do as a tissue, and I dab my eyes to relieve the pressure from within. *I'm not alone this time.* Maybe I got closer to the center of the record. Perhaps I learned something to make the challenges easier to handle. Heat flares up in my cheeks, and I roll down the window. It chatters and squeaks, so it sends shivers down my spine. The air is still cool and refreshing.

"I don't know, Luke; there is someone I need to talk to first, but hopefully, it will not be long."

"I can also come and visit you. It looked mega cool when you took off." Luke grimaces and makes a quick movement with his hand. "Thomas has shown me around up here, and do you know that you can go out on the edge of the cloud and that you do not have to wear those boots?" His little voice speaks eagerly, and I sit still and listen. "We've also been over to see Dad. I drew a little mouse for him, the kind you drew for me too." His blue eyes glow, and at regular intervals, he blows his hair away from his forehead.

"Thomas!" My voice is a bit determined with an accusing twist.

He stands in the background and innocently shrugs. We both know very well that it is forbidden to give signs to the living. He is not a notch better than grandparents who look after their grandchildren and allow them to do everything they can't do at home.

I cough a bit; I don't want to be the harsh and boring mother. "I'm so happy that you are enjoying yourself, Luke. I'm looking forward to coming back to you." My finger sends an air kiss to him. Thomas reaches over and steals the picture. "Eva, we are here, and I think we should talk as much as possible." His blue silk tunic is a bit open at the neck, so I can see the little silver bear he always wears on a chain.

"It will make it a lot easier for me." I drum on the steering wheel and bite my teeth together.

"We will keep the connection open, so you can always reach us." Luke stands with his thumbs up and dances next to Thomas. He's only five years old and has already been through so much. The way he handles it makes me so proud and reminds me of how much humans can cope with. Often, we just do not know until we try. I put my hand on my chest and feel the necklace Thomas gave me when I was told I was part of the Ring. The pendant is a diamond-shaped, deep purple stone. In the stone is scratched a faint outline of a woman with her arms over her head. He said that the stone had been passed from one seeking human to another for many thousands of years. I tighten my grip around it. The sky opens in a big bang, and rain suddenly falls on the car. I zip my coat up and try to close the window again. Now, I better get the heat fully turned up, so there is hope for just a bit more warmth. The car rumbles and snorts a few times before sending more lukewarm air out of the air ducts.

"And you can always call me too."

I wish I could have talked to Thomas more before I left, so I could have asked if he knew why Luke cannot know about Frank. It makes no sense.

"Thomas, can we talk later?" I bite my lower lip lightly.

He steps closer to the picture so that the fine lines around his eyes become completely clear. "Sure, you can call when you're ready."

Vigorously, I wave as the image fades out and the screen turns black again. There is nothing to do but try to find Frank. The next stop is his apartment.

6

A FRIEND FOR LIFE

The stairs to Frank's apartment are worn, and it smells harshly of old urine. On the floor lie several old newspapers and some used needles. The last time I was here, it looked significantly more vibrant. Now, the place seems abandoned and like a magnet for homeless people. The door is open, and the lock lies on the floor. I step carefully forward. Whether my heart is pounding because I might meet Frank, or whether it's the uncertainty pouring over me, I don't know.

The old factory hall is devoid of furniture; even the large wall lamps are gone, only the raw holes in the walls and the dust on the floor are left. There's a hollow echo as I step on the concrete floor.

"Hello, is anyone here?" I proceed cautiously. This is where Frank tried to persuade Lucy to help reveal In-Between. Fortunately, he failed. Since that day, I have not seen Lucy and must admit that I forgot all about her after going back to In-Between. My body gets light at the thought of Lucy; she was always so cheerful and happy. It was a pleasure to be with Lucy. She always brought such naivety and optimism with her.

A rush runs through my body as I feel a hand on my shoulder.

In a quick motion, I turn around and take a step back. My hands are in front of my body, ready to defend myself.

A familiar laugh echoes in the empty factory room.

"Daniel…" I lower my hands but can't help but frown.

"Hey, Princess, how nice to see you." He folds his arms and is one big smile.

I stand with my mouth open, searching for words, but can't think of anything but repeating myself, "Daniel."

"Yes, that's me," he leans slightly forward and kisses me gently on the cheek, making his day-old stubble tickle my skin. I blink feverishly just to make sure what I see is real. The tinted glass in his sunglasses makes his eyes look almost black.

"Well, I don't have to come looking for you at your place when you come here regularly." He smiles his sly, slightly mischievous smile and winks at me. He is tanned and looks like someone who has spent two weeks on a beach.

"Well…" I exclaim but don't get to say anymore.

"I can see you let yourself in." He walks into the room, lifts his arms to the sides, and turns around so that the muscles of his well-trained body can be seen under the tight-fitting white sweater.

"The door was open; it's not me who," I hurry to interject since I don't want him to think that I'm the one who broke in here. I kick a stone on the floor and let my hands slide down into my pockets.

He grabs my shoulders and shakes them lightly. "I know it was Frank himself. He called me yesterday completely out of his mind. I've never experienced him so furious before." Daniel pushes his sunglasses up into his hair and looks at me with his deep brown, nearly black eyes. There's something about Daniel that I can't resist; that's why I insisted on not seeing him before I left here last time. He makes me feel like a little girl, innocent and naive. It's not bad, just unfamiliar, and not the best when I have to be proactive and determined.

Suddenly, his facial expression becomes serious. "Do you want to go get some lunch, then I can tell you what I know?" The pronunciation of the words is elegant and exudes upper-class dialect.

I look around at the empty space. There are no alternatives that can compete with Daniel's offer. "I would like to, but what do you know that could be of my interest?"

"Later, come on, Princess, your carriage is waiting outside." He takes my hand, and before I have time to inspect the apartment for signs of where Frank may be, we are back out on the stairway. Daniel closes the door the best he can, and together we go down to his red sports car, which is parked right in front of my pile of rust.

"I'd better take my car," my tone is insistent. I know Daniel is good at persuading me to do as he pleases, so I may sound a little harsher than I would like.

"As you wish," he kisses my hand and lets it slide out of his. "But we can also pick it up later, and then you could ride with me." He smiles crookedly, and I know very well that he's hinting that his car is much more luxurious than mine, but I avoid answering with a little strained pull of my lips. "No, thank you, mine runs like a dream."

He opens the front door so that I can get in. It creaks and sounds like the whole door could easily come off in his hands. "Shall we meet at the cafe by the park?"

I stop and look at him, "Sure, but give me one good reason to have lunch with you."

"I'll let you know what Frank is up to."

7
A MOMENT OF TRUTH

There is a slight hiss, and the door slowly slides open. Shiva enters the Ring's control room, where Thomas, Luke, and Meera are already gathered. Her long jet-black hair hangs loosely around her face. She walks over to the large sofa facing the mint green chairs where the others are already sitting.

"It's really nice to see you." She puts her hand on Meera's shoulder and gently squeezes it. "Have you become accustomed to all that has happened?" Shiva's dark eyes bring infinite depth with them. One can almost touch the calmness around her. She chews lightly on a piece of green chewing gum.

Meera shakes her head slightly. "I thought it would be easy. In all the years I have struggled to keep my soul's call encapsulated, I have imagined that I was on the right path. My fight is to stop fighting." She makes a line on her trouser leg with her fingernail and avoids looking at Shiva. Thomas and Luke are each sitting in their green chair. The light is dimmed, and on the table, several candles are burning on a large brass dish. Next to it, there's a carafe of water and several filled glasses.

"All my life, I have been different, believing in the good in everyone, fighting for nature, man, and the spiritual. I have been alone in my faith but have kept going." Meera keeps running the thumbnail across her pants, leaving long streaks. "But in a way, it's easy and noncommittal to believe and fight your own little battle; there is a certainty in that too." She reaches for the glass of water and takes a sip. "Now, all I have believed and hoped for has come true, and I can't stop thinking, what now? It's actually scary because I feel more alone now, more vulnerable than ever before." The flow of words stops, and Meera glances up at the large screens that hang over the dark red table and command the entire end wall of the room. They show pictures of crowds in big cities, busy roads, and people fighting. "Now, it's real. There is nothing I need to convince anyone else about." She narrows her eyes, "It is one thing to have a deep belief that the universe is a certain way. It's something else to find out that it is the truth."

Shiva is still standing by her side. The wrinkles on her face reveal the struggles she has fought, first as a child growing up in the slums. Later as an adult, where she had to flee from a human trafficking network run by a billionaire. She has carried the pain all her life. It was her willpower that drove her forward. She studied during the day and worked at a bar in the evenings. Her challenge was to transform doubt into trust and struggle into love. She couldn't defend herself when she was assaulted late one night on her way home. She lay on a dark road for several hours, bleeding to death. She wasn't found until the sun rose. By then, it was too late. She was allowed to stay in In-Between for a longer period to receive newcomers. It was Gabriel who trained her, and it was at that point that it dawned on him that the energy of the Ring had begun to manifest itself again. That was over fifteen years ago. Time in In-Between has helped her stand firm in herself and find peace. Now, she rests like a tree, solid with deep roots in the ground.

Thomas moves forward in the chair. "Meera, you are not alone; we are here, and if it can be of any help, I feel the same way." His heart gives several small punches as if it would expand, but he does not show it. They make eye contact.

"I will keep that in mind." She wraps a strand of her long gray hair around her finger.

While they have been engrossed in their conversation, Luke has been exploring the space. He has found again that everything is not just what you can see in In-Between. His hand glides curiously across the floating white walls of the room. A section slides to the side, and a cupboard with small bottles comes into view. He lights up with a big smile and resolutely reaches for a yellow bottle of juice and tastes it. He has not noticed that Thomas and the others are looking at him and are enjoying his immediate curiosity about life—a naivety and belief that all is well. Since the slightly sour yellow taste doesn't please him, he continues with the orange bottle on the shelf below. The excitement shines out of him, complemented by sounds of pleasure.

"What's in the bottles?" Meera leans over to Shiva.

"Different frequencies that can support different states of mind. Don't worry; they are completely harmless and will only work if you need the support."

Suddenly, Yoge storms in and glances around the room. His long slim body is covered by a loose-fitting black suit that is a little too short in the legs. He looks a little puzzled at Thomas and back around the room. "Where's Eva?"

Thomas sits back in his chair and glances over at Luke to make sure he's busy with his adventure. "She's back on Earth," he almost whispers.

"WHAT!" Meera hits the table so that the glasses rattle, and she gets up. "Weren't we supposed to be ready to go back together?" The blood rises in her face, which, in an instant, goes from being completely white to dark red. "I just sat here and bared myself, believing there was a point to this...." She stands with her back to the others.

Yoge pulls up his pants and steps on his own toes with his big clogs. "I can come back with my calculations later; it's probably better."

"No, wait, Yoge, we have to work together." Thomas looks at Shiva and tries to lean on her calmness. "I can say no more right now, but there is something Eva needs to take care of, and only she can handle it. Meanwhile, the Master has given us each our tasks here." Meera has graciously sat on the edge of the sofa with folded arms. Thomas feels an inner pressure. He knows he carries a tremendous responsibility now that Gabriel can no longer oversee their gatherings. The last thing Thomas heard was that Gabriel's energy level was down to a few percent. He only has enough energy to breathe and is under constant observation. No one knows how long he will be able to hold on. Right from the start, it has been Gabriel who oversaw everything concerning the Ring. Now, his job is to stay calm and get through the next 89 days, so he is ready to be sent down again. Thomas runs his hand across the chair's armrest and feels a creeping agitation in his stomach.

"I'm taking care of Luke while Eva is gone." Warmth spreads throughout his body. Luke opens a side of him that he had displaced. He helps him get in touch with the little boy who lives inside himself but was hidden away for far too many years. He looks up. The ceiling is one large window, where both light and dark clouds hang in several layers above them. Still, there is light in the control room, where the floating walls absorb the sound. Shiva leans forward in slow motion. "My task for the next 89 days is to learn to share from my source of inner peace. I still don't know how I will manage." She smiles and looks around at the others with her warm gaze while she gently leads a loose strand of hair behind her ear. Shiva has always kept to herself and talked to as few people as possible.

It's tranquil in the control room. They sit and look at each other with the certainty that each one of them represents a piece in a giant and extremely important puzzle. Without each one of them, the whole will not work. The clouds float past and let the sun's rays penetrate. Luke is still busy examining all the bottles in the closet. On the floor next to him is a circle of bottles in all the colors of the rainbow.

"I have been to the Master too." Meera clears her throat. "Am I allowed to say what he said?" She looks at Thomas, who gives an appreciative nod back.

"Nothing." She forces a laugh. "I just had such high expectations. That was the only thing." She looks at Shiva and over at Yoge, who answers her gaze. "Right now, I don't quite know what I'm going to do with it. But there is probably a reason for that." She looks intently at the others but then holds up her hand in front of her to signal that she doesn't want them to answer.

Luke has opened another invisible cupboard. This one is filled with snacks. Thomas has half an eye on him all the time, even though he would rather be fully present either with Luke or with the others. "We have 89 days to get ready; let's use each other as much as possible. The control room is at our disposal, and we still have our corridor." He speaks in a low voice, and he is about to continue when Yoge interrupts.

"My calculations show that the energy released in each of our energy systems when we gathered in the Ring is stable. This also applies to Gabriel, but the energy his body could absorb was significantly less than the rest of us. It's just enough to keep him alive, for now." Yoge pauses and grabs a notebook from his breast pocket; it's full of numbers and calculations. He flips through it and looks up. "The Master has pointed out that the energy will begin to decrease markedly after the 89 days have passed. When we travel back with the energy, it is important that we can all accommodate it; otherwise, it could have catastrophic consequences for our nervous system when we arrive on Earth." He looks in short jerks from one to the next and continues when he is sure they are listening. "When I say accommodate it, it means that the frequency is so high that our nervous system will burn out if we are not ready." He holds back. The thin hair on his head is sticking to the sides, making his marked right parting visible. He is wearing his classic black tight-fitting high-necked sweater, making him look even taller than his six-and-a-half feet. "I'm working on doing a test so we can find out if we're ready before we move on." He looks over at Luke, who has returned to the cupboard with bottles of all sorts of colors. Now, he is in the process of tasting a blue bottle. On the floor next to him lies a pile of snacks. "Who is taking care of Luke's development?" Yoge's gaze wanders again from one to the next.

"I am," Thomas folds his hands and rests his chin lightly on them, "I have promised the Master to come by with him later today. I know he has his own plans with Luke." He reaches into his pocket and grabs his Skycon. It flashes green; he looks up at the others and puts it back in his pocket. "Will one of you stay with Luke? There is something I need to look into." Thomas gets up while still holding on tight to the Skycon in his pocket.

"I'll stay here." Shiva stands next to Thomas and puts her hand on his arm. "Just go and take the time you need."

"Thank you, see you later," he looks over at Meera and Yoge. "By the way, Yoge, will you check on Gabriel later? He was supposed to call me this morning, but I haven't heard from him."

8

LET CURIOSITY WIN

"Thomas," his image appears on the small screen. I'm sitting in the car on the way to the park. Daniel is driving in front of me. "Thomas, I don't have much time. Are you alone?" I look briefly at the little picture on the Skycon while driving, holding it so no one else can see the device.

The clouds drift in front of Thomas, who waves them gently away with his hand. He is out on a ledge not far from the Ring's control room and is standing with his Skycon in his hand. "Yes, Shiva is with Luke." He buttons his long black coat around his neck and turns his back on the wind that blows his long hair forward.

The air in the car is dense and still a bit humid. But I cannot roll down the window because it will be impossible to hear what Thomas is saying. The light in front of me changes to red. Daniel keeps an eye on me in his rearview mirror. The traffic is heavy, and there are shops on both sides of the road with people rushing in and out constantly. They are out shopping for everything from clothes to hardware.

"Do you know why Luke cannot know anything about Frank?"

My tone is determined, and I quickly look down at the screen where Thomas shakes his head no.

"It's news to me." He struggles to get his long hair to stay behind his ears and not hit his face. It doesn't look like he will win that fight.

"You haven't told him anything, have you?" An elderly gentleman in a blue Volvo drives up next to me and stares at me. I send him a polite smile and pretend to speak on the phone.

"No." The clouds pass Thomas, and the wind blows into the microphone, so it's hard to hear what he is saying. He tries to hold his hand to cover the microphone but then lets his hair loose.

"Could Luke have a connection to Frank that we don't know about?" The light turns green, and I put the car in gear. The car behind me drives very close. It's a young guy with a buzz cut, busy texting while driving. I stay focused on Daniel's car and try not to judge.

Thomas begins to walk back and forth across the cloud. He gets a little distant in the eyes. "The only reason I can think of is that it has something to do with your or Luke's development and preparation." He pauses and waits. Then he shakes his head, "I can't think of anything else."

"But," I try to protest but give up when the car in front of Daniel suddenly brakes for no reason. Most of all, I want to push the horn but control myself. The thoughts come rushing back into my head; so much for staying focused. I can't stand any more challenges, even though I know it's pretty naive to think this task will be easy. The cars move again at a snail's pace, and several vehicles change lanes, hoping to reach their destination faster.

"The best thing you can do now is to be curious while you are there and see what happens. Have you found Frank?" Thomas does not allow himself to be distracted by the intrusive wind blowing his hair in all directions. His gaze is locked on the small screen, so it feels like we have eye contact.

"No, not yet. But I'm searching. Can you look for him? He was not in his apartment. Do you think that Luke could be in any kind of danger?" My voice is about to crack. "Frank will do anything to get his way!" The traffic moves again, and the cafe is around the next corner. I flip the indicator on, and the older man in the Volvo gives way so I can change lanes.

"I will take good care of Luke and ask David to search for Frank. As soon as I have any news, I'll contact you. Is that okay?"

Daniel turns right at the intersection and into a parking lot further ahead. I follow but slow down, so the car behind me almost touches my bumper. Now, it will soon be me who is honked at.

"That's fine. I hope you find him, and thank you for taking good care of Luke." I glance at the small screen. "I have to go. I'll call you…." The button on the side gets a light press, and the image disappears. I put the Skycon in my pocket before turning into the parking lot, where Daniel is already waiting for me. I don't like to hang up so abruptly. It reminds me of the blunt way we always talked to each other in the newsroom. People could call and ask for help, and once they got it, they just hung up without saying thank you or goodbye. I did not have a choice because Daniel is not supposed to see the Skycon. He opens the front door and extends his hand. "Welcome."

I reach out and send him a shy smile.

"This way," Daniel leads me along a narrow gravel path that leads up to the most idyllic little white house with lattice windows and pink roses that climb up the walls. There are several tables outside where people eat lunch, and further ahead, a little down a hill is a large lake. The smell of freshly baked bread greets us. Further on stands a dark-skinned gentleman with a white apron, welcoming guests. Daniel walks toward the lake, where several ducklings swim. "Here," he points to a table that is almost at the water's edge. "It's our table. I just managed to call from the car." The ducklings crawl out of the water and waddle past us. "They will turn into beautiful swans one day." He looks at me with a warm and loving look. "You have also unfolded your wings. There is something special about you today. It's like you're shining brighter than the last time I saw you. What happened?" He pulls out my chair for me and then sits down opposite.

The sun is shining from a cloudless sky, and there is only a light breeze. Thomas must be far from here. I moisten my lips and try to take some deep breaths. "Cheers..." I lift the glass and take a sip of the ice-cold white wine that has already been poured into the finest old, ornate glasses. The wine is full of sweetness and the taste of flowers spiced with rosemary. "I just think I feel good..." that is the disadvantage of being with Daniel; he always has so many questions. It's not like before when I was surrounded by journalist colleagues who only cared about themselves and their accomplishments. They were highly skilled in asking questions but did not listen to the answers. They were only interested in the answers they could use. While it's nice to swim in Daniel's attention, I have to stay focused. "Tell me about Frank."

Daniel puts his hand on mine. "When was the last time you saw Frank?"

I raise my eyebrows, pull my hand back, and put it in my pocket. "I haven't seen Frank since I was in his apartment a few days ago, two or three; I can't quite keep track of time." I grit my teeth and press my tongue against the inside of my teeth.

"So, you haven't heard of his plans?" Daniel leans forward toward me.

My stomach drops, and I throw myself back on the chair. "No!"

"I'm afraid this is not good news...."

9

IT'S ALL FOR ONE OR NONE AT ALL

"This is so cool." Luke runs triumphantly down the aisle, enjoying the view of himself from all angles. His hands are deeply buried in the pockets of his jeans, and his white T-shirt hangs loosely as he makes one pose after another. Thomas stands patiently waiting where the door is very faintly marked with a small green ring.

He can feel the door to his childhood open inside him, and the pain begins to scratch at the surface. At the age of twelve, he lost both his parents in a car accident. The pain has become a constant companion. The accident ripped him out of his safe, innocent childhood into the world of adulthood. His hands rest on his chest as he quietly watches Luke. Luke's zest for life is unspoiled. Although Eva and Andreas have each influenced him in their own way, he has managed to hold onto his core essence. He is spontaneous and immediate, without a burden holding him back. Carefree, he enjoys any situation in the present. Thomas takes a deep breath. He can see himself in Luke, but as far back as he can remember, his father had done everything to change him. Recognition was only something he got for what he did, not for who he was. And he was not like his father. He was already sensitive and shy as a child. His father tried to push him and wanted him to be the best in his class. Thomas breathes rhythmically. The pain tingles within him, but there is a little more space inside him every time he breathes. He has learned to contain the pain, observe, and appreciate it. It helps him prioritize what he thinks is important. That way, it becomes his friend rather than the enemy. Although it was hard, it also taught him about other aspects of life than the ones he himself stands for. He looks with loving eyes at Luke, who is right down at the other end of the mirror aisle, investigating how he can make the mirrors reflect as much as possible

Thomas swallows and keeps breathing as calmly as possible. Images from his childhood flash before his inner eye. The house was like a fortress of lies; everything looked good and ordinary from the outside. But within the walls, fear of his father ruled. Thomas's father was a local politician and a recognized man in the community. He worked around the clock, and if he was not in a meeting, he was sitting in his office. On the rare occasions when he was with the family, his thoughts were somewhere else. He garnered great respect in the local community and often told Thomas how talented others were. Thomas's heart beats a little faster as memories slide by. Throughout his childhood, he struggled to fit in and be "right" in his father's eyes. No matter what he did, it was never good enough. His father took every opportunity to tell Thomas how important it was to carry on the family's traditions. Like, for example, when he was asked to give a speech at his parents' copper wedding anniversary. It was his father who told him that his mother would appreciate it and that it was a good quality to have: to be able to speak in public. Thomas had spent months writing the speech the best he could, practicing it in front of the mirror, standing the right way, and pronouncing the words as his father would. When the day came, he had such a stomachache that he could barely get out of bed. But he fought his way through the day, and when his mother asked him, he assured her that everything was fine. She was a sensitive person and insecure about herself. At the time, he did not understand why she was with his father. Today, he can see that she found security in the marriage and that it was enough for her.

When evening had come, and his father gave him a signal to get up, everything turned black inside him. He felt his legs disappear beneath him and his knife landed with a bang on his plate. The chair caught his body, and everything turned dark. The next thing he remembers is waking up in his bed. He could hear his parents arguing outside the door, and his father's rough voice hissed at his mother. "He is a disgrace to the family. You have ruined him with your weakness." The sound of aggressive footsteps disappeared. Shortly after, the door was ajar. It was his mother who came in. Her eyes were red and swollen. She sat down next to Thomas and stroked his hair. He took her hand and clasped it in his. He was only eleven years old.

"Thomas!" Luke comes sprinting down the hall and throws himself into his arms. His hair falls in front of his blue eyes, and he blows hard to get it away. "What shall we do now?"

The heat from Luke's little body washes over Thomas, and he lets himself be filled. Inside him still lives his own little boy, the part of him who has not grown up—the shy and sensitive part that he quickly learned to hide away. He hugs Luke and lets love from his heart flow over to Luke and to his own little boy. "We have to meet a man who means a lot to me; he is a wise man."

"What does wise mean?" Luke lets go of Thomas and lands on the floor. He wrinkles his nose as well as he has learned.

"It is a person who knows a lot about life and everything that happens inside of us."

Luke looks at him. "He sounds like Master Shifu." Luke loves *Kung Fu Panda*, and the explanation is approved.

Gently, Thomas touches the spot where there is a tiny, almost invisible green circle in the mirror. There is a faint click, and a section of the mirror wall opens. Luke widens his eyes and sneaks through the opening before Thomas has time to say anything. When

Thomas manages to step through the door, Luke has already run down to the end of the hallway, and before he can stop him, he disappears into the Master's room. At that moment, he realizes that he should not call out for Luke, telling him he should wait—and he shouldn't tell him how to behave with the Master. Luke must be Luke. Thomas takes a deep breath, and more space becomes available inside him. He's not like his father. It is possible to break free from the patterns of the past.

Deep laughter spiced with a child's laughter fills the hallway. Through the doorway, he can see Luke and the Master facing each other; they heartily laugh while holding onto their stomachs. Thomas steps in, but it doesn't seem to affect them. They maintain their connection in a space they have made together, where only they know what is happening. He watches them from a distance. There is a lightness around Luke, an immediacy that children only have before their parents begin to shape them. How Luke managed to hold onto it, he can't figure out.

The Master catches sight of Thomas and waves him over. He wipes his eyes and puts his hand on Luke's shoulder. "I see that you have brought our youngest member of the Ring with you, but that does not mean that he is the youngest."

Luke's inner peace and reflection over the things Thomas shares with him and the way he has adjusted to In-Between so fast tells Thomas that he is an old soul. All the members of the Ring have traveled through many lives. They stand in the middle of the room, where the light pours through the large windows from the garden.

"Yes, this is Luke; Luke, this is the Master." Thomas puts his hand on Luke's back.

"Do you have a real name?" Luke looks up at the Master, who smiles back so that his narrow white teeth become visible, while he slowly strokes his hand over his long white beard.

"I do, but what you call me is not important." The Master speaks with his usual calm and pauses between each word. He stands with his hands folded in front of his body. The diamonds on his watch twinkle in the sunlight and throw colorful reflections in a chaotic pattern up the wall.

"Is this your room?" Luke looks around. The books are back in place on the shelf, sorted by author. "There are so many books; have you read all of them?" Luke pulls a face and lets his eyes roll around his head.

The Master steps to the bookshelf and lets his hand slide lightly over the back of the books. "I read one a day. And this is my home."

Luke walks over to the TV and the white armchair with ears. "Do you have many channels?" He turns to the Master, who slowly approaches with almost floating steps so that his white robe with pearls around the neck wraps around his body.

"I have all the channels I need." He stops three feet from Luke.

Luke's gaze wanders around curiously, but the decor is sparse, and there is nothing interesting for a five-year-old. "Why is there no TV in my room?" He stands in front of the Master with his arms at his sides and a serious face.

"There's something else you need to spend time on while you're here."

"And you don't?"

Luke keeps looking at the Master and asking his questions until he gets an answer that he thinks makes sense. The Master answers Luke's persistent questions with no sign of fatigue or irritation. Thomas watches them both with great astonishment. Never before has he experienced someone asking the Master so many questions. Never before has he experienced the Master so jovial and playful. As he stands there looking at them, it is as if they are equals, despite the difference in size and age. There is a similarity, an energy between them, something that resonates between them.

Thomas never felt equal with his father. His father was a short chubby man, and Thomas grew taller than him by the age of twelve. But not even that made him feel equal with his father. When his father was present, he made the calls. He also did so when he was not present. It felt like he had tiny threads through his body that his father could pull as he wanted and whenever he wanted. Thomas has spotted some of the threads and has started cutting them. For every little thread he cuts, he gets a little more of his freedom back.

Luke crawls up onto the bed with the snow-white bedspread and sits down so he can dangle his legs over the edge. He crosses his arms and finds his most serious facial expression. "So, if you have the only screen that works as a television here in the clouds, can I come here and watch my favorite YouTube programs with you?"

The Master chuckles and sits down in his armchair with his hands resting on his knees. His gaze has a subtle, almost mischievous energy around it. Thomas is still standing at the door and can see that the Master cannot resist Luke's perseverance and enjoys his company.

"It's a deal; you can come here once a day for an hour to start with. Whether we watch YouTube or do something else, time will tell."

"It's a deal," Luke looks triumphantly at Thomas and lets himself fall back on the bed with his arms to the sides.

"Come," the Master walks toward the glass door to the garden where shrubs with small red shaggy flowers grow. The door opens in a sliding motion, and warm air flows toward them. The swans have moved under the shade of a large old oak tree. Luke rolls down from the bed and runs in front of Thomas. A Kookaburra is laughing in a large eucalyptus tree with a completely white trunk. Luke opens his eyes. "That is so cool. Where is it from?"

The Master looks at him. "Australia. It came after a big bushfire."

"Can I hold him?" Luke looks at the Master.

"We will see; if he wants you to, you will know." The Master walks with slow steps along a narrow path toward a small round opening. In several places, small purple flowers radiate from the bushes along the path. The color is intense and almost luminescent.

Butterflies with wings in patterns that only nature can create sit on the flowers.

When they reach a small opening, the Master turns to Thomas and Luke. His gaze is focused and filled with a powerful energy that cuts through the thin warm air.

"Thomas, your task for the next 89 days will be to heal the last part of yourself, the wounded part."

Luke stands still with his hands in his pockets and watches the Master. He doesn't say anything but listens to the words. A butterfly lands on his nose, and he gets distracted. It sits utterly still and opens and closes its wings before moving on.

Thomas maintains eye contact with the Master as relief fills his body. For decades, he has carried the pain from his childhood; now, the time has come to release it. He slowly raises his hands and gathers the palms in front of his chest while continuing to look into the Master's deep brown eyes.

"Luke will help you." The Master puts a hand gently on Luke's head and turns it back in the direction of Thomas.

Thomas always knew the past would catch up with him and that he had to deal with the pain of childhood at some point. He has tried to suppress it, hoping it would heal itself with time. It has not happened. On the contrary, the pain is encapsulated inside and intact. He doesn't feel the pain daily, but in stressful situations, it appears—particularly if he makes a mistake. It is the epitome of weakness, according to his father. The pain is like an old companion who may have affected him more than he is aware.

"There is more." The Master walks toward a white bench in the shade under the large eucalyptus tree. Luke jumps up onto the bench and sits like a tailor next to the Master. "As you know, Eva has gone back." He breathes so calmly that it is almost impossible to see his chest move under the long white robe.

Thomas sits at the far end of the bench and puts an arm around Luke's slight shoulders. Luke leans toward him and closes his eyes.

"Eva needs all the help she can get in relation to her task." The

Master holds back, "but she also has to get ready to contain the energy you have to carry back with you." One of the swans has risen from the shade under the oak tree and come strolling toward them. It walks over to Luke and nibbles on his pants. He opens his eyes and cannot help giggling. After a few nips, it waddles to the lake and glides into the water next to some large water lilies in bloom.

"If Eva does not make it in time, none of you can leave, and it will have catastrophic consequences for the development of humankind. The energy can only be carried down when all the Ring members are ready to hold it together." The Master speaks with a deep voice, and the pauses between words emphasize the seriousness of the message.

10

AN INHUMAN CHOICE

The hallways of the intensive care unit are deserted, and I can faintly hear the echo of a conversation on the floor below. The green color on the floor is worn off and no longer matches the faded, slightly lighter color on the wall. The energy-saving lightbulbs in the ceiling make everything look lifeless. After Daniel and I had our lunch, he began to talk about Frank. Just a few minutes into the conversation, I was overwhelmed by an ancient fear. It felt like it came from a distant past, a previous life maybe. I got up and ran to my car before I managed to explain or say goodbye to Daniel. And now, I'm at the hospital where Luke is hospitalized.

On my right is the cord that can make the door open in front of me. But I let it be. It is almost impossible to comprehend the grief crashing down on me. My life has consisted of hundreds, if not thousands, of choices. Never before have I thought about how every little choice affects our life and gives it the shape it has today. In a way, I am accountable for all my decisions; they pursue me and insist on shaping my life. Some choices are innocent and long forgotten; others sneak up on me like old lies I have forgotten about. I breathe as deeply as possible. A tsunami of tears pours through my tear ducts. I squint my eyes and try to hold my breath, so I don't drown.

The choices. They keep coming back to me. It's not just my actions but also the things I have said. Sometimes, I feel like I'm losing myself and doubt I'm good enough. All my life, I have tried to fit in, show consideration, and live up to the standards of others —to win recognition and respect. But the more I tried to be like others, the more I became a shadow of myself. My common sense was lost to doubt, and I swam around in deep water with no contact with myself, hoping someone would save me. Time and time again, I have struggled ashore, but insecurity has always been an undertone in my life. I gasp for breath again, this time managing to get a little more air down into my lungs. There are no people to be seen in the hallway in front of me. The tall, elongated windows in the door are filled with greasy fingerprints, and the wood around them is worn. The cord for the door moves a bit. I stand completely still and stare blankly into the air.

Thomas always talks about resources. He told me that when I lose myself or cannot feel my needs, I need to return to my resources. One of the resources is to breathe. It's easier said than done when it feels like the oxygen bottle is empty. Another resource is to find something safe to look at. Right now, there is only the door, and it is not very secure. *You need to have your tactic prepared*, Thomas has repeatedly said. Right now, I wish I had practiced a little more. My contingency plan is knowing what I can say to myself when I'm in too deep, something that will get me safely back on shore where I can stand firm. *Say only what you know*. I remind myself of the story with the old man and the horses, who were tired of the peasants' interpretations. I know Luke is in a coma. And I know I have to find Frank and stop him. That's it. I blink a few times and try to shake my head a bit.

The most crucial choice I have made in my life was to stay in In-Between. When I made it, I thought the worst was over. But that opened an avalanche of new choices. It's like it's all exploded around me ever since, and the effect will not diminish. I know I have to continue on the path I have chosen. I cannot go back; the door is closed behind me. Now, I must focus on Luke. That's what I know.

I reach for the cord but hesitate and pull my hand back. If what Daniel told me is true… I hold back and bite my lower lip; then, Frank has met some rich and powerful people who want to help him spread the knowledge about In-Between. If that's the case, it's unlikely that there is anything I can do anymore. Daniel said that Frank wants to start where it hurts the most. But he didn't know what it meant. That's when I got up and ran. I just had to come here and make sure that Luke is all right.

I'm good at getting things done; it's just that I don't always have time to think before I act. So, I just left Daniel at the lake. It was my power of action that made me become a journalist. I had an idea that I could make a difference with my stories. But it was an illusion. Nor was it the driving force when it came down to it. The driving force was to feel worthy and gain recognition. It was not any nobler than that. My willpower got me far, and I kept going where others gave up and went home. If I cannot use my willpower to solve what is needed to travel here as the Ring, I don't know what to do. I flick the cord, so it swings up toward the ceiling and back toward me.

One more breath. It's incredible how speculating makes me lose direction. I shake my head to clear it.

In a swift motion, I grab the cord and pull firmly. On the right-hand side of the hallway hangs a dusty clock. The two hands are both pointing to twelve. The third hand, counting the seconds, has its own life and moves in rhythmic jerks. There are several empty beds in the hallway, and in a bin lies a bouquet of withered flowers. I walk with almost silent steps. The first door on the left is ajar. Through the crack, I can see the back of a nurse standing bent over an elderly lady. I continue down the hall past two empty chairs and a table propped up with an old weekly magazine pressed under one leg. The sound of a woman's voice seeps out of the next room.

"I am here with you; do not leave me. Not now; we have the future ahead of us." The voice is tearful.

I walk carefully through the door and toward the woman. Startled, she turns around as I approach and resolutely wipes the tears away from her face with a tissue, which looks crumpled and soaked. She could well be in her early fifties. Wrinkles have started to become visible, and a few pounds have settled around her stomach.

"Sorry, I didn't hear you; I thought I was alone…."

Although I have never seen the woman before, I feel a strong urge to embrace her. I walk forward and extend my hands. Heat flows through my body and into my hands that meet the woman's sweaty hands. We stand still and look each other in the eyes. "If only he would wake up again; I don't know what to do without him…." Her tiny body shakes. "Without him, I am not whole."

I step closer to the woman and open my arms. Without any hesitation, she lets herself be embraced. I tense all my muscles as she suddenly lets go. Quietly, we stand next to the bed, where the woman's husband seems to rest indefinitely. This reminds me of the first day I received a soul in In-Between. That's when I realized that I could be a rock for others to lean on without losing myself.

"You just have to keep talking to him. He can hear you," I whisper into the woman's ear. She snorts several times and tightens the grip around my arm while struggling to stay on her feet.

"Do you think so?" She looks up at me. Her mascara has run far down her cheeks and makes her otherwise tight face look a bit human. "So, it's true what it said in the newspaper this morning?" She finds a clean tissue from the bag on the bed and wipes her eyes and nose. "Is there such a place inside the clouds?"

I don't say anything. I'm just looking at the woman with a loving look. "I have not seen the newspaper. But remember not to give him headphones with music; when he wears them, he cannot hear what is happening."

The woman is still a bit distant in her eyes, as if her thoughts occupy her more than my words. "Do you really think it's true that you can choose whether you want to live?" She tries to rub the mascara off her cheeks with the tissue, which quickly turns more black than white.

I frown and feel the turmoil creeping under my skin but stay focused on the woman. She has gone to the bedside table. The man is lying completely still in bed, his dark skin is shining a bit, and his brown hair is nicely straightened to the side. The woman reaches out and grabs his hand.

"If he can decide for himself, why doesn't he wake up right now? What is he waiting for? I need him here!" Her voice becomes more and more desperate. She reaches for the box of tissues; it is empty. Tears run down her cheeks and drip from her jaw onto her red ruffled shirt. "It is so unfair. I have waited all my life to find love. We fit together perfectly. Why did we only get a year together? She shakes the bed rail, and several wrinkles draw a chaotic pattern on her forehead.

I open my mouth to tell the woman she's right; it's unfair, but there's also something to learn. The words remain thoughts. Gently, I put my hand on her back and stand softly next to her, breathing calmly until I feel that she has calmed down. Then I remove my hand and walk to the door.

"Are you the angel they mentioned in the newspaper?"

I stop without turning around. My whole body stiffens like it is frozen to ice in a split second.

"Because if you are, could you ask Jack to wake up?" My inner self loosens up, and I slowly walk out of the room.

The hallway is still deserted and reminds me of an impersonal corridor in an office building rather than a place where people need to be welcomed with warmth and care. Next door, I bump into a nurse who steps out of a ward at high speed. She takes a step back in pure amazement at seeing someone.

"Hi, I'm sorry if I scared you." The nurse does not appear to be more than 20 years old. Her half-length wavy hair falls a little randomly, and on her forearm, I can glimpse a tattoo of a cat.

I try to smile casually but fail.

"Who are you looking for?" The nurse's voice is friendly but determined. Under her arm, she holds a note board with a blue pen dangling from a string.

"Luke Lancaster." My gaze wanders around, hoping to find a safe point.

"And you are…" she narrows her eyes, flipping through the list of names of the hospitalized.

"I am his aunt." My tone of voice leaves no room for questions. I try to look her directly in the eye, hoping to come across as more convincing than I feel.

"Nice that you could come; his father has just left. Luke is in the next room; you can just go in there. I'll come back later." She continues down the hall.

The door to Luke's ward is closed. I can see him lying in bed through the small round window in the door. The door is heavy, and I use all my strength to push it open. If I did not know that Luke is in In-Between and that he is well, the reunion would have been unbearable. I step almost silently into the room while holding my breath. The machines buzzing by Luke's bed seem mastodontic and frightening. There is a jumble of hoses and several numbers and graphs on one of the machines. His little face is covered with a mask that helps him breathe. Now, I can see how it must have been for Andreas, my mother, and Luke to see me when I was lying there. It becomes real in another way. I can no longer keep my emotional distance. A violent twitch from my stomach makes me double over. It's reality. A little too real. All choices create rings of consequences.

Luckily, I manage to control the convulsions, and the wonderful lunch with Daniel doesn't end up on the floor. I squat down and put my fingertips on the cold, worn floor. The Skycon shakes in my pocket, but I don't respond. Thomas will have to wait. Right now, I need to be alone with Luke and just be alone with all that has happened in such a short time. Before, I lived a pretty ordinary life, thinking everything was okay because I was saving up for my retirement and exercising regularly. I had even started eating more plant-based healthy food. The expectation of growing old watching Luke grow up and have children of his own was real.

I stand up. Luke lies so still that I can barely see his small chest move. But I know he's breathing. His bangs cover his forehead, and the duvet lies neatly over his body. I can hear the door open behind me, but I remain standing. My gaze is fixed on Luke.

The sound of steps comes closer, but I feel confident it's just the nurse from before. I reach out to stroke Luke's hair.

"Well, well, well. Then we meet again." A clammy hand rests on my shoulder, and it shudders in me like an uncontrollable explosion.

11
AN ENEMY AMONG ANGELS

Instantly, the air turns freezing cold, and it feels like tiny ice crystals rain down on me, stabbing against my skin. My gaze is desperately looking for someone who can help me, but I'm alone. Alone with Luke and… I turn around and feel a thick breath flowing toward me. Right in front of me is the person whom I, on the one hand, came back here to find and, on the other hand, loathe more than anyone else.

Frank.

"Hi, Angela, or do you prefer Eva?" He smiles his most mischievous smile and holds out his hand; he grabs my shoulder when I don't react. His eyes are prickly and icy cold.

"What are you doing here?" I put intense pressure on each word and clasp my hand around the cold, round metal bed rail. My feet will not move, so I use my body as a screen between Frank and Luke's bed.

"How nice to run into you. I had a feeling that you would be here." Frank pulls his hand back and holds onto the smile so that, if possible, it looks even more fake. "It's nice and cozy." His gaze wanders around the room. On the right is a small bedside table with small LEGO knights in battle positions, artificial candles, and a vase with sunflowers—Luke's favorite flower. Andreas has decorated the room with some of Luke's favorite things. On the walls hangs a poster from the *Kung Fu Panda* movie, and next to it, several pictures of Andreas, Luke, and I on holiday at the sunshine coast in Spain when he was four. There are no curtains, only a blind hanging loosely down on one side, where the window is ajar.

"It's too late, Frank. Forget it; you will never be a part of the Ring." I hiss so that several small saliva particles fly in Frank's direction. My gaze drills into his withdrawn eyes with such force that he takes a step back while laughing condescendingly.

"Too late…" His laughter makes me bite my teeth hard and clench my jaw. My knuckles turn completely white, and my whole body is transformed into armor with the most substantial plating where no emotion can escape in or out. "You are wrong. It is not too late." Frank's voice is like a missile trying to penetrate my defense.

In moments like these, I wish I knew of other options than using a counterattack. But there's nothing else I can do. Frank activates my entire arsenal of defense mechanisms like a virus that propagates under my armor and explodes before I even have time to detect it. He fills me with suspicion and makes me unsure whether there could be something true in what he is saying or if he is bluffing. He stands with a crooked smile and looks at me as if he knows something I don't. The way he stands makes me insecure. It's not like Frank to look so relaxed as if he has already won a battle I didn't know had started. He steps forward and past me. He walks to the foot end of the bed, where the light from the window makes his bald forehead shine. Damp patches under the sleeves of the white Armani shirt reveal that he is not quite as relaxed as he pretends to be.

"Well, this is Luke…" His gaze is fixed on me like a hawk that will not let go of the sight of its prey.

I move closer to the foot end and try to block him. I fail. Even though Frank is shorter than I am, he manages to look down on me.

"What do you want?" Each word is like a sentence with a break between the words and extra emphasis. The Master would be proud of the gaps. My teeth grind against each other, and I stay standing so Frank cannot get closer to Luke. *The task.* I have completely repressed it. Right now, my focus is on keeping Frank away from Luke. But I have to find out who's helping Frank in In-Between and who he is teaming up with here. Under no circumstances may he reveal In-Between before the 90 days have passed. If ordinary people become aware of In-Between, it could trigger turmoil and imbalance globally, preventing the Ring from performing our work. It could shift focus to matters of faith, and people who face more difficulties than they think they can handle might seek out In-Between.

Frank smiles so his crooked yellow teeth come into view. He reaches out, places a hand on Luke's duvet, and glances at all the machines standing by the wall. "Did you read the newspaper today?" He walks calmly to the devices that regulate Luke's oxygen and blood pressure. I mechanically shake my head and narrow my eyes a bit. "You should do that; I think you'll like the nice way I refer to you. There is also a lovely picture of you as Angela." Frank maintains his superficial smile.

I stand completely still and manage to maintain control of all the muscles in my body, even though there is a rebellion inside me. Like a lion roaring at his enemy, a scream rises inside me, but I hold it back. The blind in the window flutters and hits the window as the wind grabs it. Frank turns, closes the window, and rolls the blind down. It gets dark in here. My teeth run slowly over my lower lip and bite into it, so the pain keeps me alert. My eyes start to sting, but I do not blink.

It feels like being strapped into the front carriage of a roller coaster that has just made it up a very steep hill and has reached the point where the rails disappear in front of you. Ahead is a free fall. It is impossible to change your mind or get away.

Frank is standing next to the machines that monitor Luke's

condition. He runs one finger over the buttons. "You should have given me the last position in the Ring. Fancy that you chose to give it to your son. What kind of person are you, Angela? You have chosen yourself over your son and taken his life. It was my position." He sighs loudly and shakes his head superiorly.

"I…" Several drops of sweat run down from my armpits. Hoping he doesn't notice, I push my elbows against my body. I'm just about to defend myself, but that's what Frank is after. Then he will have me hooked.

"You still don't get it, Frank. I'm not the one who decides who's in the Ring." To my great regret, there is a hint of vulnerability in my voice. An opening Frank can go after, and an opportunity like that, he won't miss.

He leans over the bed and snorts. "I do understand. It's crystal clear. You wanted to be with your son, Eva. You can't fool me. And you think you can play God because you are part of a group of people you call a Ring." He moistens his chapped lips, "It's all gotten into your head, and now you think you can choose the members of the Ring. You will do anything to be with Luke. You're a sad human being, Eva."

I turn on the ceiling light, and it flashes a few times before it's at full power. The light is cold and removes all warmth from the room. Frank starts fiddling with some of the hoses connecting the machines to Luke and claps his hand on the side of the appliance. "Do you still think it's up to you to save the world?" His smile is smarmy as he straightens his shirt. "Well, Well. We will see." His laughter is scornful.

The temperature inside me is rising at a rapid speed. I don't want to play Frank's game, but I can't see how I can stop him either. I have to do something—just something to get the conversation turned in the direction I want.

"Who helps you in In-Between?" I make an effort to sound determined and energetic, even though my inner energy account is in deficit.

Frank lifts his index finger and points it in my direction. "You should have given me that seat in the Ring, Eva. It was mine." He walks along the edge of the bed and back toward me with slow steps. He does not take my bait. But I won't give up so easily.

"Who helps you?" My pronunciation of each word is exact. I narrow my eyes even more. He should not be allowed to win or get away with whatever he is doing. Too often in my life, I have given in—mainly to get others to like me or because I felt I was worth less than them. My father always said, "Eva, we must put others before ourselves." I interpreted it as important to please others and that their word had higher status than mine. If I experienced that others had opinions differing from mine, I bowed down and gave in. The only place I managed to stay firm was my work. I never gave in there. But privately, I did. For all intents and purposes, I would rather avoid a confrontation. But not today. Today, I do not bend. I'm done giving in. I lift my chin so I can look down at Frank.

"Who's helping you, Frank?"

He is standing directly in front of me, so the small scars on his skin are distinctive. "Eva, Eva, Eva, you could have won, saved the world, but you failed when your choices became personal. Your big ego ran off with you." His voice is like the fire of a dragon that inflates itself to frighten the enemy. I'm standing firm. My armor keeps his attacks out. Behind his facade is a wounded man, not just the anger and contempt he exhibits. When I focus on that, I can face him without being knocked over or trapped in his game.

I don't want to argue with Frank because I know it's the way to lose the victory, or rather lose myself. The pain he carries from previous lives, where he lost people close to him, is significant. Maybe I know better what he is capable of, how pain is his driving force. But I don't know how to reach the wounded part of Frank. That part is well hidden away. I have to try to find an opening; anything else will remain a battle. And if I fight, I will lose. He is too strong, both mentally and physically. And I don't want to fight.

I look over at the machines that keep Luke alive. There are flashing lights in red, blue, and white colors and lots of numbers.

"What do you need, Frank?" Although I want my voice to be accommodating, it's still harsh and dismissive. I try to soften it with a smile, but it's strained. My gaze is fixed on Frank, who steps closer to me.

"What do I need? Do you really want to know?" Now, he is standing right in front of me—so close that I can smell his body odor. His eyes are bloodshot, and the small scars on his face look like craters.

I stick my hands in my pockets and wait patiently. If I manage to find a crack in his armor, I might be able to reach the wounded part of him. That's my only option.

He runs his hand lightly over his chapped lips. On his ring finger, he wears a large silver ring with a "K" engraved in gold.

"What do I need?" He pauses. "When I was a boy, I dreamed of being a cop like my father. He did what was needed to get criminals off the streets." He gets a bit distant and stares into the air. Suddenly, he begins to laugh. "Do you really think I will fall for your In-Between psychology? Forget about it." He looks at Luke, who looks like an angel, lying there in bed with his eyes closed. The duvet lies under his arms, and his hands are folded on his chest. "It is everyone or no one. Am I right?" He pats lightly on the duvet as he looks at me, filling his lungs with air and sending it in my direction with a superior smile spiced with the sound of an ahh. "Say goodbye to your son, Eva."

12

LET THE DISGUISE FALL

"Don't you dare touch him!" The air is pressing so hard on the inside of my lungs that it stings. I'm frantically trying to reach over the bed and grab his sleeve. Frank acknowledges me with another sigh as he casts a condescending look in my direction. Then he raises his hand and pulls several wires out of the machine. I hold on to the bed rail and throw myself around the bed, grabbing his arm. My heart is pounding, and my whole body is flooded with adrenaline. He twists free and grabs a hose—the hose that provides the oxygen supply to Luke. I struggle to reach his hand but am pushed away like an annoying insect that must be swatted. Franks starts to pull the plug slowly, and I scream so my lungs are about to crack, "DON'T YOU TOUCH IT."

He stops, smiles smugly, and blinks a few times. "You should have given me the position, Eva. I told you. Repeatedly. But you didn't take me seriously. You only listen to yourself and your needs. It's all about you, you in past lives and you in the future. But not anymore. It's over." He turns the plug and tries to twist it out. I throw myself on his back and bite him in the neck, but he shakes me off, so I'm in free fall. The bed rail comes toward me with an eerie speed. Everything gets dark.

I lie curled up on the floor and only just manage to open a small crack between my eyelids. Frank tilts his head on its side like a bird. "Oops, Eva."

I don't move, and he kicks me with his foot, so I roll over onto my back and feel the heat from the blood running from my temple. He smiles contentedly, turns around, and puts his hand back on the connector for the machine that provides oxygen. If he pulls the plug, Luke will not get the 42 days his soul needs to fulfill the transition from Earth to In-Between, and he will move on beyond In-Between. And the Ring will not be assembled.

"What the hell are you doing here?" I recognize Andreas's voice and fight to turn my head the other way, only to see a pair of feet running toward Frank, who lets go of the plug. Frank steps over me and walks toward Andreas. Andreas grabs him by the shirt and throws him across the floor. I can only just see past the bed where Frank has landed on the floor.

He raises his arms, gets to his feet, and walks voluntarily toward the door. "Calm down, calm down now… Alright, we are all here to do good." He is still laughing in an unctuous way and looks way too gloating—as if he will not admit that he has just lost the battle.

"I have told you to stay the hell away from my son." Andreas stands with his fists clenched and is red-faced. "You perverted bastard!" He pushes Frank to the door, so he is about to lose his balance. "Get the hell out of here and stay away!" He shouts at Frank, who is still smiling as if he thinks it's only a matter of time before he can cross the finish line as the winner. This is just a minor bump on the road.

"LUKE!" I manage to say as I reach for the bed frame and try to pull myself up, but I have no strength in my arms. Only now does Andreas catch sight of me.

"What the f… are you here too? What are you doing with my son? What's going on?" His voice is filled with anger combined with wonder. Luckily, the blood makes me look like a victim, and he quickly runs over and helps me sit up. My white blouse is covered in bloodstains, and my head throbs.

"What are you doing here?" he repeats as he holds on tightly to my arm. There are dark lines under his eyes, and his short gray hair is slightly greasy.

"Luke, has anything happened to Luke?" I stammer out as I try to straighten up. The blood is still running from my temple, and Andreas hands me a tissue.

"No. What are you doing here, and why is the blind down?" He walks to the window and pulls up the blind. The light pours in and lightens the mood. Quickly, he gets all the wires back in place and turns toward me. I am still sitting on the floor, and he offers me a hand to get to my feet. Synchronously, we bend over Luke, who is lying as if nothing has happened, breathing slowly through the transparent mask fitted over his mouth. I hold my hand up to my face and feel the relief in my body. I dare not even think about the consequences it would have had if Frank had succeeded in taking Luke's life. Not just for Andreas and me but for the whole world.

A tear twists loose and gets caught by my finger. I stare at Luke and hold my hand against my cheek so that it forms a bowl that quickly fills with more tears. Andreas waits by my side.

"Where did you go, and why did you let Luke take off with his grandmother? And what was the note about?" His voice vibrates a bit. Andreas has not seen me since we said goodbye in the house the night I took Luke with me. All I left was a note on Luke's pillow that said, "I'm sorry." He could not help but find it. But right now, it's my luck that he thinks that my mother took Luke for a ride, not me. Otherwise, he most likely would not have taken it so lightly to find me here. And he would probably have thrown me out the same way he just did with Frank.

I swallow a few times and make a run-up for a conversation that I have not prepared for. When I had to tell Meera about In-Between, it did not go as I had hoped. A jumble of thoughts is drowned out by an intense pain that makes my head feel like an explosion. He doesn't seem upset with me; that is my luck. A grandmother has a more significant say than a babysitter, and he will take it up with her later if she is alive. It is as if space becomes smaller around me, and the light disappears.

"Can I have a glass of water?" I move my head in several small jerks and notice that a nerve in my left eye makes my eyelid tremble. Andreas reaches for the small table next to Luke and takes a carafe of water. I can't help but notice the leather bracelet with a silver anchor on his arm. He has inherited it from his father, and it has been passed down through generations. But I have never seen him wear it before; it has always been sitting in the top drawer next to his bed. He pours water into a glass and hands it to me. I remove the tissue from the wound, and my hair is completely stiff with clotted blood.

"Here, sit down. It looks like you've got a nasty hit to the head." Andreas pushes a stool toward me. I slump and rest my elbows on my knees. He needs to know what is going on. It is impossible to hide it from him anymore.

"Why did you let Eva's mother take off with Luke? Why didn't you call? It's not okay! Now, he is in a coma; it's also your fault." He looks at me with a very serious look on his face.

I can tell he is trying hard to keep cool. He knows he won't get any answers if he kicks me out. If only I could get to my feet, I would feel a bit more on par with him. I snap for air and try to moisten my lips so that the words don't get stuck. "I am not who you think I am…." I look down. The water in the glass I hold in my hand starts to splash as my hand shakes. After all, Andreas is the person I have been most attached to in my adult life, and he is Luke's father. He scratches his beard mechanically as he leans against Luke's bed. He tends to be tanned at this time of year, but he is winter pale.

"It's a long story, and I need you to believe me." I reach for the bedrail and use all my willpower to get up.

Andreas doesn't say anything but doesn't protest either. Instead, he starts biting the thumbnail on his right hand. Unfortunately, the left nail is completely gone.

If I only knew where to start to make it sound authentic. Hopefully, he won't think that I'm crazy. I try to clear my throat, but the sound gets stuck and turns into a cough. "I know it sounds strange, well… far out. What I'm about to tell you. But I need you to listen." I keep quiet and look straight into his brown eyes.

He raises his eyebrows, "Say what you have to say, then we'll see if I believe you afterward."

There is a long silent pause before I get my bearings and whisper. "I am Eva." The words vibrate in the room as if we were sitting in a tunnel with echoes. It fades out, and the room becomes completely silent. Andreas sits entirely still and looks at me. There is no trace of a reaction on his face—nothing. I wait. The sound of footsteps in the hallway is the only thing that breaks the silence. They disappear again.

Suddenly, his facade cracks, and he lets out a loud resounding laugh. His whole body shakes with laughter. But when he sees that I do not respond, the laughter slowly dies down. He wipes one eye with the back of his hand. "Eva…" he narrows his eyes. Almost no sound comes out of his mouth even though his lips are moving. He blinks several times to make sure it's Angela sitting in front of him, not Eva. "I'm not sure I get you. Do you mean Eva Monroe… Angela?"

I stand completely still and let him watch me. "I know it sounds far-fetched, like a bad morbid joke. To be honest, if it was the other way around, I'm not sure I would believe me… I'm dead… I mean… what I'm trying to say is…" I look down at the floor, where there are clear wear marks from the many relatives who have desperately walked back and forth next to the bed. Now, I have to choose my words carefully so he doesn't think I'm pulling his leg. I straighten up, look him right in the eyes, and lean forward a bit.

"I'm here on a mission." It came out the wrong way, and now I sound like a maniac. But before I can do anything, Andreas interrupts.

"I think you should go now." He walks closer and kicks the stool, so it falls over. He grabs the door handle and is about to pull the door open. "I can't stand such neo-religious bullshit. Get out!"

"No, no, it's the truth." I insist and grab the stool. In a shift move, I sit down and hold on to the edge of the stool. "When I was in a coma, I went to a place called In-Between. I was given the choice of waking up or becoming part of a group of people who can help the world to the next level of consciousness." The words come out at such a high speed that there is no room for pauses between them. My gaze is fixed on Andreas, and I do not blink.

He looks at me as if he can detect if I'm telling the truth. Then he closes his eyes and lets go of the door—for now. He walks right past me over to the window, where he opens the hasps and gives the window a push, so it is about to fly off the hinges. The cold wind hits his face. He stands completely still and lets the fresh air give him renewed oxygen to the brain.

"I know it sounds far out and like some scam and hoax. But it isn't. You know how critical I am with that kind of… You know me, Eva…." I grab the corner of the bed rail and pull myself back up. He stands with his back to me, looking out the window. There is a large dark stain on the back of his shirt.

"I can prove it. Ask me anything that only the two of us know." He turns, so we stand on either side of the bed with Luke between us.

"What was the first thing you said when Luke was born?" His voice is determined.

"That he had a dimple in his chin similar to yours." My answer falls promptly without hesitation. I look over at Luke, lying still in bed, unaware of what is happening around him. He still has a small dimple in his chin.

"What other name did we consider for Luke?" He looks at me

without blinking like a predator ready to bite if the prey shows weakness.

"Ruben, because he is our ruby."

Andreas scratches his beard and rubs some of it between his fingers. "What did you say to me the day you wanted to divorce?"

"That we should always be there together for Luke even if we lived separately." I hold back and try to swallow, but my mouth and throat are like sandpaper.

Andreas walks with slow steps around the bed while sliding his hand over the bed rail that leads him directly to me. He walks right up to me and looks at me as if he wants to see if I am real. Then he runs his hands steadily through his short gray hair and over his day-old stubble.

"Do you believe me now?" I manage to get small chunks of fresh air down into my lungs.

"You may have questioned Eva's mother or Googled it."

"Come on; there are limits to what you can Google."

"Are there?" He narrows his eyes. "Last question. What is the one thing that Eva did not want others to know about her?"

So many times, I have regretted telling him that. It happened right after we met. A late night when we had had a little too much to drink. In a weak moment, I made myself vulnerable. I look into his deep brown eyes. "That behind my perfect facade, I felt alone and insecure."

He keeps his gaze on me as if trying to look behind my exterior.

"And that one," I point to his bracelet. "You haven't worn it since your father gave it to you. It's been in your bedside drawer." I wait. "Do you believe me now?"

"Do I have a choice?" He is about to bite the nail on his thumb, but it's already all but gone, and instead, he chooses the index finger. Our gaze meets in a union of two worlds.

"Luke is in In-Between, and he's fine!" I point out the window, which in no way can make sense to Andreas because he knows nothing about In-Between. He has never heard of the place or felt the enchanting silence there. "In-Between is a place inside the clouds where people who die suddenly travel. They get an opportunity to say a proper goodbye to their life on Earth. Those who are in a coma." I manage to stop myself before I reveal that they get to decide whether they want to wake up or continue on their souls' journey. "Those who are in a coma are there too."

Andreas doesn't seem to notice that I am repeating myself. His eyes are blank, as if he is inside himself examining the new information. The window slams shut with a bang, and he gives a slight twitch with his head. The machines flash tirelessly, and Luke lies just as still in bed.

"Luke is part of a Ring that has taken thousands of years to reassemble. It's a ring of ancient souls who must carry a higher consciousness back to Earth. But for now, Luke will be in a coma for 42 days." I don't want to tell Andreas that I will ultimately decide if he wakes up; it will have to wait. Andreas still says nothing. I can see in his eyes that he hears what I am saying, but since he has no objections, I continue. "Do you know Frank?"

"Who is Frank?" He pulls a face.

"Frank, the idiot who was here before...." I wave my arms energetically and point to the door.

"Do YOU know him?!" Andreas's tone becomes suspicious. "What the hell is he doing here?" Anger shines from his eyes, and he lifts his fist into a striking position.

I quickly lift my hands in front of me to make him calm down. He would never consider hitting me, but he once became so angry that he slammed his hand through the drywall in our living room. "Yes, I know him, but he is not my friend. In fact, I cannot stand him. How did he find Luke?"

Andreas shrugs. "I don't know, but he was also here yesterday, sneaking around disguised as a doctor. I recognized him from before, so I asked him to leave."

I reach out and lay my hand on Andreas's, hoping that he won't remove it. He looks down at my hand and pats it. I place the other hand over my mouth and slowly let a deep breath seep out between my fingers. "Frank wants to be a part of the Ring. He thinks I gave the position to Luke instead of him."

"Did you?!" Andreas's words are cold and direct. He becomes restless.

"NO! I would never do that!" I shake my head feverishly. "It was not up to me at all, and I had NOTHING to do with Luke and Mom's accident."

"Is your mother involved too?" He starts walking restlessly across the floor.

I keep shaking my head. "She came to your house the night I looked after Luke. My mother is not stupid. She figured out who I am."

"Does she believe you?" He stops.

I nod.

Andreas slaps his hand against the bed rail, shaking the whole bed. "She did it on purpose, your mother. She took Luke's life on purpose!" The stool gets a kick, sliding across the floor and hitting the door.

"No, no." I shake my head dismissively and let go of the bed rail to approach him. It swims before my eyes, and I'm losing my balance. He grabs the other stool and pushes it back toward me. I sag down. "No, she would never do that." How do I explain it to him so he believes in me? There are no words convincing enough. I know that from Meera because she didn't believe me either. "Luke is still alive...." I whisper. "My mother didn't want to hurt him; she would never do that."

A ray of sunlight finds its way into the room and lands on Luke's face. I look out the dirty window where the clouds drift past and draw a chaotic pattern in the sky. *Thomas, help me, say it's not true; my mother did not do it on purpose. Give me a sign, something.* I fold my hands in front of my chest and push them further up to my face, so Andreas won't think I'm praying.

"Where is my mother? Have you seen her? Is she well?" Hopefully, Andreas will answer. It will turn the conversation around, so I have time to get my thoughts under control. I just need a brief time out. I need to know whether Andreas believes me.

He stands with his side toward me and stares at Luke, who is lying completely still. "She's fine under the circumstances." He keeps hitting his hand against the edge of the bed in a steady rhythm. "That is why she is not upset that Luke has been injured. She knows he's fine." Andreas gestures with his arms, "What kind of people are you!" he shouts into the room.

I begin to laugh in relief but sense that it is totally inappropriate and could send a wrong signal. I hold back. My mother is alive. If I were in his shoes, I don't think I would leave it at shouting. I think I would go crazy in powerlessness and despair. But Andreas retains his composure. For now. Maybe he is still in shock and doesn't completely understand what I'm saying.

I look at him, and my gaze becomes blurred; how can I convince him that there is a meaning to it all and that I am not a bad person? The worst thing about it is that I can understand him well. I take a sip of water and try to rinse all the thoughts away to see clearly again.

"Andreas, you'll have to help me. Frank's completely insane, and he will do anything to expose In-Between and apparently also take Luke's life." The glass is empty, and I place it on the table next to me.

"I have not said I believe you." He starts walking back and forth across the floor again. He stops, pours water into the glass, and swallows it in a mouthful.

"I'm sorry, but it's not just for my sake. Think of Luke." I pull myself up. My head screams in pain, but this time I ignore it and cling to the bed rail. Now it's about making a plan so Frank doesn't get anywhere near Luke again.

"We have to call the police." Andreas stops and clenches his fist so that his knuckles turn completely white. "Frank has been following Luke for a long time. I also saw him at the Kindergarten, and one day, he talked to Luke in our garden. I just thought it was random, but I'm not taking any more chances."

"No! We cannot contact the police. NO ONE must know about In-Between. It could ruin everything." I look intently at Andreas, who crosses his arms. "You can't tell Emma about it either… No one. You have to trust me."

Andreas starts laughing. "I'm not planning to; she would have me hospitalized." His laugh infects me with a burst of liberating laughter that reminds me of the days when we were just the three of us with our whole lives ahead. Everything was easy and innocent, and one day took the next without much significance. Now, I know that every day counts, every minute, every single moment is precious. The power of now.

Andreas stops his laughter abruptly, "But we can't watch over Luke all the time. We need help."

I walk toward him, keeping a firm grip on the bed rail. We stand facing each other. "I know who can help us."

13

A THIN RED LINE

The car rumbles on the bare country road, where the asphalt has been worn off in several places. There are no trees along the road, only the open expanses, which seem endless and tiring. I keep the gas pedal on the floor of the little red car, which means I can just get it above 65 miles per hour. I still have several hours of driving left. With me, I have the hope that I can persuade my mother to come back with me to take care of Luke at the hospital. Only now does it begin to dawn on me that my mother has survived the car crash. Andreas's suspicion awakens the thought of my mother driving off the road on purpose. I must admit that I have thought the same but pushed it away. No matter how spiritual she is, she wouldn't do that. My head falls back on the small hole in the headrest. Darkness envelops the car, and the headlights throw two light cones on the road. I feel totally alone in the world. There is no one else here—only me and the darkness. The darkness has never scared me, but there are so many unresolved questions ahead and answers I would like to find.

Before leaving the hospital, I told Andreas about my very intense months. First in In-Between, where I followed him and Luke very closely, and later here on Earth. I cannot figure out if he really believed me or was just in shock and eventually acknowledged everything I said. I hope for the first and ignore everything else. Several bumps on the road make a spring from the worn-out seat poke into my bottom. I ignore it and quietly stare at the endless road that refuses to twist but cuts right through the landscape and divides the world in two.

In a split second, I see a glimpse of a crowd coming toward me on horses. The dust rises from their hooves. I blink and shake my head frantically, but there is no one but me on the road. I switch to the high beams, but the image comes back. This time, the horseback riders are closer. There are hundreds of men on horseback, all with black armor and tormented expressions on their faces. I know that picture. That's the glimpse that came to me the night Luke came to In-Between. I ease my foot off the accelerator, tighten my grip on the steering wheel, and straighten up, concentrating.

The darkness becomes even more enveloping, and a cold wind seeps through the crack from the closed window. Suddenly, I step on the brake; the wheels scrape along the asphalt and send a scream into the night. The car slides off the road, hitting the hard shoulder and the uneven grass along the side of the road. It shakes so that all the loose parts clatter. I hold on as best I can. Right in front of me, I can see the crowd and feel the darkness storming toward me. The car stops, and a cloud of dust rolls over it. The image changes, and out of the dust comes a young man in beautiful long bright clothes riding on a completely white horse. I sit still and stare straight ahead because I recognize the young man. My whole body is tense. All I can see is the young man on the horse surrounded by the darkness and the dust around me. He rides toward me, and it's like he jumps into another time when the horse sets off and disappears. The dusty smell is still here, the heat comes creeping in, and the dust settles like a blanket on the car. Seven crosses appear. In a brief glimpse, I can see the young man on the horse hanging on the cross to my right.

It's Luke.

It gives a start through my body. There are several small glimpses of a few seconds. A man is standing in tattered clothes, speaking to an assembly. A knight with a red cloak, a white shirt, and a cross on his chest. A woman with herbs and medicine. These are glimpses of Luke's soul journey. He, like me, has previously been at the forefront, trying to enlighten the world, and has also experienced being persecuted, hanged, and hunted because he dared to live in a different way than most. The flashes are like flipping through an old book in a foreign language that suddenly makes sense. My heart is pounding in my chest, and my body temperature is screwed up completely, so the sweat is soaking my shirt.

Luke preached about higher consciousness, about a new world. The less conscious people were afraid of him and wanted him gone. The pictures in the book show it clearly. He dared to take the lead, speak out against those in power, and follow his heart. I recognize that from myself. Through several lives, we have both died for speaking our truth and challenging those in power. We have been on the run and been persecuted, but only by people who felt threatened and had based their wealth on the exterior. I start coughing and gasping for breath. It is as if the cabin has run out of oxygen. A picture of Frank emerges in a flash. He represents the people afraid of the new consciousness, even though he feels attracted to it. He is divided. The anger and hatred in him apparently win.

If I get it right, I might be able to reach Frank. All people are born with a good heart; our history and imprinting govern our choices, but it's not just this life I have to face. I have to believe that behind all the pain, there is love. And behind the mist of unconsciousness, there is clarity.

I close my eyes; the flashes are gone, but I still feel them in my body like an invisible burn mark. I lift my blouse away from my body to dry, but it sticks to my skin. That's why the Master doesn't want Luke to know about Frank. He has met him before, but not only in this life. It feels like the threads of the past have constricted around my neck and are tightened. I kick the car door open and go out into the field. A scream grows explosively from within me, a cry that cuts through the dark night and dies away. My lungs sting, but I keep screaming at full force. The scream sets the pain of the past free, and my body feels lighter. I scream louder and more fervently. The darkness engulfs the screams. My soul is filled with so much pain that it feels like several pounds are taken off my shoulders when they are sent off. It is as if shadows of myself from past lives stand in a row behind me and send the pain through several lives and into the present. I extend my arms and tilt my head back. After what feels like an eternity and several tons of pain, I pause. It is completely still—no wind, no sounds, and no other people. I collapse in the field and lie on my back, looking up at the stars. What if the Ring will face the same resistance in the world this time? *What if people are not ready? What if the unconscious people will not evolve and choose to hold on to fear and hatred?*

My skepticism was previously great. I mocked my mother for her belief in angels and past lives. It was so easy to drown out my body's stress signals or fatigue with bustle. I continued as I thought was best. Thomas told me at one point that if we don't listen, the messages will just become louder. I wonder if that's also collectively, or does it only apply to the individual? I lie still and feel the straw tickling my body. The insight we need to bring back, I wonder how it unfolds? When I look back on my own life, I can doubt that the work of the Ring will succeed. If most people are like I was, they will not be ready or listen. It takes a lot of power or will before people stop and look beyond the life they live. I have always been able to feel the longing, like a delicate calling in my inner self. But I have stared purposefully at what was tangible and could be proven. The longing has been deep inside me, and at times it has surfaced. I have been good at soothing it with work and convincing myself that others knew better than me, especially those who are well educated. I sit up and look out over the field where the grain sways gently from side to side. The moon casts a bright light and breaks the darkness. Despite all that I have been through, I can still doubt myself and doubt whether the world is ready for the Ring to return—doubt if I have something worth sharing. If what I know is good enough. But maybe it is my luck that I know what it feels like to be a skeptical non-believer.

14
THE BALANCE OF THE MASCULINE AND FEMININE

"Thomas." My hoarse voice dies out. I rub my eyes, slightly swollen from the tears that came with the screams. My whole body is limp yet light. The pain is gone. It's like a wall that has held me back is cracked, and now I can breathe more freely and easily. I am sitting on the moist cold soil in the field, surrounded by darkness. My car is still parked on the roadside. The moon's glow reveals that dust has settled like a duvet covering the red color, and all the windows now look gray-toned. There's no wind, and in the air is an exceptional scent of moisture and grain.

"Thomas…" I tap the Skycon lightly with my index finger and clear my throat, hoping to get some voice back. It flashes green. Then, there is hope that Thomas will respond. A quiet buzz of anticipation rushes through my body. The screen changes, and the image of Thomas fades through.

"Eva, how are you? I tried to get ahold of you earlier. Frank approached Luke's ward at the hospital. Is everything okay?"

I lay the Skycon on the ground next to me and pull the picture up in front of me. What should have been a sigh of relief drowns in frustration. If I had responded to Thomas's call, I would not have put myself and Luke in danger, and then I might not have been forced to reveal my identity to Andreas. I close my eyes and shake my head. Slowly, I let myself fall on my back.

"What's up?" Thomas holds the Skycon closer. All I can see are the fine lines on his face and the endless blue eyes with the distinct white ring around the pupil. He looks at me and gives me time.

I lift my arms above my head. "It's a long story. Can you tell me something wise, then I will tell you what happened afterward?" My arms fall to the side, and I lie still and look at the picture of Thomas with the stars in the sky flashing as a background.

He begins to speak calmly; the words come precisely one after the other without hesitation. "I don't know if this will help you understand what is happening." He's inside the control room, and it doesn't seem like there is anyone else there. I can see the green chairs behind him and the edge of the red table. He has put his hair up in a ponytail, highlighting his distinctive cheekbones.

"As you know, all people have a male and female side. When we are in balance, the distribution is close to fifty-fifty. Most people have a predominance of one quality or another."

We talked about the masculine and feminine when I was first attracted to Annabel. Then, Thomas explained that it has nothing to do with whether I am gay or not but with my longing to open up to my feminine side and the qualities I miss.

He is sitting on a floating chair that slightly sways as he moves. The ceiling light is on, and the sky looks dark. On the table are several glasses and a slim blue bottle. "Most people are not aware that their male or female side is out of balance. It has consequences for the way they live and the choices they make." Thomas pauses to make sure I'm listening. "When the female qualities are out of balance, people start to compete and compare with others and experience jealousy. It can happen to both men and women. If the masculine qualities are out of balance, one will be attracted to going to war, fighting, and taking revenge." Thomas leans back in his chair. Behind him, I can see that Luke lies on the couch, asleep as if nothing has happened. I lie in my little nest surrounded by tall grain, forming a wall around me. The straw I lie on is soft and keeps the moisture from the soil away.

Thomas pours from the blue bottle into a glass and takes a sip. "When men and women go to war, it's because they no longer have contact with their healthy masculine qualities. They are out of balance and only feel that they can accomplish something by fighting others. Unfortunately, it could not be further from the truth." He leans forward and sets the glass aside. A small gold sticker on the blue bottle says, "Clarity."

Even though I am lying on the straw, the cold and the moisture eventually start to seep through, and I sit up. I can only just look over the straw if I straighten my back. "But what if they are in balance?" Something in me awakes. It's the part of me that grows every time Thomas shares his knowledge of human psychology. It's like drinking from the source of wisdom, a source that is much deeper than learned knowledge.

"The female highest quality is love, and the masculine is meditation. In meditation lies presence as well. When the masculine rests in his presence, he or she is at home. When the feminine rests in love, acceptance and compassion will surface. The feminine is like a bowl that holds everything the masculine can dream of. The masculine is like a rock the feminine can lean on. The worst thing that can happen to the masculine side is if the feminine side does not respect the masculine. For the feminine side, it is to be ridiculed." He holds back. "These are the basic layers, and when you are in touch with them, it feels easy. But there are many nuances around it."

His words resonate inside me. Not because I know much about my male or female side, but I recognize the feeling of being ridiculed. It has kept me from expressing my opinion from the day I started school. First, I hid behind my shyness, so I avoided being noticed. Later, I pushed myself into situations where I had to be visible to prove myself. One way was to speak in larger gatherings, putting my name on an article in the newspaper or a feature on TV.

It was intimidating at first. Luckily, I got used to it and found out that it didn't kill me. But the fear of failing or being humiliated was always lurking. I can see that I have repeatedly held myself back from saying something because I thought others knew better. Once they had made their point, there was no reason for me to say anything too. Maybe it was the fear of being laughed at, not being good enough, or being measured against others.

Thomas speaks softly and with his usual calm. His crystal blue eyes light up the image. I cannot help but think it has something to do with his process. "It may be easier for you to recognize the female sides, but try to see if you have struggled in your life or been attracted to control or winning. It's the male side out of balance. In the beginning, it is not always easy to identify."

I don't say anything. Thomas has hit the spot again. It's like he's looking right through me. "Are people really so easily transparent and similar, yet so complex in expressing their pain and imbalance?" My voice breaks the silence. The grain sways around me every time a breeze picks up.

Thomas laughs out loud. "You can just look at yourself, Eva." He turns around to see if he woke up Luke, but he continues to sleep calmly. I bite my lip. All my life, I have tried to maintain control. Once I had things planned and in place, I could relax easier. My inner warrior was tasked with protecting me in situations I could not control—and maybe even in cases where I just became insecure. It's my inner warrior that Frank brings out. The control is like a spider web with an infinite number of threads. It infiltrates my thoughts and actions without me being aware of it and gives me false security. I take a deep breath and pick up a piece of straw. The clouds slide in front of the moon. The only thing that breaks the darkness is the image of Thomas. The sky is pitch black. I pull down the sleeve of my blouse, which stretches a little bit and reaches beyond my hands.

I know the anger and being identified with the struggle to win. Earlier in my life, I was engulfed in thoughts of revenge if a colleague stole an idea of mine. One time, I was thoroughly obsessed with outing a person who I believed had signed into my account and read my ideas for stories. I succeeded in the end. One day later, he resigned. I got my triumph. But it didn't taste good; the sweetness of victory had become sour, and now I know why. I lost myself, and my masculine side went to war to win. I sit completely still and run the fine straw between my fingers. Something is fascinating about looking at my life with higher consciousness. It all suddenly becomes so simple and readily transparent. But Frank is still struggling. He wants to win. And so do I.

Thomas sits still and waits until he can see that I am present again. He drinks the whole glass of blue juice. The light behind him changes. It's hard to know if it's early morning or late evening where he is. "Everybody is looking for love. That's why we keep trying even when we get hurt in a relationship. The longing is great. Humans are created to be together and survive in groups. Balance in the feminine and masculine can be a great advantage, so we don't have to depend on finding a partner who will compensate for our shortcomings or help us create balance."

"I simply don't understand what you are saying." It has become too cold to sit down, so I get up. The picture follows me and lights up in the dark. If I didn't know that the car was parked to my right, I would feel a little lost here.

Thomas doesn't allow himself to be influenced by me and continues. "Let's say you long for more acceptance and love in your life; then you can choose to go out and find a partner who can give it to you."

That is a perfect example. I laugh a little to myself and start walking around in my little circle.

"You can also shut off your longing, and either live by yourself or start comparing yourself to others, mainly women. Then envy, jealousy, and not least, lack of acceptance easily become a part of everyday life. That means you can be extra tough and judgmental toward yourself… or others." Thomas pauses and looks over his shoulder to make sure Luke is still asleep. He has turned over to his other side and pulled a brown blanket with a light pattern up over his shoulders.

"But you can also give love and acceptance to yourself. Imagine your masculine power as an inner man and your female power as an inner woman. Both live inside you. You can let your inner man see your inner woman. Be present. Give her space for care, vulnerability, and love without making her feel wrong or weak."

"Yes, but how do I do just that? Do I have two people running around inside me?" My tone doesn't hide that I find it a bit strange.

He rocks lightly back and forth on the chair, looking at me with a caring gaze. "You have to go exploring and find out what your female side needs and what your male side has to offer. That way, you can better meet all your needs and understand why you react the way you do. There is no list of facts, but there are some general features we can lean on."

"Yes, please," my laughter surprises a sleeping flock of birds, and they take off from the field.

Thomas continues. "The feminine qualities are love, acceptance, forgiveness, and vulnerability. The masculine is drive, presence, inner peace, and willpower. For me, my father nurtured my drive, but it got out of balance. He didn't recognize the feminine qualities and considered my mother to be weak. That's why I hid them."

I step out of my circle into the darkness and walk toward the car. Even though it sounds complicated, I will have to stay curious. Otherwise, I will be like the people I fear will meet me with resistance when we hopefully return to Earth as the Ring. At least it is my inner man who is a journalist, and he had the drive that created the results. But probably out of balance, as Thomas says. Have I used him to hide my vulnerability? Have I been running after achievement and recognition to make him feel accepted? Have I used my inner man to hide my insecurity? My inner woman, who is she really, and what does she need? I think she needs care and love, and if what Thomas says is true, then I need to be more caring and loving toward myself. I stop and feel a raindrop fall on my nose. It's impossible to see the colors of the clouds; everything is dark. The straw slaps my pants as I set off in the direction of the car. I just manage to throw myself in the front seat and slam the door before there is a huge bang and the sky opens up in a big flash of light.

There is no doubt that I have lived my whole life from my masculine side in the past, even though others probably don't think so. But I have controlled, fought, and been anything but present. My female side has woken up in In-Between, and it's the part of me that doubts myself; it's she who's afraid of not being good enough. And when I was with Andreas, she felt safe, and my inner man didn't have to work so hard.

"Does it make sense, Eva? The image begins to flicker. I realize that the Skycon lies on the ground in the crop circle. I can still see Thomas, but the sound begins to scratch. My hands hit the steering wheel, and the spring in the seat is extremely intrusive. The windshield is flooded as if someone is standing with a garden hose and spraying water on it. "Thomas, wait a minute."

I rip the door open and run in the direction I came from. I can't see anything. The rain is pouring down on me, and I am soaked after three steps. A lightning bolt cuts across the sky. Further ahead is my crop circle. I leap forward like an antelope on the run from a lion. There is another loud bang, and it howls in my ears afterward. The picture of Thomas follows, but he says nothing. He sits still and lets himself be entertained. The buzzing sensation from the grain hitting my pants is gone. I've reached the circle. Under several fallen pieces of straw lies the flashing Skycon. I pick it up and kiss it.

"Okay, I'm back again." The light from the car headlights makes it easy to find my way back. I'm soaked, so there's no need to hurry. The raindrops tickle my skin, and the cold sensation awakens my insides. My clothes stick to my body, but I feel free. It throbs where I hit my head earlier, and the blood runs mixed with the rainwater from my hair. I washed my face before leaving the hospital and luckily had a clean blouse in the car. "You asked if it made sense?"

Thomas has moved and is sitting next to Luke. He lightly strokes his hand over his hair. Luke opens an eye and closes it again. "For all people, the more the two sides are in balance, the easier it is to act appropriately and draw on the balanced qualities from each pole. When the feminine, masculine, or both are out of balance, we are driven by the behavior linked to the imbalance.

"So, both the feminine and the masculine side can be out of balance at the same time in a person?" I ask, wondering, and dry the rain from my face.

"Yes, and they can both be in balance too. There are four poles. Once the sides are in balance, we can seriously begin to spread our wings and present ourselves in the light authentically and genuinely. But it requires practice. You're well on your way, Eva. I say this only so that you may become even more aware of it. It seems like Frank is identified with his masculine side out of balance—with the struggle, the war, and the anger. So, the more feminine you can be…."

"I hear you. It makes sense. Annabel should have been here instead of me; then Frank wouldn't stand a chance." I blush a little and continue, "or Shiva." The car is only a few feet from me now. The rain pours down, and the sky becomes illuminated at regular intervals. My hair sticks to my skin, and all my clothes are soaked.

"Eva, there is a reason it's you. You are outgoing and have access to your masculine side. Shiva has never used it in the same way as you, and she has her learning. Without your masculine side, you will not succeed. But see if you can use your acceptance, care, and vulnerability more toward Frank, and remember that he longs for respect."

I bite my lip lightly and feel my discomfort just at the thought of showing Frank respect.

"Eva, why do you have red streaks on your face?"

The car is right in front of me. Before I get in, I grab the bag with extra clothes that I always have in the trunk and throw it on the passenger seat. At the bottom of the bag is a towel. I wipe my face and check in the rearview mirror that all the blood is gone. "It doesn't matter." My hand is looking for a dry blouse and a pair of pants. "I need help. As long as Frank is after Luke, there has to be someone with him all the time. I'm on my way to fetch my mother."

"That sounds like a good plan; are there others you can trust and ask for help?"

My gaze gets distant as I scan my inner gallery of characters and stop at Lucy—my lovely friend. Lucy doesn't know about In-Between, even though she has been there. I'm not sure if it would be too risky to ask her for help. "No, there is no one else I can think of. Well, maybe Daniel, but he is also Frank's friend...." I let silence take over and keep scanning.

"We will help you all we can. But you are closer to the people there, and it's easier for you to sense what is needed. I trust you will do what it takes to stop Frank."

The windows slowly mist up, and the air inside the car becomes humid. The engine makes a noise with the ventilation, which struggles to send out heat. This mission would be so much easier if Frank didn't exist. There is no doubt that his two poles are out of balance, but I wonder if he is jealous of me and therefore fights me. Is it his feminine side who is fighting against me?

Luke starts to move, "Eva, we can talk later if you want to."

"Certainly, I will call you. Hug Luke from me." The picture dissolves, and I am alone again. I quickly peel off the wet clothes and hang them over the back of the passenger seat to dry. I run my damp shirt over the windshield but can only see as far as the light cone reaches. The car gives a jerk as I put it in gear and continue out on the infinitely long road.

15

A JOINT CHALLENGE

Thomas moves back and forth on the floating chair, shaped like half an egg and braided like a bird's nest. He sits in front of the big screens in the Ring's control room. The dark red color on the wall behind the screens makes them stand out. They are turned off. Right now, he needs a moment without impressions that affect him. He closes his eyes, places both hands on his heart, and sits completely still. Although Eva coped with the situation with Frank, she is still vulnerable, and there are limits to what he can do to help. His father's voice shouts in his head if he is not very attentive, like a devil sitting on his shoulder commenting on his life and actions. He can hear him say that he doesn't have the ability to oversee the Ring—that he will fail, and "in our family, we do not fail." The door slides open behind him, and he turns around to see Yoge and Shiva. The windows in the ceiling let a diffused light cast soft shadows down on the floor behind them.

"What's up?" Yoge is heading directly toward Thomas and doesn't see Luke lying on the couch sleeping. His long thin legs cannot fill his pants, and his movements are gawky. The pen is in its permanent place behind his ear. "You have…"

Thomas puts his finger in front of his mouth, and Yoge lowers his voice slightly. "You have asked us to come. I was right in the middle of a major calculation around the frequencies Frank has used to travel back and forth."

Shiva has followed and stands next to them, forming a triangle. Her hair hangs loosely around her face. She wears a long light beige dress with delicate white markings of flowers and a dark brown shawl over her shoulders, making her feminine side stand out.

Thomas looks from one to the other and nods toward the sofa. Luke is still asleep and has not registered that Shiva and Yoge have arrived. They move to the dark red table in front of the screens. Thomas glances up at the sky and takes a deep breath.

"Frank is after Luke." He whispers so the words can hardly be heard. "But let's wait until Meera arrives, and I'll tell you everything I know."

The concentration causes Yoge's face to cramp up and look even narrower. Shiva says nothing. She puts a piece of chewing gum in her mouth and tries to chew on it discreetly. Thomas knows that she only chews gum when she is under pressure. Whether it's because of Frank, Luke, or her process, he doesn't know. On the table are several bowls of snacks; these are the remains of Luke's adventure earlier.

"How are you doing in your process?" Thomas looks at Yoge, who is immersed in his notebook of calculations. It seems that he doesn't hear the question. And then at Shiva. She stops chewing. Her gaze becomes distant. It is as if she disappears into herself to pick up the answer. "It's going well. I enjoy it. Silence nourishes my soul. It's easier to look inside when I'm alone."

It's completely quiet in the control room. The clouds slowly drift past the large windows in the ceiling. After a while, Yoge grunts and clears his throat.

"I take one day at a time. All that silence and isolation, it's not me. But I am coping if that is what it takes." He turns on the chair and looks at the door. "Where was Meera when you called her?"

"She was asleep," Thomas smiles, "maybe you weren't?"

"No, I need to make the most of my time here, and when my morning goes by in silence, I have to take the nights into use." He rubs his wide nose with the back of his hand and flips diligently through his notebook. When he finds a blank page, he grabs the pen and writes several rows of cryptic equations.

Heat flares up in Thomas; he knows that Yoge is always busy with all sorts of calculations and experiments. It is a vital necessity for him, a significant part of him, and his whole soul's potential. He leans back in the chair, which floats slightly across the floor and follows his movements. Tiredness fills him, and he closes his eyes. If only he could sleep now and get a time out. But it's just a way to avoid the feeling of turmoil that reigns inside him, a way to escape from what's important right now.

"What about you, Thomas? How are you doing?" Shiva gently puts a hand on his leg. Luke begins to move a bit and makes small noises. It sounds like he's dreaming. After a few minutes, he turns over and sleeps heavily.

The most delicate energy of care vibrates around Shiva. The source of feminine energy is infinite, and she always pours generously of it—like a field of dandelions whose seeds are set free and float in the air. Her big challenge is finding the courage to share the energy with more people, so the field is not only for those close to her but accessible to all.

Thomas opens his eyes, so their gaze meets. "I think it's difficult. After all, there are things I have happily avoided looking at—episodes in my life I always knew would catch up with me one day." He runs his hand over the armrest to smooth it out. But it is already smooth. "It's easier to push things in front of you than embrace them. But I can see that the time is right." He pulls up the sleeve on the always perfectly ironed blue silk tunic and glances at his watch—a large blue watch with glittering stones around the edge and gold hands. It's been more than twenty minutes since he called Meera.

Thomas doesn't mind talking about himself, but it's not often that someone asks him. He is always busy helping others. It makes him warm inside, and his energy bubbles. His soul finds meaning in being there for others and showing the way.

A quiet hiss makes them turn toward the door. Meera squeezes through the door before it's all the way open and walks briskly toward them. She grabs a chair, and the triangle turns into a square. Under her eyes, she has black marks, and her hair is tousled. She is wearing a black training jersey, which is too big and inside out. In her hand, she has a half-filled coffee cup. "What's happening? Why do we have to meet now? It's the middle of the night." She casts her gaze from Yoge over to Shiva and ends up at Thomas. Her voice is determined, and she leaves no pauses between the words.

"We each have a process of development we have to go through before the 90 days have passed. But…" Thomas holds back. "Eva…" He wants it to sound informal, but he also knows he can't or will not hide his concern from the others. "Frank is after Luke."

"Who is Frank?" Meera rubs her hands over her face and downs the coffee in one mouthful. She opens her eyes wide and puts the cup down hard.

Shiva puts her hand on Thomas's shoulder. "What happened?" Her voice is still calm and gentle. Thomas tells them how Frank showed up at the hospital and tried to remove the tubes that keep Luke alive, how Eva fought and was knocked out. And that she had to reveal her true identity to Andreas and tell him about In-Between. Together, they got the tubes back in place and got rid of Frank, for now.

"I've spoken to Eva, and she's on her way to see her mother, who might be able to help her." He looks over at Meera. "Frank has been in In-Between before and has found a way to travel back and forth. He is angry that Eva did not give him a place in the Ring."

Meera shoots her chin back and makes a mess with her hand in her hair. "But I don't understand; it's not Eva who decides who is in the Ring. Or did I get it all wrong? Who's that moron?"

"No, it's not Eva's decision, but Frank doesn't believe Eva."

Thomas looks down and lowers his voice a bit. “Frank insists he should have a position in the Ring if one becomes vacant.” He pauses and takes a deep breath. “If he kills Luke, there will be a vacancy.”

“That’s crazy,” Yoge throws the pen on top of the notebook. “The frequency of that man is so low that he would short circuit at the first energy level.” He makes a pair of scissors that cuts with two fingers, which indicates that it can lead to a nervous breakdown in the brain.

Shiva says nothing. She sits with her mouth slightly open. The tiny hairs on her arms have risen. She hands the packet of chewing gum over to Meera, who takes a piece.

“As I see it,” Thomas gets up, “it’s the anger that has taken over in him. When anger takes over a human being, it is impossible to hear the message. The recipient will always see it as an attack or attempt at cheating.” He looks at the others, “I think we all recognize that. But in Frank’s case, anger just goes back many lives, and he can’t control it.” The others listen quietly. This time, no one interrupts, so he continues. “Eva has had several glimpses of past lives where both she and Luke have met Frank. There is an old score that is unfolding and needs to be settled. It’s not something we can change or interfere with. It’s part of what Eva must learn in this life.”

Luke is still in a deep sleep and doesn’t notice what is going on.

“Isn’t there anything stronger than that?” Meera reaches for a glass, points to the carafe of water on the table, and blows a bubble with chewing gum. In an easy motion, Shiva stands up. She runs her hand over the floating wall so that a section slowly slides to the side.

“Yes,” Meera leans forward and gets to her feet. The chair hangs and rocks gently in the air. Her arm strokes Shiva’s as she eagerly reaches into the cupboard for the red bottles. “Two of them, then I’ll be more functional at this inhuman time of day.” She marches back to her chair and sits contentedly down again. It only takes her a moment to finish the first bottle and open the next.

Thomas waits until Shiva is back too. "Although it's Eva's job to transform her baggage, there is more at stake: the Ring. The Master has asked us to help Eva the best we can. Otherwise, we risk that she will not have time to get ready before we have to gather. She is challenged on many levels."

Yoge moves forward in the chair, making clicking noises with the pen. "We can set up an auto-monitoring of Frank that we can all follow on our Skycons, and I suggest we make a roster."

"Then you better have the evening since you are so busy sitting in silence every morning." Thomas laughs lovingly at Yoge, who snorts back.

"But who is helping Frank up here? He can't travel back and forth by himself, can he?" Meera looks slightly confused. It's all new to her. Just getting used to the thin air, the easy walk, and all the new possibilities that open up in In-Between is a big upheaval for her. She has plenty to do to get ready to take her place in the Ring.

Shiva leans over toward Meera and places a hand on her back.

"Before you traveled here, we talked to several people, but no one knows who is helping him," Shiva speaks in a low voice, nearly whispering. "It's a mystery. We investigated while Eva was finding you and Luke. That's when we discovered the challenge."

Meera collapses in the chair. "Maybe I can try." She looks up at Thomas. "I mean, I'm new; maybe I will have more luck. Nobody knows me, and it doesn't hurt to have a pair of fresh eyes." She blows another bubble that bursts and plasters the chewing gum over her mouth and cheeks.

"As long as it doesn't interfere with your process, so you don't have time to get ready." Thomas reaches for a glass on the table and fills it with water. He takes a sip and looks at Meera with an intense look.

"It will not." Meera looks determined and keeps eye contact with Thomas as she peels the chewing gum off her skin. "I'm honored to be here." She speaks slowly, and her voice is more relaxed. "It's my duty to do everything I can to bring the Ring together." She pauses and looks over at Shiva, who is still resting her hand on her back. "It's like coming home to the place inside of myself that I've felt all my life but also struggled with." Shiva lowers her hand and folds her hands in front of her chest as she blinks slowly. She knows that feeling. For her, life was about survival, but in flashes, she saw a different way of living that she just couldn't reach.

"Doubt. It has always accompanied me as a faithful companion." She takes the chewing gum out of her mouth and puts it in a napkin.

They all sit and let the silence fill them while the light descends from the enormous windows in the ceiling. The stars hang over them like luminous dots, and the gleaming white floating walls and the light floor help to see everything more clearly.

"Thomas, please let me know if you need help with Luke." Shiva pours water into his empty glass. "That's probably where I can be the biggest help. Strategy is not my strong point."

The cold water fills Thomas's mouth, and he swallows. "Luke is a gift to me; he helps me in my process. He is the best help I can imagine. He is also with the Master every day."

The large floating screens turn on. Yoge's index fingers eagerly press on the keyboard. A picture of Eva emerges. She is parking her car outside a small yellow half-timbered house surrounded by yellow and red roses.

"She is with her mother, Janet, for help. Janet already knows about In-Between." Thomas puts down his glass and moves closer to the table. With an easy touch, he pulls up a picture on the screen from inside Janet's house. She lies asleep, unaware that she will soon be visited. "Janet was with Luke when he came here. That's why she's bruised and battered."

Her entire cheek is black, and she has a bandage on her left hand, which rests on top of a small floral fleece blanket.

"I can stay here with you until Luke wakes up." Shiva looks at Thomas, moving over next to him. Luke is still fast asleep.

Meera rubs her hands over her face and tries in vain to wipe away the tiredness overpowering her. "Tomorrow, I will see what I can find out regarding Frank." She tries to shake one more drop out of the red bottle. It's empty. "But I need to get some sleep…."

Thomas knows it will be difficult, but it's worth the effort. Meera is right; she is not a known face in In-Between, which could be an advantage.

"I will try to find out what kind of frequency Frank uses. There must be something we are not seeing." Yoge has filled an entire sheet with numbers while they were talking, and now he is searching diligently for a blank page… numbers that only make sense to his quirky brain.

On the screen, Eva's mother is awakened by the sound of the doorbell. She rubs her eyes, reaches out for her dressing gown, and is on her way to the kitchen when it dawns on her that it was the doorbell and not the egg timer that rang. On another screen, they can see Eva standing outside the door. Her breath is white, and she claps her hands together to keep warm.

Thomas takes a deep breath. "Shiva, I'll stay here with Luke, so the rest of you can get some sleep and take over later." He looks over at Meera, who is struggling to stay awake. Shiva gets up and embraces him gently. He inhales her high frequency of love which vibrates with a delicate frequency.

"I'll be back," Yoge places the pen behind his ear. He mumbles to himself, working on his calculations as he disappears out the door.

"Are you sure you have the time to look for those who are helping Frank?" Thomas releases Shiva and turns to Meera.

"Yes," she struggles to get up from the chair and sways on her legs.

With the gentle tone of love from an infinite source, Shiva steps forward, takes her hand, and whispers, "Let us know if you need help."

"And remember, even though we are in In-Between, you can't trust everybody." Thomas looks at her with intensity. She answers with a nod.

16

WHEN THE UNIVERSE TAKES OVER

The sound from the bell dies. I take a step back. A tile under my feet is loose and rocks as I step on it. Even though it's dark, I sense that the garden is more overgrown than usual. Weeds are growing everywhere in the flower beds. Wild grass has turned the ordinarily elegant and proper garden into a mess. Only the roses along the wall seem to get attention.

"Who is it?" the voice only just reaches through from the other side of the door. I step forward. "It's me, Mom, Eva...."

There is a clink of keys, and a chain is taken off the door before my mother appears through a small crack in the doorway. "Eva!" She gropes for her glasses that always sit in her hair when she is not wearing them, blinks repeatedly, and squints her eyes to see better in the dark. The bulb in the lamp above the door is broken, and a touch of light from the lamp inside the hallway falls on her cheek, revealing the black marks on her cheek and around her eye. The door opens slowly, and she steps aside so I can enter. "Don't pity me," she points to her face. "It's not as bad as it looks." She extends her arms and pulls me through the door and into a big embrace.

"I haven't quite gotten used to your new look yet," she caresses my cheek. "What in the world are you doing here?" Her hands grab my arms, which also get a good shake. I pat her lightly on the shoulder, trying to step back. "I need your help." My voice is low, and my gaze falls to the ground. She squeezes my arm and pulls me further into the hallway.

The hallway is dark, and the smell of old age has settled in the walls. She closes the door behind us and walks into the living room, which is further ahead. There is a sparse light from an artificial flickering candle, and she fumbles a bit for the switch to a floor lamp. Before it reaches full power, the light flashes and is almost suffocated by the green lampshade with fringes before it lights up the living room. She sinks into her flowered sofa with huge pillows. She looks so tiny and weak as she sits there, but I know she's not. On the table is a plate with leftovers and a cup of coffee. Next to it is a picture of me with Luke from our vacation to Crete. That was right after Andreas and I got divorced.

"How are you?" I point to her hand.

"It will be all right. I'm not complaining. It will probably be okay again."

"And what about your head?"

"It's still attached." She laughs a little, so the small square glasses slide forward on her nose. "It scares people away when I'm out shopping. I get plenty of space."

I sit down on the chair opposite and move a little closer to her. The wrinkles on her face have multiplied, and she is not only black under the eyes because of the accident. The last few weeks have added some years to her body age.

"I need your help." My gaze is urgent. As I sit there, I remind myself that I don't know if she knows that Luke is in a coma—or if she drove off the road on purpose. The light gradually begins to penetrate through the dirty windows. The sun is rising on the horizon.

Her gaze tries to dodge mine, and she takes the plunge to talk but instead fiddles nervously with a button on the couch. "How is

Luke?" she stammers out, looking at me in a quick glance and away again. I cannot figure out whether she's scared of my reaction if she drove off the road on purpose, or she's just nervous.

"Luke is in a coma. He's fine and has arrived in In-Between." It's hard to elicit a smile, but I try. I'm lousy at not telling the whole truth. It's for sure that I will never be a good strategist or politician. I'm too honest for that and too easy to see through. As a kid, I always lost when we played cards. I distinctly remember a time when my father looked at me and said that all the aces had been played. At that moment, I felt cheated. Did the others keep track of which cards had been played? That possibility had never occurred to me.

"Who decides if he wakes up?" She raises her head and looks anxiously at me with her brown eyes. "At least you can tell me. It was me who sent him off to that place."

She's right. Whether it was on purpose or not, she drove the car. If she had not lost control of the vehicle, a rock might have fallen on it, or a tire could have been punctured and the car gone over the edge. If Luke was supposed to travel to In-Between, it was just a matter of time. The forces of the universe are somewhat stronger than our will. I have gradually learned that—both with Meera, with myself, and now with Luke. I have to trust my mother. If she is to help us, she must know the truth.

"I do." I look out into the garden, where several sparrows and buzzards are pecking at a ball made of seeds hanging in a net from a branch on the big apple tree. It's one thing that it's an unbearable choice I have to make; it's something else altogether to be confronted with it. My heart almost shrinks inside my chest and feels like a hard rock. I await her contempt and speech about how I can allow myself to make that choice on behalf of another human being—on behalf of my son.

"Choice," she says. "There are choices everywhere. And we have no idea what consequences our choices have. We think we make all these clever decisions, but we are just pieces in a bigger game. But as long as there is hope." She pauses and reaches out for my hand. Her fingers are warm and soft as silk as she squeezes my hand. The heat radiates up through my arm and meets my heart.

I can sense her looking at me. A part of me had just forgotten how spiritual she is. All her life, she has been preoccupied with the part of life that still feels new to me and can challenge me. She has always talked about the meaning of life and higher powers, that there is a divine power that determines our destiny; perhaps it's the panel she has referred to without knowing it. According to Thomas, the panel consists of those who have the spiritual oversight of all souls. And who keeps an eye on us all. Maybe it's also the part of the universe that comes together when there is something you really want and take responsibility for it to happen. It doesn't seem as challenging for her as it is for me. My gaze is fixed on the window facing the garden where the touch of the sun is melting the frost off the grass. After all, I'm just an ordinary woman with an extremely challenging task who got yet another choice to make that I don't want to.

"I can see you haven't decided yet," she speaks softly. There is no anger or blame to be felt. Silently, I gather courage as one gathers stones at the beach. At one point, they weigh so heavily that I can tell more.

"But that's not why you're here." She speaks as she can see that I have no intention of saying anything. My mom is just as impatient as I am. Things should preferably happen now, and it's like a punishment to wait. For that reason, she could well have taken responsibility for Luke moving on when I couldn't. She didn't know if Luke would end up in a coma or die. But she knows that if you end up in a coma or die suddenly, you go to In-Between. I have told her that.

"Luke is in a coma. I've come right from the hospital. But there is a challenge." I tell her about Frank and the experience at the hospital and that Frank has leaked a story to the press about In-Between. She listens patiently to me. I cannot see what is happening inside her; her face is inscrutable. She has always been great at keeping the facade. As a child, I could never tell whether she was angry or happy. She could look satisfied but at the same time have knowledge that made her angry. She has always been cautious not to let her emotions get in the way of others; whether they were positive or negative, most of it was going on inside her.

"I need your help to be with Luke when Andreas is not there. We cannot risk Frank getting close to him again."

She gets up and walks into the adjoining room without saying a word. I sit back and do not quite know what to do with myself. I Take the Skycon out of my pocket and hold it in front of me. It flashes green. It's nice to know there's a connection. The next moment, she comes out of the room with a bag in her hand and a coat over her arm.

"Shall we go?"

17

TWO SILENT WARRIORS

We sit in the car like two silent warriors on their way to the front, where the enemy is hiding and waiting. Silence hangs between us. In a way, it's wonderful to sit here with my mother. It reminds me of when we went on a trip when I was a child—just the two of us. My father was always busy, so my mother and I went together. It was innocent, I thought. But behind it was a hidden pain in my mother—a broken dream about a real family where you did everything together. She did what she could, tried to give me lots of love and attention. She succeeded. There's another seriousness about our trip now; we both know that. We are far apart in many ways and yet on the same path.

I would previously have sworn that we were not. I always thought I was like my dad. He valued the tangible and measurable. My mother has always been more into the airy stuff, angels and intuition. Now, it's about balance. Heaven and Earth. The masculine and the feminine. I look over at my mother. Her eyelids have become too heavy and have closed. Her glasses bounce slightly on her nose every time there is a bump in the road. The sun hangs alone in the sky right in front of us. We are back on the straight road, where the grain sways in the wind as far as the eye can see.

There are so many things I want to say to my mother. All this time, I had not understood her perspective on life when she asked the universe for help or waited for a sign. The realization that I have been rude and made fun of her hurts. It especially hits the feminine —the vulnerable and subtle part of me that I have had hidden well away. She has not taken it personally and never turned her back on me. On the whole, she has never paid attention to what others think of her and her outlook on life.

I look at her. Her head has fallen forward, and I just manage to save the glasses before they fall to the floor. Although there is natural ventilation through the cracks in the car, I roll the window down a bit. The fresh and clear morning air hits my face. The smell is sweet, the way it can only smell in the morning before the air is polluted again. Right now, I don't know how to deal with Frank. One thing is to get my mom to look after Luke; another thing is how Frank will react when he finds out that someone is with Luke all the time. I also don't know what his plan is and whether his revelation of In-Between will have any bearing on the work of the Ring. But I can feel that I'm keen to find out and do what I can to keep him from destroying the Ring's mission.

"What is troubling you, Eva?" My mother has suddenly opened her eyes and straightened up in her seat.

I quickly look at her and back at the road, which has started to wind in front of us, without answering.

"Is it the mission and Frank?" She fiddles with her bag and finds a tissue. "It's not your responsibility. You can't take full responsibility for whether the Ring succeeds on your shoulders." She blows her nose, and the sound drowns out the engine rumble. The tissue is thrown down on the floor, and her hand continues up into her hair, reaching for the glasses. I point down into the compartment under the air ducts where the glasses are located.

"Well," I try. My words die. I take a deep breath. Deep down, I know she's right. But if I could just fix it—get Frank to disappear or realize that there is no free choice of seats in the Ring. It is not first-come, first-served, or those who bid the highest.

My mother looks at me. "There is so much we don't understand, so much that is greater than us. Sometimes, we must surrender to the forces of the universe and float along. I think there is meaning to everything." She straightens the little hat she has fished out of her bag and places it on her head. The purple color matches her scarf and jewelry and makes her face light up. She looks elegant as she sits there, despite the color of her face. She is a real lady and radiates greatness as if she had blue blood.

Go with the flow; it's easier said than done. It's just so annoying to hear. *Go with the flow*. The words resound in my head. The balance between trying to control life and taking action, and the opposite pole; letting go. I think it's hard. I tighten the grip on the steering wheel and, without thinking about it, press the accelerator. The engine acknowledges with a loud hum, and the slats in the air vent rattle.

Out of the corner of my eye, I can see her gaze resting on me, but I don't react. "Do you remember when you were little, and your father was always busy?"

I pull a face, "Yes."

"For many years, I tried to change him. I took for granted that when you were born, it was because we wanted to raise you together. But his interests were different. He needed to work and wanted to reach the top—get external recognition. Power. Money. Things that have never meant anything to me." She pauses and fiddles with her scarf. "I think our opposite sides attracted us to each other." She keeps looking at me, and I keep looking at the road. The sun still hangs right in front of us like a fireball and dazzles me. With a quick movement, I tilt the sunshade down. A small yellow piece of paper drops down onto my lap. I fumble but can't get hold of it, as my gaze is still on the road.

"What is that?" My mother reaches out and grabs the little yellow piece of paper. She unfolds it and exclaims, "What a scrawl!"

"What does it say?" I have no idea where it came from. Maybe it's the previous owner's.

"I love you, Princess," she almost shouts, "it's signed with a big 'D' ha—it must be for you." She folds it and puts it in my pocket.

The words entice me to shift focus from the task to Daniel. It's tempting to think about how life could have been with him. He makes me feel safe and allows my inner woman to show. I shake my head and roll the window a bit further down and notice that I am now sitting with the handle in my hand. I toss it over my shoulder onto the back seat and continue to stare at the road disappearing under the car. The sun blinds me, and the sunshade doesn't help.

"Here, take my sunglasses." My mother dives into her bag and finds a pair of sunglasses that look like something Prince would have worn. Purple, of course, they match the hat and scarf. I reluctantly put them on. The sky is transformed from blue to light purple and the grain from brown to dark red.

She smiles smugly. "They suit you. Anyway, when I realized I could not or should not change your father, we got divorced. We were too different, and that's fine. It has given you a door to both worlds. But you have always been like your father with that journalistic work."

I smile a little and lean over toward her. "I don't know if that is a compliment."

"It's not."

My Mom never sugar-coated things. I have definitely inherited that from her.

After four hours of driving, we turn into the hospital's parking lot. My heart starts beating faster as we approach. There has been complete quiet for the last few hours. I try hard not to overthink what can go wrong. My mother is the world champion of worrying, and I'm happy to let her keep that title. Thoughts swarm around

Luke anyway. Doubt visits me again and again like an old friend I can't get rid of.

I park right next to the entrance. If there's one thing I hate, it's when I can't get one of the spaces closest to the door. I can't help myself competing, but I am also convinced that there is a vacancy precisely because other people think there isn't. It's better to drive around one extra time than to discover that there was a space closer to the entrance. Every time I find a place close to my destination, it feels like a victory.

"Are you ready?" I look over at my mother, who is busy putting on lipstick.

She looks very charming as she sits there—bruised and wearing a lovely purple hat. One thing I can say about my mother is that she is always there for you. I have never met a human being who, like her, put her loved ones before herself. But it has also had its costs, like the years when she had virtually no money for food or rent because she helped a friend who had been injured and was not covered by insurance. My mother has never learned to say no or prioritize herself. But she has also never complained about anything. I think that's what gives her soul meaning, even if it sometimes has great costs for herself. This time it's Luke who benefits from her endless love and desire to help.

I remember as a child when there was something we had to share, and everyone else got more than her. She always bought new clothes for me, my sister, and my father, and she wore clothes that were over ten years old. There was nothing wrong with it, she said. Now I can wonder why I never appreciated my mother. My focus has been on living up to my dad's expectations about money and business, and I have not been able to see what my mom was offering. It was as if it had no value. It doesn't in ordinary society either. Helpfulness, gratitude, and care do not weigh as heavily as status, money, and results. What she gave could not be measured or weighed.

The hospital appears empty, and there is no one to be seen. If I didn't know better, I would think we had come to the wrong place. Unfortunately, we have not. We walk to the second floor and along one of the long sterile corridors, where the words are engulfed by the silence and where everyone walks slowly and with stiffened eyes. Here in the intensive care unit, the patients lie and hover between life and death. Imagine if the relatives knew they were in a beautiful place and would come back if that was the intention.

Further ahead is Luke's ward. I grab the door, put my shoulder on it, and push it open. It feels like a knife is being drilled into my stomach, and my body freezes. There's Luke's bed. Luke's machines. My mother bumps into me from behind; she has not registered that I'm glued to the floor and have stopped.

"Excuse me," she mumbles as she writhes past me and into the ward. "Where is Luke?" She looks at me with a look that demands an immediate answer. But I have no answer.

18
CLOUD CLIMBING

"Luke, it's this way," Thomas points to a high mountain of clouds. "The one who gets to the top last is…."

"An old man," Luke laughs and sets off running toward the mountain. They run side by side, and the sound of their breath quickly reveals who is in the best shape. "Can you climb to the top?" Luke looks wondering up at Thomas, who smiles as he tries to keep up. "…without falling through?" Luke makes a face, revealing that he is not entirely comfortable with the situation.

"Yes, if you know the secret magic formula," Thomas laughs. "And without it, you will be the old man."

"NOOOO," Luke picks up speed. He is stubborn and purposeful. His short legs sprint away, and for each of Thomas's steps, it takes at least two of Luke's.

The cloud mountain rises like an almost vertical wall further ahead. Luke's gaze is locked on the top. The mountain glistens in the sun as if it were covered with stardust. The wind tries to tear small pieces of cloud off the mountain but must give up.

"Give me the formula!" Luke places a fist in Thomas's stomach, but Thomas doesn't say anything before they reach the foot of the cloud that rises steeply in front of them.

"You already have it; you just have to find it inside you." Thomas breathes and bends slightly forward.

Luke looks at him and takes the first step up the mountain. His gaze is locked on his feet, which step on top of the cloud without falling through or slipping back. He breathes gently and takes one more step. It works. Then he turns triumphantly toward Thomas, "It wasn't that hard." At that exact moment, his foot slips, and he slides down, only stopping because he bumps into Thomas's legs.

Thomas breaks out in loud laughter. "Maybe it takes a little more searching inside yourself, but what it is, you need to find out for yourself. That is today's task."

Luke clenches his fist and slams it into the cloud, which swirls up around it. "Can't you just say what it is?" He jumps up, ready to make one more attempt.

Thomas smiles and shakes his head slightly as he smooths out a small cloud hanging next to him. "But I will be waiting for you at the top…." He starts walking up the cloud mountain. "…Old man."

Luke takes a run-up. The first three steps are at high speed, and he is doing well. But suddenly, it is as if the cloud is smoother than ice, and in no time, he is back where he started at the foot of the mountain. He looks up. Thomas is already a third of the way up the mountain, and he is not slipping. Luke stomps a few times in the cloud, takes another approach, and sets off. With the most determined steps he can take, he sprints toward the mountain and reaches six feet before running on the spot. Grunting, he lets himself fall forward on the soft cloud and slowly slide back down again. He has crossed his legs and looks up at Thomas. Then shoes and socks are ripped off. He rolls up his pants and stares purposefully up at the top. In a quick motion, he sets off running—this time with small steps that quickly replace each other.

Thomas is halfway up and has sat down. Above him hangs the sun alone in the sky. Luke snorts and lets out the worst swear words he knows. His small steps move him at lightning speed up the mountainside, further than the two previous times. He's closing in on Thomas. "I want to catch him; I want to catch him." The words seep out between his clenched teeth, and he stares at the top. But at that moment, his feet lose their grip on the cloud. He gives up and lets himself slide down back to where he started. Thomas has now reached the top. Next to him, he has made a chair shaped out of a cloud for Luke, who is getting ready for his next attempt. The same thing happens every time. The first part goes well, but then suddenly, a change occurs, and he loses his footing and has to start all over again. He has always been stubborn, and right now, he is not going to give up. One approach after another in all possible variations, but the outcome is the same. The light slowly turns red, and the sun disappears on the horizon. Thomas walks casually down the mountain as if it were the most natural thing in the whole world. He stops next to Luke, who lies exhausted on his back. "Well, my friend, do you want to call it a day? We can try again tomorrow if you like."

Luke nods but can't stand up. His whole body is dog-tired after the many attempts, and his will is used up. "Why can you just walk up the mountain when I slide down? You are CHEATING." He sits up and looks at Thomas, squatting next to him.

"That's what you need to find out. Let's continue tomorrow." He extends his hand to Luke, who lets himself be dragged up.

"Are you carrying me home?" He looks at Thomas with his most pleading eyes and turns up the charm as only he can. "Pleaseeee."

Thomas pulls him up and puts him on his back. Luke lets himself fall forward toward Thomas's back and oozes with satisfaction; that was today's small victory. Thomas's pocket vibrates, and he pulls out the Skycon. Eva appears on the screen.

"He is gone!" She is red-faced and out of breath.

"What do you mean? Who is gone?"

"Luke is missing. I can't find him. Frank must have taken him."

19
MISSING

I run frantically out into the deserted hallway, where the only thing I can see is the few pieces of furniture that stand along the wall and scream loneliness at each other. I turn to my mother, who is still standing with a blank stare. "Stay here," I look at her and wait for a nod, so I know she has understood the message.

She keeps staring at me. "Where is Luke? Do you think…?"

She doesn't manage to complete the sentence before I interrupt. "I will find him; stay here. Okay!?" I run down the hallway in no time to the office where the staff has their breaks. With a firm push, I open the door and let my gaze wander, searching the room to find someone who can help me. It's empty. And nothing indicates that anyone has been here today—no coffee cups on the tables or chairs that are not in place. The door slams behind me, and I stand in the hallway, where there are now only two options left. I can run right or left, hoping to find someone who can help me. As my mother stands in the hallway to the left and has begun to pick off the leaves of some withered plants, my common sense tells me that the smartest move is to run down the hallway to the right. She can stop any member of staff at the other end. I rush through the revolving door and out into the stairwell. The atmosphere is different here, noisier and messier. As soon as you leave intensive, it is as if the pulse of life returns. There are more people here, but it's all patients or relatives on the move. I run toward the next set of doors. "Neurology Department" sounds advanced, but I try my luck. Inside the hallway, I grab the first nurse I see. A middle-aged woman with fiery red hair pulled back in a ponytail and a face carpet-bombed with freckles. She is standing at a high counter filled with yellow patches.

"I can't find my son; can you help me?" I stare at the woman, who looks a little overwhelmed by my desperate way of approaching her. For every step she takes back, I step forward.

"Who is your son?" She looks at me wonderingly and starts fumbling with a bundle of keys.

"Luke, Luke Lancaster. He was in intensive care. He was there yesterday." I can't stand still and look feverishly up and down the hall. People are waiting, and there are far from enough chairs for all of them.

She shakes her head so that her ponytail swings from side to side. "Unfortunately, I have nothing to do with intensive care, sorry."

"But you can look him up on the system, right? There must be a file...." The intensity of the words is about to knock her back, and she grabs the edge of the table, looks up at the clock on the wall, and casts a glance toward the staff room. It's five minutes to midday. "Come with me," she walks toward an open door. Inside the small space, which most of all resembles a converted broom closet, there's a computer.

"How do you spell his name?"

I'm standing right behind her because there's no room for both of us in there.

"L-u-k-e L-a-n-c-a-s-t-e-r, it's straightforward." I tap nervously on the wall and feel how turmoil has taken control of my body.

The computer searches. It takes forever. She shakes her head and sighs loudly. "This is always the case. The system never works.

The government is constantly cutting back funds, and if it's not on the staff, it's the machines."

Even though the turmoil rages inside me and my legs cannot stand still, I hold onto the best version of myself. "I'm sorry to hear that. Thank you so much for trying to help me."

She glances down at her watch, where the hand has struck twelve. A swarm of green and white coats rushes toward the staff room. There is a brief buzz in the hallway before it becomes silent again.

It must be deeply frustrating to go through years of education to help other people and constantly live in fear of being fired or failing due to time pressure or machines not working. I remember my mother always told me that gratitude is one of the most important qualities we can learn. When I was younger, I thought it to be foolish. Because when you grow up and have enough of everything, it's easy to take it all for granted. I've been feeling that lately. Everything I have taken for granted has been taken from me. But it's so easy to tell others that they should not take their lives and children for granted. Or even simple things such as walking, smelling, or holding onto a knife. It rarely changes anything before what we take for granted is gone. Then we wake up, but it's too late. If only I knew how to get people to wake up before it's too late. Thomas has also spoken several times about gratitude. But along with gratitude comes other emotions. Humility. How can I be grateful if I am not humble? Is that why it's so hard to be grateful? Are we taking things for granted? Do we really have to lose everything that matters to us in order to wake up?

"Sorry, I can't help you." The nurse shakes her head and interrupts my thoughts. "The system is not working." She turns to me. We stand right in front of each other, so close that I can smell her sweat and see the tiny pearls on her upper lip. I move back so she can get out of the broom closet.

"Thank you so much for taking the time to try." I smile at her and place my hand gently on her arm.

She presses her lips together so that they become completely white and tries to smile back. "I know there is ward round in intensive at 12:10; it's in five minutes. Maybe you can find someone who can help you find your son."

"Thank you." The temperature rises a degree in my body, and water is about to overflow into my eyes. I blink a few times to make it go away. But why can't I allow her to see that her help touches me? I set off, back down the hall, through the door, over to the other side, and through the next set of doors. When the last door opens, I can see my mother. She is talking to an older man in a white coat. I run as fast as I can.

"Do you know where Luke is?" I tumble into the conversation without introducing myself.

The man bends his head forward and looks over the edge of his glasses as he raises his thick eyebrows, "And you are?"

My mother jumps in, "This is Luke's mother." She straightens her little hat and smiles proudly at me.

He flips through his papers. "It says that Luke's mother is dead, but maybe you have resurrected?" We are the only ones in the hallway. The plants in the windowsills look more dead than alive, and the bit of light that comes through the windows drowns in the light from the LED panels in the ceiling.

"Ha-ha," I exclaim, "that would be funny. No, I am…." Now I have to choose my words carefully, so we don't create more confusion than necessary. "I am his aunt. And this is my old mother, who can't always remember who is who. I've always been very close to my nephew. Like a mother." I smile, so it hurts in my jaws. "Are you a doctor? Do you know where he is?" I use the age-old diversion strategy because I need to know where Luke is. Now.

"Yes." He looks at me calmly as if time is not important to him. He doesn't know that Frank is trying to destroy the mission for the Ring, nor does he know what consequences it will have for the whole world.

My mother grabs my arm and pats it lightly with her other

hand. The constant restlessness in my legs subsides, and I try to stand still for a moment.

"I am a doctor." He takes a break that feels like an eternity. "And I also know where Luke is." He will win the World Cup in long breaks if he doesn't say any more soon. Not even the Master comes close. I try hard not to melt him with my gaze.

"Luke has been in intensive care for a long time, so we have chosen to move him." He flips through the papers. "He was transferred to a highly specialized neurorehabilitation hospital yesterday."

Relief flushes through my body. Luke is safe, and Frank is nowhere around.

The doctor continues, "It says here that his father has approved the transfer. Do you know him?"

I must remember what I have learned and refrain from sending a rude comment back. I have a choice in every single moment. Will I respond out of fear or trust? Will I fight or seek peace? I remind myself of the power of gratitude.

"Of course, we know him; he's a nice man," my mother answers before I have time to find the right words.

"Thank you, thank you for your help." I smile at him and look over at my mother. "We have to get ahold of Andreas!"

20
THE REGAINED JOY OF LIFE

The phone rings tirelessly, but Andreas does not answer. My mom starts fiddling with her scarf. "Do you think something has happened?" We are still in the intensive care unit. The doctor has gone to see another patient. A porter comes past us with a patient who has given up his life.

"No, he's probably just with Luke. Let's see if we can find out where they are." I pull out my cell. It was still in the car, a leftover from the last time I was here. Quickly, I write "highly specialized neurorehabilitation hospital" and press search. There must be a limit to how many there are. Seven. Only two are within a 125-mile radius; one specializes in treating children. "This is where he is!" I hand the phone to my mother. She pushes her glasses into place and wrinkles her eyebrows. "I think you're right. Let's go there." The phone suddenly starts ringing loudly. She gives a twitch and drops it on the floor. I bend down and pick it up. It's Andreas.

"Andreas, is Luke okay?" I shout, so it resounds in the hallway. "Is he with you?"

"Hi, Angela," he laughs a bit. "Yes, yes, he is here with me. Do you want to say hi?"

My heart skips a beat. I stand completely stiff and let my jaw drop. "Is, is he awake?" I manage to say.

I can almost hear how Andres smiles through the phone. "No, no. But you don't know if he can hear you even though he is in a coma." There is complete silence.

I collapse and lean against the wall, which is already stained with dark vertical marks. It has frequently been used as a backrest. The floor is dusty, and I draw a heart with an "L"

in the middle. On the one hand, I want with all my heart that Luke should wake up and be allowed to live his life, but on the other hand, it would be a life without me, and the Ring would not be completed.

"Hi, Luke," I stammer. "Where are you, Andreas?"

My mom is in the process of straightening a picture on the wall before pulling a chair next to me.

"We are in the pediatric ward of a specialized neurorehabilitation hospital; I can just send you the address. It's a much smaller hospital and good for Luke." He sounds calm. But he always is. Andreas has always been able to remain calm in the most aggravated situations. When Luke was little, I sometimes panicked if he got something stuck in his throat or was about to fall down a flight of stairs. And even though I knew he had to explore the world, it was horrible to lose control that way. Now, I have waved goodbye to any kind of control. After all, control is basically just the absence of trust. Trust feels like a bigger and more solid rock to lean on than fear does. It's as if the control can disappear under your feet when you least expect it. *Trust*, I say to myself as I exhale slowly and empty my lungs of air. *Trust*.

"I will text you the address and wait here until you arrive." Andreas has put down the phone and is rummaging with something else while we talk.

"I have my mother with me." She has sat down next to me and starts waving at the phone.

Andreas hangs up without saying goodbye. It's typical of him. I fold the phone and put it in my pocket. "Andreas is with Luke," I look at my mother, who has heard it all.

The pile of old weeklies on the table is now neat. She looks at me, "Let's get going. There is no time to waste." Before I get to my feet, she is long gone. I run after her.

"When will my mother be back?" Luke looks up at Thomas and over to the door to Eva's room, which is right next to his. The light from the moon falls on the wall and draws a sharp shadow over the images of two angels playing. It's completely quiet, as quiet as it's only possible to be in a place without traffic or people. Thomas strokes Luke's forehead. He is warm, and his hair is slightly damp at the hairline.

"She will be back in 40 days at the latest. They're going to go by fast."

"How do you know that?" Luke blinks his bright blue eyes, trying to blow cold air up into his hair.

Thomas looks at him in amazement and smiles so much that he can hardly utter the words. "I don't, and you are absolutely right. I do not know. But I know that time flies when you are having fun and learning new things." He stops and smiles even more, if possible, "And it's always great with good company." He grabs Luke and tickles him, so he screams loudly and twists around in bed.

"Is this where you are most ticklish?" His fingers grab right under Luke's arm. Luke howls and twists so much that he is about to fall out of the bed.

"I will pee in the bed if you don't stop." He struggles to get free.

Thomas will not risk it, so he stops, and Luke looks triumphant because his move worked.

"Peace." Luke holds his hand up in front of him.

"Peace," they both gasp for breath.

"What are we going to do up here? Is there a Kindergarten?"

Luke has settled into bed again and pulled the duvet all the way up under his chin to avoid a new round of tickling. On the table next to him is a vase with sunflowers, and there is a pile of Donald Duck comic books.

Thomas gets up and slides his hand over the window, which opens to let in a cool breeze. "You must learn to climb clouds." Thomas sits down next to Luke, who pulls the duvet over his head as he shouts a resounding no. His laugh fills the room and reminds Thomas of when he was a child before it dawned on him what life is all about. Back then, he could wake up in the morning and be captivated by a tiny beetle on the floor and spend several hours studying it, building a house, and finding food for it. The whole world was all about the small beetle. Being one with time and just being is what he practices rediscovering within himself. But there was more than that—the joy of life—the fine and pure, unspoiled joy of life. He can feel that Luke has it, but he doesn't. It feels like something inside him is guarding that place and that he cannot get in touch with it. But the time with Luke helps to pry open the lock. He sits completely still and smiles at the duvet next to him. Gently, the duvet is pulled down, and the top of Luke's hair appears, followed by a very red and sweaty face. Luke groans.

"Say, we have to do something other than climb on clouds." He looks pleadingly at Thomas.

"What else would you like to do?" Thomas awaits his reply.

The expression in Luke's eyes is the same as one would get if you let a child into a toy store and tell them they are free to take any toy they want. "Can I think about it until tomorrow?"

"Of course, you can." Thomas removes some of the wet hair from his forehead and turns off the light next to the bed, making the moonlight visible in the room, and says goodnight to Luke.

"Are you not singing for me? Mom usually does."

No one ever sang for Thomas when he was a child. He even went to bed and got up in the morning by himself from the age of seven. Thomas scratches his hair. "How about I tell you a story instead?"

"Great, I love stories." Luke snuggles closer to Thomas.

"Well, then close your eyes." Thomas sits down with his back up against the wall. "There once was a young boy…."

21
FALLING THROUGH LAYERS

The Skycon flashes. It's Meera. I touch the side, and her picture comes to life in front of me.

"Hi, Angela." Her voice is a bit restrained. She has the hood of a pink sweater pulled over her head. The whites around her blue eyes are bloodshot, and the wrinkles around her eyes are marked.

"Hi, Meera, how are you?" I'm sitting in my car parked down the road from Daniel's castle. Seven large black muscular horses are walking along the fence by the road. They seem to enjoy their freedom within the boundaries of their paddock. They have become accustomed to me parking here because I have done so every day since I dropped my mother off at the hospital. Time is a strange thing. When I need it most, it disappears between my actions, and when it just has to pass by, it will not disappear. Right now, I would like to be able to fast-forward or at least look into the future—just three months.

I cannot help but smile at myself because I know it would be the easy solution, but it's tempting. My old grandmother always said that time should be used wisely. I'm not sure if she had thought more profoundly about it or whether it was something she had heard from her parents. But there is some truth to it. I have wasted a lot of time on things I did not feel like doing or thought I should do because others expected it. Basically, it had nothing to do with others but everything to do with me. The interesting thing is that we can all stop and change direction, but excuses often line up to prevent us from doing so. If we have unexpected time to think about life, we fill it with all sorts of chores that we suddenly invent. We wait until we have no choice and there is no other way. As long as we can survive, we will continue to live as we do, even if we are not happy. I stayed in the relationship with Andreas for too long and even began to think about having another child. That would have kept me busy but could never save our relationship.

The horse outside the car neighs loudly and lifts its front legs. Then it gallops away across the field. The other horses in the herd follow. I agreed with my mother and Andreas that they would work out who should be with Luke and when. Andreas wasn't too happy about seeing my mother; he definitely blames her for what happened. But I'm sure they will get through it, and if problems occur, they will call me. It allows me to concentrate on Frank and has led me back to Daniel. He's the only one I can think of who can help me find Frank. But he has not been home the last several days and does not answer my calls. I also circled the old hospital to see if Frank would show up and combed all the newspapers, just in case Frank succeeded in disposing of more stories. So far, I have not found anything, nor have I been able to find any more online. But I sense it's a matter of time. Frank has not given up. Probably the opposite. Resistance gives him the energy to fight. Now, I have chosen to camp here until Daniel shows up. Time goes by, and there is nothing I can do to change it.

"Angela," Meera coughs gently. "Am I disturbing you?" She is in the control room. I can see the couch behind her. It looks like she's alone. The reflections from the screens in front of her cast shifting shadows on her face.

My head gives a jerk, and I am present again. "No, sorry, what did you say?"

I move her picture up onto the inside of the windscreen, so I can see her better while keeping an eye on Daniel's castle further down the road. "I spoke to Thomas about Frank and who is helping him here. We want to try to help you the best we can." She pauses and takes a sip of a coffee mug that looks full. "We are completely blank. I have spoken with the people I have eaten with." She holds back. I wait and know I have to give her time, even though I want to ask her to fast-forward to the conclusion. Not because I have to go somewhere, but sometimes I get so impatient. It's one of those days. The clock is ticking.

She moves closer to the picture, and the deep wrinkles between her eyes become more apparent. "I've been eating at different tables and trying to ask people about Frank. No one knows me up here. But no one knows Frank either." She shakes her head.

The seat scratches my back as I lean back. "Why can't anyone remember Frank? It doesn't make sense. Meera, how many people have you talked to?" My tone could well be interpreted as accusatory. It wasn't meant that way.

Meera pulls a gray strand of hair free from the hood and runs it around her finger. "A lot, both people who have been here a long time and some who have just arrived. You know how easy it is to tell the difference." She smiles shyly at me. There are several red bottles on the table next to her and a brown one that I haven't seen before.

When people arrive at In-Between, they always walk around with huge eyes and careful steps for the first few weeks. It takes time for the brain to come to terms with not falling through the clouds. I pull a smile and remember how I struggled the first few days. It's beyond comprehension when one has not tried it. Walking in the light, bright cloud dust, the almost transparent walls that float smoothly and define the spaces, the perspective on life and death is turned upside down, and you suddenly see everything from above. It is a great upheaval for the brain.

All the souls in In-Between are there because their lives somehow ended abruptly. Just acknowledging that one's life ended before you expected it is a challenge that can take a long time. At first, you deny it, and when the seriousness dawns on you, you get angry. Angry at life, at God, and not least at yourself. The last battle is the most difficult one because you realize that you could have done something about your life instead of constantly postponing what was important. I empty my lungs of air, wait a moment, and then let them fill again so that they expand. But it is easier to blame God, society, or others for your shortcomings or misery. Then you don't have to take responsibility. It feels like my throat swells, making it harder to swallow. I was given a choice to come back because I was in a coma. Not everyone gets a choice. Those who die suddenly cannot return to their lives on Earth. But in a way, it might be easier because they don't have to take responsibility for their choice to live or say goodbye.

The muscles in my neck tense up even more, and my heart gets heavy. If I had taken care of my development and learned from life, would I have ended up here? If I had stopped by myself. It's impossible to say, and no one knows the answer or the challenges we must face, so there is no reason to pursue it. But one thing is for sure: I have made many choices in my life that have kept me from feeling myself and my needs. My choices have implications for the evolution of the world, even though I make up only a microscopically tiny part of the universe. Everything is connected. But even though I'm just a tiny piece of an enormous universe, it doesn't give me the right to abdicate the responsibility to live my life every day. There, I failed. I lived in the past and the future.

I could always find something to complain about or something that should be different than it was. The constant longing for things to change made it difficult for me to be present and appreciate what was. That's the fight—the battle that everyone who comes to In-Between is struggling with. The struggle with regret, guilt, and grief. But then it's too late. Therefore, it's easy to see who is new and who has been there for a long time. Once the amazement and fascination have died down, the inner struggle begins. People become quiet, walk by themselves, and have a fragile vibration around them. Those who have been there for a long time find it easier to laugh; they are more social and relaxed. They enjoy the freedom they have been given, but it only happens when they let go of the struggle.

"Meera, there's a guy you can try to talk to. He is quite clever with the technical stuff and getting the system to do things you are not supposed to. His name is Ian, and he is often in the control room at night when everyone else has left. You can recognize him by his jet-black hair that he always wears in a tight ponytail. Thomas had previously talked to him about Frank, but he didn't know anything then. Maybe it's worth another try. He may have heard something or know someone you can reach out to."

She makes a note on a piece of paper lying on the table. "It sounds good; I'll find him. Is there anyone other than him you can think of?"

I jump in the seat when one of the horses sticks his head through the open window and gives my shoulder a loving push. It has seen my packed lunch on the dashboard. Before I know it, its whole head is inside the car, and I push it back out to save my food. My mind scans through the gallery of people I have met in In-Between. There's also Allan from Alabama, but he is too innocent, and all he wants is to be with his girls, and Heidi from Sweden; she is too naive.

"Ian is my best bet; I would start by getting ahold of him. Go easy on him; otherwise, he closes up. He can do a little bit of everything, and yes, let me put it this way, it's probably not all quite in accordance with the rules. But he's okay; there's nothing sneaky about him."

"Thank you, Angela, it is a great help. I feel a little lost here sometimes and need to find my bearings." Her vulnerability shines through in the picture like a lamb that only just got on its feet for the first time. My compassion grows. It washes away all other emotions and leaves me here with Meera.

"How are you doing, Eva?"

"It's not easy. I cannot find Frank and have no idea where to look." When she's so honest, I want to be too.

Meera shakes her head, "Unfortunately, I cannot help you. Only Yoge knows how to use the surveillance, and I heard him swear over it earlier tonight."

I can sense someone coming into the room. Meera is absent for a moment and moves to the side, making space for Thomas.

"Hi, Eva…" his clear blue eyes shine brighter than usual. There is more life in them—as if a bit of spark has been ignited.

I move forward in the seat to get close to the picture, "Thomas!" A bubble from my stomach grows into a smile. "How is Luke?" My voice is eager, and I hardly pause between the words.

Thomas chuckles, "He's having a great time. He is currently learning to climb cloud mountains."

I know exactly what he's up to. Thomas did the same with me. It's one of the best exercises to be in the present and let go of control. It took me weeks to get up the cloud mountain, and Thomas walked up there with ease every day. I wanted to win. My urge to win removed focus, so I lost. "How is he doing?"

"He is tenacious like his mother. Just as stubborn. And just as eager to come first. There is no doubt that he is your son." Thomas winks at me. "And how are you?"

"It could be better…." I fall back into the seat that scratches my back with the old nubbed fabric. A spring from the car seat digs into my buttock.

I tell Thomas and Meera about the experiences of the last few days. About how Luke has been moved to another hospital and that it wasn't Frank who took him. And that my mother is with him now. "But I'm stuck. I don't know how to proceed. Should I keep looking for Frank, and what should I do to stop him if I find him? I can't arrest him." My shoulders almost reach my ears, and I shift uneasily on the seat.

Thomas holds his gaze, and his chest rises and lowers at a perfectly calm pace under his blue silk tunic. "Do you remember when you were looking for Meera and were about to give up?"

I remember it as if it was yesterday. The struggle inside me, the frustration that was eating me up. The worst feeling of all: powerlessness. I gasp for air. Is that the feeling that's hitting me again? The cursed powerlessness? It's the feeling of standing at a dark dead end.

"But I made it easy for you," Meera smiles at me, trying to lighten the mood. She takes the brown bottle and slides it into her pocket with one hand while drinking from the coffee cup with the other.

"Yes, at least I didn't have to push you off the mountain," a dry laugh is all I can evoke.

"Eva, what kind of feeling is challenging you?" Thomas looks at me with his usual calm.

"Powerlessness," I mumble.

He bends his head slightly forward so that the long, dark blond hair covers his face. With a light stroke, he removes it. "So, the question is whether you have learned to deal with that feeling or whether you should have one more round with it?"

Sometimes, Thomas is so annoying that I could whack him one, but that's only when he hits my sore pressure points. I know he's right, but that does not mean it's funny.

"What did you do last time you met the powerlessness?" His words reach out to me.

What did I do? Strangely enough, I don't remember. I can only remember the struggle.

"It happens to most people. We focus on survival, and when we encounter an emotion that we don't like, we rush on to something else in life. A feeling can be experienced so strongly that we think we can die from it." He pauses and looks over at Meera, who reciprocates his gaze. When she asked the Master about her task and the answer was nothing, she was also struck by powerlessness. She didn't know what to do. Should she start inventing a task or just let it go?

Thomas gets up and walks to the cupboard full of drinks. He takes a small orange bottle and comes back. I can see a frequency number on the side of the bottle, but I'm not sure what it means. "There are seven basic emotions. Joy, sadness, shame, anxiety, disgust, anger, and surprise." He speaks calmly and clearly.

"Inner calm is something we experience when emotions are in balance, and we can observe them and are in touch with ourselves."

Every single word resonates in me. Seven basic emotions, then the task of getting to know them is not that big. "But where does the powerlessness come in?" I interrupt his pause.

Thomas can't help but smile; he knows me and my impatience. "Underneath each of the basic emotions lie several others, kind of cousins." He borrows the paper from Meera and turns it over. He draws what looks like a family tree for all the emotions and their cousins.

Powerlessness lies beneath sadness. He holds it up and points so I can see it better. "I always thought it was the hardest emotion of all. Here you are, checkmate. I can easily relate to your battle." He looks directly into the Skycon.

That's exactly how I feel. I feel like I have run out of moves and that Frank wins no matter where I move on the game board. For every move I make, he has a better counterattack that I have not anticipated.

Thomas reaches out and turns on a dim light in the ceiling. Now, it is clear that there is no one but him and Meera in the room. I can see several bowls on the tables with snacks and empty glasses. There are also a couple of red bottles with extra strong energy liquor, while I only have my worn-out water bottle with lukewarm water and a plastic bag with a day-old sandwich.

"Eva, working with emotions is pretty simple. Usually, we struggle to get rid of the difficult emotions. We wrap them up and hide them away, hoping they will disappear." Thomas holds his hands up in front of him and shapes them like a small ball. "But then the opposite happens. They stay inside you and become more and more out of balance." He pauses and reaches out for two glasses. First, he pours water for Meera and then himself. He holds up the glass in front of the Skycon. "Imagine me pouring a handful of sand in the water; then it will be hard to see clearly. It's the same with emotions. Once they have taken over inside us, we cannot see clearly, and they control us and not the other way around. But if we wait, the sand will fall to the bottom and settle. Slowly, the water will become clear again, and now we can more easily make the most appropriate choice."

He puts the glass down on the table, where it makes a small mark. Meera sits next to him and rocks calmly back and forth on the chair. She has taken off the hood so that her thick gray hair falls loosely around her face. "When we get stuck in an emotion and hide it away, it gets out of balance. In the long run, unbalanced emotions can turn into diseases."

I have heard Thomas say this before, and I can feel the truth in it, even though a part of me still thinks it sounds a bit too weird. Is there really such a strong connection between our soul and body? The escape from my vulnerability, the struggle, the anger, and the doubt of trust have led me away from myself. I've been working overtime to keep them down, so others won't see them. Imagine if they got out when I couldn't control them—my body shivers. The thought of others being allowed to look behind my controlled facade makes the smallest muscles in my body tremble. I glance out the window at the horses now grazing under a tree. The large castle with spires looks uninhabited. There are no tire tracks on the driveway or lights in the windows. I have practiced accommodating my anger, anxiety, and sadness. But I have not succeeded in falling completely through the layers down to powerlessness. Naive as I am, I thought that when I could accommodate my sadness, that was enough. But the truth is, unfortunately, that I have kept the sadness under control.

Thomas interrupts my thoughts, "You have come a long way, Eva. Powerlessness is the last feeling most people wrestle with. When you can embrace it, you are about to reach the finish line."

That is the good news of the day, I think, trying to be a little bold. "Well, then there is still hope."

Meera has started drawing small skulls and bombs with lit fuses on the paper. I don't know how many emotions she has to work with, but there is plenty to address for most people. She unscrews the lid of the small brown bottle and pours the contents into the coffee.

"Thomas, why is it so important that we get to know all our emotions?"

"If we want to change the world for the better, we need to start by getting to know our emotions. We all make our choices based on emotions, and if we do not know them, we don't know what our choices are based on. Emotions are like a kind of fuel for our development and our actions." He glances at Meera to see if she's listening. She has started drawing on a new piece of paper. "The brain is designed in a way where we have far more resources for our emotions than for our reasoning. The emotions are also 'cheaper' to use; for example, they don't require as much energy as changing behavior." He gets up, walks to one of the screens, and pulls out images of war. "Is it reason or emotion that starts a war?" It's as if the ring around his pupils becomes stronger and glows as he speaks.

"It isn't reason; that is for sure," I mumble, glancing in the rearview mirror to see if the ring around my pupils also gets brighter. It doesn't. My leg starts to move up and down, and my finger drums on the steering wheel.

"I'm not saying that people have no common sense. We do. But our choice is nearly always based on emotion—positive or negative." He flips through the pictures and stops at pictures of huge trees that are cut down by the roots and fallen in a line like domino pieces. "Is it common sense or emotions that decide to remove a rainforest?"

“It must be greed,” there is a bit of wonder in my voice, and I am unsure if greed is an emotion. The springs in the seat continue to chafe my butt, and I try to shift my weight onto the other side.

“We have to assume that, but we don’t know. Greed is not an emotion; it is controlled by our ego rather than our heart. There is a deeper emotion that controls greed.” He places his hands flat on top of each other, moving the top down below the other.

“Anxiety,” I suggest.

“Exactly. It’s one layer deeper.” Thomas flips through the pictures. “The fear of missing out lies deep in the human brain. It was designed to help us survive many thousands of years ago, but now it’s killing us.” Pictures of famine fill the screens.

I look at the pictures and feel a fragile tingle in my heart. If only more people were aware of their emotions and the deeper layers, then their choices would probably be different.

Thomas looks at Meera to make sure she’s listening too. She isn’t. She has fallen asleep in the chair and is sitting with her mouth open. He reaches out, takes the little brown bottle, and holds it up so I can see it. “Whiskey.”

I can’t help but smile; I nearly did the same when I arrived at In-Between.

“Part of our job is to help people understand their feelings. It’s one area where we need to raise awareness with the energy and light we bring back. That’s why it’s important that we are all completely familiar with our egos, our emotions, and our souls.” Thomas speaks as if he can read my thoughts.

“What do we do now?” I open the car door to get away from the spring in the seat and stretch my legs. At that exact moment, someone honks intensely. Daniel has just passed me and waves eagerly from his open red sports car.

“Thomas, I have to go. I think luck just caught up with me and the answer arrived!”

22
A JOURNEY INTO THE DEEP

"To what do I owe this honor?" Daniel has parked his shiny red sports car in the driveway and comes strolling toward me. His cap faces backward. The castle lies behind him like a magnificent backdrop, with the sun falling on the brickwork. His footsteps crunch in the loose stones on the driveway. I know I owe him an explanation. The last time we were together, I left him by the lake after we had lunch. He wanted to tell me about Frank's plans but didn't get that far. He mentioned Luke first, the panic gripped me, and I hurried off to the hospital without hearing everything he wanted to tell me.

He lifts his sunglasses and places them on top of his cap. "Well, how long will you stay this time, Princess?" Elegantly, he steps forward and kisses me on the cheek. I'm holding my breath. The way he pronounces the words always reminds me of the upper class you see on TV in fancy series. There is no trace of anger or bitterness in his tone of voice. Right now, I need all the help I can get, and Daniel is the only one I know who is close to Frank. He looks relaxed in his jeans and pink sweater. I wish I could borrow a little of his laid-back attitude.

"I'm so sorry I left you by yourself the other day. I don't know what got into me. Am I forgiven?" I kick the stones on the driveway and make a small hole in the ground.

"Of course, you are forgiven. But what happened?" He holds up his hand to shield himself from the sun. Then, he points to the side of my head where the wound from the collision with Frank is still visible.

I shake my head defensively. "It's nothing. Do you have time for a cup of coffee?" I smile at him and hope that is enough to change the subject.

"I always have time for you, Princess. Let's go and sit in the garden." He reaches out and takes my hand. His skin is silky soft—like skin that has never done any physical labor. We walk across the courtyard toward the old wooden gate with large carvings to the castle's right. A path leads to the garden, which is more like a park. Here are open expanses with yellow fields to the left and huge beech trees as far as I can see to the other side. It's like a painting where the imagination is unleashed. The last time I was here was the day I met Daniel and got the first glimpse into past lives. I've never been here in the daytime. The pool area is more prominent than I thought and surrounded by palm trees. We walk down to a nook next to the pool, where roses climb up a fence and form an oasis filled with pink colors and the sweetest scent. There's a table set with cups decorated with small blue flowers and a jug with a convoluted spout. There is also a small bowl with round chocolates wrapped in gold paper. Nothing is there by chance. On the right is a wooden chest, and on top of it are several Indian woven rugs in light brown colors.

He pulls a wicker chair with off-white cushions out next to me, "Have a seat."

I let myself fall into the chair, which is stiffer than is comfortable. Daniel pulls a chair over and sits down opposite me. He could easily be arrogant and self-righteous with so much money, but he isn't. He is always sweet and helpful and never puts his own needs first or bears resentment. I love watching him. His movements are elegant, and his pronunciation of words is more solemn and precise than mine.

"What can I do for you?" He leans forward, puts his warm, soft hand on mine, and looks me in the eyes. "I've been thinking about you, and I'm sorry if I scared you with my message about Frank."

I shake my head. "No, no, it's all right." I look down. "But do you know that Frank tried to turn off Luke's respirator?" Pain from my lower lip rushes through me as I bite into it.

Daniel pulls his hand back. "WHAT!" He pushes the chair back firmly and gets up. "It makes no sense. Why would he do that?" He takes off his cap and hurls it on the chair.

I have never seen Daniel react so ragingly before. He cannot stand still and walks back and forth on the spot while clenching his fists. I stay seated and look at him. "Frank said it was all or none. And when I didn't want to give him a space in the Ring, then no one should have it." My voice is low, and I look down. "But I can't give him a position in the Ring; there is no freedom of choice. And it's definitely not up to me."

Daniel walks to the railing next to the roses. He stands with his back to me. Silent. With his eyes locked on the horizon. I stay seated.

"I was with Frank yesterday." He slaps his hand against the railing. "I asked if he had seen you, and he said no." In a quick motion, he turns around. "I was worried about you, and I know Frank doesn't always tell the whole truth." He takes the chair and moves it right next to mine. "Did he do that to you?" He points to my wound. I don't get a chance to answer before he continues.

"Frank has always been economical with the truth. It was the same when we were young. I have always stood up for Frank because I have known him since we were children. I feel sorry for him. He has not had it easy." He pulls up the sleeves of his sweater and starts pouring from the pot.

"But that's no excuse for being an idiot," I say with a determined voice.

"Easy now, warrior, you are about to kill the wrong person." Daniel moves away from me, leaning back in his chair. An elderly lady with short gray hair appears at the castle. She walks toward us with small steps. Her legs are shorter than her arms, and she is dressed completely in off-white clothes with a small blue apron.

"Do you need anything?" The voice is friendly, and Daniel smiles at her.

"No, it's so nice. Thank you for making it ready for us." He looks at me, "I hear you have been waiting for me for several days." He makes a cunning grimace and moves his fingertips lightly against each other.

It's hot today; the temperature is already over 86 Fahrenheit, and even in the shade, you cannot avoid sweating. I pull off my sweater, and Daniel follows. He has a white T-shirt underneath. His body is tanned and physically fit—every little muscle has the proper definition.

"I have to stop Frank or at least keep putting him off for 37 more days until Luke is out of his coma. Can you help me?" My voice is about to crack, but I manage to control it.

"How do you know when Luke will wake up?" He squints at me and takes a sip from the cup. "Are you also the one in charge of people in a coma?"

I reach out for one of the chocolates, unwrap it, and let it slide into my mouth. I have said way too much already. I don't know how much I can tell Daniel. Basically, I don't know if I can trust him or if he is just a skilled psychopath who uses every little trick to win my trust. "Is it coffee?" I must be desperate to change the conversation because I don't drink coffee and never have, and definitely not in this heat. I grit my teeth and hope Daniel has forgotten that little detail.

"Nope, it's iced coffee," he says slightly teasingly. "I also have gin and tonic."

"Iced coffee is fine," as long as it doesn't taste too much like coffee, I finish the sentence inside my head. The scent is round and soft, with a touch of caramel. As a precaution, I add two teaspoons of sugar.

"This is my new favorite." He smiles at me and holds the cup with his fingertips.

I take a sip, and the full creamy taste explodes in my mouth. I look at him.

"There's also a little chili in it." He laughs so his white teeth that sit perfectly in his mouth become visible. "Angela, I don't want you to tell me anything you're not comfortable with." He pauses and is about to laugh, "But the more I know, the easier it is for me to help you."

I know he's right. But is this a clever psychological trick to get me talking anyway? Before my thoughts have finished negotiating with each other, it spills out of my mouth. "Yes, I ultimately have to decide whether Luke should live or die." My emotions break out of the prison that has held them inside. I can no longer control them. My eyes are flooded, so everything becomes blurred. I cover my face with my hands, and it blackens my gaze. The only thing I can feel is my body shaking. It feels like letting go of a branch and falling into a rushing waterfall that pulls me underwater and through the river with an outrageous force. I let go of all the emotions and let myself be dragged down into the depths. The more I sob, the less air I have. Then I feel Daniel's arms around my back, and he pulls me up to the surface where I can get some air before the current grabs me again. Everything is swirling around inside me—light and darkness, pain and joy, perseverance and abandonment—fear and trust. It all gets rinsed together into a black mass, which is the only thing I can see. Daniel keeps holding me, and the tears run freely down my cheeks. I gasp for breath. I stay seated and let myself be flooded by the black mass.

If this is what Thomas meant by getting to know the feelings, I'm well on my way. It's dark here, and I fall further and further into the depths. At the same time, I can feel Daniel's firm grip around my body. How long I'm sitting here, I don't know. But when I finally open my eyes again, the sky is fiery red above us. I lean toward Daniel, who is just sitting completely still next to me without saying a word. He reaches for a blanket lying on the wooden chest behind us and wraps it around me. I look at him, "I don't want to be the one to choose the fate of my child."

He looks at me and wipes a tear away from my chin, "I don't understand very much of this, Angela. But I don't think that any human being should decide the fate of others. What happens if you do nothing?"

The thought had never occurred to me. If I don't give them an answer, what then? I straighten up. It's just an easy solution, so I don't have to take responsibility. "I don't know." My voice blurs itself, and my body shakes. Not because I'm freezing, but the whole trip down the waterfall has taken a toll on me.

"Have a drink, here…" he hands me the cup. "Unfortunately, it's not that cold anymore." Daniel smiles at me, and I can't help but smile back. My eyes are swollen, and my nose is filled with snot. "Is there anything else you need?"

I exhale so my lips vibrate, "A tissue, and then I need to find Frank."

23

DO YOU SEE ME?

We have moved inside and are sitting on the couch in front of the open fireplace in the large living room. The furniture is heavy and belongs to a different time. The air is warm, and the door to the terrace is open so we can hear the birds singing. My pocket vibrates, but I can't look at my Skycon. Although I have to believe that Daniel wants the best for me, I can't tell him how I contact In-Between. The less he knows, the better. At least, that is what I'm telling myself.

"Frank." Daniel is lighting up the fireplace. Even though it's hot outside, the thick walls keep the house cool. "We have been friends since we were children. I've always seen the funny side of Frank. We had fun together, got drunk, scored each other's ex-girlfriends, and followed each other through life. There is something special about the people who have known you all your life. They become like family to you." He flicks the lighter, and the fire catches. "Even if you grow apart, somehow you choose to ignore that."

I have pulled my legs up underneath me. Daniel puts the rug around me and sits down next to me. The fire crackles and begins to send heat to us. Outside, the sky is burning red, and the clouds form several beautiful patterns in bright colors outside the large windows.

"Frank has always liked success. He has talked a lot about people with money and power in a way I never understood."

I can see it's getting harder for Daniel. The pauses between his words get longer, and he stares into the fire.

"When I had chronic stress, Frank was there for me as a brother. My own family was no support. They thought I was a weakling and just needed to pull myself together. My parents made it clear to me that having a weak son damaged their reputation. I come from the working class, but my parents have always pretended to belong to the upper class. We didn't have much money, and what we had was used to make others believe that we were wealthy." Daniel shakes his head. "It has never been a wish for me to be rich because I saw what the illusion did to my parents. They were never happy."

"But you have a lot of money...."

"Yes, and that's fine. I've been lucky."

I sit completely still and listen to Daniel. He's never said much about his life before. It's like being allowed to look behind the facade.

"It was easy enough to make money but hard to go from being successful to not even being able to get out of bed in the morning." He shakes his head in despair. "Frank has never been successful, and therefore it was perhaps easier for him when I had a breakdown." His voice is monotonous, but the pronunciation is still elegant. "Frank loved being the one on top when I lost my energy." He gets up, takes a log, and puts it in the fireplace, even though the fire has only just got hold of what's there already. Over the fireplace hang several family photos—Daniel with his mother and father. They stand in front of a small red house with a flat roof. The mother is sagging, and there is no life to be seen in her eyes. The father holds his chin high and has folded arms. Daniel is probably about seven years old and standing with his blue bicycle in another picture next to it. There is also a picture where he is standing with an elderly lady with thin white hair. Her face is wrinkled, and she is wearing tiny round glasses.

He pokes at the wood, so the flames increase. "I'm privileged; I'm not missing anything. I live in the present and do what I feel like." He turns his head and smiles so that the fire reflects in his eyes and brings back the spark. "But Frank, he has never been the success he wanted to be. He's full of desire but has no power. No one appreciates him, and he doesn't get the recognition he is longing for." In an elegant leap, he lands next to me and takes my hands. The heat gives a tuck in my stomach. "All Frank has said to me is that he is part of the Ring. The only way he can make you realize that is through Luke. I don't know what that means."

"I do." I grit my teeth hard. "Frank is obsessed with the idea of becoming part of the Ring. I have to find a way to make him realize that I'm not the one who hands out invitations." My fingers run back and forth across my forehead, "But I have no idea how." The blanket suddenly seems clingy, and I throw it to the side.

Daniel shakes his head slightly, "It's straightforward. You just have to figure out how he feels successful, gets recognition and power." He smiles at me, "Good luck with that," his loud laugh fills the room.

I know the longing for recognition too well; it has been my driving force all my life. It made me become a journalist and take on life-threatening assignments in war zones around the world. It made me unravel stories of cheating and fraud, hoping to win the ultimate prize—the Pulitzer. The times I have sat at awards ceremonies as a nominee, waiting in excitement for the moment when the name of this year's winner was announced. Year after year, the award went to someone other than me. It was like passing the finish line and being able to taste the sweetness of victory only to realize you have been overtaken at the last minute. Instead of a trophy, I got a bucket of ice water in my face and sat there defeated. But still, I crawled back on the horse and kept going because maybe I could do even better next time. And the following year, I sat there with butterflies in my stomach that died and had to be buried next to the hope of being seen and recognized. Whether I gave up eventually or just stopped feeling anything, I don't know. But there was a long period in my life where I just was. There were no significant fluctuations. When I look back on it, my desire burned out because nothing made sense. My spark of life was extinguished. Still, I made another attempt after I divorced Andreas, and I must admit that I did think I would succeed when I sat on the plane on my way home. When I came to In-Between, the meaning returned, but in a humbler form. I don't want to triumph over my position in the Ring. I don't want the whole world to know that I and six others are the chosen ones.

On the contrary, I would very much like no one to know. Maybe I'm starting to acknowledge myself; I can't help but smile to myself. At that exact moment, Daniel tears me out of my thoughts.

"You have to understand that Frank has not managed to succeed with hardly anything for any length of time. He has held several top jobs in the financial sector, but after a short time, he has resigned."

"Why?" I pull up one corner of my mouth and wrinkle my nose. The sleeves of my blouse are pulled down around my hands. I did that as a child whenever I felt insecure, and it has never stopped.

"I think it's the fear of not being able to deliver results. It is easier to give up before someone discovers that he has more in his mouth than his abilities can live up to."

It has become dark outside, and the stars are hanging scattered in the sky. The glow from the fireplace casts several red and orange shadows on the large white walls. If the conversation were about anything other than Frank, it would be cozy here.

I look at Daniel with the most charming look I can come up with, "But you have several companies; why don't you offer him a job and hire someone to praise him?" I smile all over my face and even think my plan is slightly ingenious. "You'll get interest from your efforts on your karma account."

Daniel laughs heartily with his deep timbre. "I need no interest;

I want to help you because I can feel it's important to you." He takes my hand and kisses it. "But then you must stay here with me too."

I cannot. I freeze inside.

Daniel chuckles, "You should see yourself. You look like a deer in highlights."

I try to force a little laugh but don't succeed. There is a knock on the door behind us, and the older lady with short gray hair trots toward us. In her hands, she holds a silver tray. On it are two small glasses with a gold edge and a bottle of gin. Fortunately, there are also water glasses, a blue jug, and a glass bowl with ice cubes. She puts it down carefully on the table.

"Thank you, Laura," Daniel sends her a smile and loving nod.

"Are you thirsty?" He reaches out. "Water or Gin?" Before I get to answer, he continues, "I know you can't stay here; don't worry." He squeezes my thigh, takes the ice cubes with the tongs, and drops them into the glasses. In one glass, he pours Gin and Tonic.

"Water…" I have to stay focused.

"As you wish, Princess." He hands me a glass of water—the ice cubes rock on the surface. I lean back and let the velvety soft fabric from the sofa embrace me. There are only embers left in the fireplace, struggling to stay alive.

My thoughts spill over each other—the Mission, Frank, and Daniel. It's like I'm being pulled from three sides. "I'll be back in a bit." In a resolute motion, I push off the couch with my hands and get up, heading for the toilet. If Frank wants recognition, it must be from someone he respects. The door closes behind me. I know he doesn't like women and that I have met him in several lives where he has always carried fierce anger. He wants power and influence; maybe it's his anger that drives him. I open the tap, make a bowl with my hands, and fill it with ice-cold water. It tingles on my skin as it hits my face. Daniel has to help me. Frank trusts him; that must be my rescue. On my way back to the living room, I hear Daniel talking to someone. When I open the door, I stop abruptly, and my whole body freezes to the floor. Daniel is sitting on the couch with my Skycon, talking to Meera.

24
THE OLD MAN

"Come on, Luke, you can do it." Thomas is halfway up the cloud mountain. Luke stands at the base and looks up. His gaze is fixed on Thomas, and his fists are clenched. He closes his eyes and takes the first step. His foot lands on the cloud without slipping. He sets off and takes the next step. His small nostrils vibrate as he breathes, and his face is concentrated. Every little cell in his body is focused on getting up the mountain—one more step without slipping down and starting over for the one hundred and twenty-seventh time, for the fourth day in a row.

"Looking good, Luke; you are on your way." The sun is already high in the sky. They enjoy breakfast together each morning before Luke spends an hour with the Master and the rest of the day with Thomas. They have found a mountain cloud out of sight from the central area of In-Between, where there are only the two of them and no unnecessary disturbance. There is almost no wind, and only small pieces of cloud detach from the top.

Luke's feet slip under him at that exact moment, and he takes another slide on his stomach down the cloud, leaving him with his head hidden in the cloud. Thomas sits calmly on the mountain, observing him. He knows that it takes total concentration, presence, and confidence to climb a cloud mountain, and his job is to teach Luke precisely that. Complete balance internally, where you don't do it for others to see, but because you get in touch with a place inside yourself, you feel the balance between the two poles, the feminine and spacious, and the masculine and energetic.

Luke gets on his knees and looks up at Thomas. "Why are you disturbing me? Now, I don't want to do it anymore." He crosses his arms. His face contracts and he resolutely turns his back on Thomas.

"There will always be someone or something that can upset you. The art is not to be disturbed." Thomas speaks in his warm, calm voice.

Luke doesn't respond. He sits perfectly still at the base of the cloud mountain. Like a closed clam, he has withdrawn into himself. Now, he is sitting there waiting for it all to pass. Thomas looks at him; he knows exactly what's going on. He can clearly remember how he felt as a child when something was difficult. When his parents were killed in a car accident, he was only twelve years old. Growing up in an orphanage without his parents was a daily challenge. Although his father was tough and his mother didn't say much, it was safe and what he knew. The day he was picked up from school by two police officers and told that his parents had died, he suddenly woke up to the brutality of life. That same day, he had to choose the most essential things from his room that he wanted to bring, but no more than what could fit in a small suitcase. He stood there, five feet tall, and looked around at his little world, which was big enough for him, and had to say goodbye. How could he decide what he wanted to bring? The tiny houses he had built for the animals he found in the garden? The sticks he had spent hours cutting while waiting for his father to come home from City Hall? The LEGO castles that had taken days to build while his father worked in the office next to the living room, where the smell of his mother's cooking filled the house? No matter how he packed it all, it could not fit in his little blue suitcase—the suitcase his parents had given him for the family's first trip together—an excursion for local politicians, where they could bring their families with them for half price. He struggled to hold back the tears as he reached out for a small glass ball with a picture of them together in an amusement park. The gold glitter swirled when shaken. It was the first and only trip they had all been on together. He stood with the glass ball in his hand and hugged it as if he was trying to bring the memories to life and, together with the memories, also his parents. But then one of the officers came into the room and asked him to finish.

Thomas takes a deep breath and lets himself slide down the cloud—down to Luke. He wraps his arm around Luke's tiny shoulders, and Luke disappears into his embrace.

If only there had been someone who had held him back then. He remembers it like it was yesterday. His whole body became petrified, and he disappeared into himself, like a clam hiding in its shell. He continued to use the same strategy throughout his life whenever he met resistance. Exactly the same way Luke is doing right now, even though the challenge is of a different magnitude, the strategy can still be used. It was like withdrawing from the world and becoming a spectator from a place where others cannot reach you—a way to protect oneself from the pain, whatever it was. The warmth from Luke's little body slowly seeps into Thomas, and he acknowledges it with care and reassurance. Thomas sits completely still and feels how it's possible to transform the pain, which goes back to when he shut himself in, away from the outside world, to survive. He notices how caring about Luke helps heal himself and how Luke's energy helps him open up and allow the mussel's transformation. Without a single word, they sit at the foot of the cloud mountain. Out on the horizon, several clouds slowly drift past. Above them, the sky is blue and infinite. Thomas opens his eyes and looks at Luke, who opens his eyes at the same moment.

"Come on, let's reach the top." Thomas hugs Luke, and he looks up. Gone is the petrified face and empty gaze. The glow is back in

Luke's cheeks and the sparkle in his eyes. He gets up in a leap, throws his jacket on the cloud, and looks at Thomas, "The last one to the top is still an old man," then he sets off running up the cloud mountain. Every step he takes lets him take a new one. The cloud dust swirls up around his sneakers, and he runs, almost floating toward the top. Thomas gets up and sets off in pursuit. By the time he is halfway, Luke is very close to the top.

"I'm right behind you." He tries to distract Luke as much as possible—not to be cruel, but to make sure he maintains his inner calm and balance. Luke continues toward the top; his little feet only briefly **touching** the cloud before setting off again.. He looks straight ahead without being influenced by Thomas. This time, he does not slide down but continues toward the top—fifteen feet to go. He increases his speed and almost floats up the side of the mountain. His breathing is calm, and even though he is running fast, his body is relaxed. Thomas stops and looks at Luke. He is flooded with pride and admiration. If only we get the support we need, we can unfold our potential. He takes a deep breath and sets off running again. Twelve feet. Luke's gaze is still fixed on the top, and not even the flock of birds soaring past him can disturb his concentration. Nine feet.

Thomas gives everything he has to catch Luke. His breathing hisses, and it tears in his lungs. It's too late. At the same moment, Luke leaps triumphantly up to the top with his arms as high above his head as he can. He jumps up in the air, spins around, and sees Thomas sprint toward him, only six feet further down the mountain. Luke's eyes are like a firework of excitement. He cannot stand still and hangs in a victory jump when Thomas reaches the top and grabs him. He swings him around over his head in outstretched arms while the sun's light falls on both of them and almost sprinkles triumphant glitter down over them. Thomas keeps turning around while holding onto Luke's hips, and Luke spreads his arms out as if flying. His long bangs blow away from his face, and his blue eyes twinkle in the sun. He beams and laughs his innocent childish laughter that comes all the way from his stomach. Thomas slows down and lets Luke slide down into his arms. Their gaze meets. At that moment, Thomas notices how Luke shows him the way through his pain from childhood and back to the pure life of energy and play.

"I made it!" Luke's voice is full of excitement. "*You* are the old man."

Thomas is one big smile and hugs Luke toward him while he whispers. "You're right. I'm the old man."

25

AN UNEXPECTED GUEST

"I think I know who to look for." Daniel speaks into the Skycon as if it were an iPhone on a facetime call, "or rather where to look." He lies sprawled on the sofa in the glow of the embers from the fireplace. The floor lamp next to him is dimmed, and outside, several torches are lit and flutter in the wind.

I'm still standing frozen in the doorway of the living room. My Skycon must have fallen out of my pocket and ended up in the crack between two cushions on the couch. It's too late to panic, so I don't.

Daniel holds the Skycon in front of him and is looking at the small picture of Meera. "Frank once mentioned something about a group of people working on making it possible for you to travel back before your time is up. I reckon it must be this group that is helping him get back and forth." He pauses, turns around, and catches sight of me. "I'm just talking to your girlfriend on your weird gizmo."

Stiff as a stick, I go and sit on the edge of the couch. "Hi, Meera." The muscles in my neck tense, and my tone becomes strained. I pull the picture up in front of us and take the Skycon from Daniel. He sighs as if I robbed him of a new toy.

"Hi, Angela," Meera waves, "I'm sorry if I interrupted you in the middle of something important." She looks at us with an expression that indicates she thinks there is more going on than just searching for Frank.

"You're not disturbing anything. I can see that you have met Daniel." She's sitting outside at the table inside the maze surrounded by flowering bushes.

I give Daniel a push, so he moves and makes space for me next to him on the couch. "I know Frank can send people from In-Between to Earth, but I never figured out who is helping him. The people who sent Frank back here?" I look questioningly at Daniel. "What did he tell you about them?"

"It started with him being angry that others should make decisions about him. In fact, I think it all started with him feeling mistreated in a round of layoffs." Daniel looks at the picture of Meera hovering in front of us. "Have you met Frank?"

Meera shakes her head. "I've only heard of him."

"Then you may have also heard that Frank is a little, let's say peculiar, sometimes. He has very entrenched ideas and beliefs. I've known him for a long time, so I've learned to listen to them without taking it too seriously." Daniel looks over at me with an almost apologetic look. I nod back, so he senses that it's okay for me and that I'm not judging him. I have also known people whom I have chosen to ignore some of their less charming sides because we had a history together. One of my good friends from journalism college went ruthlessly after revelations of people who cheated the system or had personal tragedies. She got close to other people and their fate. But when the stories weren't always tasty enough, she twisted the headlines and bent the participant's words. I didn't say anything because I could understand her eagerness to have her articles on the front page. But there was something about her methods I just couldn't reconcile with back then and definitely not now. I run my hand through my hair and pull it back in a ponytail. Sometimes, it's just easier to focus on what you like in others and ignore everything else.

Daniel interrupts my thoughts. "Frank said too much once. He said he was in a group called Kingston." He frowns, "And I don't know what that means. But I could see from his expression that he immediately regretted telling me."

I turn the Skycon toward me, so we are both inside the frame. "Find David. He can help you search for Kingston. He helps Thomas and knows about the Ring. He's our technical guru and was an indispensable help when we had to find you. He almost lived in the control room all the time I was here searching for you."

Meera makes a thumbs-up and notes his name. "I'll get ahold of him right away. If you come up with anything else, let me know. The traces of Frank are like breadcrumbs that have been removed."

It doesn't seem that Daniel has more to offer, so I take over. "Frank has always been good at covering his tracks. It took me a long time to figure him out. You should not expect to see Frank in In-Between; he knows it's too risky." I try to sound convincing, but I can feel the doubt swirling around in my body like a virus. "Just call if you need help."

She moves closer to the picture. "I'll do that."

I wave, and Meera and Daniel do the same. The small screen turns black, and the large image in front of us dissolves.

"Nice friend you have there!" Daniel smiles at me, waiting for me to share more about Meera and In-Between. When I say nothing, he continues. "Is she one of the seven?"

I press my lips together. "She was the one I came to find when I met you." I tell Daniel about the encounter with Meera at Lucy's place, our journey to the Himalayas, and how I found her dead. He sits still and listens, completely present. He creates a safe invisible space around me as I open up. Somehow, it's a bit similar to what Thomas does.

"Daniel." My voice is very determined, leaving no doubt about the seriousness. "You have to help me find Frank." The embers are about to die out. Daniel reaches out and lights the candles on the table.

"Princess, of course, I will help you. Would it be useful if I tell you that he will be here for lunch tomorrow at twelve?"

I sit up with a jerk and hammer my fist on his shoulder. "WHY didn't you say that before?"

Daniel bursts out laughing, "I was just waiting for the right moment, and then you went to the bathroom. Well, and then I got caught up talking to your girlfriend. Tell me, is she also dead alive?"

"Very funny!" I put on my most strained smile. "What do we do when Frank arrives?" I stare at him, so my eyes sting, demanding an answer with my gaze.

He leans forward, pours gin and tonic into the glasses, and hands me one. Since I'm not moving, he takes a sip. "Okay, okay. I'll greet him and serve some delicious food, and the rest is up to you." Daniel looks at me teasingly. I give his other shoulder a firm punch, so the gin is about to splash over. Slowly, he leans forward toward me. His face approaches mine, and I can feel his breath. My whole body gets flooded with heat. He stops as his mouth is right next to mine. Looking into my eyes, he says, "I wish the circumstances were different." He leans slightly forward, and our lips meet briefly. I pull away. I need to stay focused and cannot let Daniel distract me now.

I take the glass from his hand and down it in one gulp. "When Frank comes, you lure him down to the dungeon and lock him inside. It's a proper castle you have with a dungeon, right?"

"Do you mean the space I use to chain women who behave indecently and even ask for a slightly different treatment?" He lifts his eyebrows, and I know what he's suggesting. He waits and tries to get me to take over the conversation so he can play cat and mouse with me. But I say no more.

He gives in and continues. "You are right; there is a dungeon. It holds my very best wine. I'm not sure I'd dare let Frank in there."

It would otherwise have been an easy solution. First, put some sedative in his glass, and then lock him up so I can go back to In-

Between and concentrate on Luke and my process. I'm completely out of ideas, but I'll have to find the right move now that Frank's coming. This time, I must be prepared for the worst and most manipulative attack from him.

Suddenly, Daniel's facial expression changes from smiling to frozen. I turn around in a swift motion. There, in the door to the garden, stands Frank. My heart skips a beat, and I briefly consider whether to hide behind Daniel. But I don't manage to do anything before Frank enters the living room and smiles his mischievous smile.

"Now, look who's here. You have a visitor, Daniel."

26
THE GAME

I slide my hand into my pocket and squeeze the Skycon. *Give me strength, give me strength.* The glow from the fluttering torches on the terrace sporadically lights Frank up from behind. He has put on his most smarmy smile, and if I didn't know any better, I would think he was a man of the world as he stands there in his expensive, completely smooth dark blue Armani suit. Daniel steps resolutely in front of me and walks toward Frank like a knight protecting his lady from the enemy. But to Daniel, Frank is not an enemy; he is an old friend, and I don't know whose side he is on when it really matters. I get up behind Daniel because I don't want to greet Frank sitting down, letting him look down on me. Frank gives Daniel a hug as he looks at me over Daniel's shoulder. His gaze is icy cold. I stand completely stiff and wish the others from the Ring were by my side. Frank lets go of Daniel and moves toward me. He lifts his arms out to the sides so his belly skin appears where the buttons cannot hold the fabric together in the already too-tight shirt. I cross my arms firmly and stand completely stiff with my eyes fixed on Frank. My eyes sting as they run out of water, but I ignore them.

"Hi, Angela. Good to see you." His arms fall to his sides, and he avoids my rejection. "Sorry if I'm a little too early" He looks over at Daniel. "Had I known you had a grand visitor, I would have come even earlier." His scornful laughter resounds hollowly. "How's your head, Eva? I hope it doesn't hurt too bad; such a shame how you tripped."

Every little muscle in my jaws is tensed so that I don't send off a hostile remark. Even though I didn't manage to prepare, I have to be tactical.

Frank looks at me with his prickly eyes. "Angela, I just need to have a man-to-man talk with Daniel. I didn't know you were going to be here. Sorry." He smiles so that his yellow teeth become visible.

You're not sorry. I still control myself and try to melt him down with my look.

"But I have something that might cheer you up in the meantime." He opens his black attaché bag and takes out a newspaper. "I think you'll like the article on page thirteen." He slaps the newspaper against my stomach, and I reluctantly take it. "Come, Daniel, there is something I would like to share with you. It's not suitable for delicate female ears. Let's go out into the courtyard?" Frank starts walking, but Daniel stays standing.

"No."

Frank stops and turns around in amazement. "No?" He walks back toward Daniel. I step back too and stand out of Frank's reach.

"No?" Frank repeats and is now quite close to Daniel, who's not moving. He narrows his eyes and looks at Daniel wonderingly.

Daniel gives him two quick pats on the shoulder. "We can go to the kitchen, my friend." He steps past him, and Frank looks snortingly at me.

I stay standing until they leave the room. Then I let myself drop down on the couch. If only I knew what Frank was up to. If only I could feel confident that Daniel is on my side. The door closes behind them, and I grab the Skycon in my pocket and tap Thomas's icon. He responds immediately, and the image appears on the small screen.

"Hi, Eva." The wind lifts his hair, and the cloud continues indefinitely behind him. "I'm sitting here enjoying the view with Luke."

"Hello, Mom!" Luke leans into the picture and beams with excitement. "I made it to the top of the cloud mountain." His voice is eager, and he holds his head close to the Skycon so I can only see his eyes and nose. The image floats back a bit.

I pull out the picture, so it gets a little bigger but not too big, just in case Frank suddenly returns. "You are so clever. I'm super proud of you, Luke." A warm, rushing feeling overwhelms me, and I forget for a moment about both Daniel and Frank.

"And I came first." Luke jumps up with his arms in the air.

"Way to go; you are my shining star!" I hold the picture even closer and wish I could disappear into it, just for a moment. "Are you enjoying yourself?"

Luke nods eagerly, "This place is so cool. When are you coming back?"

"Hopefully, it won't be that long." I mean that sincerely and try to believe in it, but I know it will be longer than I want. But no more than 37 days, because then I have to decide if Luke should wake up. The sound of voices in the hallway is getting closer. "I have to go."

Thomas turns the picture toward him. "Is there anything else you wanted?"

"Yes, but it's too late. I'll call you later." I wave to Luke and Thomas. I turn off the Skycon and put it back in my pocket in a hurry. At that exact second, Daniel and Frank enter the living room again. I get up so fast that the candles on the table flutter.

"Well, did you read the newspaper, Angela?" Frank smiles at me contemptuously, making the scars on his face look more distinctive. I don't move a single muscle and look straight through him. He tries to inflate himself and make himself taller than he is. It just makes him look even more ridiculous in his slightly oversized suit with shoulder pads and tight blue shirt.

Daniel puts his arm around Frank's shoulders as you do with your best friends. "I told Frank about my new investment adventure in the Middle East and asked if he would be in charge of it." Daniel looks at Frank, who smiles smugly. My shoulders drop a bit, and I try to control my smile.

"That sounds interesting."

Frank stands perfectly still and looks at me, icy calm. "But that was not why I came today." His gaze is fixed on me like a missile locked on its target and approaching at a frightening speed. "I came to talk to Daniel about how we can get the last position in the Ring." He pauses and turns his head toward Daniel. "And strangely enough, he offers me an exciting job very far from here."

Daniel lets go of Frank's shoulders and gives him a proper thump on the back. "What's up with you? Don't you like the heat, or are you afraid of success?" Daniel looks relaxed, moving elegantly around the explosive landmines in the field of tension between us. "Or would you rather chase the illusion of a Ring like another Indiana Jones?" He chuckles, and Frank sees no other way but to laugh along. "If Frank says yes to my offer, he will be at the forefront of what could be the next revolution in artificial intelligence. But I can also go look in the basement; maybe I have a whip laying around and a hat if you'd rather borrow that for your treasure hunt." Daniel looks over at me. I blink slowly to indicate that I understand what is behind it. *Daniel is on my side*; there is no doubt about that anymore. The question is just whether that is enough.

Frank maintains his poker face. His aftershave bites into my nose, but I keep my eyes fixed on Daniel so that I can see Frank out of the corner of my eye.

Daniel gets a pat on the shoulder while Frank's stinging eyes are fixed on me. "I'm not as interested in success and recognition as you are; for me, the most important thing is that I contribute to making the world a better place. I have to use my skills where they do good." Frank smiles cunningly. "It is a fine offer, brother. And if I need an assistant, maybe I can call you, Angela?"

Skills, I think I'll throw up. The only skill Frank has is arrogance, spiced up with self-importance. That cocktail is by no means particularly charming. I stand completely still like one of those street performers who can stand for hours without moving a muscle no matter how much passersby try to provoke them. I bite my teeth together hard and press my tongue against the back of my teeth, making sure not to say something I will regret later. I need to play the game tactically.

Frank turns to Daniel, "It was great to see you, brother. About your offer." He shifts his gaze to me. "Shall we say that you will have my answer within 37 days?"

27
A QUESTION OF FAITH

Frank is gone. I crawl into the corner of the couch and wrap the blanket around me. A wave of chills forms goosebumps up my arms, and my body gives some slight twitches to shake off Frank's sleazy energy. The blanket smells of Daniel—vanilla with the sweetness of tobacco leaves. He has gone out to the courtyard to see Frank off. I reach for the newspaper and resolutely turn to page thirteen. A large image of me as Angela and one smaller where I'm Eva with a cloud in the background adorns one side. The headline reads: "Is there more between Heaven and Earth?" I skim the text. It describes how I ended up in a coma and later came back to life. Frank states: "There is a life after death, but more importantly, there are people who play God. They decide whether people should wake up from their coma or die." To the right is a frame with the headline: "The Ring." The Ring is described in detail, and it says that the members of the Ring aim to return to Earth to help people get to their next stage of development. There's no mention of who the members are.

I throw the newspaper to the other end of the couch and rub my hands on my jeans. To be completely honest, if I read something like that when I was alive, I would think it was bogus or the desperate invention of a madman. But there is a journalist who has agreed to write it and an editor who has approved it. They must have judged that the story is of interest to their readers. My fingers run across my forehead. Will it affect the assembling of the Ring? It's impossible to predict, but now I know there's a risk that people will recognize me. Fortunately, Luke was not mentioned in the article. That means it's me people will seek out if they believe the story.

"He's gone," Daniel steps into the living room and sits down next to me, so I move up a bit. "Did I pass?" He puts his arm around me and smiles his most charming smile.

"It depends on whether Frank says yes to your offer." I bite my lower lip. "What now? I don't know what he's up to!"

"Maybe I can help you." He reaches into the pocket of his perfect jeans that are worn in just the right places. "This is for you." He hands me a cell phone.

"I have a phone, thank you." It's hard to keep the frustration at bay. Frank was here, and I had the opportunity to wring information out of him and eliminate the threat to the Ring. Now, I'm back where I started. I do not know what Frank's plan is or where he is.

"Look here, Princess, before you start growing thorns." He leans toward me. The scent of vanilla and the sweetness of tobacco leaves become more intense. "Here." He opens the phone and presses an all-black icon with an exclamation mark in it. "Now, you can track what Frank is doing."

I take the phone out of his hand and look like a big question mark. There is a map, and a red dot indicates something that is moving. "Is it…?"

"Yes, it's Frank's car." He reaches over me and presses the phone. "And the other dot is a signal from his jacket."

"But…"

Daniel smiles very confidently. "Are you happy now?"

I kiss him on the mouth. He looks just as surprised as I am. "Yes, but how?"

"I knew he was coming, and I knew you wanted to get ahold of him. So, I had arranged with my employees to put surveillance in his car while he was here." He sits perfectly still and looks at me, smiling. The embers in the fireplace have died out; only the floor lamp next to the sofa lights up a dim circle around us.

"Unfortunately, he came a little earlier than expected, so I had to get him to the kitchen, where I had a small tracking device in a drawer which I could attach to his jacket." Daniel opens the drawer under the coffee table and puts two new candles on top of the burnt ones. A box of matches is on the table; he strikes one and lights the candles.

I can't help but shake my head. "Cheers, James Bond." I reach for the glasses of gin and tonic. The ice melted a long time ago. The glasses clink as they hit each other. "Thank you, Daniel."

"There is one more thing." He pauses for a moment, which fortunately is not long enough for me to get nervous. "My people could not check the equipment before he arrived, so I hope there is enough battery on the devices, so they will work for the time you need."

"What now?"

"Now, you can keep an eye on Frank while we have fun." Daniel throws the pillow down at the end of the couch and lies down on his back with his feet on my thighs. "Feel free to massage my feet while you are sitting there anyway." He looks like someone who thinks he's got the best idea in the world. I have to kill it. Although it's cozy, I can't stay here. I must go back to Luke and my mom and make sure they're okay. Thomas also needs to be filled in on what has happened. I lean toward Daniel and kiss him on the cheek. "Thank you for your help. I'm deeply grateful for everything you have done for me."

He touches my cheek. "In another life, maybe."

"I would love that." He is by far the sweetest, most charming, and most attractive man I have ever met. I use all my strength to keep my arms outstretched while his charm tries to soften them.

There is something unique about his mix of masculinity and femininity—a presence that dances with love, with easy steps of care and strength. In many other people, they stumble over each other. This also applies to me; my masculine side can easily run off with me without me noticing it. But that doesn't happen for Daniel. He reluctantly gets up. "Well, then I have to hire a tall, beautiful blonde to massage my feet."

I pull a face, knowing full well that Daniel is just teasing. He puts his arms around me and pulls me close. "Take care of yourself, Princess." At that moment, the feeling of separation pours over me. Most of all, I just want to stay in his arms. The separation feels unbearable. The void leaves rips in my heart; it stings, and loneliness invades me. I recognize the feeling; it always comes insidiously when I have to say goodbye and move into something unknown—alone on a journey. As a journalist, I experienced it when I completed an assignment I had been engrossed in for a long time. We always had a sense of togetherness in the team, and when it suddenly had to dissolve, we stood there in no man's land. Or the days when I worked at home and had taken Luke to Kindergarten. The void when I got home required me to distract myself, so I wouldn't fall into it and feel completely alone. Now, the shift is there again—the separation from Daniel. Although he's not part of the task, he is a rock and a friend. Now I'm moving on, alone. I push myself free from his embrace and look him in the eye.

"Thank you." I place a hand on his chest. "You have been a huge help, and I will miss you."

"Will I see you again?"

I shake my head, "Don't count on it."

28

THE UNKNOWN JOURNEY OF THE SOUL

The sun is setting, and the light is beginning to fade away. Thomas is sitting in the control room as the door slowly slides open. Shiva enters, pushing Gabriel in a wheelchair. Thomas gets up and runs to them, "Here, let me help you." Gabriel is completely pale, and his skin is sagging. He is gray around the eyes, which have only a tiny glow left.

"How are you?" Thomas is sitting close to Gabriel, who blinks slowly. It takes too much effort to speak. He must prioritize his words.

"I'm not… going to… make it…." Gabriel almost whispers the words. Shiva and Thomas move closer to make sure they hear every little word he says. He closes his eyes. They sit perfectly still while his breath hisses and reveals the difficulty of passing through his throat. On the big screens behind them run images from the seven continents of the world: elephants in chains walking with tourists on their backs, a refugee camp, the Sacred Valley around Machu Picchu, and the Great Barrier Reef. Thomas slides his hand over the chair's armrest as if he could wipe the nervousness away.

Gabriel has always been the anchor of the Ring. It was he who found Yoge, Thomas, and Shiva and gained insight into the Ring. He is an old soul who has traveled through many lives. In previous lives, he has ruled in large parts of the world and has impacted world history. Now, his energy is being used up, and his soul is moving on. Most of the time, he is in a room where Yoge has created a special light that helps to keep him alive in In-Between.

Thomas looks at Gabriel's crumpled body that hangs limply over the armrest of the wheelchair. He knows that Gabriel will do everything he can to get the Ring assembled. His willpower is crucial.

"Where is Luke?" The words tremble a little. Shiva looks at Thomas with her loving gaze.

"At the Master's, he's there twice a day; I have to pick him up in half an hour." Thomas keeps his gaze fixed on Gabriel. "Luke has asked to go there twice a day instead of once." His hand still glides back and forth over the armrest.

"I don't think there is anything we can do to help Gabriel. I get no visions or messages." Shiva grabs a piece of gum from the package she always keeps in her pocket and puts it in her mouth. "Gabriel, do you know how long you have left here?"

He opens his eyes slightly and makes an effort to find strength. "Eva…" He holds back. "It's not what she thinks." His eyes close, and his head falls forward.

Thomas moves very close, so his ear is right next to Gabriel's mouth. But Gabriel sinks into the chair even more if possible. He is so thin that his ribs show under his gown. His lips slide apart, but no words come out. Shiva gets up to fetch a glass of water and helps him take a sip. Several drops run down next to his mouth. The light descends slightly from the ceiling and settles gently on his bald forehead.

"Forty-five," he whispers, after which he closes his mouth again.

"We have to get him back to his room." Thomas looks at Shiva as he holds Gabriel's head, so it doesn't fall forward again.

"I know. He insisted on coming here, but he's overworked."

"Let me take him back; then I can pick up Luke afterward." Thomas gets up and grabs the handles of the wheelchair. Gabriel has closed his eyes and seems to be sleeping.

They look at each other.

"Forty-five?" Shiva puts her hand on Thomas's and whispers. "Do you think he's alluding to how many days he has left?" She tucks her hair behind her ear. "I can't see the answer...."

Thomas looks up at the sky. "I don't know, but if it is, the time has just been reduced by half for all of us." Thomas tries to drown his nervousness. He reaches out and puts his arm around Shiva, who falls into his chest.

"We will make it," she whispers and steps back. Their gaze meets in an intense moment where they both know what's at stake. "It's not your responsibility or fault if we don't make it." The calm around her vibrates unaffected.

Thomas would like to borrow a little of it. If they don't succeed this time, it's not certain that they will ever succeed. Inside his head, his father's devilish voice shouts his eternal sermon that failure is a sign of weakness. No one knows where the souls go when they leave In-Between. If Gabriel's soul gives up, it's unknown if they can ever find him again.

29

WHERE THERE IS LIGHT, THERE IS DARKNESS

Thomas walks down the aisle leading to the Master's corridor. It's completely quiet. For a brief moment, he notices that he is walking faster than usual. Hopefully, Luke is still there and hasn't gone back to his room by himself. Even though he's been in In-Between for a week, he could still get lost. Thomas looks at his watch; he is fifteen minutes late. Being on time was one of the many things his father permanently imprinted. Never be late; it's a disgrace to yourself and, more importantly, to others. It's the seventh time in his life he is running late, and it's not easy. It was hard for him to leave Gabriel, not knowing if he will make it. But there wasn't anything else he could do. The light from the tube Yoge created for him made the gray color on his skin fade a bit. As he approaches the door, it slides up easily. He carefully enters, stops, and runs his hand slowly through his hair. Luke is sitting in the garden on a white bench next to the Master. They are both sitting with crossed legs. He walks toward the door to the garden with almost silent steps but stops when he feels the intense energy. A completely golden light has wrapped itself around the Master and Luke and frames them most finely. Behind them is the mirror-shiny lake with a metallic blue tinge. The large eucalyptus trees stretch toward the sky, and several shrubs surround the lake with small red flowers. To the right is an opening in the bushes where a path of pale stones begins.

"We know you are here." It's the Master's deep calm voice. "Come closer." Thomas walks over and sits down next to them.

Luke opens his eyes and tries to frown. "Are you here already?"

Thomas glances at his watch; he's half an hour late. "What are you doing?" He knows what they are doing, but he is curious about Luke's perception.

Luke blows his hair away from his eyes. "We practice doing nothing." His blue eyes glow in the sun, and he smiles all over his face. "It gives us more energy to do everything else we want to do, doesn't it?" Luke looks at the Master, who is sitting still without saying anything. "It's very cool; it's called mediation." Luke looks very serious and brings his palms together in front of his chest.

"Is it hard?" Thomas folds the sleeves of his black silk tunic precisely.

"Nope." He raises his head and holds his chin up so that the pride beams out of him. "It's easier than coming up with something to do when you're bored."

Thomas can't hold back the laughter and strokes Luke's blond hair. "Would it be alright for you to do a little more meditation while I take the Master for a walk around the lake?

"Sure." Luke immediately settles down and closes his eyes. "See ya."

The Master grabs Thomas's arm and gets to his feet. They walk toward the small opening in the bushes. A swan comes striding toward them. It chooses to slide into the lake before passing them.

"Gabriel is very weak," Thomas speaks softly, so he's sure Luke doesn't hear him. He holds the Master's arm under his arm as they walk side by side on the small path around the lake. "I'm awaiting a status from Eva, but Gabriel had a vision where he was troubled."

The Master listens as he takes small steps. A white robe covers his slender body; on the back, a thin gold thread draws the image of a ring with a swan inside. His breathing is almost silent. They continue slowly past several swans sitting at the water's edge, resting. No wind is moving, and the sky above them is entirely blue.

"Eva will be ready in time. It's not her we should worry about." The Master stops and looks Thomas straight in the eye with his gaze cutting through any ambiguity. "It is Frank and Luke who are vital in the question of whether the Ring can be assembled or not." He starts walking again. "The rest of you are well on your way, and your development is going better than expected." The Master speaks slowly and with pauses between each word, indicating the weight of his message. Thomas feels the relief in his body and takes a deep breath.

"Is there anything we can do to help Eva?" Thomas looks over at Luke, who is now on the other side of the lake. He sits completely still with his eyes closed. The swans walk around him curiously, but that doesn't distract him.

"Eva must decide if Luke should continue on the Ring's journey. It's her last task before she can join the Ring herself and participate in the final tests." The Master runs his hand down his long white beard. "There is one more thing." He stops. "Luke *must* spend his 42 days in a coma. If he is short of time, it is not certain that his soul can contain the high frequency of energy that you must carry down to Earth." He holds one of his long pauses, and Thomas knows he can't interrupt, even though questions are queuing up. "While he is in a coma, his soul has the time it needs to deal with the transmission from the energy on Earth to the energy up here. Those who are not in a coma need time alone to adjust. They often sit in silence for the equivalent of 42 days. Luke must handle the energy change and get ready to be part of the Ring. He can only do that as long as his body is in a coma."

Thomas knows what he is talking about. He died suddenly and spent more than 42 days in silence before accommodating the subtle and high-frequency energy. There is a part of In-Between dedicated to those who arrive suddenly—an area where they can be at peace until they are ready to be a part of In-Between until they have accepted their sudden death and are prepared to look inside. "But Meera came here suddenly too?" Thomas looks at the Master, wondering. They can still see Luke over on the other side of the lake. One of the swans has crawled up on the bench next to him and is sitting with its neck outstretched.

"That is why her job is to do nothing. Right now, she's the weak link. But she is a very old soul, and that helps."

"And Luke?"

The Master smiles so that his eyes twinkle. "He is older than both of us."

They continue around the lake at a slow pace. Thomas doesn't know how long Gabriel has left, and if Luke needs his 42 days in a coma, then it is at least one more month.

"It is the biggest puzzle in the universe that needs to be completed. Getting seven souls to meet at just the right time with the perfect timing in their development requires a precision no one can interfere with. Trust. It's the only thing we can rely on." The Master's words hang in the air between them.

"And Frank?" Thomas looks questioningly at the Master. "Why is Frank a part of it all?"

"Frank represents the darkness. Where there is light, darkness is amplified. Without one, the other does not exist. Frank is a natural reaction to the fact that the Ring is gathering."

Thomas stares at the Master in surprise. At no time did the thought occur to him that Frank is a reaction to the Ring being gathered.

"To experience true joy, you must experience sorrow. To value relationships, you need to feel loneliness. When the light comes, darkness is magnified. Yin and yang." The Master brings his hands together and folds them in front of his chest.

"Take Luke with you and come back tomorrow at eight. We will continue; help Eva as much as you can in the meantime. Time is short."

30

ONE STEP AHEAD

Thomas and Luke are walking down the empty hallways, side by side. Nobody else is here, only the stars in the sky that occasionally twinkle outside the enormous windows. Luke balances the best he can on the yellow stripe on the floor and sometimes disappears into the wall only to reappear a little later. If Frank turns off Luke's respirator, he will not be ready to be part of the Ring. It's crucial that Eva stops Frank. Thomas walks in his thoughts and observes Luke's playful lightness. If Gabriel can't last long enough, Eva has to come back before her time is up, regardless of whether she manages to stop Frank or not. But that doesn't change the fact that Luke has to be in a coma for another 37 days. If she succeeds in stopping Frank, it also requires the others in the Ring to be ready to gather ahead of time.

"What are you thinking?" Luke jumps right in front of Thomas, who is about to fall over him. "I can see when you think wisely; then you get such a deep wrinkle across your forehead. Does it have anything to do with my mother?" Luke narrows his eyes and looks insistently at Thomas, who is unprepared for the question.

"Yes, Luke, your mother has a task that is a little challenging." He tries to be as honest as possible without scaring Luke.

"What kind of task?" Luke stays in front of Thomas and puts his arms out to the side. He tries desperately to frown.

"It's a kind of mission that she has to solve." Thomas can't think of anything to compare it to, hoping Luke doesn't ask more questions.

"Is she coming back then?" Luke lets his little hand slide into Thomas's palm. They walk along the empty aisle where the color of the stripe has changed to blue. Most of the screens outside the doors have the names of the current occupant on them. Opposite the wall is a large window where they can see several white lines from planes passing beneath them.

"Yes, she will." Luke's tiny hand is warm; Thomas squeezes it.

"Is there anything else we need to do today? I'm just so tired after all that mediation." Luke makes his most pleading eyes, "Can I go to my room?" He starts dragging his legs across the floating white floor.

They have reached the door to the Ring's corridor. A section of the wall slides opens slowly and silently.

"Of course, Luke, I'll come around and say goodnight later. I'll be right inside the control room if you need me."

Luke leaps off and gives Thomas a thumbs-up. When he has disappeared into his room, and the door is closed behind him, Thomas takes his Skycon from his pocket and presses Eva's picture with a little eagle in the corner. It connects and rings, but she doesn't answer. He lets it ring, hoping that she is all right. She sounded uneasy when she called before. Thomas looks out over the hilly landscape of clouds drifting past. Although he has spent many years working on his personal development, he can feel that a climax is approaching. It's like a knot is tightening up for him and also for the others. They move toward the center of the record at high speed, closer to themselves. Thomas holds his hand over the button to the control room. The door slowly slides open. He still doesn't understand why Luke can't know about Frank, but there is no reason to challenge that part; it's the Master's decision. Meera, Yoge, and Shiva are sitting on the couch. He stops at the door and feels a quiet shiver underneath his skin. They get up, gather their hands in front of their chests, and bend slightly. He reciprocates the greeting and sits in the green chair opposite them.

"I got ahold of the others as agreed," Meera looks at Thomas, pulls the green hood of her tracksuit over her head, and takes a sip of coffee. If only Thomas had had time to talk to Eva so that he knew what she wanted before. He looks over at Yoge, who is busy with his notepad, where yet another page is filled with equations and numbers.

It's completely quiet in the control room. The table is set with glasses, water, and a tray with fresh fruit.

"Let's try to get Eva to join the meeting," Thomas presses his Skycon, and this time she picks up.

The image of a worn headrest appears. Through the car's windows, he can see several large old beech trees with rugged trunks. "Hi, Thomas!" Eva tumbles into the picture so that it shakes.

Her long brown hair with natural highlights gently wraps around her narrow face. The cheeks and the small nose are so different from Eva's, who has slightly less marked cheeks and a few gray hairs. Thomas puts his hand on his heart and fills his lungs with air. The picture widens so that Eva can see that they are not alone.

"Hi, Eva; good to see you again." He smiles so the fine lines around his eyes become more apparent.

"Wow, is there a family reunion?" Eva pulls the picture up in front of her and places the Skycon on the dashboard. "Where's Luke?"

"Luke is in his room," Thomas quickly looks around at the others, continuing, "I have gathered you because our time horizon may be changing." Yoge looks up most graciously as Thomas lets his gaze wander between them. Shiva doesn't say anything. Her energy resonates more powerfully than it has in the past as if she has opened up even more to her inner source of love. Eva's picture floats next to them, so it looks like she's present in the control room with them.

"Gabriel is more weakened than we thought, and he doesn't have much time left." Thomas pauses and swallows. "It could be a matter of days or weeks before his soul releases his body, and the energy is used up."

A sinking feeling runs through the room as if the light dims and then increases in intensity again. Yoge has placed the pen behind his ear and put the notebook on the table.

Thomas continues, "It's important that Luke remains in a coma for all of his 42 days so that he can be ready for the next journey if that's what you decide, Eva."

Eva sits completely petrified, and her gaze has become blank. They are all waiting for Thomas to say more, but there is no more to be said.

"If we have 45 more days to complete our process," Yoge grabs the pen and taps a few times on his notebook. "And Luke has forty-two in total in a coma where five have already gone, then that gives Eva thirty-seven more days on Earth before she comes back. Then we only have eight days together to get ready." He speaks without a single pause between the words, rubs his wide nose with the back of his hand, and snorts a few times.

Thomas nods at Yoge, "That is also my conclusion." He looks around to make sure they all agree. No one objects. "It means we have to work even more intensely with ourselves so that we are ready to bring the higher consciousness back to Earth." Thomas stands up. "We must ensure that we don't let our egos or past affect us." He speaks as much to himself as to the others. "Our energy needs to be completely pure."

They all sit perfectly still and listen to his words. The seriousness resounds in the control room, and the light is intense.

"Eva," Thomas pauses. He closes his eyes briefly before

speaking again. "You must understand that it's your choice whether Luke should continue his old life with Andreas or he should be part of the Ring." He walks to her image. "We will support you no matter what you choose." He raises his palm toward the picture.

Eva is sitting in her car. Her jaw is tense, and her eyes stare straight ahead. Thomas wishes he could reach through the picture and put an arm around her, but the image just moves as he steps closer. From the corner of his eyes, he can see Meera pouring juice from the gold bottles into the glasses. She takes a sip and tightens her mouth. The golden bottle contains pure ginger juice.

"I don't know what to do." Eva bangs her head softly back against the headrest. "Should I give Andreas Luke back and let them live their lives without me? Or should I hand over Luke to a mission that may not succeed and I don't really know a lot about? We don't know if we will be ready in time. And what if we end up in jail or are killed for bringing higher consciousness to Earth? Is it worth it? Can't I just do what's best for me and get back to In-Between?" Thomas lets her talk because, between the words, she often finds the answers herself. In conversations like this, Thomas and Eva are usually alone. But right now, it doesn't seem to bother her that the rest of the Ring is also listening. She grabs a water bottle and takes a sip but spits the water out the open side window. No one says anything. All the screens in the room are turned off, and the light is dimmed. Thomas reaches out and takes one of the glasses with ginger shots. He drinks the juice without grimacing, and so do Yoge and Shiva.

The wind starts to shake the trees surrounding the car, and there is a noise on the roof as several twigs sprinkle down. Eva leans out of the picture, and it sounds like her hand is groping for something on the floor. When she sits up again, she has the window handle in her hand and tries to put it back on so she can close the window and stop the increasing wind from blowing in. She zips her jacket up to her neck and wraps her arms around herself.

Minutes pass before Meera clears her throat, hesitating a bit, and then speaks. She is still a bit insecure when the others from the Ring are all there, knowing that she was the last to join apart from Luke. "I have good news." The light from the windows above adds shine to her gray hair. "I found Kingston!"

"Kingston?" Thomas looks at her in wonder.

"Yes, Kingston. The group of people here who help Frank. Eva's friend helped us."

Eva straightens her back in a jolt and hits the car horn in her zeal. It lets out a cramped hiss.

Meera doesn't allow herself to be distracted and continues. "I found Ian in the control room as you suggested, Eva. He had heard about them." A smile creeps in, but she grits her teeth and chokes it.

Eva has moved very close to the picture. She sits still without blinking.

It's so quiet that you can almost hear the light falling from the ceiling. They are all looking at Meera. She runs her hand under her bangs. "Ian had heard that there's a group who meets at the other end of In-Between, out on the edge."

The edge is where In-Between ends, and it can be a dangerous place to stay because, in bad weather, parts of In-Between can tear loose. The detached parts dissolve and disappear. It was out on the edge that Eva met Frank for the first time. Maybe it was no coincidence that she met him there. Thomas reaches for a green bottle and pours it into his glass. He looks over at the others on the couch. Yoge has drawn some numbers on a screen next to Eva's picture. "Look here. These are the frequencies we communicate with from In-Between to Earth." He points to a few thin lines that almost disappear in the crowd of other lines. "The green lines are the communication we have up here, and the orange lines are where we listen in on Earth from the common control room. He enlarges the picture. "The thin red lines here are the frequencies used to communicate with you on Earth." He looks over at Eva and divides the picture in two to see the control room and the graph. "I have not been aware of them as the lines have matched our communication with you."

"What does that mean?" Thomas looks at Yoge, wondering.

"That means that someone has hacked the system and put their communication right next to ours, so it is almost impossible to see that they are also communicating from here to Earth." He rotates the graphs so that they stand out from the screen and zoom in even more. "That's why we haven't been able to find Frank; they've put a blockage around his frequency." He kicks the table with his clog and runs the pen across his forehead, leaving a blue line. "It also means they can listen to all your conversations, Eva."

"How long have you known this, Yoge?"

"For forty-two seconds." He flips through his little pad. "Numbers are not just numbers."

I sit completely still in my car. Every tiny cell in my body is on high alert. That's why Frank is so calm and condescending and why he was not surprised that I was with Daniel. He knew. And he also knew that Daniel had spoken to Meera. I blink slowly and breathe only the most necessary air. Every breath I take feels like there is less air left in the car and that I am being suffocated slowly. I pull the handle on the car door and kick it open. Clouds are gathering, and the sky is darkening. It seems like two weather fronts are entering a battle—the heat against the cold. The hot air has become clingy. I fill my lungs as if it was the last air I can get.

Yoge continues to turn the graphs, which show a picture of In-Between from above with red dots in the places where communication has taken place. "Meera is right. They meet on the edge."

Thomas takes a piece of paper and writes on it. He holds it up so they can all read what it says. *Can they just listen, or can they see our picture too?*

Yoge touches several of the red dots and writes some codes that start a search process. He takes the pen from Thomas and writes: *they can only hear us* on the paper.

"Eva, we continue as previously agreed." Thomas is writing on the paper as he speaks. He holds up a note in front of him.

They can only hear us, not see the picture.

I read it and nod to Thomas. I have to continue where I left off. Frank will notice if anything changes. I run my hand through my hair several times.

"Go to Luke and stay there until we talk again," Thomas calmly speaks as he continues to write.

I rip the glove compartment open to find something to write on and with. There is an old pen. In my bag are several receipts and the newspaper. As I pick up the newspaper, the wind grabs it and spreads it to all sides. I pull the front door and close it with difficulty as the wind is so strong and provides maximum resistance.

We must disconnect from you. Thomas holds up a note, saying, *You MUST get Frank's Skycon. Until then, we can't talk to each other!* Thomas clutches the note in his hands so that his knuckles turn white. He is right. I look down at the only page of the newspaper that didn't fly away, the one with Frank's article. I'm completely blank and don't know what to write as I stare at the picture of myself and swallow a lump in my throat.

Thomas holds up another note. *You need to turn off your Skycon so they can't track you.* He takes the paper down and writes again. *Take care of yourself,* followed by a heart.

I feel exactly like when the plane crashed, and I frantically fumbled for my oxygen mask. It couldn't save me.

31
LONELINESS IS KNOCKING ON THE DOOR

The wind pushes the car door open, and I step out into the strong wind, which throws dirt in my face. It crunches between my teeth, and I manage to spit most of it out. My hair is thrown in all directions, and I turn up the collar of my jacket to shield my neck from the wind. There is an opening between the tall trees. I hurry to find shelter under the dense treetops with trunks so substantial that it would take several people to embrace them. A narrow path leads into the woods away from the small parking lot where the car is parked next to other wrecks, which seem to function more as bird nests than means of transportation. I narrow my eyes and look up at the high trunks, which sway slightly from side to side. As my hand touches the trunk, I feel a deep vibration in my body. They stand firmly anchored with their roots, as they have stood for several hundred years. I lean my back against the trunk and take the Skycon from my pocket. It balances between my thumb and forefinger: *goodbye connection, goodbye lifeline.* I turn it off with a hard push, and it stops flashing. If I felt alone when I said goodbye to Daniel, it doesn't compare to how I feel now. It's like being sucked into a downward spiral of loneliness. As if all the bonds that bind me to others are cut, and I stand all alone. Again.

You are not alone. It's the sound of my voice inside my head. I shake my head slightly and push away from the tree with my leg. I am alone, separated from everyone else but maybe not from myself. The warm, humid air fills my lungs, and I walk further into the woods. The trees are dense, and the crowns don't let much light through now that the dark clouds have gathered above me. We are created to survive in groups, not alone. Is that why it hits me so hard when I say goodbye to others? I have never thought about it in detail, but I always had this unrest when I separated from others and could not predict the future. I felt lost but free. Contradictory, mainly because it has always been my own decision. Like when Andreas and I went our separate ways, I regretted it a hundred times. Was it the deep fear of not surviving on my own that struck me? In a way, the pain of being with someone else even when you are not thriving can be less scary than the fear of being alone. Raindrops begin to fall from the trees. It's refreshing when they hit me and almost tickle my face.

Several times, Thomas has talked about falling through the layers. If separation is the top layer, then what lies beneath? There is a fallen branch on the path. I pick it up and draw a line on the ground. Under separation lies loneliness. I draw one more line. And beneath the loneliness… there's no immediate answer to that. I look up and get a drop of water on my forehead right between my eyes —*the fear of being left outside*. Slowly, I draw one more line. My chest moves slowly as I breathe. I kick lightly below the line with the tip of my shoe. *Vulnerability*. The branch gives a cracking sound as I break it over my leg. "If we do not dare to let others into our lives and be vulnerable, we will always be alone." That was what Thomas said to me the day we talked about the feminine and masculine. Now, it makes sense like a piece that finds its place in the puzzle.

Vulnerability has always been a foreign word in my family's vocabulary. I have learned to manage everything myself, and if I kept others at a proper distance, I could control my emotions. But it was precisely through this that the pain arose. I can see that now. I did not let others all the way in. Luke was the first to knock on the door to my heart, and later Annabel managed to open it too. Vulnerability is a loss of control, and that's not my strong side. I kick a fallen branch on the path. It's easier to break a branch off a tree than to put it back on. The same goes for relationships. It is easier to keep your distance than to let others in.

Although I feel alone, I am not. I can visit Daniel at any time and can call him right now if I want to. I put my hand on my heart and close my eyes as I walk along the path with small steps. Luke, Thomas, my mother, and Annabel—they all live in my heart. We are all connected on a different level. It's like tiny golden threads connecting our souls and hearts.

I open my eyes slowly. Of course, it's not the same as being physically together. I have been with many people in my life where I have given nothing of myself. The risk of being together is also that you easily lose yourself or compromise to fit in. Meera had an open heart when I met her. She dared to show her vulnerability and stand by what she believed in. She didn't care what others thought. That was what I was attracted to and why I went with her to the Himalayas. I continue along the forest path, where the rain has formed several puddles. *We see in others what we long for ourselves*. It's as if the heavy, moist air dissolves with every drop that lands on the ground. Moss spreads from the forest floor up the trunks and forms a dark green surface. The path becomes narrower and more overgrown as I advance into the forest. An owl hoots, so it resounds between the trees. It's not to be seen anywhere.

Vulnerability feels like standing exposed and alone on thin ice as your feet slowly melt it. The fear of meeting the icy water makes you protect yourself with a layer of shields—drink alcohol, eat sweets, do extreme sports, or hurry to find someone to be with. All of these can be ways not to feel vulnerable. At the thought of sweets, I put my hand in my pocket because, if I'm lucky, I have a caramel. I could use it right now, but unfortunately, I ate it when I did not need it.

I continue down the narrow winding path that has turned to mud sticking to the soles of my shoes. Further ahead, a clearing appears. The rain forms a wall where the trees end. I look up. The tree crowns are so dense that they act like an umbrella full of small holes. *Trust.* I whisper to myself. *Trust.* My steps are heavy and slow. For every step I take, I try to inhale the word a little more. The clearing is close, and I continue to focus on it. My shoe lands in a puddle, and slowly the water seeps in.

In the same way, trust penetrates my heart and gives the control a ten-count. My arms lift slightly from my body out to the side. I put my head back and close my eyes. It's calm inside me. I managed before; I will make it this time too.

32

GOODBYE TO THE EGO

"Yoge, shall we go to the edge and see if we can find Kingston's meeting point?" Thomas looks over at Yoge, who is preoccupied with the graphs of communication frequencies. "YOGE."

With a tap of the pen, he dissolves the picture and puts the notebook in the back pocket of his oversized pants. "What, uh, yes?" Their gaze meets. "It's a possibility." Yoge prefers to be alone and disappear into technical calculations. His big challenge is that he has to meditate every day. It challenges him just as much as being with others.

There is a low hiss, and the door to the hallway slowly slides open. Thomas notices that Shiva and Meera are still sitting on the sofa immersed in conversation and immediately thinks about whether Luke has woken up. The Master enters the room with short, floating steps. There is an extraordinary light around him like a vibrating shield. They all get up and greet him with their hands folded in front of their chests and a gentle bow. He returns the greeting and sits down in the chair next to Thomas. Shiva, Meera, and Yoge sit opposite on the couch. They have moved forward and are completely present. The Master's slender figure almost disappears in the chair. He takes a deep breath before speaking as if waiting for the words to come to him from somewhere else. Then, he closes his eyes briefly and begins to talk with the most profound calm.

"You have all worked on the challenges I have given you so that you can be ready to travel back to Earth with the new consciousness." He pauses and looks at them individually. "The next phase can begin." The pauses between his words are precise and underscore the importance of his message. "If you are to be ready in 45 days, we need to intensify the training." The light becomes clearer in the room, and above them, more stars appear through the window that occupies most of the ceiling.

"Before you gather in the Ring, it is crucial that you all have reached development stage five." He pauses. "There are five stages of development, where five is the highest and where the individual is as close to being enlightened as possible. Reaching it requires that you each go through an intense personal development, where you are confronted with your ego's ambitions, feelings, thoughts, and not least, the potential of your soul."

They all sit completely still and listen to the Master's words which hang in the clear light from the moon. "Since you can still not help Eva, you have the opportunity to concentrate fully on yourself and the task. A unique program has been prepared for each of you, which you must follow for the next 35 days." The Master pauses and breathes calmly. He doesn't give anything away while speaking. It's impossible to see if he believes the mission can succeed in such a short time. "You will be allowed to leave your program to monitor Eva from here."

Meera leans forward and awaits the Master's nod before she speaks. "What does the program consist of?"

"The program is designed for you individually to help you raise your awareness. You will be challenged on your attitudes, emotional wounds, ambitions, and consciousness." He holds back. "I can say no more." He slowly looks around at each of them as he runs his hand down over his beard. "The program will hopefully help you reach development stage five in time."

Thomas leans forward. "And what about Luke?" He reaches out for a glass of water.

The Master smiles, "Luke is going to be with me. You have already helped him a lot, but now you have to focus 100% on yourself." His words cut through space like a sword. Thomas feels the unrest creeping in. He knows very well that he must be confronted with his lack of life energy and fear of failing with his father's grip on him. The Master's eyes twinkle. In a way, he seems happy to spend more time with Luke.

"And if we don't reach developmental stage 5 in the 35 days?" Yoge leans back on the couch. Both legs and arms are crossed, and the wrinkles on his face deepen.

"Then you cannot continue the work of the Ring. In the last phase, you must unite the energy and together lift it to the highest level—the energy that you must bring back to Earth. But this is also where you need to coordinate your efforts. Cooperation as one complete unit is crucial for your success." The Master rises. His robe moves lightly around his body. "Your training starts in the morning. You will be picked up from your rooms at six a.m. and led to your training areas." He folds his hands in front of his chest, bows slightly, and walks with slight floating steps toward the exit. The door slowly slides open as he approaches, and he disappears into the hallway.

"Well, am I the only one getting a little nervous?" Meera gets up and walks with purposeful steps to the cupboard. There are more than twenty different bottles to choose from, all of them of varying colors. She quickly skims the names and reaches out for a green bottle. "Soothing" is written on the label. She brings a bottle for each of them and places them on the table. "What if I can't do it?" she says as she empties a bottle into a glass, spilling a bit on the table because her hand is shaking slightly.

Shiva gets up and walks with easy steps toward Meera. She reaches out and takes her hands between hers. "None of us can be sure that we will make it. Each of us must do our best and take responsibility for our process. There is nothing more we can do." The calmness of her voice resonates like a soothing embrace. She looks with her loving eyes at Meera, placing one hand on her cheek. Meera looks down and gives Shiva's hand a soft squeeze.

"If it can be of any help, I had a vision the other night. It showed paths leading to different corners of the world, and each had a golden ring hanging from a string." She slowly braids her long black hair and is absent for a moment. The energy vibrates strongly around her body and lights up like a silhouette around her. "Hope," she almost whispers. "We have to hold on to hope."

Yoge looks up as if he had been somewhere else and has just returned. "What are we going to do with Kingston? Do you still want to go to the edge and look for them?" he mumbles, so the others have to make an effort to hear what he is saying.

"We can do nothing," Thomas speaks calmly. "We have to trust that Eva finds Frank and gets his Skycon so we can stop him from communicating with the people here. What happens then is up to the Master."

"That sounds like a good plan. Take care of yourselves." He mutters the last words so that they barely escape his mouth and disappears toward the door.

"Are you ready?" Shiva looks Meera in the eye and pulls her close into a gentle embrace. They stand completely still for several minutes. Thomas sits in the chair and looks at them with a caring look. He knows most people do what they can to avoid looking inside. It takes a lot of courage to take that responsibility. But he also knows that the development of humanity won't make any progress if the focus is not changed from constantly having to perform to working with personal development—from results and measurements to well-being and thriving, not just mentally but right into the soul. It's a big task that lies ahead of them. It's one thing to work with oneself; it's something else to show others the way.

33

ONLY THE ONE CAN SAVE THE WORLD

I drive into town and constantly keep an eye on Frank's position on the phone that Daniel gave me. It's important not to get too close or too far away. I feel like an undercover agent on a surveillance mission. My car is great for the job; no one will suspect me of being part of any intelligence service. It's harder in every way than I thought to keep track of another person moving. It always looks so easy in movies, but I have to act naturally and keep an eye on the distance from the car in front and everything else around me. The light turns red, and I press the brake. The vehicle makes a few small jerks before stopping. It gives me a moment to take a closer look at the screen. I'm not familiar with this town, but it looks like Frank is in a building three blocks ahead and to the right. The car rattles as I put it in gear.

Further on, a large SUV pulls out, leaving a nice empty parking space. *Perfect*, I smile and indicate a right turn. There is not much power steering in the old wreck, so I must use all my effort to maneuver it into place. I set the parking brake, an old habit. Why I bother, I don't know. No one knows how to send parking fines to In-Between.

The wind has calmed down a bit, but it's still shaking the flags and signs on the street. I grab my phone, Skycon, and jacket. Even though it's early morning, there are people with empty staring eyes at a high pace everywhere. I manage to jump into the gaps between people and get from the car over to the building. Here, I can stand in peace and survey the area. I get on my toes to see what kind of building Frank is inside. I can't see it from here, and instead, I find another gap in the stream of people and go with the flow down the street. Two more blocks, then I'll be outside Frank's position. A strategy would do wonders now, but that has never been my strong side. I have always been impulsive and fast, and my curiosity and naivety have driven me. But right now, it doesn't seem like the best tactic to run into Frank and pretend it's a coincidence. The advantage this time is that I know he's eavesdropped on us. Now, Frank doesn't know he's being monitored. I smile triumphantly to myself, feeling a rush in my stomach as I'm a step ahead of him for the first time. A young man with ultra-short shorts and a headband whizzes toward me on roller skates. He sends me the widest smile as he passes me.

I can see the building where the GPS indicates Frank is. I stop at a red light. As the crowd in front of me moves, I manage to cross the street in a hurry. I can see the store marked with a red dot on the phone and squint. It's a tailor that makes custom suits. There is no way I can just walk in there pretending it's a coincidence. Instead, I head to the corner of the building, where there is a kiosk. The kiosk wall is decorated with T-shirts, caps, and fridge magnets; on the top shelf is a black cap with an eagle embroidered on the side.

"That one." I point to the cap.

The old kiosk man with high temples and a chin that is one with his neck is dressed in everything imaginable from the shop: a T-shirt, watch, brooches, and, of course, a hat. He lights up as he sees the possibility of a sale, even if it's modest.

"Would that be all?" He smiles all over his face, exposing the only few teeth left in his mouth, while the small bells on his chest ring lively as he moves. "If you buy one more, you get one for free."

"No, thanks," I reply politely and pay. I pull my hair back and put on the cap. Now, I feel a little more undercover.

He looks at me curiously. "It's you from that article, isn't it?" He coughs like he's been smoking twenty-five cigarettes every day for his entire life and leans forward toward me. "Is it true what it said in the newspaper?" His breath smells of the smoke that has etched his vocal cords for years.

I look down the street and try to dodge the question.

"Is it true? Is there a place inside the clouds like it said? And can you take people there?" He grabs my arm.

I know it's rude, but I grab my cap, hurry away from the kiosk, and ignore him. In a movie, the heroine would probably have had both the energy and the correct answer to deal with the situation, but I have neither. Attention is the last thing I need right now. I pick up the pace.

"HELLO, LADY, is it true?" The kiosk man has taken to the street, shouting at me. People around us begin to turn and look at me. I pull the cap down over my forehead, but I'm surrounded by people with mobile phones, taking pictures in no time. They stand around in a circle and move closer and closer. I bend over, roll a stroller carefully to the side, and squeeze through the crowd. Quickly, I rush into an adjacent parking garage. The GPS signal from Frank's car shows that it's parked further ahead. I glance over my shoulder to make sure no one is following me. The dot doesn't reveal which floor the car is on, nor do I know which car Frank is driving. But maybe I'll be lucky that he forgot his Skycon on the front seat and failed to lock his car. I smile to myself. My mother has always said that I was born under a lucky star. Why should luck fail me now? There are voices in several areas of the parking garage, but it's difficult to say where they are coming from as the sound is thrown around between the thick concrete walls. Everything looks gray and lethargic, and it seems that it's essential to get as many cars into as little space as possible. The sound of a horn makes me fly behind a concrete pillar. When I stick my head out, it turns out that it was a good move that I jumped into hiding. Frank comes walking down the ramp toward a large black Chevrolet with tinted windows. I look at my phone, but I can still only see the car's GPS. Frank must have left his jacket with the tailor. Carefully, I sneak a peek past the concrete pillar. Frank rummages for something in the glove compartment.

The Skycon!

If I make a massive tackle combined with a moment of surprise, will I have a chance against him? That's probably unlikely, even though I'm taller than him. My head thumps lightly, reminding me how easily he knocked me over in the hospital.

"Hi, Jimmy, what's up?" Frank's voice is sloppily spiced with a nauseating sweetness. He's holding a phone up in front of him, but I can't see who he's talking to. I can only hear Frank's words. He's about five parked cars from me. The light from the fluorescent tubes flashes, and half of them turn off. Luckily, there is still light where Frank is standing and darkness around me. *Thank you*, I think, sending off a thought to the universe.

"It was what we could have expected, but it doesn't change the plans." He leans against the car, which is gleaming clean. His white shirt sits tight around his stomach. "I'll take care of it from here if you just keep an eye on the others in the Ring."

I dare not budge from the spot, even though I am tempted to sneak closer to hear better who he is talking to and what is being said. I'm trying to breathe completely quietly, but it sounds like I have asthma. Several cars drive past me, and people who pass by look at me a little puzzled. I take no notice and just look down at my phone regularly, so no one suspects anything.

Frank laughs out loud. "Yes, Angela. No, no, she's not going to be a problem."

I close my eyes and clasp my hand around the phone. He touches the screen, ends the call, and puts the phone in his pocket and the Skycon in the glove compartment. Then he slams the front door and walks directly toward me. I squat down and lean my back against the concrete pillar. If only I could get to his car before it locks. Quietly, I sneak along the back of the cars parked up against the wall. I can see Frank's feet under the cars and do everything in my power to stay hidden. Now, there is only one car before I reach Frank's. I stand up a bit and can see his back at the ramp to the next floor of the parking garage. At that moment, the lights on his car flash, and the side mirrors fold in. I hammer my hand against the cold hard concrete floor and let myself fall back, so I sit down with a bump on the floor. How do I get into his car? It's completely impossible! Petrified, I sit on the cold floor and look up at the yellow fluorescent tubes flashing above me. The light from them is sparse and makes everything look lifeless and gray.

"Do you need help?" A handsome gentleman in a gray suit steps up beside me. "Have you fallen?" His black hair is styled nicely to the side, and the dialect exudes upper class.

I look at him in surprise, "Uh, yes." He offers his hand; I take it and get to my feet. "Thank you," I manage to stammer out and brush my pants. He smiles kindly at me, and I straighten my jacket to look a bit more proper.

"Are you injured?"

"No, no," I shake my head dismissively. "I must have forgotten to look where I was going." I smile back persistently.

He opens his shiny attaché case and takes out a business card which he hands to me. "Here is my number in case you need help."

"Thank you, thank you," I smile at him and can't help but wonder if he means it.

"Well, I hope you have a wonderful day." He walks on toward the exit to the street. I look at his card, Lawyer Steven O'Connor, and put it in my pocket. Then it was probably more business than compassion. The car next to Frank's backs out and leaves me a clear view. I walk over and look through the windows. It is spotless: no marks, dirt, or personal items. With easy steps, I walk around the car without touching it. The rear windows are tinted. On one seat, I can see a brochure. My nose is almost completely flat as I press it against the window to see what is written on it. It's from a hotel. It says, "Drive in," but I can't see the rest. It's not that important either; I can follow Frank with the GPS signal.

"Well, look who's here?"

It gives a start in my body; I know exactly who is behind me.

"Hi, Frank," I say as I turn around and try hard to pull the corners of my mouth up in a smile, but they refuse.

"What a coincidence to see you here. Are you also parked here?" He smiles and tilts his head a bit.

He knows very well that he is ahead on points, but he doesn't have to rub it in. I manage a strained smile and straighten my cap. "What are you doing here?"

"It's my car, Angela, but I think you know that already."

Discreetly, I try to wipe the mark from my nose on the window away with my sleeve. "It's a nice car you got there. You have done well." I have to try to make conversation with him and see if I can get him to reveal something about his strategy.

"I have started a collaboration with some people who want the same things as me. And they want what's best for me." His withdrawn eyes sting when he looks at me, sending chills down my spine.

"Anyone I know?" It hurts my cheeks to smile so strained, but I keep going.

"No, Angela, this is not for you. These people want to save the world for real, not like you and your ring of illusion." He laughs scornfully and pats me on the shoulder.

"Does that mean you have given up on being part of the Ring?"

He looks at me, so his gaze drills into mine. "Look, this is where our little friendly conversation ends, and we go our separate ways."

My breathing is as calm as possible when your worst enemy is facing you. "But if you don't want to be part of the Ring, you don't need the contact to In-Between, do you?" My question catches him out, and even though he tries desperately to walk away from me, he can't help turning around.

"Only one of us is going to save the world," he laughs sneeringly. "And it will not be you, Angela."

34

ONE LAST OPTION

I have one last Joker in my hand—one person I know Frank likes and who I might be able to persuade to help me.

Lucy!

I'm back in the car. My fingers drum frantically on the steering wheel, hoping that a bunch of great ideas will fall in my lap. The last time I was with Lucy was when Frank wanted to reveal In-Between to her, and she refused to hear him out. I can't be sure that she will listen or help me. Another challenge is that she lives over 400 miles from here!

The glove compartment gets a punch on the side so that it opens. Under an ancient service book, I have a mobile phone with my contacts. If I want to persuade Lucy to help me, I have to convince her that it will also affect her and her child if she doesn't. I hold the phone in my hand, ready to dial her number, but something is holding me back—a feeling of being paralyzed and just locked into the situation. I flip through my contacts, land on Andreas's number, and press it instead.

"Hello?" His dark voice sounds a bit rusty.

"It's me."

"Eva?" he says, followed by silence. "Yes, sorry, I have not become accustomed to the idea that you have risen from the dead again."

I continue to drum on the steering wheel and don't feel dead. "How is Luke?"

"He's sleeping. That is what you do in a coma." Andreas pauses. "I'm not that privileged. I don't get much sleep at the moment."

"But isn't my mother there to help?" A roaring motorcycle pulls up next to the side of the car, and I push the phone closer to my ear to be able to hear Andreas. It accelerates and moves on. It's followed by several cars in a constant stream.

"Yes, she is, but I can't sleep at night; my head keeps swimming. And Emma…" he hesitates.

I don't say anything. I'm waiting. It's like sitting in a place where there is a buzz around you without being a part of it. Only the passers-by who are looking for a parking space notice me. I turn my back toward the road to escape the accusing glances of parking-space-hungry drivers.

"Emma senses something is wrong, but I can't say anything. You said I'm not allowed to." He swallows a yawn.

Emma rolled her eyes when Meera spoke about past lives the night we met at Lucy's. She doesn't believe there is anything between Heaven and Earth other than what can be proved. She would just entertain her friends with stories about In-Between and ridicule it. "Can you wait a bit? Just a short time?"

Andreas doesn't answer.

"For old time's sake. For Luke…"

"How long will this go on? Did you find the idiot?" I can hear quiet music in the background when Andreas pauses. A rhythmic beep sound complements the music. It comes from the machine that keeps Luke alive.

I swallow and run my teeth over my lower lip, so it stings. "Thirty-six days." There is almost no sound to my words that are drowning in the traffic noise from the passing cars.

"Excuse me?" Andreas raises his voice, and the sound from the speaker is distorted.

A car is honking next to me, and a man deliberately points at his watch. I look away.

"One month…."

"And what happens then?"

The silence almost pushes me back into the seat and presses on my chest like a heavy-weight disc. I can hear Andreas breathing. But the words are stuck in my throat and will not leave.

"Eva!" Andreas starts to sound impatient and raises his voice even more, so I have no doubt it's time to answer.

I try to answer, but my throat is parched. "I don't know what is going to happen." My voice is low, and that is partly true.

Andreas doesn't answer. I know him well enough to know that he can figure it out, that I can't say it, and that he must wait for an answer.

"I'm not sure I can handle the pain of losing Luke," he speaks softly. "It was one thing suddenly being alone with him when you went into a coma. But having to lose both you and him." The music stops in the background. "I thought all hope was gone. But when you were suddenly here again, hope came back."

"Who are you talking to?" It's my mother shouting in the background.

"Eva, is that you?" There is a brief pause before my mother continues. "I'll take care of Luke and Andreas. Concentrate on what you have to!"

It gets quiet, very quiet. I know my mother is right, but I have a hard time surrendering to it. In a way, it feels like standing alone on a ledge and having to jump off. It is the only way forward, and the enemy is catching up with you from behind, so it's only a matter of time.

"Eva," Andreas has recaptured the phone. "Your mother is right. Do what you have to do, and don't worry about us."

I'm trying to force words out of my mouth. There is no doubt that it would have been my escape route to drive to Luke instead of throwing myself into the abyss of uncertainty. Now, both Andreas and my mother are pushing me over the edge.

"Call if there is anything I need to know about Luke." I hold onto them a little longer, so I avoid being confronted with my next move: Lucy. The reason it feels so scary is very simple.

Rejection.

If she doesn't want to help, I simply don't know what to do. It's easier not to ask and avoid the risk of a no. I switch on the engine, which rumbles, and turn the air to full force. "Thank you, promise to call if anything happens or if Frank shows up…."

"We'll call if there's anything new. You can be completely sure." Andreas's voice is a bit hesitant.

"Yes, we will," shouts my mother from the background.

Andreas hangs up, and I sit all alone in the car. Without thinking about it, I put the car in gear and drive out onto the road. The sound of a honk and squealing tires doesn't make me stop. Now, they can have my parking space. Lucy is the only option left. Lucy. No matter how many others I call, it doesn't change it. I disconnect my brain and turn on my willpower. No more discussions with myself, no more fights or fear scenarios. "Go!" I say in a firm tone to myself, pressing the accelerator hard. With that speed, I should reach her place by evening.

35

I KNOW WHO YOU ARE

I park the car one block away from Lucy's street. The large street lamps light up the road with their bright white lights. There are no people to be seen, but parked cars are everywhere. I was lucky to get the last space behind a large gray van. The city is divided into two—one part with housing and one with huge government buildings. The vast majority who live here either work for the state or live with someone who does. It dawns on me that Lucy never talks about Tim's job. She only talks about how great he is. When we met in In-Between, we hadn't seen each other for six years and had so much catching up to do, and I never thought to ask about his work.

Hi, Lucy, there's something I just need to ask you. You remember Frank; would you help me steal a little thing he's taken from somewhere I can't tell you about? I doubt that Lucy will buy it. She doesn't usually let herself be persuaded by half stories or anything against her beliefs. Family is the essential thing for Lucy, her highest priority. That'll be my opening strategy.

Down the road and around the corner, then I'm there. A homeless dog with ribs as distinct as a washboard and a rat sitting on a pile of garbage searching for dinner are watching me. The tall houses stretch up toward the heavy clouds, and in many of the windows, the lights are on. In several places, I can see silhouettes of residents. A cat crosses the road and looks startled, surprised not to be the only one out hunting. The wind shakes my jacket and throws an empty beer can around.

Farther ahead, I can see Lucy's front door. A lady opens the window on the ground floor as I pass by, and the smell of burnt pork spills out. It's number twelve.

The lamp outside the front door dazzles me. There are a large number of buttons with names that belong to the different apartments. My finger runs down from the top. Sixth, Peter and Janice. Fifth, Tom and Ben. Fourth, Lucy and Tim. Quickly, I cast a glance up and down the road; it's still empty. I lean my back against the door as I stare at Lucy's name. My hands sink into my pockets, and I bend one leg, letting my foot rest on the door behind me. If Frank can't get help from above, he is alone and easier to neutralize.

Imagine if he went to the press with the Skycon to prove he's telling the truth. It would overthrow the whole of In-Between, and the mission might fail. The thought makes chills run down my spine. If the development of the world is to be reversed, the only possibility is a higher consciousness; that was what the Master said. When I see headlines in newspapers with wars, destruction, rich people getting richer, and nature getting poorer, it makes sense. Many people line their own pockets who already have enough for themselves, thinking short-term for their own gain. Egos inflate and want to be seen, get "likes," and be heard. Before, many parents were not at home because they worked. Now, many parents are not with their children because they are absent. It has consequences, the Master said. The weeks I was in In-Between allowed me to see it all from a distance, and I began to understand what the Master means. My life was a small bubble, and I thought no further than what I needed. It's scary to look at the larger perspective. Many people keep the challenges in check because it's difficult to relate to and understand one's role in the big puzzle.

The door suddenly disappears behind me. I let out a slight squeal and reach out feverishly for something to hold onto but land with a bump on the stairs. It gives a jolt up through my back, and my butt hurts. I collect myself for a moment and look up at a big belly. The woman whose stomach I am looking at takes a step back. She has bags full of empty cans in both hands and a blue cowboy jacket hanging open.

"Angela!!!" The bags fall to the floor, so they rattle loudly, and she throws herself over me in a big hug while I try to get on my feet again. "Angela, why didn't you tell me you were coming!" Lucy shakes me from side to side in an embrace, and her big belly pushes me back. When she releases me, she stands with glowing eyes and pats my shoulders simultaneously, so it feels like they are getting narrower. "It's great to see you." She keeps patting me on the shoulders, and I can't help but laugh. "I was just on my way out, but that doesn't matter. Come, come, let's go and see Tim; he's at home." With difficulty, she bends down to pick up a couple of the cans that have fallen out of the bags, puts them back in, and places the bags under the staircase. She takes my hand, says, "Come," and pulls my arm. "You've never met Tim, have you?" I shake my head, but I know very well what he looks like.

The staircase is bright, and the steps are wide. It looks newly renovated. There are no marks on the walls or wear on the steps. We've only just reached the second floor when Lucy stops.

"There are some extra pounds to drag along." She bursts out laughing and caresses her stomach. Her golden-brown hair sits in a ponytail, but a strand has torn loose and falls over her chubby cheeks. "It's so strange; every time I see you, I think of my old friend, Eva." She shakes her head, "I'm so sorry; I hate it when people mistake me for someone else," she laughs again. What are you doing here? Why didn't you call? And where did you go? I wanted to contact you but didn't have your number."

I just smile back and have just run out of words. Cheeky remarks are also sold out. Lucy gasps for breath and sets off up the stairs. "No, don't tell me until we get up, then I can listen better." She pulls herself up the stairs, pauses on the next landing, and so it repeats itself for each landing until we reach the fourth floor.

"Here we are," Lucy looks triumphantly at me. "It's an achievement when you're carrying forty extra pounds."

I clearly remember how it was. She puts her finger on a fingerprint reader on the door, and a little later, it opens. "Tiiiiiiiiim!" She walks in, and I follow right behind. We enter a large room. There are no internal walls, just one big space, and Tim is nowhere to be seen.

"Here, hand me your jacket." Lucy already has a hanger in her hand and places our clothes on small hooks that hang down from the ceiling on almost transparent cords. My gaze continues to scan the apartment. I can sense that it's an old property, but they have renovated it in a modern way. There are high ceilings with moldings all the way around the edge. The kitchen is to the right and blends in with the rest of the room. On the entire back wall are windows with a panoramic view of the city away from the main street. Outside is a balcony, where I can see a silhouette. Lucy struggles to take her shoes off, "Just go in, I'm coming." She laughs again. "Everything turns into a project with this one," she pats herself on the stomach and gives me a light push, so I'm about to stumble into the living room. In many ways, it's so liberating to be with Lucy. She never takes things too seriously or makes life complicated. Her laughter is contagious with sincere joy.

"Tiiiimmm, where are you?" She shakes her head and grimaces at me. There is a large brown corner sofa with large pillows to the right, and now I can see a single door in the extension of the bathing area; it must be the toilet. After all, they do need a little bit of privacy. Lucy overtakes me, heads straight for the terrace, and slides the door quietly to the side.

"HA! Caught red-handed."

The silhouette jumps and turns around, "I thought you went out shopping." It's Tim. He looks very ordinary with smooth brown short hair that is trimmed to one side, a round face and a small nose. He hurries to put out his cigarette and looks apologetically at Lucy, "It was just two pulls."

She crosses her arms and purses her mouth. "Just a pity that you'll be sleeping on the couch tonight." She turns and walks back toward me.

Poor Tim, he looks like a homeless dog and hurries to get rid of the cigarette butt. I'm still standing in the living room; Tim has not seen me.

"You have to meet Angela; I told you about her some time ago. She is the one that reminds me of my old friend, Eva, whom I have not seen in a hundred years. You haven't met Eva. She's dead."

Tim smiles as he sees me and comes toward me with an outstretched arm. I smile back, and our hands meet. His hand is small and a little rough. He is wearing a green knitted sweater that fits snugly and marks his small belly top. He looks me straight in the eye. "How nice to meet one of Lucy's friends." He shakes my hand, and I follow.

Lucy is in the kitchen and has already made two cups of coffee and one cup of tea. It's all on a tray with a bowl of jelly beans, licorice, and chocolate. She looks apologetically at the bowl as she puts it on the table. "This is my pregnancy weakness." She lets out a loud laugh, "I can't help it. They almost pursue me. I can wake up at night and just crave chocolate. She points to the pieces wrapped nicely in shiny silver paper. "It's an experience to be pregnant." Tim has sat down at one end of the corner sofa. From here, you can look out over all the city roofs. I sit at the other end. Tim pushes a pillow to Lucy so that she can support her lower back.

"How far along are you?" My brain calculates at high speed. There are no pictures on the walls, only a huge TV of at least 85 inches. On the wall facing what I think is the toilet, there are several thin lines.

"Five months and a bit too many pounds." She shakes a roll of fat around her waist, "I used to be skinny and super fit. It's a drag to be fat."

"You'll lose it again; just wait." I reach for the bowl of chocolate. "Are you excited?" The paper crackles as I unwrap it.

They nod synchronously. "It's a dream come true." Lucy suddenly looks distant in her gaze and is enveloped in sad energy. She looks at me, "When the accident happened, I didn't know I was pregnant. I could have lost the baby."

Tim reaches for her hand. "But you didn't." He sits still and looks at her with loving eyes. I remember how she told me she wanted to have a baby when we met in In-Between. But Lucy doesn't remember, and at the time, she didn't know she was pregnant.

She takes a jelly beans. Her face lights up. "What are you doing here? It's great to see you." She chews and reaches out for another one. Tim also looks at me and awaits an answer.

"I was just passing through," I look away, trying to cover up how terrible I am at lying.

Lucy leans forward, lights a candle on the table, and takes her cup of coffee, which is still steaming. She pushes the cup with tea toward me. *Well remembered*, I think, without saying anything.

I reach for the tea but hesitate. "There's actually something I need to talk to you about."

"Ha!" I knew it; it's no coincidence that you're here. No one comes to this city by chance unless you're married to someone like this one." She slaps Tim on the thigh, snatches three gummies from the bowl, and throws them in her mouth. "Well, what is it then?" Lucy moves excitedly forward on the sofa. "Are you pregnant too?"

I shake my head defensively in a hurry. "No, no… Lucy…" I stop myself and look down at the floor as I rub my hand across my forehead and start bouncing my leg up and down. If there's one thing this journey has taught me, it is that honesty pays off. I don't want more lies or cunning stories. I look up and say, "I need your help."

Lucy sits still and looks at me. I stop and look from Lucy over at Tim. It's impossible to get him out of here, so I have to count on him to understand what I'm going to tell them in a bit.

"Oh, no, as long as it has nothing to do with that clammy guy, Frank." Her laughter fills the room but abruptly stops as I don't respond. "It has!" She moves forward on the sofa, so she is about to fall off the edge. "Is he after you?" Her gaze is inquisitive. "If he bothers you, just tell me. I have some contacts from my past I can draw upon." She bends her arm and indicates that they are strong. "And Tim has some very important friends."

"Frank," I stammer.

Lucy breaks in and looks at Tim. "Frank is the weird guy who wanted to tell me something creepy." Tim listens, and he seems nice but doesn't say much. Calmly, he sits and looks at Lucy while he drinks his coffee. But Lucy also takes up space for two, so if he wasn't quiet beforehand, he might be with her.

"Frank has taken something that doesn't belong to him."

Lucy laughs again. "You make it sound like a crime story." She raises her hands in front of her and waves them.

"Lucy, I'm not the person you think I am."

Her laughter freezes. "You're getting a little scary." She jerks back on the couch and wants to pull her legs up under her but can't because of her stomach. Instead, she grabs the pillow she leans on and hugs it.

I sit down on the edge of the couch. "Sorry, I don't want to scare you, but for you to understand the seriousness of what Frank has taken, I have to tell you something."

"What is the matter with you people!" She hits the pillow and throws it away as she gets up. "First Frank, and now you." She walks to the window. "The last time we were together, you said I shouldn't know. Is it the same thing Frank wanted to tell me? Then, you are no better than him."

I hurry to her, "Lucy, I would never say anything if it wasn't extremely important. Something has changed, and I have no one else who can help me. You're my only chance."

She slowly turns around and looks straight into my eyes. "It's all right. I know who you are."

36

IN-BETWEEN

My tea is cold, but I still take a sip. Tim stares at me as if he's seen an alien for the first time in his life.

"I don't quite think I'm getting this." He gives me a strained smile and fiddles with the fluff on his wool sweater. "You're Angela, Lucy's girlfriend, but now you say that you've also Eva, Lucy's old friend who's… dead." He raises his eyebrows to his forehead.

"Yes…"

Lucy has sat down next to Tim, and that's probably a wise decision because he's the one under the most pressure right now. It looks like his brain is searching for a logical explanation or connection, but he can't find anything he can use. He keeps staring at me as if he's afraid I'll disappear if he blinks.

"I'm dead."

Tim rolls his eyes and suddenly bursts into a very fake laugh. "You're pulling my leg. That is great; you nearly got me there." He looks over at Lucy and back at me, and over at Lucy again. "What day is it today? International fib day?" Neither of us changes expression, and Tim sits completely petrified on the couch with his eyes widened. "You're not kidding." He stays seated. Lucy leans against him and lays her head on his shoulder. He doesn't move a muscle. "Yes, you are."

I shake my head. "Tim, I know it sounds far out, and it is. If it can be of any comfort, it also took me a long time to get my head around it." I reach into my pocket and grab my Skycon. "One of these," I put it on the table. "That's what it's all about." For others, it may look like a very ordinary gadget, and yet not. The material is different, and the design is not like a regular phone. It is smaller, weighs almost nothing, and only has a few buttons.

"May I?" Tim points to the Skycon. I hand it to him. He looks inquisitively at it as he turns and twists it between his fingers.

"Where did you get this?" He looks like a little boy who got what he wanted the most at Christmas, just in an even better version than he knew existed.

I cannot help but smile inside because I just told him I'm dead and still sitting on his couch.

He takes the Skycon, holds it close to his eye, and gets up. In the kitchen drawer, he finds a magnifying glass and continues to study the Skycon closely. Neither Lucy nor I say anything.

"I have never seen anything like this. What is it made of?"

I shrug.

Lucy takes the bowl of jelly beans and empties it into her hand. She puts as many as possible in her mouth and still manages to say, "He's an IT nerd beyond the ordinary if you were in any doubt." Tim is wholly engrossed by the Skycon and ignores Lucy. "Take a look around. Anything with a bit of electronics in it, we have it." She laughs heartily and carries on chewing. "Tim is a professional hacker for the Department of Defense."

The frame on the wall, the TV, the fingerprint reader on the door—it all makes sense. There is probably more that I haven't noticed. I cough as I get some saliva down the wrong way in my throat. "Can you be a professional hacker?"

That was Tim's cue; suddenly, he is present again. "They need to have the best hackers on their side," he starts pressing the buttons on the Skycon.

"NO, don't turn it on." I fly off the couch and pull it out of his hands. If Frank finds out I'm with Lucy, I will have wasted my last chance. Tim takes a step back and holds his hands up in front of him, "Sorry...."

"It's okay, but Frank can hear our conversation if it's turned on." I look over at Lucy.

"That idiot shouldn't listen in." She pats the pillow on the sofa and indicates that Tim should come and sit with her.

"How did you find out who I am?" I change the subject and look inquisitively at Lucy. The Skycon is on the table—turned off.

"My dreams." She hesitates and takes a deep breath. "At first, it was vague, but then suddenly." She pauses, looking over at Tim. "Suddenly, it was like being somewhere else, a place where you were too. But you were Eva."

She's talking about In-Between. Right now, she just thinks it's a dream, and she doesn't know that she has been to In-Between. She has just connected the dots.

"There is something special about the light around you. It's the same whether I see you as Eva or Angela." She caresses her stomach softly.

I look down at myself and cannot see any light.

"There is a special vibration near you, and the same was in the dreams. They were very vivid. It was as if you were merging into one person. That sounds far-fetched; I know that. But when I saw you in the stairwell, I had no doubt." She looks down and shakes her head. "But I don't understand much of it." She takes a sip of her coffee and spits it back into the cup. "Yuck, life is too short for cold coffee."

"Well, anyone want something a little stronger?" Tim looks at me and walks over to the wall with the thin lines. He presses it lightly, so a door opens. There are several drawers and above them is a bar cabinet with bottles and glasses. He takes out a bottle of whiskey and looks over at me.

"I'm game."

"What do you want, Lucy?"

"Hot coffee, please." She hands Tim the cup. He makes fresh steaming coffee and pours whiskey into two low glasses with a flower pattern on the side.

"Cheers." I take a proper sip, which rasps down into my stomach.

"Cheers, whoever you are." He shakes his head slightly. "It's a strange day." Lucy and I can't help but laugh. I lean back on the couch. So far, so good.

"There is a place between life and death where people who die suddenly or people who are in a coma travel to." I take another sip and make sure they are with me. Both Lucy and Tim sit perfectly still and look at me with expressionless faces. "That's what you remember; it was not a dream, Lucy. You were in In-Between after your accident. That's also where you first met Frank." My heart gallops away, so much that I fear it will jump out of my chest. Heat spreads through my whole body. There is still no reaction from Lucy or Tim. I continue telling them about In-Between, about the people, the place, and the challenges you are allowed to face. It's like floating in a marvelous tale with Lucy and Tim. I lower my voice and approach the landing. "There is a Ring which consists of seven selected people. The Ring has not been assembled for thousands of years, but now it's assembled again." Still no reaction from Lucy and Tim. The room is completely quiet. It's like all sounds were left outside, and space absorbs my words, making room for the next. "I am one of the members of the Ring. Meera is also one of them, and my son, Luke."

Now, Lucy reacts and widens her eyes. "You are kidding!!! That is so crazy, Angela!" First, she slaps herself on the thigh and then Tim. "Give me a glass, Tim; the little one can handle a small sip." Tim reaches for his glass and forces the last drops into his mouth before taking the bottle and filling Lucy's glass. Then he lifts the bottle straight to his mouth and drinks. Suddenly, what he is doing dawns on him, and he looks completely bewildered. "I don't usually do that."

My glass is still half full, and I drink it slowly. "We all need to work on ourselves to get ready to come back to Earth with a new energy that will help people become more aware." It must sound like a script from a Hollywood movie if you didn't know any better. But both Lucy and Tim seem to buy my story. "The challenge is that Frank has stolen one of these." I reach for the Skycon. "He will reveal In-Between and, in that way, make sure that the Ring is not assembled in time." I hold back and swallow even though it's difficult. "He thinks he should have a place in the Ring, but that can't be done. That's why he has gathered a group of people to oppose our work. He also gets help from above, in the most literal sense."

Lucy slams her hand on the table. "He must not succeed!" And then she hits Tim's shoulder. "This is the future of our child we are talking about. Frank must not fuck it up!" Lucy's face changes color, and she becomes completely ruddy. "Frank is an idiot. He's only interested in himself," she snorts.

I take a deep breath. It feels like a large barbell has been lifted from my chest, and I can breathe again.

"Tell us what you need. Tim and I are ready to help you. Right, Tim?" Tim says nothing but nods mechanically and takes another swig from the bottle.

37
KINGSTON

Both Lucy and Tim needed to compose themselves, so after answering all their questions, we agreed to go to bed and wait until the morning to plan our strategy. I picked up my bag with clean clothes from the car and the phone that monitors Frank. Now, the sun is shining right into my face. The sky is entirely blue except for a small cloud that hangs alone outside my window. My body is light, and joy tickles like sparkling wine after talking to Lucy and Tim yesterday. I'm so relieved that they took it overwhelmingly nicely. Tim was somewhat skeptical, but eventually, he said that if Lucy believed me, so did he. I don't know if it was his curiosity about the Skycon or my story that caught his attention. He had a tough time letting go of the Skycon, and I almost had to wrestle it from him when we went to bed. Now, the big question is, what do we do from here? Although I know the responsibility is mine, I rejoice in feeling like a team and no longer being all by myself. I wish I could talk to Thomas and hear what he would suggest concerning Frank. There's a light knock on the door. "Are you awake, Angela?" It is Lucy's voice.

"Yes, I'm coming now." I'm in a sleeping area behind the

kitchen that I didn't discover yesterday. The door is made to disappear into the wall and look like part of it. From here, you cannot hear a sound from the living room. I put on my white cotton blouse and jeans in a hurry and go to the kitchen. Lucy and Tim are already seated. There are eggs and bacon, and juice is in a jug on the high counter.

"I hope you're hungry." Lucy starts scooping food onto my plate. The tea is already steaming in my cup. The room is much bigger than I sensed last night. It's very bright, and there is a view of the whole city. The empty frames have been transformed into images in chaotic patterns and vibrant colors with lots of life. It looks expensive.

"How long have you lived here?"

"Not very long," Lucy puts her hand on top of Tim's. He is sitting next to her on the opposite side of the table. "We got the place through Tim's work." Tim doesn't say anything. "Well, it's actually a secret, but now you have also told us your secret. Everything about Tim's work is mega secret, isn't it, honey?" She winks at him and slaps him on the hand.

Tim nods. He is a man of few words. "I just needed a fresh start after the accident, and this is perfect."

It's hard to disagree with, I think to myself. There is no doubt that Tim would love In-Between with all the technology that is far ahead of Earth. The eggs taste delicious, spiced with a strong aftertaste of chili.

"Here, have some juice; it's homemade." Lucy hands me a glass of yellow juice. An intense taste of mint spreads in my mouth and rinses the strong aftertaste from before away.

"Delicious."

"Yes, the eggs are a bit intense," Lucy smiles, "but good for your health. Not that it matters to you."

"What's going to happen now?" Tim moves a little forward on the chair and puckers his dark tousled eyebrows.

"I know where Frank is." I take a mouthful of juice to stall a little. I don't know if Lucy is ready to be confronted with Frank. She eats with a colossal appetite and is already on her second serving, which is as big as the first one. "I need your help to get the Skycon from Frank." I gently place my hand on her arm.

"What do you want me to do?" She speaks with her mouth full of food. I shrug my shoulders and must admit that I have no plan or idea of how to proceed from here.

"How do you know where he is?" Tim begins to fidget in the chair. He looks like he's concentrating. It's obvious that his brain is working overtime behind the blue eyes.

"There's a tracker on his car and his jacket."

"Do you know which tracker?" He looks thoughtfully at me.

I shake my head and reach for my bag, where Daniel's phone is. "Here. This is where I can track him." He opens the phone and quickly finds the program. Two small dots are flashing a fair distance from here. "Where did you get this from?" He narrows his eyes so that his eyebrows almost meet.

"From a friend." The heat flushes up my cheeks. "Is it okay?"

Tim laughs for the first time. "Are you crazy? It's some of the best surveillance equipment you can get your hands on. It's almost impossible to track." He looks like someone who just won the lottery. "And even better, it allows me to hack his phone as long as he has it on him close to his jacket." Tim picks up his laptop and connects the phone to it. His fingers dance across the keyboard. "Here we go," his voice is triumphant. With a quick motion, he turns the screen so both Lucy and I can see. "This is Frank's camera."

An image appears: a huge hall, where enormous paintings with wide gold frames mark the walls and tall statues reign in the corners. The light is dim. Several men dressed in all-black suits sit around a large old wooden table. A chandelier hangs down from the ceiling with lit candles dripping onto the large rustic table. It looks like they are in the middle of a discussion; the atmosphere seems intense.

"It's Kingston!" I stammer.

"Didn't you say it was Frank?" Tim looks at me wonderingly.

"Frank is part of Kingston, a group of people helping him. Can you get some sound too?" I stare at Tim, who looks very concentrated. It scratches a little before the sound comes through. The sound is diffuse, and it is difficult to distinguish the words from each other. I close my eyes and make an effort to hear what is being said. The high ceilings and reverberation throw the sound around the room.

"Where is Frank?" My gaze wanders from the screen over to Lucy and Tim, who doesn't know who to look for.

"I can't see him either," Lucy shrugs.

"It's his phone. He has it in his breast pocket, so the camera points toward the others; that's also why the sound is so diffuse." Tim types fast on the keyboard; he might as well be writing in Russian. None of it is understandable to ordinary people. But it must mean something because the sound changes and becomes clearer. The screen splits in two, and a picture emerges from a different angle. "It's unbelievable how careless people are with their safety." Tim shakes his head. "They almost invite us to watch."

I lean forward in the chair and can barely get my face closer to the screen without touching it. "There he is!"

"Hey, move a bit so the rest of us can watch too. "Lucy gives my shoulder a push and moves the chair too.

I feel the warmth in my cheeks and move to the side. "There," my finger diligently points to the screen where Frank is sitting. He looks earnest. The bald forehead disappears almost completely in the contrast of the image. His eyes are lifeless and look like two dark holes. He sits and listens to one of the others speaking.

"It doesn't help to dress expensively when you look like that." It flies out of Tim's mouth.

Lucy and I look at each other and smile; we probably both thought so without saying it aloud.

Tim points at the screen. "The guy speaking is the director of one of the world's largest pharmaceutical companies; they make vaccines for third world countries." The picture zooms in to the right. "I don't remember his name, but he is a weapons giant." He pans to the left but can only get half a head in view. That is enough to see that it is the president of one of the world's superpowers. I lean back and stroke my hands over my face.

"That's quite a company Frank has joined!" Tim continues to type on his computer, and he manages to connect another camera, so we have the whole table covered. There are twelve men in black suits and one woman, all dressed in charcoal gray shirts in the finest material. Smooth, polished, and without any kind of facial expressions or expressions of emotion, they look like dressed mannequins. Seriousness radiates from them. At the end of the table, a dark man with completely black slicked hair chairs the meeting. He speaks loudly and with accentuated words. The others look at him and listen without interrupting.

"If nothing happens soon, we need to start the next phase. Frank, you have to take care of the threat you mentioned. It's time for you to show your worth. Use your influence and your contacts. We cannot have an opposing movement where people start believing and hoping for a better world." He pauses and looks around at the others at the table. "We need to focus on fear to maintain the grip on the direction. It's the most effective way to strengthen our economic position and influence." The others clap in a controlled way without moving a muscle on their faces.

"Now, we know what we're up against." Tim's attempt to be bold goes down like a lead balloon.

"If we want to stop Frank, we need to get his Skycon." I look over at Lucy. Tim closely studies the picture.

"I don't think that is the only thing I would be worried about."

"What do you mean?" My hand continues to run across my forehead, and soon I will have red streaks on my skin if I don't stop.

"With that group of people and their influence on the world's agenda, they are probably not just betting on Frank being able to communicate with In-Between and getting the story of your existence leaked."

I stop the movement of my hand. My jaws hurt as I clench my teeth.

"Coffee, anyone?" Tim gets up and heads for the coffeemaker as he continues. I shake my head, and Lucy nods. "Angela, you say that all seven of you must be ready to come down here again. But what if you or Luke don't return to In-Between? What if you're not ready in time because you are busy chasing Frank?"

A shiver runs down my spine. I sit completely still without saying anything. Tim uses my silence to lay out the scenario even more clearly. "What if he's winning because you're running after him? What if you are acting precisely as he hoped?"

I sit completely frozen on the chair without blinking or breathing. If Tim is correct, that I'm losing because I'm afraid of what Frank will do, I'll spend all my energy trying to stop him, and at the same time, he's winning. "But…" I stop myself.

"Just think about it for a moment. You said he wanted to kill Luke, but he failed. He leaked information about In-Between to the press, but it's not a story that has caught on so far. What are his options to stop you now? It's to keep you busy." He empties his glass of juice, "And it seems to be working very well."

"But…" I try again. "But Luke can't die. Then he wouldn't be ready to join the Ring. He must have the 42 days to get ready. That's how long the energy transition takes when you leave your life on Earth." My gaze stares blankly into the air, hoping that I will find the answer. "If people get to know about In-Between, we risk upsetting the balance and too many taking the back door from here. In-Between won't be able to cope. The pressure will become too great and the curve too steep."

"Then there is the last option. You, Angela." Tim sits still and looks at me.

"What do you mean?"

"What if he comes after you?"

My stomach gives a rush, and I gasp for air. "It makes no sense. He has already been close to me several times."

The doorbell rings, and both Lucy and I jump half a yard. Tim places a cup of coffee in front of Lucy and heads for the front door. I hold my breath and look over at Lucy. Our gaze meets. I can see that she is thinking the same as I am. Neither of us has time to do anything before Tim opens the door.

"Hi," it sounds from the hallway. "There's a package for you." Tim signs for it. He brings it back and places it on the table. We sit completely still and stare at the package. Then Lucy starts giggling. "Stop it now; it's just a package. Frank doesn't know you're here." She reaches for the package, but Tim stops her. "Have you ordered something? Because I haven't."

Lucy withdraws her hand. "No, not that I remember."

Tim takes the package, goes to the kitchen, and puts it in the sink. He turns the water on full force. When the parcel is soaked, he opens it gently and holds up wet diapers and a pacifier. "Lucy…"

"Ohhhhh, that was probably the welcome gift I got from the supermarket. I totally forgot…."

We all break out in laughter, making the mood go from freezing to a more comfortable temperature.

"There's one more thing we need to pay attention to. As long as Frank has the Skycon, I cannot contact In-Between because he's eavesdropping on it."

Tim extends his hand. "Hand it to me again."

I reach into my pocket and hand him the Skycon. He fetches a small hand-held scanner and moves it over the Skycon. Nothing happens. He keeps moving it back and forth and turns it around—still nothing. Then he shakes his head. "It shouldn't be possible. I can't measure any signal from it."

"But it's off," I try with my common sense.

"It doesn't matter; devices always send a tracking signal. But this one has a frequency I can't measure." He keeps scanning it and switching the settings on his handheld scanner, but nothing helps. "I would love to keep it," he smiles at me, and I just smile back.

I reach out, and Tim reluctantly hands it over. "If I turn it on, I cannot speak freely to the people in In-Between."

Lucy breaks in, "But is it important?" She looks concentrated and more severe than what suits her face.

"Both yes and no, I have to stay here until I have control of the Frank situation. But it's also important that I get ready to join the others. It helps to have contact upwards." I smile at her. "Another thing is that I have to coordinate my return; otherwise, I'm stuck down here, and this body cannot last."

"We can utilize that Frank doesn't know where you are. It's to our advantage." He throws the scanner on the table, "Then I can keep this one when you're done." He grunts smugly and holds onto the Skycon.

I'm just about to answer when he holds his hands up and indicates that he knows it's not an option. The men on the screen begin to leave the room. They walk toward an area with parked cars in a large courtyard. One of them goes over to Frank. "You have to stop that Ring. Tell me if you need help."

"What the f…." Tim gets up so fast that the chair falls over with a loud bang. Lucy looks terrified. "What is it?"

Tim is fiery red in the face, and his hands shake as he points intensely at the man in the picture Frank is talking to. "That is… it is…." He stammers. "That's my boss."

38
THE MISSION

Tim pulls the sleeves up on his green knitted sweater. He has a long tattoo on his forearm, consisting of zeros and ones. He has poured whiskey to the top of a glass and empties it in one mouthful. It's ten o'clock in the morning, and he looks at me with a grimace which indicates that this is not normal, neither drinking at this time nor the people he has just seen gathered on screen.

"Fuck, fuck, fuck." He walks back and forth on the floor in front of the long row of panoramic windows.

"Here, have some chocolate," Lucy grabs a selection of mixed chocolates from the drawer under the table. I've only just eaten my breakfast and am pretty stuffed, so I shake my head defensively. "Maybe later." She takes two pieces herself.

"We can't do anything about that group of people or their businesses." Tim has walked up to the high table where we sit. "But we can stop Frank. That would be a setback for them." He waits for me to nod appreciatively, so I do.

"If stopping Frank means they get less goodwill for their politics and plans, then I agree." I look over at Lucy, who is happily munching on two new pieces of chocolate.

"I'm ready," Lucy speaks before she has time to finish chewing. "Maybe it can help you get together and oppose that nasty group of men." Lucy looks at me urgently, "The world needs to be a better place for our children. If we cannot stop them, we have to delay them as much as possible." She strokes her stomach and grabs two more chocolates.

"It's also the only option I can see." I take a deep breath. "But I don't know if we will succeed with the Ring."

"You will." Lucy's voice is very determined. "Meera sacrificed her life for it."

I have too, but I don't need to point it out. And if I also have to sacrifice my son, it can't be in vain.

Tim takes glasses, plates, and the empty chocolate bowl and puts them in the dishwasher. "Let's get going; we can't waste any more time. I just need ten minutes to find the equipment we may need." He is already on his way to the bedroom. "We'll make a plan along the way."

After driving for five hours, we reach Frank's position. It's not far from where he met with the Kingston group, but luckily, it's in the city. The plan has been made. Lucy must, quite by chance, run into Frank. On a nearby street, there is a cafe, and she has to lure him there.

Meanwhile, Tim will try to hack the car's locking system and gain access to the glove compartment, where we will hopefully find the Skycon. It sounds nice and straightforward, and with a bit of luck, it will be. My job is to keep watch.

"Are you ready, Lucy?" I lean forward in the front seat. We are driving in Tim's company car; it's way more comfortable than my old wreck. If Frank were to see us, he would not suspect anything either. My car can be recognized from a long distance. Luckily, there are lots of people on the street, and the shops are still open.

"I'm ready." Lucy turns to face me. "I'll try to keep him talking for as long as I can so you can do your part." She grabs my hand. We turn down a small side street, where rubbish bins from the restaurants occupy the parking lots. Here, there is no one to be seen.

I try to ignore the restlessness in my body, which comes creeping in as I stare at the small map on the screen in the car.

"But if we succeed, it could be that Frank will target you or Luke in desperation." She looks at me urgently.

I don't say anything because what should I say? That Frank has already tried to take Luke's life? If I tell her, she may change her mind.

"Give me your phone," Tim looks over at Lucy, who hands him the phone. "We have to look after you both," he lets his gaze fall on her stomach and calls himself. With a single tap, the speaker is turned off. "We can hear you, but you cannot hear us." Tim looks with loving eyes at Lucy, "Here, put it in your pocket; then we'll be with you." He puts a tiny earpiece in his ear and gives me the other one; then, we can both listen in. "Clear?"

"Yes," we say immediately simultaneously, and we get out of the car. Lucy has a small bag over her shoulder and a jacket that hangs loosely over her floral dress. A small dot on the phone indicates that Frank has parked his car on the main street, not the best location for us. The second dot shows that he is moving toward us, so Tim and I need to go around the block to get to his car without meeting him.

"You have to keep him occupied for at least ten minutes, okay?" Lucy nods. "I love you." Tim kisses Lucy, and she gives me a quick hug afterward.

"Thank you," I whisper into her ear, and she acknowledges it with a kiss on my cheek. "Take care of yourself, and if there is the slightest risk, walk away from Frank. Okay?" I say firmly.

"Understood, Chief, see you," Lucy starts walking down the sidewalk in the direction of Frank. In no time, she is absorbed by the crowd on the main street. Tim takes a small black suitcase out of the trunk; its contents are like a data center filled with technology.

We set off running down the side street. Several people look at us wonderingly. We ignore them and head for Frank's car five blocks ahead and to the left. We can hear Lucy's breathing and rapid footsteps on the sidewalk in the earpiece. "I can't see him yet," she whispers. Tim and I run as fast as we can. There are still four blocks until we are at the car. Hopefully, he hasn't turned around and is on his way back again. I try to ignore the thought and focus on my breath instead.

"What the hell? If it isn't…." That's Frank's smarmy voice.

"Wauuu, Frank, is that you?" Lucy plays her role, perfectly surprised.

The microphone scratches. It sounds like something is hitting the pocket. "Long time, no see. What are you doing here, Lucy?" Frank's voice is ingratiating as always.

"I'm out shopping for baby equipment," the microphone scratches again as she pats her belly.

"But you haven't bought anything?"

"No, not yet, and now I have to pee desperately. You don't happen to know where there is a restroom nearby?"

You're brilliant, Lucy. If there's anything Frank wants to be, it's gallant. We're still running as fast as we can, and now there are only three blocks before we reach Frank's car.

"I know a nice cafe right over here. May I buy you a cup of coffee?"

"Yes, but only if they have a restroom." Lucy laughs and seems completely normal.

"They do."

We can hear their footsteps and suddenly quite a few more voices. They have reached the café, so the plan is running like clockwork. Tim and I are just two blocks from the finish line and turn the corner down the main street where Frank's car is parked. Now, I can glimpse it further ahead.

"What would you like?"

"Just a cup of tea. The little one doesn't like coffee." The sound scratches as if she's taking off her jacket. It hits the chair leg, and I press at my ear to try to hear better. "I better find the restroom. Is it that way?" There is no answer, just a lot of voices in the distance and a bell ringing every time someone walks in or out of the cafe. We slow down so that it doesn't seem suspicious that we stop right next to Frank's car. There is a cable box on the wall by the sidewalk where we can sit unnoticed.

"Here." Tim looks at me. "You're on guard." He puts the black suitcase on the cable box and squats down with his back to Frank's car. Inside the suitcase are some antennas that he points toward Frank's car, after which he sets a program to scan. He is entirely in his own world.

I keep pressing my hand to my ear so I can hear if Lucy is back. There is a hollow sound like a bathroom. "How are you doing?" I turn to Tim, who shakes his head slowly.

"It may take some time. The safety of the car is quite advanced." The machine continues to scan. A constant flow of people passes us. Nobody cares what we're doing. They stare ahead with faraway looks.

"Here I am," it's Lucy. I can hear in the tone that she is smiling. Her voice is closer, so she must have put the phone on the table. "Do you live around here?" It's still Lucy who's talking.

There is a rattle with a cup. "No, not around here." Frank's voice is a little harder to hear and drowns a bit in the crowd of other voices in the café. "Maybe you're out shopping too?"

The sound of Frank's unctuous laugh is unmistakable. "No, Lucy, I have more important things to do."

"That's a nice ring you have there. What a beautiful symbol. Did you get it from a girlfriend? Kirstin, maybe?"

I wish I were a fly on the wall in the cafe. Poor Lucy. She has to be with Frank and pretend to be interested. She seems to be succeeding. I look over at Tim, who is shaking his head. My watch shows that we have spent 12 minutes so far. If only Lucy can hold onto him a little longer. Further down the road, I can glimpse two officers on horseback. They're riding in our direction.

Frank doesn't respond, and I feel the unrest spread in my body. It seeps out into my arms and legs and makes me shake inside. We must succeed in grabbing Frank's Skycon. Suddenly, there is a loud thud. The alarm on Frank's car has gone off. Fortunately, the officers have turned down another street and are out of sight. I look over at Tim. He pretends not to hear it and is busy with his suitcase. It's impressive how fast he moves his fingers.

A cup is placed right next to the microphone and distorts the sound. "No, Lucy, this is the symbol of freedom. I see it as my duty to make this world a better place. That's what I wanted to tell you the last time we saw each other. But back then, you would rather listen to Angela." Frank's voice is louder now; he must have leaned forward toward Lucy.

"Angela? I haven't seen her since last time either. I have no idea what she's up to. Do you? She can be a little weird, you know."

"I didn't say I had not seen her." Frank still speaks in his unctuous voice. The doorbell ringing when people go in and out, and a buzz of human voices are constantly in the background. "Angela is doing what she can to sabotage developments in the world."

"Is she?" It's typical Lucy. She can make everything sound true. I can hear Lucy sipping her tea.

"You can consider whether you want to help make a difference in the world. There will be some action soon that you can be a part of." He puts something on the table, and I hear her picking it up.

"That's exciting; let me think about it. Can you tell me more?"

It seems that several people have lined up close to their table, their voices sounding like a buzz in the background.

"Lucy, I'm sorry, I have to go now," the sound of a chair sliding across the floor cuts through the speaker. "Let me just pay; this is on me."

"Thanks, Frank, what a gentleman you are," Lucy knocks on the phone. That's the signal she can no longer hold onto him.

I look over at Tim, who still has had no luck getting the car unlocked. He hits the keyboard, but nothing happens. Sweat begins to run down from his forehead and gets caught by his ruffled eyebrows. I can't stand still anymore and start walking back and forth on the sidewalk. Several people send me angry glances as I break their flow forward.

"Thanks for the tea, Frank. Let me just think about what you said, and then I might get back to you."

"You will not regret it, Lucy." The sound scratches again, and it sounds like Lucy is putting the phone back in her jacket pocket.

"Frank, do you know how I can get ahold of Angela? Her number no longer works."

"Stay away from her," he hisses the words out close to Lucy. "Call me. You have my number. You will soon have one more to think about; our children must grow up in a safe world—a world we can trust."

"Frank, I couldn't agree more. I'm so glad that we ran into each other today. When can we meet again?" Lucy tries hard to hold onto Frank.

"Call me, Lucy. I'm counting on you."

"Sure, Frank. See you."

Now, there is only car noise to be heard, replaced by another knock on the microphone. It's a clear sign that Frank is on his way to us.

I take the earpiece out and walk to Tim, who has taken his out long ago to concentrate. "Frank is on his way," I look down at the phone showing his position. He is three blocks away. Now, it's just two blocks.

There is a click sound. Tim looks up at me, and I run to the car's front door and tear it open. There is one more click, and the glove compartment opens slowly. I throw myself in the front seat and reach into the glove compartment. It is empty, as in completely empty. Tim rubs his sleeve over his forehead, which is filled with beads of sweat. My hand fumbles back and forth in every little nook of the glove compartment. It remains empty.

"DAMN IT." I slam it closed, get up, and shut the car door behind me. The dot on the phone is gone. I turn to Tim. "We have to go. Now! Frank could already be at the traffic light on his way to us. If he sees me, he will put two and two together."

"What happened to the surveillance?"

I shrug, "I think the batteries died." Daniel did mention it could happen when he gave me the phone. Luckily, it was just now.

Tim quickly packs all the equipment and slams the suitcase closed. We don't say a word to each other. The volcano inside me is erupting. My whole body is about to explode with anger and frustration. As soon as we are out of sight of the main street, we stop. I'm looking at Tim. He doesn't say anything.

"Thanks for the help," I make an effort beyond the usual to be polite.

"We have not lost yet. We can try again," he puts a hand on my shoulder and shakes it lightly. I try to smile, but the corners of my mouth don't obey. If there was a scale for how disappointed and frustrated one can be, I just blew it up. Lucy is already sitting in the car when we get back. She waves to us. I make a strenuous attempt to wave back, but it just turns into a nod. Most of all, I feel like kicking all the bins on the road, but I control myself and keep my eyes on Lucy.

Tim opens the trunk and puts his suitcase in while I jump in the back.

"It wasn't there," I speak in a low voice and can barely get the words out of my mouth. Tim gets in and looks at Lucy. "We managed to crack the alarm system and the locks. It was really hard."

Lucy sits perfectly still and doesn't change her expression. Then she starts laughing. "You two, you look like someone who's been to a funeral."

There is no way I see anything funny about it. Neither can Tim, even though he succeeded in his part of the plan.

Lucy extends both hands toward me. “Choose one.”

I’m not in the mood to play and slap reluctantly on the right hand. She turns it over and opens her hand. It’s empty.

“Try the other one.” She jumps slightly in the seat and looks excitedly at Tim.

I slap it, if possible, even more reluctantly. She turns her hand and opens it. I open my eyes wide. There is Frank’s Skycon. “WHAT! LUCY! HOW!!!”

She’s one big laugh, “It’s for you. No, not you, honey.” She slaps Tim’s fingers.

I move forward between the two front seats and grab her, so she is about to tumble into the steering wheel. She gets the biggest hug, and tears start rolling down my cheeks. I allow them to run because I’m busy hugging Lucy and cannot let go again. I’m filled with gratitude and release a shout of joy as I embrace Lucy. Only when she pats me lightly on the back, do I loosen my grip.

Lucy is still bouncing in her seat. “When Frank went to pay for our drinks, I thought I’d better check the pockets of his jacket that he had hung on the chair. You know, just in case. There it was.” Her eyes beam with pride.

I put my hands on her cheeks. “You have no idea how grateful I am.”

Lucy chuckles. “It’s always great to be able to help.”

39
THE SWEET TASTE OF VICTORY

I have thrown myself onto Tim and Lucy's oversized brown couch, which I am almost engulfed by.

"Here, this is to be celebrated." There is a loud bang as the cork from the champagne rises into the air, almost reaching the twelve-foot-high ceiling. Tim pours my glass and fills a glass for himself. "You have to toast with us, Lucy. But I'll get you something else." He reaches out for a bottle of alcohol-free sparkling wine.

Lucy drops down into the corner of the couch and sinks, if possible, further down than I did.

"Cheers, mission accomplished." It's clear that it suits Tim well that we won over Frank and that he has a little agent hidden in his stomach. His eyes are filled with the glare from the tiny champagne bubbles, making him look even happier.

Lucy and I raise our glasses, "Cheers."

"What is next, Angela?" Lucy looks at me and smiles. "What are you going to do now?"

That's a good question. It's one thing that we got Frank's Skycon; it's another thing that Frank is still trying to spread fear and destruction in the world. There is no doubt that I need to get ahold of Thomas to hear his assessment. But right now, I just want to enjoy the victory with Lucy and Tim.

"I actually don't know," I hold back. The light in the living room is dimmed, and the large copper lamps above the table are off. Around the floor are clusters of smaller lamps of different sizes, which look like half eggs plated with gold inside. They provide a warm and cozy light. I look out over the city, which is lit up again. It's fascinating with all the lights and all the fates that wander around, each in their own little world, unaware of the plans very influential people are devising, unaware of how people with power exploit their position for their own gain. If I didn't know better, I would not believe it. It would be beyond my comprehension, and I would insist that no one would do anything like that. Unfortunately, that is not the case.

"When the Ring is assembled, we will be sent down here again." I look over at Lucy. She has put her legs up on the sofa. Her half-length golden hair falls easily around the chubby cheeks, and the gaze in her deep brown eyes is filled with calmness. Even though it wasn't her mission to solve, she looks relieved. "The Ring's job is to raise people's consciousness. Hopefully, it can stop wars, people who kill because of religion or race, and the spread of fear." I swallow and moisten my lips with the tip of my tongue. "I don't know how we will succeed, but I know it's the last chance to stop the wave of fear and selfishness washing over the world."

Lucy hits Tim's legs, so it gives him a twitch. "Do you remember the other day in the supermarket?" She looks over at Tim, who has sat down at her feet. "We were standing in a long queue, and next to us, they opened another checkout. Tim and I moved toward it as a lady with several layers of makeup that almost crackled on her face overtook us. She pushed herself past us." Lucy makes a tight mouth grimace, raises her arms, and makes pointed elbows. "In front of the new queue stands a younger woman talking on the phone. The make-up lady also pushes her way in front of her." Lucy starts laughing, "The younger woman looks up from her phone and tells the make-up lady nicely that she is also in the queue. You should have seen the make-up lady's facial expression. She rolled her eyes and, if possible, tightened her mouth even more so that the makeup cracked. Do you know what the make-up lady then said?"

I shake my head excitedly.

"Life is a constant battle that we must each fight."

I frown, "A fight?"

"Yes, a fight. For her, everything was a fight, and that included shopping too. I was quite shaken." Lucy leans back on the couch, which embraces her gently. I look over at Tim, who nods, acknowledging her. He puts his feet up on the black coffee table and puts down his glass.

"Humanity needs help." Lucy puts both hands on her stomach, "If it's not too late. I get so provoked by people who only think of themselves. And even more by those who pretend to be saviors but are really big lying egoists."

"Lucy! It's not too late; don't say that." I try to straighten up, but the couch is so soft that it's hard. "Have you thought about how the universe always creates balance? Our Ring has not been gathered for thousands of years. Do you think it's a coincidence that it is happening now?" I was puzzled the first time Thomas spoke about how natural disasters, economic fluctuations, and diseases, in the most marvelous way, can be reactions to destruction or overconsumption.

Tim sits still and listens without saying anything. I can't figure out if he thinks it's all nonsense or if there is an open crack in his soul where he can feel what we are talking about.

"Listen, I've been a hardcore fact-based journalist with both feet planted solidly on the ground. But there is just more to life than that." I begin talking faster. "I have relied on research, investigation, and science, but time and time again, I have to admit that it's also only a small part of the larger whole. All research is a selection of information, and an opt-out of others, based on what the individual researcher chooses. And who says scientists are more conscious than others?" I take a sip of my champagne. It tickles in my mouth. "My world view, sure, and self-image have changed markedly. The researchers make studies based on criteria they set themselves. They get paid to do research, and surely, they want to deliver results too." Tim fills up my glass, and I take one more drink. "Some of them are just people who also want to be known for their research because then they get more funding." I can hear that I am getting a little black and white. It's one of my weaknesses when I get engrossed in a case and want to emphasize the point.

"Are you saying we can't rely on research?" Lucy looks at me questioningly.

I shake my head. "All I'm saying is that many scientists have, through decades, been looking for something greater than themselves without being able to prove it or explain it, so other people understood it. I'm trying to say that just because there is something science can't prove, it doesn't mean that it doesn't exist. Take In-Between for an example.

"We must not just rely only on research and believe that it is the whole truth—that everything can be measured and weighed. There are so many examples of research results we have spoken about in the press, where later it has turned out not to be the whole truth. That part of the story is rarely told." I hold back and feel the temperature rising in my body. "Research cannot stand alone and can become convenient to assess what is true and false. There is more to life than what we can see and measure with our common sense." I swallow. "I know for sure."

"But how are you going to decide what is true then?" Lucy hands her glass to Tim, who fills it halfway.

"That is the problem, and here consciousness comes into play. The more conscious people become, the easier we can see what comes from the ego and what is coming from the heart—what is based on trust and what is based on fear. But it requires a lot from all of us. We must learn to distinguish between ego and soul. Only then does the balance arise. A human being is a human being. If there are a hundred people who die of water shortages in Africa, it is just another day. If it happens in Europe, it is a catastrophe. But the pain is just as great because no matter what color we are on the outside, the feelings and needs inside are the same."

Lucy and Tim sit still and listen intently to what I say, forgetting all about the champagne. The frames on the wall are dimmed. In one of them, Tim has put a picture of a fireplace. The other two have an abstract pattern in golden colors.

"Have you thought about how people driven by desire have been successful for many years?"

Lucy shakes her head.

"But they have. They pretend that their work is for the service of a higher cause or that it is for the sake of others. It's their egos and desires that drive them. They want to be seen and recognized and want others to look up to them. And then they will make lots of money. But you will hear them say that money doesn't matter." I hold back, trying to slow the tempo and intensity of my voice. "People driven by desire will find it difficult when consciousness is raised. But if Frank wins, they will get lots of tailwind." I empty the glass and put it on the table.

Lucy claps her hands and reaches for her glass. "Cheers, Angela, you'll be a super great representative of that Ring."

I can't help but laugh because I sound completely preachy, which is the last thing I want to do. There's just so much I have realized in the past few weeks. The blinders that have narrowed my view have been removed, and my perspective on life expanded.

Tim coughs softly to get my attention. "Now that you have two of those gizmos, would it be possible for me to have one of them?"

I wink at Tim, "Nice try, but unfortunately, no." I wait just a moment without saying anything before continuing. "But I can show you how it works."

Tim opens his eyes wide. "YES, that would be awesome." A reaction so genuine you usually only get it from children.

I take my Skycon out of my pocket. Tim moves over to the

couch next to me, so we sit shoulder to shoulder. With a light tap, I turn on the Skycon. It starts flashing. "It's making contact."

"Just a moment," he gets up and picks up his scanner, "Is this okay?"

"Sure." He can scan all he wants. He won't get much out of it; In-Between transmits at such high frequencies that it cannot be measured with equipment from here.

"Ready?"

Tim nods eagerly. I tap on Thomas's picture. It doesn't take long for him to appear on the screen. With a slight movement, I pull the image up in front of us. Lucy moves over next to Tim.

"Hi, Eva," he speaks in his warm voice, so I get soft inside. It reminds me how much I have missed him and how alone I would feel without him if it weren't for Lucy and Tim.

"Hi, Thomas. We've got company today. This is Tim, and you know Lucy. They've been helping me get the Skycon back from Frank." I suddenly realize that my heart is beating fast. Hopefully, Thomas won't get upset because I have allowed Tim and Lucy to watch.

"Hi, Lucy, nice to see you again. You look good." He smiles at her, and she smiles back at a stranger she doesn't remember having met before but says nothing. "Hi, Tim," Thomas's voice is still calm. My heart calms. "That is great news that you got the Skycon from Frank. Now, we can talk freely." Thomas is sitting in the control room. The reflection from the images on the screen casts different shadows on his face.

I can see that Tim has not gotten used to me being two people and wrinkles his ruffled eyebrows. Fortunately, he is more interested in the gadget than my name and earthly incarnations. The scanner is working at high speed, and he is moving closer and closer to Thomas's image out of eagerness. Every time he tries to stick his hand through the picture, it floats to the side.

"It's the most extreme quality. It looks like we're there, totally

4D without being that." He shifts between rubbing his eyes and scratching his hair.

"Thomas, Frank is a member of a larger group who is corrupt and wants to spread fear here on Earth. They are manipulating the economy, diseases, and the environment. It's the inner circle of Kingston; they are here. Those people in In-Between are just helping them." My voice keeps breaking. "What do you want me to do?" It feels like a victory that we got Frank's Skycon, but I know that we haven't reached the finish line yet.

It becomes completely quiet. Only the wind whistling from the balcony can be heard. We all sit and look at Thomas's picture—waiting.

"There is nothing more you can do." He pauses. "It's not your task alone. It's a common task. Whether we succeed or not, time will tell." He sits completely still. The screens behind him float from the red wall and create a backdrop of oceans.

"But what about Frank?" I fight my way up from the couch and walk to the kitchen to get a glass of water. If I drink any more champagne, I won't be able to think clearly.

"Let me check with the Master and get back to you." He keeps his eyes fixed on me. His hair is pulled back into a ponytail, making him look older and more chivalrous as he sits in his blue silk tunic.

I sit down again and am about to spill the water as the couch envelops me. "How is Luke?"

"He's having a great time." Thomas laughs. "Luke understands, if anyone does, to take advantage of the opportunities up here." He moves very close to the picture. "You can look forward to seeing him. He has really evolved. But right now, he's with the Master. We have entered the next phase and have all been given new tasks."

My body gets warm, and I feel a quiet bubble of happiness spread through my cells.

"I will speak to the Master and get back to you. Until you hear from me, you can relax and enjoy it."

"I will do my best." I wave to him and end the call. Tim also hesitantly raises his hand. The image dissolves itself, and he reaches out for it.

"And he is… where did you say he is?" Tim looks at me with a bit of seriousness in his eyes.

"Inside the clouds. Up in the sky." I point out the window to emphasize my point. The clouds hang intermittently in the sky in small clumps.

"The screens behind him—they did not look completely normal." Tim narrows his eyes.

"There is nothing you would call normal in In-Between."

40
A WISH

If you could prepare your farewell here on Earth, what would it be like? I lie in bed and look up at the bare white ceiling lit by the moonlight. The duvet rests heavily on my body. Next to the bed is a narrow window from floor to ceiling. The lower part is tinted. On the bedside table, a slim lamp lights up by itself when it gets dark. Lucy and Tim have also gone to bed. They have had their share of adventure for today.

I braid my fingers behind my head. There is probably a reason why we are not always allowed to prepare for leaving here. It's difficult enough to say goodbye to old friends or family you don't see so often, but you know there is a possibility that you will see them again. But if we knew, we wouldn't. It must be one of life's strategies. My brain is busy, and I know why. I pull down the duvet a bit and put my hands on top of it. My time here is once again running out. And I am in a completely unusual situation that I know and can prepare myself for it. People who die suddenly cannot. Those who take their own lives can, but they are often filled with so much pain and despair that they don't look their loved ones in the eye and tell them what they have in mind. Unfortunately, because then it could be that they would find help. If the Ring is reunited, I'll be back. But I have no idea whether it will be as Eva, Angela, or a third person, or if I will remember any of this. Death is a bizarre thing. My chest rises as I breathe, and I pull the duvet up under my chin. The purple Sugilit necklace lies heavily on my chest, it's like it's starting to vibrate harder, but that's probably just something I'm imagining. The color is deep and intense.

Most of all, I want to gather all those people who have helped me this time before I return to In-Between: Daniel, Lucy, Tim, my mom, and Andreas, and thank them. But I know this is not an option. Farewell is one of the hardest things, and it tears the heart to pieces. It's like hearts are made to merge. Unfortunately, humans are just not that good at it. I swallow and push the duvet aside. It's hot in here. Carefully, I open the door and step out into the kitchen. Out on the patio, I can glimpse Lucy's silhouette. There's a glass on the table. I take it, fill it with water from the tap, and put ice cubes in it. The door to the terrace slides open easily and silently as I touch it.

"Are you smoking!" The words fly out, and Lucy gives a twitch. She turns and hides the cigarette behind her back.

"Angela, are you not sleeping?"

I'm obviously not. "Lucy, you can't smoke when you're pregnant."

"A little cigarette doesn't hurt."

"Yes, it does." I take the cigarette out of her hand and smear it out on the tiles. "This is exactly what I'm talking about. Consciousness, Lucy."

She looks like a question mark making an I-am-offended-and-only-five-years-old grimace where her mouth narrows and her eyebrows almost meet. But I don't give up.

"Lucy, you are gambling with your child's life."

"And you are not?"

Point taken. I shake my head slightly and pull the corner of my mouth to one side. "I have no choice. I have been required to choose. I would rather not." I glance beyond the many lights of the city.

"Who cares, Angela? I just needed to relax a little. The last few days have been mind-blowing with the dreams, you, and Frank." She turns away from me and faces the view of the city. Her long hair hangs loosely down the back of her pink nightgown. I walk over and stand next to her. We stand shoulder to shoulder. I'm wearing my long white night T-Shirt and have bare feet. In front of us lies the city like a blanket of light. It's still warm—one of those evenings where the heat will not let go.

"What do you need, Lucy? What are you dreaming about?"

She shakes her head in despair. "I just want to live a normal, uncomplicated life."

"Normal and uncomplicated?" I can't help but laugh and give her shoulder a push with mine. She doesn't say anything. There's no wind, and the heat embraces us like a sweater you can't take off. The city is a sea of light in all possible colors—small dots that turn on and off. Some move; others stand still.

"I haven't been able to understand my dreams, and they have returned night after night." She holds back. "There's something inside me that just thinks it's too far out."

I know exactly what Lucy is talking about. I can clearly remember at the TV station when we occasionally brought features with something a bit spiritual; then, there was laughter and ridicule. Once upon a time, there was a feature on Feng Shui. When the feature finished, the presenter turned to the weather host and asked if he had more warm air ahead. Back then, I thought it was pretty funny. Now, I can see the arrogance and how unconscious people use scorn and harshness to demean the fine energy that is in the spiritual. Maybe Thomas is correct; if the feminine is spiritual, it can be kept down with masculine ridicule. Lucy is far more conscious than she is aware. She seeks an explanation for her dreams without judging them. It's often those who are the least conscious who resist the most. Sometimes, people realize that their hearts have been closed and that there is more to life. But that doesn't change the damage they have done on their way there. Lucy has no resistance to the spiritual. She just doesn't know much about it yet.

I put my arm around Lucy's shoulder. Our energy melts together as we stand there: two warriors looking out over the battlefield, where the unconscious battles are fought, and people fall without knowing why.

"Now that you're back, it all makes a lot more sense. But what is it like in In-Between?" Lucy speaks in an almost whispering voice, keeping her gaze out over the city. She is definitely not one of those unconscious people. On the contrary, she seems like an old soul. Maybe that is why she can recall the energy from In-Between.

"It's quiet in In-Between in a pleasant way. The energy is extremely high, and it feels as if you are being lifted inside. Everything feels easier. The light is magical, so clear and intense. And you are closer to the stars at night." I smile and look up at the sky, which is covered with stars tonight. "In-Between is an intermediate station for most people. Like you." I stop and wait for her to react. She still looks out over the city, and I continue. "When you die suddenly, you get 42 days to go through a learning process. Those involved in an accident and in a coma can choose to wake up or continue on their soul's journey."

She turns her head toward me and smiles, "Soul's journey?"

"Our soul travels on to a new life when it's ready." Did I really say that? Half a year ago, I would run away screaming from someone who said anything like that. But Lucy is not running anywhere. She stands calmly by my side and listens. "There are many who stay longer than the 42 days because the learning is so intense and uplifting. The light in In-Between makes it easier to see one's survival mechanisms, the ego's agenda, and all the excuses for not living the life we dream of and unleashing our potential."

"That doesn't sound nice then." Lucy strikes a gentle laugh, leaning her head against my shoulder. I pull her close. I'm a head taller than she is, and my arms can just reach around her. Her hair smells of sweet flowers with a touch of jasmine.

"The idea is not nice, but the process is amazing. For many, this means that they can clean up their inner baggage and move on in the development of their soul. Then there is not much struggling left when they come down here again and more surplus energy for development." We stand completely still, and the heat from her body burns on my bare arms.

"I don't think I'm struggling." She relaxes and sinks further into my arms.

Lucy is right; I've never seen her fight. She is always happy and positive, playful and laughing, and curious about life too.

"It's only the dreams that keep coming back. They've been pursuing me somehow." I can feel the baby kick in her belly and cannot help but laugh. She catches it. "He wants to let us know he is here too." She breathes slowly before asking, "Was I in doubt if I wanted to return to life?" She raises her head a little.

I shake my head. "You could not return fast enough. You just wanted to get back to Tim." Lucy doesn't know that she met Frank in In-Between, and he gave her the opportunity to go back ahead of time. I stand for a while, wondering if I should tell her. But who will it benefit? Her or me? What would she use the information for, besides getting upset that she's been close to an alliance with Frank? There is no need to say it unless she asks.

A light breeze picks up; it brings some cool air with it. We both suck it in and start laughing.

Lucy raises her hand over her belly. "I'm thrilled with my life; I have everything I could want."

How nice it must be to feel that way. I have always lived with constant turmoil inside me—a restlessness that always set in after a short time if nothing new happened. Whether it was a job, boyfriend, or housing, I somehow felt compelled to make a change. I was never really happy. It was like trying to capture and maintain an illusion of happiness, but it kept disappearing in front of me like sand between your fingers. An invisible inner force kept pushing me forward, even though I didn't know where I was going. It must be nice to feel like Lucy, not to have to go anywhere. Our souls are on different missions.

"I will miss you, Angela. Or Eva. Or both of you." Lucy pushes herself even closer to me.

"Me too." I tighten my grip around her shoulders.

"Do you get magical abilities when you are in In-Between? Will you become a little God-like?" She can't hold back her smile even though she's trying hard and starts to chuckle.

"There is a guy up there who knows a lot about the lottery winnings, but we must not interfere with life on Earth."

"Hey, we would like to win the lottery." Lucy lets go of me and looks me in the eye. "Can you fix it?" Her eyes sparkle. I can't help but laugh.

"Let me see what I can do. I can't promise anything."

"Yes!" She claps her hands delightedly together, and a shopping spree beams out of her. "Don't worry. I'll use them wisely."

"Yes, and not on cigarettes."

She salutes, "Yes, ma'am."

There's a shooting star in the sky. We both see it. "What do you wish for?" I look at Lucy.

"Are you allowed to tell?"

"Why not? Then it will probably just manifest more strongly."

"A long, happy life with Tim and the little one." It doesn't require a long period of reflection, and her voice is sincere. "What about you?"

I hold back. What do I want? I actually don't know. My expiration date is long overdue, and I can't return to my life here. The air expands my lungs, and I exhale. "That we succeed in uniting the Ring and make a positive difference in the World."

"That is pretty modest." Lucy smiles at me, "I hope so too. Not just for you, but for all of us. Look," she points. "Another shooting star. Then your wish will also be mine."

41

IT'S YOUR CHOICE

"Hi, Eva," Thomas's voice is as calm as always, sending a stream of soothing vibrations through to me. How long I've been driving, I don't know. The inner autopilot is turned on, so I can neither feel if I am tired nor hungry. The road is infinitely straight, and it feels like I'm not getting anywhere. The same landscape just repeats itself over and over again.

I said goodbye to Lucy and Tim this morning. It was sad in every way because, deep down, we knew we would not see each other again. And if we do, I will probably not be able to remember them. I have been consumed by my thoughts for hours, just wanting to be alone. In a marvelous way, experiences and emotions land like pieces in a bigger picture when I sit here in the car all alone. It feels like looking at myself from the outside. I can observe without interfering. The pieces are tested in different places by themselves, and I watch them and let them find their way to the correct position.

"How are you?" Thomas looks at me expectantly with his crystal-clear gaze. I pull over to the side of the road next to some vast fields with sunflowers that stretch toward the sun's rays.

"I think it's going well." I can't help but smile. "I just sat and let things fall into place inside myself, here in my office." He laughs and moves closer. The fine lines around his eyes are only faintly marked. He walks outside on a cloud. "That sounds great. Now, we can have contact again; that's good." The clouds lie in layers behind him like a duvet you can step on. There is no one else to be seen, so he must be some distance from the main area.

I'm one big smile. No doubt it's great to be connected again.

"I have spoken to the Master." He pauses.

"And?" I break into his pause.

"He will let you decide your next move." Thomas folds his hands in front of him so that his fingertips meet.

It is completely quiet here. There's not a car on the road, and no wind moves. There are streaks inside the windows from earlier when I impatiently tried to wipe the dew away with my sleeve. I deflate like air going out of a balloon that punctures. "To hell with that." I hold my hand up to my mouth. "Sorry."

Thomas laughs, "Eva, you're just saying what others would also think; that's what makes you so likable."

I run my hand over my face several times. If only I could erase the doubt. "I don't know, Thomas. I really don't know." I shake my head and tighten the grip on the steering wheel. Should I turn right or left? I have no idea. It's impossible to see what is best. The fog has settled before my inner gaze.

"Let me help you." His words reach out to me. "What opportunities do you see?"

"I can stay here on Earth or go back to In-Between." My thumb drums lightly on the steering wheel, and I have difficulty sitting still. The seat scratches through my thin blouse.

"What will make you stay?" Thomas's voice is filled with warmth and care. He walks on as we speak.

"Frank and Luke." It's that simple. But I know what Thomas is fishing for too well: my real reason for staying. Fear or trust? We've talked about it several times—that we always have a choice. And that all choices are based on fear or trust. It can be difficult to see for yourself, and there are often both emotions and many layers associated with it.

I fill my lungs with air to the breaking point and let the air seep out as I say. "The fear that Frank will ruin our mission or that he will hurt Luke." Saying it out loud usually helps the fog clear so I can see better. Right now, it's still foggy and impossible to predict what is best in the long run.

Thomas has walked up onto a high cloud and sat on top. The sun's rays fall on him, and the contrasts between light and shadow become clearer than usual. "Well, in terms of trust, it's important to remember that it must be pure and not forced. If we force trust, it's not pure, then some emotions are repressed, and trust will not be rooted in our soul but in our ego. Our choice will be based on a feeling that will be controlling the thoughts and then our decisions."

"But is it also important to be critical?" I sit completely still in the car. Sweat runs from my chest, and the back of my blouse is soaked. The old nubbed fabric cover on the seat keeps scratching insistently no matter how I sit, so I try not to move unnecessarily. Most of all, I feel like ripping off all my clothes and throwing myself into an icy lake, but there are none nearby.

Thomas's eyes shine brighter than usual. It is as if the blue color becomes less intense, and the white ring takes over. "The critical sense is incredibly important. Many people forget it because they think it's the salvation to be positive. That's not the whole truth." He leans forward. "The positive path in our brain helps us solve problems, cooperate, and open our hearts. The negative path lets the fear in and shuts down our ability to take responsibility and believe in ourselves. The paths in the brain are like paths in a forest. If you keep using them, you maintain them. If you choose other paths, they will disappear in time." A cloud hovers over him, and for a brief moment, he is completely gone. Out in the distance, several dark larger clouds are heading toward him. He gets up and starts walking down the cloud. "So, what weighs heaviest, the fear of Frank or what might happen to Luke?" He holds his hands up in front of him like old-fashioned weighing scales as he walks.

I sit for a while, staring blankly out of the windshield at the lonely road in front of me. A pickup with a dog in the back passes at high speed. The dust from the road whirls up and envelops the car. It seeps through the cracks and makes me cough. "I think the hardest part is saying goodbye." I swallow. It has gone so fast the other times, but now I suddenly have time—time to say goodbye or stay a little longer.

"No one expects you to know the answer. But keep in mind one thing, if the Ring is to be assembled in 42 days, you must be ready. Are you?"

It feels like lightning strikes me. How will I know that? I have been so engrossed in Frank that I have not given my development a thought.

"We all have to go through some kind of test before we gather in the Ring to ensure that our nervous system can cope with the transformation that happens when the Ring is gathered. Once we pass the test, we enter the final phase; none of us knows what it entails." Thomas turns his head away, his dark blond hair floating slightly to the side. He holds his hand up, and I sense that others are in the area. Shortly after, he returns and looks directly at me. "There is no knowledge of the last phase, so we go in blindly." He pauses and becomes a bit absent as he reads something on a note. I couldn't see who gave him the note. "I have to go. I'll call you tomorrow. Maybe you'll have decided by then." His face gives nothing away.

I wave to him. He waves back, and the image dissolves itself. The car is like a sauna, and I push the door open, so the handle to the window lands on the ground. The road in front and behind me is endless and disappears in hot ripples. I spread my arms out to the side and put my head back.

"Help! I need some help here."

42

A FINAL GOODBYE

Making a decision is like walking through a door and closing the others next to it. Before you enter, you can still see the other doors, but as soon as you step through the chosen door, there is no way back. Doubt washes over me like a tsunami and swirls me around in a centrifuge of doubt, guilt, shame, and fear. Once the first wave has subsided, the ego sets in with all the survival strategies that justify my choices or actions and downplay what I choose not to do. This effective strategy maintains the ability to believe we are doing the right thing or at least convince ourselves of it. In the long run, the beliefs become the truth. Like when you don't get around to voicing your opinion and convince yourself that what you wanted to say was also uninteresting. When you want to lose weight and yet fill yourself with sweets and tell yourself that there is no need to try to lose weight because you'll fail anyway and deserve something sweet after a long day at work. Or when you know that you are unfaithful to yourself but cannot contain the truth and build a wall of excuses around it so you can't feel the pain they are hiding.

I drive into the parking lot outside the hospital. The visitor's car park is marked with signs. A car pulls out right next to the entrance. Today's first small victory has been achieved.

The thoughts tumble over each other in my head. I'm fickle. On the one hand, I want to influence all decisions, but a part of me just wants to be free of that responsibility and leave it to others. If only I could get a glimpse into the future, blow a bit of the fog away and see what will happen further down the road of life. Then, the choice would be easier. But I can see no further than the fog allows.

A big red heart on the double door leading to the large entrance hall splits in the middle as I get closer, and the doors open. Luke is my strategy. If I see him, I might be able to figure out what to choose. *A little help in making the decision would be nice,* I think to myself, and send a wish out to the universe.

Time goes by, and if I wait long enough, I'll have to go back to In-Between. A decision is also waiting there. Should Luke be a part of the Ring or go back to his life with Andreas? Whatever I do, I run head-first straight into life's most unfair choices. No matter how much I search, there is no way around it.

The hospital welcomes me with colorful pictures on the walls, large windows that let in light, and smiling people. I greet a few nurses on the way to Luke's ward. The corridors do not seem as long and closed as in the other hospital. There are tall wooden tables with orange chairs around them and round lamps that cast a dim light down the tables. Outside, there are green areas and, on several walls, hang succulents. In every way, there is more life and less death. I can see a large fitness center through the windows where people of all ages exercise their way back to life. They've got another chance. Whether they use it, time will tell.

I'm standing in front of Luke's door, 33a. It opens easily when I push it. The light from the window opposite dazzles in, and I hold up my hand to be able to see. At that moment, it feels like an explosion of lava crashing against a glacier inside of me. I stand completely still with my hand up in front of my mouth.

"Hi, Mom." It's Luke's frail voice. He is sitting in the bed, resting his back on a pillow and smiling at me. His eyes are gleaming, even though there are a few black marks under them. He is completely pale, almost transparent.

I'm standing there frozen. There is a complete short circuit inside me. All connections are torn, and no signals are working. So, I just stand.

My mother gets up and comes toward me, making a slight smacking sound with her lips. She grabs my arm and pulls me toward Luke. "He woke up a few minutes ago. I was going to call you." She looks at me urgently. "No one else knows."

I'm moving like a robot. My legs are stiff, and my feet drag across the floor without me lifting them. "Luke...."

"When is Dad coming?" The fringe falls over his eyes, and he blows it lightly to the side. His eyelids shut, and he struggles to open them again.

"Here, my darling." My mother helps him so he can lie down. "You are tired. Rest, my dear. We are here with you." She takes his little hand in hers. I walk closer to the bed, take his other hand, and hold it in mine. I'm looking at Luke and feeling all my love melt the ice inside me and transform it into a liquid love elixir. My whole body gets hot, my throat swells, and tears roll down my cheeks.

Luke breathes slowly so that his small chest moves slightly up and down.

"Where are all the machines?" I whisper and look over at my mother. The room is not very big, but bright. Opposite Luke's bed hangs a TV on the wall. Next to the bed stands a small table with a vase filled with sunflowers. There are a few machines, but not to the extent that there were before. One measures his heart rate; that much, I understand. The one next to it is off.

"I had a feeling he was going to wake up. It was as if you could feel that he was on his way back." My mother holds Luke's hand and strokes his forehead. "I've talked to him a little bit before you came and explained about you. That's why he recognized you when you came. I have also told him what he is a part of, but it was as if he already knew." She fails to look at me. "Eva, his soul, knows the way. I think he knows."

"What do you mean?" I raise my eyebrows and wrinkle my nose while shaking my head from side to side.

"You know what I mean, but you're trying to push the reality in front of you." She looks me straight in the eye, and it feels like being impaled, so the whole illusion that I have a choice cracks and opens up to an even deeper place inside me.

Luke opens his eyes again and looks over at my mother and then at me. "See you, Mom." Then he closes his eyes again and dozes off. The heartbeat machine beeps slower and slower.

It's as if he knows that we are here. He has been waiting for us and is holding onto life a little longer to say a proper farewell. I feel a hand on my shoulder and turn around. "Andreas."

"Hey."

"Thank God you made it." I move to the right and make room so he can get close to Luke. His stubble looks more than a day old, and the wrinkles on his face are marked.

"I'm here, champ. I'm with you." Andreas gently places his hand on the center of Luke's chest and closes his eyes. My mother closes her eyes too, and I follow. We fall into a synchronized breathing pattern. It feels like space with no time or direction, only presence.

"Hi, Dad."

We all open our eyes at the same time. Luke lies still in bed with a small crack between his eyelids and looks at us.

"Luke!" Andreas leans forward and hugs him. I cannot hold back the tears.

"Dad, I'm fine," he whispers. "But I have to move on." He lays completely still, looking like an angel.

Andreas is not moving. He holds Luke with both arms and has his cheek against Luke's.

"I will miss you, Dad." The sun's rays fall gently on both of them through the window. There is a very special light in the room—almost luminescent.

I stand completely still next to Andreas with my mother next to me. She takes my hand, and I put my other hand on Andreas's back.

"I love you, Luke." Andreas's body begins to shake as Luke closes his eyes.

The door is torn open, and a man in a white coat rushes in. There are a few crumbs from his lunch in his dark full beard.

"What's going on?" He rushes over to the machine and then looks at Luke. "Has he been awake?" He looks at a small screen he is holding in his hand, where Luke's heartbeat is monitored, and an alarm goes off if there are large fluctuations.

None of us says anything. I hide my face and quickly wipe my eyes on my sleeve. My heart beats twice as fast as usual.

The doctor calls for help, and before we know it, there are three nurses in the room; one is very young, and two are older. They measure Luke's heartbeat and heart rate and check his drip. The sound from his heart continues to slow. Andreas stands with his eyes fixed on Luke. He does not allow himself to be interrupted by the doctor; he is completely present with Luke and only Luke. This is his chance to bid farewell to his only son. He knows he got a second chance, and there won't be a third.

"I don't understand." The doctor looks over at the young nurse, whose lips are unnaturally large and her face devoid of facial expressions. "There is nothing that indicates why there was a marked fluctuation." The two elderly nurses are busy checking the drip and getting the oxygen mask ready.

"I do," mumbles my mother, who insists on being right next to the bed and still holds Luke's hand. It feels like my neck has swollen to double the size. Each little muscle in my body is tense so that no one can see that I'm shaking inside.

The nurses and the doctor exchange several words and look over at Andreas. "We can't see that anything is wrong. Just pull the string if you need us." Then, they leave.

"Thank you," Andreas's voice trembles. There are large dark stains on his shirt under his arms.

As the door closes, we all move very close to Luke. My fingers throb, and my heart beats so hard in my chest that it feels like a knife being stabbed and pulled out repeatedly. Luke's chest moves more slowly. His energy gets weaker and weaker as if he is gradually starting to leave his body. Andreas sits opposite my mother and me. He clutches Luke's hand in his and taps the other one in a rhythmic rhythm on the railing. Snot runs from his nose, and his eyelids are swollen. We all sit with our eyes fixed on Luke.

A long beep sounds, and it becomes completely quiet. Luke is gone. His chest no longer moves. He has traveled on. The question is just where and in what condition?

43

LUKE'S DECISION

The Skycon flashes and flashes, but there is no answer. I just went to the bathroom, which is adjacent to Luke's ward. The door is ajar, and through the crack, I can see my mother and Andreas on either side of Luke's bed.

"I could feel it as I was driving here." Andreas rests his hand on Luke's cheek. "It was as if the small fine threads between our hearts began to dissolve."

My mom pushes her glasses up her nose. "I wonder what happened." She speaks so softly that I need to make an effort to hear her words through the crack in the door.

I slide the Skycon back into my pocket and return to the ward. Luke lies peacefully with closed eyes and his blond hair out to the sides. If I didn't know he traveled to In-Between, I would have completely fallen apart. I look over at Andreas. He will never see his son again—no more trips to the playground, no more laughs and evenings where Luke cuddles up close to him. I swallow with difficulty and can feel that uncertainty creeps under my skin. But what if he is not in In-Between? What if he has traveled on?

"What are you thinking about?" My mother tears me out of my thoughts.

"Nothing." I look at Luke and try to avoid more questions.

"Do you think anything has happened; shouldn't he be here for 42 days?" She is annoyingly insistent.

I keep my eyes on Luke and shrug. There is a very special light around him that I have only experienced in In-Between: golden but still completely clear. The doctor and nurses arrived in a hurry shortly after Luke left his body. They tried to revive him, but nothing helped. From looking at their faces, it was clear that they didn't understand why his heart suddenly stopped beating. Until now, he had been stable, and there had been no sign that his heart would give up. They left again, giving us space and time to grieve. I stare blankly into the air. A mixture of relief and unrest fills me. The relief of not having to decide Luke's life, but the uneasiness that Luke has left here, and I don't know for sure where to.

Luke's death is my signal to move on. There is nothing more for me to do here. The time has come once again to let go of my life on Earth and concentrate on getting ready to be a part of the Ring. I look up, first at my mother and then at Andreas, who is pale and sitting with a petrified expression in his eyes. He puts his head on Luke's stomach and holds him. They both know about the Ring and In-Between, but that doesn't mean it's easy to let go of your child or grandchild. I know. I wait and give him time before I get up.

"My time is up too." I look at my mother, who is struggling to hold back her tears. Her lips quiver, and she straightens her glasses even though they are in place.

Andreas hits the bed rail hard several times before getting up. "We've already said goodbye once, and I'm not quite used to your new look." He uses his last efforts to smile at me. "It was good to see you again—and hard." With a firm grip on the railing, he walks around the bed and puts his arms around me. "Take care of our son." He holds me tight as if he could squeeze a bit of Luke's energy out of me and hold onto it a little longer before it's too late.

I reciprocate his embrace. My mother stands next to us. She is completely still and waits for Andreas to release his embrace, but he doesn't. He holds onto me, and for how long we stand, I don't know. I give him the time he needs. Andreas's body starts to shake, and I can feel his tears land on my shoulder. There is nothing I can say that will make it easier, and the best thing is also to allow the emotions to flow freely. My mom sat down next to Luke, caressing his chin. She is talking to him, but I can't hear the words.

I was not prepared to leave today. Naive as I am, I thought I had more days before heading back to In-Between—more days in my old life. Time has passed so fast. Andreas lets go of me, and I turn to my mother and hug her. She begins to sob, and her body collapses. She will fall to her knees if I don't hold onto her.

"No matter what you believe, it's not right that your children and grandchildren should leave life before you." Her voice trembles.

She's right, and it's hard to justify it with a higher reason. I don't know what to say, so I don't say anything. We stand utterly still and exchange energy. I feel safe with Andreas and my mother. They are, in a way, my rock to lean on here on Earth. I close my eyes, and it gets completely dark. My mother's heart beats hard against mine. It feels like we are floating in an empty place with lots of space. I open my eyes a bit and see that Andreas has sat down with Luke. He bites his nails while the tears run down his chin.

Suddenly, he gets up. "It is too much to carry for one person!" he shouts out into space. My mother jerks and lets go of me. "It's your fault!" His voice rumbles through the room toward me. He stays standing and holds onto the bed. "You could have saved him! I know you could save him. Why did you not do anything?" Then he falls to his knees, clenches his fist, and looks up toward the sky. "You could have taken someone else. Damn you! He was the only one I had left." A scream propagates in the room, and he hits the floor hard.

I hold onto my mother so she can stay standing. We don't say or do anything, knowing that he has to go through the pain and there is nothing we can do to ease it. His scream dies out.

My mother walks over to him and extends her hand. He manages to get up and sit down on the chair next to the bed. She hands him a glass of water, which he downs in a mouthful.

"There must be something you can do?" He looks intently at me.

I shrug, "I don't know what has happened, but now there is no way back. If all goes well, then both Luke and I will return in a while."

It doesn't seem like Andreas can get his head around what I'm saying, and I don't really want to go further into it.

"See you again, one way or another." I smile the best I can.

"I'm sure of it." My mother wipes her glasses and forces a smile. "I'll see you again. You can't hide from me."

"I hope you will succeed with the Ring; the world needs you." Andreas gets up and looks at me with his deep brown eyes. "And give us a sign when you're back." He winks at me and snorts a few times.

"It's a deal." I want to leave but stand firm.

"See you," I force a smile even though it requires great effort.

"Eva." Andreas pulls up his sleeve and takes off his bracelet. It's the bracelet he got from his father when he was young. There is a silver anchor on a solid leather cord. He hands it to me, "Will you give it to Luke? It is very special to me. Men in my family have carried it through generations. My grandfather said that the anchor carries a special strength. It helps the one who carries it stand firm and be true to oneself. I want to give that strength and support to Luke on his journey." He lets go, and I put it in my pocket.

Our gaze meets. None of us says anything. We stand for a while before I break the connection between us and walk toward the door. I can feel the Skycon vibrating in my pocket, but I let it shake. If I don't leave now, I'm afraid I will not leave at all. My gaze is locked on the door, and my steps are focused. I grab the handle. Hesitant.

Blood pumps around my body. Pull, look straight ahead and enter the hallway. A moment later, the door closes with a slight noise behind me. The door to this life, the door to this mission, is closed. Slowly, I walk down the hall. People greet me, smiling. My face is fossilized. They can't see what is happening inside me. If they could, their smiles would probably stiffen.

It's raining cats and dogs when I step outside. I pull the sweater over my head and run as fast as possible to the car. The huge raindrops soak my sweater and hair in less than the time it takes me to reach the car. The clouds are pitch black and are illuminated by several huge flashes of lightning followed by thunder that makes the earth shake. The windshield is completely misted as I close the door, and the humid air fills the car. I start the engine and turn on the vent to full blast. It makes a noise like a hurricane has taken over my cabin and whirls everything around. I need to get out of here—out of town so I can find peace, both inside myself and outside myself.

The lights of the city slowly disappear behind me. The road is wide. There are cars everywhere and in several lanes. I'm sitting in a queue, moving at a snail's pace at 10 miles per hour, and the restlessness increases at the same pace as my thoughts.

Large raindrops hammer against the windshield and form a continuous layer of water, which the wipers struggle to keep away. The drumming makes the cabin feel smaller than usual. I turn the wipers to the highest level just to be able to see the car in front of me. The queue moves slowly, and, judging by the snake of red lights in front of me, it may well take a long time before I can speed up. I reach for my jacket pocket and get the Skycon. I press the side, so it begins to flash. The cars in front of me come to a complete stop. I quickly look to the sides to check if anyone is watching me.

Next to me, a man is engrossed in a conversation with a woman, who, judging by the intensity, is probably his wife. Those in front and behind cannot see me clearly since the rain covers the windows. I tap on Thomas's picture. It's ringing. And ringing. *What is happening? Why doesn't he answer?* At an almost tireless pace, it keeps ringing.

No matter how much I stare at it, nothing happens. The sky is periodically totally illuminated by huge lightning. The rain starts dripping through the gap at the edge of the window. I take a scarf, which is lying on the back seat, and stuff it into the crack. *Luckily, I will get rid of this wreck soon*, I mumble to myself, hoping that I will get a nicer car when I return. A Tesla would be appropriate. It would suit me—a white one. Smaller cars would also do; in fact, anything would be an upgrade. There is a huge bang right above me, and I crouch down into the seat.

It's impossible to get back to In-Between without making contact, so right now, I'm stuck here, both on the road and as Angela. Miraculously, I start to run out of thoughts. They almost disappear with each breath I take, leaving space for more calmness inside me and clarity. There is nothing that disturbs me, nothing that draws my attention. It's just completely quiet. My hands are resting on the steering wheel, and I look straight ahead. The sound of the rain drumming at its own chaotic pace fills the cabin. Still, no thoughts to disturb my silence, no emotions screaming for attention. There is nothing. I breathe with greater ease and feel as if I am a spectator of the world. I can hear what's going on around me, feel the temperature in the car, and feel my body, but I'm not one with that. I look from the inside out, but not through thoughts and feelings.

The queue in front of me starts to move, and even though I speed up, the feeling of clarity doesn't disappear. Not even the bad weather can distract me. The light burns through, becomes stronger, and melts the fog away.

I shift to third gear for the first time in an hour and see my exit further ahead. It will take me away from the traffic and onto the road leading to the coast. The light from the highway disappears as I turn and drive into the darkness. Suddenly, Thomas's picture flashes on the small screen of the Skycon. I pull the steering wheel, so the car skids off the road onto the hard shoulder. The cars behind me have to make a quick swerve to avoid bumping into me and flash their lights angrily. When the vehicle comes to a complete stop, I hit Thomas's picture.

The control room appears, and I can hear several voices in the distance. I wait and stare at the picture I have pulled up in front of me. My eyes start to sting, but I still don't blink as I am so engrossed in seeing what is happening in In-Between. Right now, all I can see are the big floating screens with pictures of several big cities.

"Eva." Thomas throws himself into the picture, gasping for breath. "So good you are here." He moves his hair away from his face. The blue silk tunic sticks to his upper body, and small pearls of sweat run down from his hairline at the temple. I sit entirely motionless and say nothing. The stubble is visible on his cheeks. I've never seen him like this before.

"Luke? Have you seen Luke?" His voice is hectic. His usual calm is on timeout.

I nod and still cannot find words. The drum of rain on both the roof and the windshield is so loud that I have to concentrate on hearing Thomas. As the sun sets behind the dark clouds, the darkness around me becomes more intense and embracing now that the light from the street is gone and the lightning has begun to subside.

He gets distracted and disappears out of the picture. I move a little in the seat and try to get rid of the spring drilling itself into my butt with no luck. He is back. I'm about to put on a smile but realize that it might be inappropriate. The voices in the background are gone. Now, it is completely quiet.

Thomas turns his face toward the Skycon. I have never heard him speak so rapidly and with such a concentrated gaze before. He runs his hand over his forehead. "I'm glad that you are here." He repeats as he exhales and tries to stand still. "You know what happened to Luke, right?"

I tilt my head slightly from side to side. "Yes and no. I was there when he suddenly woke up."

Thomas interrupts me, which he usually never does. "Kingston. They found out you had taken the Skycon from Frank, and it triggered a chain reaction to their Plan B." It seems like his whole body is flooded with adrenaline. He walks back and forth on the spot as he runs his hand over his stubble. "They sent Luke back. That's why he woke up."

I roll my eyes and feel my heart beating fast. "But what then… He died."

Thomas steps close to the Skycon. "Meera was on the trail of Kingston. Ian had told her to look for a ring assembled with a 'K' engraved—a gift they receive when they are accepted into Kingston. She had sat down at a table next to some young men in the cafe; they both wore the ring. When she later saw them walking with Luke, she knew that something was wrong. But she also knew she couldn't handle it herself." He keeps going back and forth across the floor at a high pace. The pictures follow him. "Two of them are big, muscular men with shaved heads like skinheads that don't exactly signal peace on Earth." This is the first time he smiles throughout the conversation. "The last guy seemed to know Luke but didn't look that comfortable with the situation. Luke has become so familiar with In-Between that we saw no problem in him exploring by himself. He has a Skycon if he gets lost." He reaches for a glass of green juice on the table and downs it in one go. "By the time Meera had fetched Yoge and me, they had already sent Luke back. That's why he woke up."

I must look like a giant question mark with an open mouth and a jaw that falls further and further down. The bolts of lightning hang out on the horizon like small glimpses. The rain has subsided slightly, so it's easier to hear Thomas.

"When we got the Kingston people away from Luke, we slowly pulled him back here." He pauses, wiping a tear about to escape from his eye. "I was about to break down inside when we had to pull Luke back. I knew he was awake, but I didn't know who was with him."

"We were all there. My mother, Andreas, and I." My voice is about to snap.

Another tear builds up in Thomas's eye, this time running free over his marked cheekbones. "It was not meant for you or him to go through that. I should have taken better care of him. It's my fault." He hides his face in his hands and sinks into the floating chair. His whole body shakes like a frightened animal.

I sit silently in the car and look at Thomas. If only I could reach out to him and comfort him as he has comforted me so many times when I have needed it. "It was such a beautiful farewell, and he was so settled and calm." The feeling of free fall takes over, and I hold on to the steering wheel as if the event's seriousness is catching up with me, and only now do I realize how close we were to losing the Ring. Nausea overwhelms me, and I swallow the best I can while tightening the grip on the steering wheel further.

"Eva, Luke made the decision himself," Thomas speaks softly. I open my eyes gently.

"When he came back here, he asked what had happened. He didn't mention that he saw you, but he said he was ready to let go."

"What does that mean?" The words fly out of my mouth. "Where is he?" The seconds before Thomas has time to answer feel like an eternity.

"Don't worry; he's here with me. But you know people in a coma have 42 days to decide whether they will wake up or continue on their soul's journey? It was you who should have made that decision for Luke." Thomas pauses. "He made it himself and is ready to be part of the Ring." Thomas runs his hand over his hair several times and frowns. The spark in his eyes is extinguished, and they look lifeless.

"But..."

"I know very well that the Master has said that he needed 42 days in a coma for his system to be ready. We made a scan of his energy system that showed he is ready. He doesn't need time in a coma, as we thought." He fills his glass with the contents of another green bottle—the one with the soothing elixir.

"But..."

Thomas shrugs and wipes the tears away from his face with the sleeve of his blue silk tunic. "There's so much we don't know and can't predict right now." He takes a sip of the elixir.

I open the car door, lean out into the rain, and throw up on the ground next to me. It stings in my throat, and my stomach contracts in several convulsions. I sit completely still and slowly let myself be soaked by the rain.

"Now, we are only missing you, Eva."

44

THE JOURNEY HOME

The sun's rays break through the gaps in the clouds and are reflected over the sea, where mist hangs like an almost transparent veil over the water. I have parked the car in a small, deserted parking lot surrounded by tall spruce trees. A path leads through the dunes down to the wide white sandy beach that stretches for several miles in both directions. Through the trees, I can glimpse the open sea. I look around. When I parked here yesterday, it was completely dark. The car park is the most difficult one to get to on the coastline. My strategy was to find a deserted place where I would not be disturbed. It seems to have worked. There is nothing but seagulls as far as the eye can see.

The sand is already hot and nestles around my feet as I walk down the dune toward the water. I carry one of my mother's yellow blankets under my arm and a water bottle in my hand. The water is calm and reflects several seagulls gliding through the morning mist while screaming. The light is golden, shimmering as if the air were filled with microcrystals. I hold out my hand and let the light surround it.

It's only a few minutes past six. There is still time. When I return… I stop myself. Who says I'll be back? Who says it's not over when I get back to In-Between? On the steep part of the dune, my legs set in motion. The wind caresses my skin. In front of me is the turquoise sea. To the left, the horizon is broken by some green islands. Several clouds hang scattered in the sky and help to refract the light. It looks like a photo where the intensity and contrast of the colors are turned up.

I stop and inhale the light and energy from the ocean. I stand as still as possible and breathe in through the nose and out through the mouth. *When I come back.* I try to continue the thought without interrupting myself, wondering where I'll end up. In which country or continent? Hopefully, it will be a place where it's warm—a place where there are positive, open-minded people. It's definitely my turn to get an easy task. I smile again, and the smile turns into a laugh that makes a flock of seagulls further down the beach take off. It seems that I disturbed their breakfast gathering. They disappear over the sea. Hopefully, Luke will also get an easy task. The yellow blanket lands on the sand; I unfold it and sit down.

It's not certain I'll get to see Luke or know where or who he is when we return. I don't know much about it all, other than that we are going to raise consciousness on Earth. I pick up a handful of sand and let it quietly seep out between my fingers; the grains are so fine and white. Thomas will call at seven o'clock, which gives me time for a quick dip. I throw all my clothes on the blanket and run at full speed, totally naked, into the water. My hands hit the water, and I dive under. It's silky soft. The water is crystal clear and has just the right temperature to be refreshing without being too cold. I lie on my back and float. The sky above me is infinite. A small cloud drifts in front of the sun. It will soon be time to say goodbye to Angela and my red junk car. It will end its days in the parking lot like an old corpse while my body will dissolve and no traces will be left. Only the yellow blanket will be here. Next week, Luke will be buried beside me; Andreas and my mother will take care of that. With calm strokes, I swim back toward the shore. The sun glitters on the surface of the water. When I reach the shore, I spread my arms to the side and face the sun. The water runs off my body, and I dry slowly in the sun. *Where there is light, there is hope*, I say to myself, and let the heat penetrate me.

The time is five minutes to seven, and I quickly get dressed. I'm making sure that I have both my own and Frank's Skycon. What a disaster if I had lost one of them. I hold one in each hand. Mine begins to flash on the stroke of seven. I activate it, and Thomas shows up in front of me. He is shaved, and his tunic is perfectly ironed.

"Are you ready?" He smiles at me. "We look forward to your return."

Luke sticks his face into the picture. "Hello again, Mom." His eyes light up the whole picture, and my heart bursts with love flowing out into every tiny cell of my body. "Hi there, Sweetheart. As ready as I can be."

"Then we will see you here in a few minutes. Do you want to lie down?" Thomas looks at the keyboard and is about to enter a longer code.

I lay on my back on the yellow blanket, which still smells a bit of my mother.

"You know the drill."

I do. I close my eyes. It's still completely bright around me. Then my body starts buzzing. Slowly, the quiet vibration spreads from my feet up through my legs. I'm lying completely still. The sun's rays pierce my closed eyelids, and I breathe calmly and get more and more tired. Now, the heat flows through my body like a rushing river. At once, the feeling of lying on the blanket disappears. There are lights everywhere—bright white light. It feels like being lifted at breakneck speed—the opposite of the rides in fun parks where you hang high and suddenly drop in a free fall before going up again. The "let go" machine Andreas and I called it. This is just the opposite. I am being pulled upward, up toward the light and the infinite. How long it lasts is impossible to say; there is no time here. I can't tell whether I hang there for a fraction of a second or several hours. It's as if time doesn't exist here, only the light—lots of completely transparent clear white light.

Suddenly, the heat begins to return. Very slowly, it floats, not around me, because my body is not shaped. It hovers, and the light is getting brighter and brighter. There are no sounds, only the light and the heat. Now, I am starting to feel something that I can best describe as a thin shell—a kind of framing of energy, crystals that find each other and create a form. The shape gets filled with heat, and I can sense something soft beneath me. The light disappears slightly, and I open my eyes in a pinch. Luke is sitting right in front of me.

"Wauuu, that was cool." His face is one big laugh, and he throws himself on top of me.

I have not fully gained control of my body and don't know what signal I should give to lift my arms and embrace him. It will have to wait. Thomas stands right behind Luke and watches. He lights up. "Welcome back, beautiful soul."

45
LET THE ANGELS SING

We're sitting in the control room. It's bright and light, and as always, there is a very special feeling with the floating walls and ceilings. Luke has tucked himself under my arm. My body is exhausted; every little cell has been through an intense transformation and is drained of energy. Thomas puts a glass of bright orange juice on the table in front of me.

"Drink this. It will do you good." He's got the spark back in his eyes. "It's Yoge who has discovered that it can be helpful when our energy system is overloaded."

Before he finishes, I take a sip and am about to spit it out again. "Yuck!" My stomach cramps and I try my best to keep it down.

"Sorry, I didn't warn you." Thomas shrugs. "That's what happens when you're a fast mover."

It tastes like something in between grapefruit, celery, and banana. And if there's one thing I cannot stand, it's celery. They should have left that down on Earth.

"May I taste?" Luke looks at me curiously, reaching for the glass.

"It's at your own risk. I warned you."

He takes the world's smallest sip, and his whole face knots.

"You're right, Mom. It's gross." He tries to wipe his tongue off on the sleeve of his shirt.

"Where are the others?" I look at Thomas, who is fetching some water. The big screens are turned on and show a beach filled with plastic bottles washed up from the sea, a highway where the queue of cars stretches endlessly, hungry people on the run, and thirsty animals. Another screen shows endless forests with cascading waterfalls, the sea where dolphins play, mountains stretching toward the sky, and people walking hand in hand on the street. Contrasts of the world. The clean and the polluted. The natural and the manipulated. Thomas sits in the chair opposite us. I slip further down on the couch; it's nice to sit across from him instead of watching him on the Skycon.

"We're all in isolation in shifts." He fills the glasses, and I take a big mouthful of water to get rid of the awful aftertaste of celery. "We're working intensively with ourselves to get ready for the gathering of the Ring," Thomas speaks calmly with his soft, warm voice. His tone is like a caring embrace. He must have processed some of his guilt concerning Luke's awakening. Maybe that was part of his learning. Thomas hasn't said anything, and I will not inquire into it. I turn to Luke and hug him. "Have you had fun while I was gone?"

He jumps out of my arms and sits in front of me. "It has been so much fun, Mom. I've learned to climb clouds, I can meditate, and I can turn off my thoughts. Look. Now, it's on." He stares at me with his blue eyes. "Now, it's off. Isn't that smart?"

I can't help but smile. "It's so clever. Do you think I can learn it?"

He nods eagerly and moves even closer to me, whispering, "Everyone can learn it, Mom. It's not hard at all." I put my arm around his small shoulders, pull him close to me, and dig my nose into his hair. The scent is like magic for my soul; it makes love melt all fear and worries inside me. We sit completely still on the couch. I close my eyes and inhale his scent, so all my small depots are refilled.

"Do you know what the plan is now?" I lift my gaze.

"You'd better talk to the Master yourself." Thomas sits straight back in the chair opposite us. A very clear white light hovers around his body.

"And what about Luke?"

"I'm going to the Master too. We can go together." He looks at me with a look that seems much older than he is.

The big screens catch my attention. Why is the world created so that it is far easier to destroy something than build it? It is as if we humans are constantly being tested whether we act from the heart or the ego: love or hate, trust or fear. It almost seems like choosing hatred and fear is free of charge. The dark. Completely dark. The place inside people where they are unconscious and where the light doesn't reach. The part that controls their fears without them knowing it and gets projected out on others. And the place that makes people act inexplicably. Like when parents kill their children, people terrorize each other, or someone scams the innocent and helpless. It's a war in a different disguise where the enemy they are fighting is themself, but instead of looking at their pain, they create a conflict around them. It's the same darkness that Frank carries. Just the thought makes my heart beat faster, and my body moves into alert. I shake my head slightly and shift my focus back to Luke, who is a love generator without even knowing it.

"I just have some things to do." I look over at Thomas. "Can we meet later tonight?"

He reaches out, and our hands meet. "That we can."

"Luke, would you like to come with me? I'm going to see how Dad and Grandma are doing."

"Yeah. It's so cool in the large control room." He jumps off the couch. "I know a shortcut there."

I frown and look over at Thomas. He raises his hands reflectively while pulling a face that signals that he didn't know. Has Luke followed my journey from the control room? Does he know much more than what we have told him? I blink a few times to let go of the thoughts.

"See you, Thomas, shall we say at nine p.m. in the café?" My back is already turned to him as Luke pulls me toward the door. I turn my head and just manage to see Thomas waving and giving a thumbs-up.

Although Thomas's juice tasted disgusting, it worked. My energy is back, and we run hand in hand through the bright, airy hallways.

"Go right here, Mom. This is the cool way." He pulls my arm, and we turn into an area I have never been to before. I wonder what Luke has been up to while I've been away, and who's shown him around here? There are so many questions that I would like answered in the next few days when I have settled in. The light is slightly different here, a little darker without being completely dark. The stripe on the floor is light purple. It's quiet, and the few people we pass smile back at us.

"Look," Luke points out the window where the moon hangs to the right, luminous clear, and completely round. He lets one hand float into the cloud that forms the wall. I'm holding his other hand and am not letting go: two souls on their way through the long corridors where time disappears, and the light carries us forward. The craters on the moon are clear. It appears to be closer than it is—as if we could take a leap and easily land on it—so close and yet so far away—a bit like our Ring. It's as if I can feel that we are approaching the Ring's gathering, yet it's so unreal.

We turn again, this time into an opening that is not easy to see. Luke looks up at me, and his eyes light up with pride. I smile back at him and squeeze his hand. He slows down, walks directly into one of the walls, and disappears. My hand jerks as I stop and nearly let go of Luke's hand, but he tightens his grip. Slowly, I slide through the wall, and in front of me stands Luke with the biggest grin.

"You have a lot to learn yet." He shakes his little head. My body is still sore from the transition, but I ignore it as best I can. The next moment, we are standing in the square in front of the café. It abounds with people. Some walk with ease; others have big eyes and tread carefully. Above the door hangs the huge screen full of names of the people who arrived and those who departed.

"There's something else I just want to show you," Luke pulls my arm, and we walk quietly past the cafe. At first look, there is no one I know here, which is quite nice. Right now, I just want to be with Luke without having to relate to others or anything. When we get a bit away from the cafe, he turns through another wall. This time, I'm a little more prepared and glide confidently along. On the other side, there is the sound of the most beautiful voice singing. No one is to be seen here. The singing comes through an open door further ahead. We walk slowly and almost silently, and Luke signals to me not to say anything. When we reach the door, we sit next to each other on the floor with our backs against the wall. I know the voice and the voice that complements it. Everybody knows the voices—the most beautiful pure timbre from a woman and an incredibly intense voice from a man. I look at Luke. He dances even though he is seated and rocks with the rhythm. Does he know the voices?

I have to get a peek in there and slide slowly toward the door. As I am right next to the door, I stretch my neck forward and look through the crack in the door. The woman who is singing—it is her. "The Queen of Soul" with black hair and chubby cheeks. The room is full of people, and my eyes are nearly rolling out. They are all here. John with the round glasses and long hair, George with the cross hanging from his ear and the iconic leather jacket, David with the different colored pupils, and Michael.... I scoot back toward Luke and sit completely still next to him while we listen.

"Do you know them?" I whisper into Luke's ear.

He shakes his head, "But it sounds cool." His body is full of movement.

He is right in every way. They must have chosen to stay here for a longer period instead of traveling on. I had no idea they were here and have not given it a thought that they could be here, and I have definitely not seen them in the cafe.

"They're super nice." Luke has pulled my ear down to his

mouth and whispers the best he can. "They have said it's okay for me to sit here and listen, as long as I don't tell others where they are." He zips his lips and makes a face, "but I'm allowed to tell you." He lets go of my ear. His little body cannot sit still at all. The rhythm moves inside him, and he gets up. It's like seeing a dancing soul with no restraints holding the energy back—pure movement. There are no inhibitions or reservations that hold him back. That's how I see Luke as he stands there on the floor and follows the rhythm. Now, a new voice takes over. Unfortunately, I also know that one. Is her daughter here too? Although the voice is beautiful, I'm sorry she's here. It's way too early.

"Let's go." Luke grabs my hands. "I want to see how Dad is." He makes small moonwalk steps on the spot.

Although I could sit here for the rest of the evening, we better move on to the control room. We go back the same way we came, and before I know it, we are standing in front of the door. Luke really knows his way around. It would have taken me much longer to get here. He walks toward the door, which slides slowly open as he approaches.

"Here, this way, Mom." He has already distanced himself from me and has gone up to the right, where one can look out over the entire control room. There is an infinite number of screens, large and small. My old seat is down in the front, but I'm following Luke. He has settled in and is eagerly pressing some buttons on the screen. There, right in front of him, the picture of my mother crystallizes. She is sitting in the hallway outside Luke's hospital ward on one of the orange chairs by the high wooden tables. Luke turns the picture around so we can see who she's talking to.

"Frank!" Saliva flies out of my mouth and hits the screen.

Luke looks up at me, "Who is that? He doesn't look nice. Why is Grandma talking to him?"

I grab a chair and place it next to Luke and reach over, pulling another screen toward us, where we open a picture of Andreas. He is at home sitting on the sofa with Longlegs.

From the corner of my eye, I check on Luke, who is more interested in his father than Frank. He clearly doesn't remember Frank, not from previous lives or when he visited him at Kindergarten and Andreas's place. But the memories may come back after some time; I know that from myself. He seems settled that he is in In-Between and that his father is on Earth. Right now, I don't know what I can say or ask him regarding Frank. I'll have to wait until I've talked to Thomas or the Master. It's too risky to shake up something that is not necessary or to say something that could affect Luke's process. I move the screen to the left, out of Luke's field of view.

"It's cool that I can see Dad." Luke sits up, jumping a little on the chair. "Do you think Dad can see us?"

I shake my head and stroke him lightly over his fine blond hair. "He can't, but he knows that you are here and that you are well."

"Does he? How does he know that?"

"I told him so." I take a deep breath. "He loves you and wants all the best for you. But he misses you too." I put my hand in my pocket and pull out the bracelet from Andreas. "This is for you from Dad," I hand Luke the bracelet. He takes it without saying anything, and I help him put it on. It's big enough to reach twice around his wrist.

"It's cool. It will always remind me of Dad." Luke looks at the bracelet. "I miss Dad too, but I just imagine I'm there with him. Then it helps and becomes almost real. Dad can just do the same with me."

I smile. A child's logic is the best, so simple and straightforward.

The control room is nearly empty; most people are probably having dinner in the café. There are a couple of people in the rows further down. No one says anything.

Emotions are hanging in the air here. You can almost touch them like a mobile with various pieces moving. The room seems bigger this time, maybe because we're sitting in the back and have an overview. Or because I am not engrossed in the emotions but can look at it all a little from the outside. I zoom in on the picture with my mom and turn up the volume a bit, though I probably shouldn't since Luke is sitting here, but he's engrossed in looking at his dad on the other screen.

"And where did you say again that Angela had gone?" Frank smiles his mischievous smile.

My mother looks at him with overwhelming kindness. "I didn't say," she takes her bag in her hand and gets up to leave, but Frank grabs her arm and stops her.

"I want to know where Angela is!"

Her gaze is mild. "Then you'll have to start searching." She tries to get free, but he holds on and tightens his grip. Quickly, she turns her head away from him and calls out to a man in a green coat, "Young man, can you help me? I need to get my bag to the car."

Frank snorts and reluctantly lets go of my mother's arm as the porter approaches. "It's right in here." She turns to Frank. "Have a nice day." She straightens her hat and walks with the porter into Luke's ward. My focus is on Frank. I'm still not comfortable with him and what he might come up with.

He sits down in one of the orange chairs in the hallway, picks up the phone, and presses a name I can't see. Slowly, he takes a lighter out of his pocket, holds it up in front of him, and turns it on and off, on and off. Someone answers and Frank hisses into the phone. "We have to move to plan C." Then he puts the phone down. "Are you watching, Angela? Plan C."

46

THE CHOICE BETWEEN TRUST AND FEAR

I'm sitting in my favorite corner of the café. This is where Thomas and I always sit when we meet. The large windows behind me frame the semicircle of the café. On the walls, the colors change gradually and smoothly. Luke has gone to bed and is comfortable being alone in his room. He also has Meera, Shiva, and Yoge further down the hall. The rooms have been moved around, so Thomas and I live on either side of him. My gaze wanders around the cafe and the people sitting here. There's no one I've seen before. The flow through In-Between is far greater than one imagines.

As a child, I only experienced people dying of old age. Today, it's different. People die of so many different diseases, accidents, and violence, and it feels like more people are dying—like me in a plane crash. They all travel through In-Between before moving on. And then some stay, the people who want to learn more before moving on. There is something extraordinary about In-Between that cannot be described—the light and the vibration in the energy. It feels like love just in version 2.0 and with a higher oscillation. To many, the place seems like a key to one's heart that is slowly being opened so that you can see yourself and the world from a different perspective.

The perspective changes from being only about oneself to being about all of us: you, me, nature, the animals, and our children. From being about here and now, it's going to be about the larger whole. It just doesn't include Frank and the others in Kingston. I take a sip of the fresh apple ginger juice I got from the bar. It scratches a little in my throat and trickles through my body.

"You're here already," Thomas sits down on the couch next to me. I had not seen him come in because I was so busy looking at those sitting at the other tables. There is a young guy with tattoos on his hands, arms, and up to his face. His skin is dark, with the prettiest brown eyes and soft features. The tattoos are in stark opposition to his feminine appearance. He sits alone and looks thoughtful. At another table sits a man in his late fifties. He sits completely still and stares at a picture. He begins to tear the picture to pieces in slow motion and eventually puts all the small pieces in a small pile on the table.

"How are you?" Thomas turns so he is facing me. He is dressed entirely in white. I rarely see him in anything other than his blue silk tunic and black coat, but white suits him and makes his skin look darker.

How am I? This is a good question that I have not had much time to deal with lately. One moment has taken the other. Our gaze meets and connects our hearts. "I feel like I have played the final of the Super Bowl, but the result is kept secret."

"Let me help you." He takes my hand. "You have done so well. Because of you, it seems that we can gather in the Ring and that Frank doesn't have time to establish the forces that can oppose us."

My shoulders drop a foot down, and I feel five pounds lighter.

"But it was a close call." He stops and slowly runs his hand through his long dark blond hair. "Meera was looking for Kingston and discovered where they met. It was out by the abyss where the Skycon has no signal. She followed them and was there when they couldn't get ahold of Frank and realized that you had taken the Skycon from Frank." He pauses and looks around the cafe to ensure no one is listening. Those who are here are either preoccupied with themselves or with those they sit with. "They yelled at each other and nearly got into a fight. It seemed like one of them was getting cold feet. But the two guys with tattoos overruled him, and before Meera gathered us, they were heading for the main area. She dared not do anything but follow them." He pauses again and moves a little closer to me. "They went straight to Luke's location. They had been monitoring him and knew exactly where he was."

"But…" I can't help but interrupt. "How did they get Luke into the launch room?" I pull my legs up under me and hold them tightly with my arms.

"They knew him."

"What! How could that happen?" I can see the agony in Thomas's eyes. He lowers his gaze and breathes quietly.

"It's my fault." He raises his gaze. "I left Luke on his own. He was so confident and wanted to explore by himself." The wrinkles deepen on his forehead.

"It's not your fault; Luke has a lot to learn, and he trusts everyone he meets. We must not destroy that." I put my hand on his leg and look him straight in the eye. "I mean it."

More people have entered the café, and we no longer have our long table to ourselves. An elderly couple has sat down at the other end. They are identically dressed in green jogging clothes. She is wearing red glasses; his are black. They don't seem to be interested in anything other than finding a place where they can sit.

"Would you also say that if it had gone wrong?" Thomas speaks in a low voice.

I hesitate for a moment but have no doubt in my heart. "Yes." I know that Thomas wants what is best for Luke.

He leans back, and I follow. We both sit and look straight ahead.

"My father didn't accept mistakes. If you failed, you were weak and looked down upon. It was crucial for my father to have status. All my life, I struggled to do what others expected, trying to fit in. Daring to fail has been one of the most difficult challenges to handle." He breathes slowly. "Even though it was terrible, it has been a good learning experience for me. I made the worst mistake I can imagine." He looks down.

I don't say anything because Thomas processes the words as he speaks. I rarely hear him talk about his challenges. He sits for a while before continuing.

"Since Luke knew one of them, he went along. They took him to the dispatch room and, of course, did not tell him what it was all about. They had hacked the code to the door."

The chills make my body spasm. My mouth hangs slightly open, and I try to comprehend what Thomas is saying—coming to terms with the fact that some people are so cunning that they will exploit a child—*my boy*—to get their will in the world. It's beyond my comprehension.

"When it dawned on Meera what they had in mind, she contacted us. We ran as fast as we could toward the dispatch room. But when we got there, it was too late. Luke was awake." Thomas shakes his head slightly, and a tear twists free from the corner of his eye. "I have never experienced such powerlessness in my entire life. It was like running into an explosion and being thrown back. I wanted to move, but my body was not listening. Fortunately, Yoge was not affected in the same way. He shouted out for Luke, and it was like the dark-skinned guy then realized who Luke was. He ended up helping Yoge. Together, they kicked the two Kingston people out of the room. It cost him a few bruises, but it gave us...." Thomas can't help but smile; he turns his head toward me, "...less than a minute to figure out what to do."

I sit, paralyzed, listening to Thomas's words. The powerlessness also hit me when Luke woke up.

"But wasn't the dark-skinned guy part of Kingston?"

Thomas shakes his head. "They just offered him a large sum of money to help. He couldn't resist it. His conscience is broken. This was his chance to give his daughters an education and a better life since he can't be there to support them."

I sit quietly and try to understand the enormous power that pain and guilt have over us. And how it can make us do almost anything even though we know deep inside that it's wrong. I look Thomas in the eyes. "I was there with my mother when he woke up. He knew who I was and had come to terms with it."

Thomas's gaze is intense, "Yes, he had seen you on the screens as Angela several times and could remember it. How much Luke himself is aware of what happened, I don't know. But we pulled him back, as you know."

"That's why he fell asleep again in the hospital bed."

"Exactly." Thomas wipes his cheek with a napkin. "When we got him back here, and he woke up, he said he would not return and that we should close the door to his life on Earth. There was no doubt in his voice; it had the same power and depth as if he were a hundred years old." He pauses. "Normally, everyone should have 42 days to learn and experience before deciding whether to wake up again or continue their soul journey." He takes a sip of his juice. It's stronger than he expected, and he coughs. "Luke was completely clarified. I think his time with the Master has helped him."

I lean closer to Thomas, and he puts his arm around me. "I'm not complaining. I was released from making the most horrible decision of my life." Thomas hugs me. I love how all emotions can be present simultaneously with Thomas. One emotion doesn't exclude another, and nothing is right or wrong. We are here with what is right now.

"If I understand correctly, Frank can do no more harm to Luke." I look up at Thomas.

"Luke is safe here. And those who helped Frank up here told us that they only helped Frank because he had promised their families money. The Kingston guys both left children behind who needed expensive medicine and wives without an income. But the families have never received anything...."

I sit up straight. Our faces are so close that I can feel Thomas's breath smelling of mint toothpaste. "Did he bamboozle them?" That is so unfair, even if they helped Frank.

Thomas narrows his eyes and gets a cunning look on his face. "Well, there is a teaching in it for them as well, and we don't want to interfere with that. But we will help their families so they have the opportunity to get back on their feet and the surplus to take responsibility. Who knows? Maybe they will win a small amount of money on the Lottery one day?"

I give him a proper slap on the thigh as I've seen Lucy do to Tim. "Did you arrange it?"

He jerks and looks at me in surprise. Then, he shrugs his shoulders innocently. "Better that they win the Lottery than that Frank wins over us."

"What's going to happen to the Kingston people?" My voice gets eager, and I tense up my body. We slide through an enormous cloud, and the light in the cafe is automatically turned up, so it doesn't get dark in here. A bolt of lightning cuts through the sky right in front of us—this time at eye level.

Thomas continues. "They get most of their rights removed—no contact with people on Earth and no Skycon. In addition, they simply have to continue their development process as before. Frank and the rest of Kingston on Earth won't get any more help from here."

"No punishment?" I drum lightly on the table.

"No, here we don't punish souls. We only help them to evolve. And no soul develops through punishment or fear." He winks at me.

I know that, of course, but a month in isolation would have been in order for endangering something as crucial as the Ring and my son. I keep my thoughts to myself and smile a little strained at Thomas, who has undoubtedly seen through me.

"So, now what?" I drink the rest of my juice, which I shouldn't. Thomas cannot help but laugh at my facial expression.

"Now, we must be ready to assemble the Ring." He takes my hand.

"Thomas, there is something I need to tell you." I let go of his hand. "When I was in the control room just before, I heard Frank talking on the phone. He said to start Plan C. It was aimed at me like he knew I would be watching."

Thomas looks intently at me before answering. "There are two options. Either he's trying to scare you, or Kingston is speeding up several of their actions. There is nothing to do about it. We have to trust that the energy we'll bring back to Earth is stronger than theirs."

We sit quietly opposite each other on the couch and keep eye contact. I can feel the hairs rise on my arms and that it trickles cold down my spine.

"I choose to trust."

"I do, too," Thomas leans forward and embraces me.

47

LET GO OF THE RESPONSIBILITY

Thomas is at the bar picking up food and something a little more harmless to drink than the juice I had ordered. There is a constant flow of people in here at all hours of the day. But there's something special about being here at night and the clarity that arises as the day draws to a close. You look back and know a little more than when you woke up. The light in the morning brings the crisp, fresh, slightly naive start to something new, but here in the evening, you can retreat and look at it all from a distance with a greater perspective. It's as if the moon and the stars bring a different kind of clarity with them than the sun's light does. The arched windows all around provide the most adventurous view of the starry sky. Below us, I can see spots with tiny dots of light in all sorts of colors. Maybe Lucy is living in one of them.

"Here is some food for the hungry souls," Thomas places a tray on the table with two bowls of smoky hot orange soup. It smells sweet. "It's carrot soup with ginger; I noticed you are very fond of that." He pushes a plate toward me. Parsley is sprinkled on top, which brings out the contrasts. "Here," he hands me a plate of Naan bread. "It just came out of the oven."

"Thank you," I take the plate. Thomas sits down on a chair opposite me with his back to the cafe.

"What's going to happen now?" I blow on the spoon with soup before putting it into my mouth. It's still hot, and I have difficulty tasting the different ingredients.

"Now, we must each prepare for the test." He takes a mouthful of soup.

"How will we be tested?" The bread is still steaming. I rip off a piece.

"I don't know."

"Well, it's hard to prepare for something when you don't know what it's all about." I dip the bread in the soup and hope it will soften the strong taste of ginger a bit. A drop falls and lands on the white tablecloth.

"It's no different than in life; you don't know what will happen here either, but every day is a preparation for the next."

He may well be right about that. "Why are we being tested when we are already a part of the Ring?" A tall young guy with a knitted hat pulled down over his ears is heading straight at us. He has a big silver ring on his index finger and carries a tray. I straighten up and squint, and he looks in my direction. There are two large slices of chocolate cake on the tray, two tall mugs with steaming chai, and a bowl of nuts. Without saying anything, he puts the tray on the table in front of us. It feels like a clammy hand is being laid on my heart. I stare at the ring. It has a heart with an M in the middle, and I breathe a sigh of relief. For a moment, I thought it was one of the Kingston guys.

"Here you are," he speaks without looking at us.

"Thank you," Thomas moves one plate in front of me and waits until the guy is two tables away. "When we return to Earth, we will carry a very high frequency of energy, which will help us spread consciousness in the world. If our body and soul are not ready to contain the energy, it could short-circuit our nervous system."

"What does that mean? What could possibly happen?"

"Then, you will go insane." Thomas says no more, and I don't exactly know what to say. So, I grab a piece of cake, and he does the same. We sit still and wait for one of us to speak.

"When are we going to be tested?" I can feel unrest spreading in my body. Just before, I felt that the finish line was within reach. Now, it's returned further into the fog.

"No later than ten days before the Ring is to be assembled."

"Why is that?" I put down my fork.

Thomas shrugs and continues to eat calmly. "I don't know; I only know what I have told you. It's the Master who said it." He seems content and speaks with a light emphasis without any hesitation.

"But aren't you scared?"

Thomas takes my hands. "What can I do? Nothing. Either I float along or resist."

It always sounds so easy and straightforward when Thomas says it, but a battle has started between trust and fear inside me. Trust that everything will work out and that I'm going to pass, and the fear that this is the end because of me.

Thomas reaches out for a candle on the table and places it between us. "It's actually quite simple. The light allows us to see, but when it disappears, the fear sneaks in." He blows out the light. "The smoke creates a veil that removes our ability to predict the future, which made us feel safe—a kind of fog. That fog stresses the brain." He lights the candle again and easily blows the smoke away with his hand. "When the fog clears, we can see clearly, and then we feel safe again." He pauses for a moment until all the smoke is gone. "But most people live in constant fear because they cannot maintain control. That takes them into the fear that creates the fog." All the smoke has disappeared between us, and he looks me in the eyes with his clear, bright gaze. "There is only trust or fear, and we have a choice in every situation. Fear is the easiest to choose. It's created to help us survive dangerous situations, but we have spread the danger into many aspects of our lives, all situations. We live in fear, and it makes us narrow-minded. Fear is easier to choose because the brain is programmed to survive, and the fear center is made to survive through primitive conditions. And it's not updated to the complex world we live in with the challenges we have now. So, if we don't re-wire our brains, we will always choose fear over trust under pressure. Fear is more than three times as strong as trust. That means you have far more power and more resources to be negative and destructive. Today, the greatest danger is ourselves, not nature. But our brain's structure and capacity remain the same.

"Well, that's insane. It should be the other way around." I interrupt him and accidentally push my plate, so cake crumbs fall out on the tablecloth next to my glass.

"It's a condition. The brain was created over 100,000 years ago. That is the newest part of the brain, mind you. The other layers are much older. Our oldest brain is designed to help us survive, and it was perfect a thousand years ago when the dangers were markedly different." He pauses for a few seconds. "The newest part of the brain that deals with rational thinking and behavior changes is harder to use, so many people choose not to."

"How is that possible?" I move closer to make sure I won't miss anything.

"People can just choose to do what they have always done. But then they won't progress. Unfortunately, when they are busy, and life is challenging, many people choose the routine. You also need to keep in mind that we have limited capacity in the smart brain."

"What does that mean?"

"It means that people have on average 33 minutes of clever brain time available per day."

"What?! Then it's no wonder that the world is going in the wrong direction." I throw myself back on the sofa and consider for a brief moment whether he is joking. But he looks dead serious.

"We check in and out of the clever brain during the day, but most people have used up their 33 minutes by lunchtime. And then, of course, some people never use it. That is why so many people struggle to change their habits and handle changes." He takes a sip of water.

It makes so much sense because I have often wondered why some people were so primitive in their thinking or could always only see the negative.

"We live with an ancient brain and have to navigate an ultra-modern world?" I manage to say with my mouth full of cake crumbs.

"It's crazy to think about, isn't it?" Thomas looks out the window; from here, it looks very idyllic. Most things do from a distance, just like most people seem perfect on the surface.

We sit for a while and watch the world from above. Lights turn on while others are switched off. On the roads, there are long lines of red lights from the rear lights of the cars. Occasionally, there are dark spots. Slowly, the lights disappear, and it's dark below us.

"The next layer of the brain controls our emotions and consciousness." Thomas takes a sip of the dark brown Chai, which smells sweet and spicy at the same time. "That part of the brain also has a lot of capacity. But it also has a function called the Amygdala."

"Amygdala, what kind of name is that?" I notice myself frowning and try to look more relaxed.

"The Amygdala is the brain's watchdog. It keeps track of all the dangerous situations you have experienced in your life and helps you steer clear of similar situations in the future."

Clever, I just manage to think before he continues.

"The challenge is that the Amygdala hijacks your common sense to make you focus on the danger, and it only allows you to use your primitive brain to deal with the situation, not the clever brain. The Amygdala controls the survival mechanisms: fight, flee, or freeze." He takes a few nuts from the bowl. "The Amygdala intervenes when *it thinks* there is danger ahead, often due to a situation that you have experienced many years before and happily forgot. This means that you are not free to choose the most appropriate way to react in the situation."

I take a handful of nuts and place them in two rows in front of me. "Is that why there are so many disagreements and wars in the world?"

"It's one of the reasons. The second is that it is easier to infect people with fear than with trust. Just look at Frank and how easily he can spread fear and get others to buy into his plan. Fear spreads like a virus and takes over very quickly if we are not very attentive."

"But what can we do if those are the options we have?" I sit perfectly still and listen to Thomas. The light is dimmed again, and the bustle is settling down.

"The more we focus on trust, love, solidarity, responsibility, and gratitude, the more we will get and begin to see all the good it brings. But it takes time—far more time than it takes to create paths based on fear, negativity, and mistrust."

"But I still don't understand why the balance is like that. It should be the other way around." I eat a few nuts and make a hole in one row on the table.

"Agreed. But thousands of years ago, it was all about survival. If we did not see the saber tooth tiger, we would die. Today, it's the complete opposite. If we do not start to see the good, we lose the zest for life."

I can feel how fear can take over inside me instantly and control thoughts and emotions without me knowing why. It's like a spark that gets lit, so I can suddenly only see everything that can go wrong.

"We can even train our brain to act differently. But it's a deliberate act." Thomas reaches for one of my nuts.

"How?"

"By simply focusing on the positive, gratitude, and what makes us happy. But it can be tough for people who are used to seeing flaws and limitations everywhere." He gets up and walks over to a table next to us, where two young guys are playing dice. He gets a piece of paper from them and comes back. "Have a look here." He draws a line across the top end of the paper and one down the middle. "Here to the left are the positive paths, and on the right the negative ones." He points to the paper and writes *x 1* next to the positive and *x 3* next to the negative. "When we focus on the positive, we get more energy, we see opportunities and become better at cooperating and thinking as a 'we' rather than 'me.'" He points to the right side. "Here, we form the negative paths that strengthen the fear of what can go wrong, the mistrust, the limitations, and here we think short-term—only about ourselves and our own gain. We are selfish and will go to great lengths to 'survive' ourselves."

He has just sketched out the world situation with such a simple drawing. I sit back without saying anything while the light from a plane flashes out on the horizon.

He points to the left side of the line. "Over here, we can call it the green path; we take responsibility for our development and our lives. On the other side of the line, let's call it the red path, we blame others for whatever goes wrong." He slides his finger from left to right. "People who live on the red path will do anything to spread fear and mistrust. They often think short-term. People who live on the green path think long-term and try to spread love and trust."

"We need to get more people on the green side." Maybe it's that simple, and humans just make everything complicated. "So, what you are saying is that the more I focus on trust, the more love and energy I get."

Thomas looks at me and gives me a moment to take it all in before continuing. "When you use one of the qualities from the green side, it also helps you strengthen the paths for the other qualities on the same side. With many positive paths in the brain, you get a greater ability to handle challenging situations, the 'red' ones. It becomes easier to hold onto the positive no matter what challenges you face. All people will occasionally be challenged in life. But it is the way we handle the crucial challenges that matters."

Although I have been challenged recently, this is what I have felt

—a deeper anchoring of trust and belief. As a journalist, I was always critical and looking for mistakes. It became a habit that I eventually wasn't aware of.

"But it's important that we are also critical," I interrupt my thoughts.

"Certainly, we need to be critical. But there is a big difference between being critical and only seeing what went wrong or what is wrong or being critical and looking at opportunities for improvement and learning." Thomas points to his paper. "When you are on the red path, the negative one, it is easiest to stay there. It's not resource-demanding, and you can easily infect others with your opinion. Over here," he points to the left. "The green path demands more of you. You sign up and take responsibility for the challenges that you experience. It requires a conscious effort that most people are not born with."

"But there must be some people born with more of those green lanes than others, and some who have a harder time switching the balance between them?" I straighten up and can sense that I am in my critical corner. We still have the table to ourselves, and there are several empty tables around us. I take another sip of the chai, which is getting colder. The lights on the table flicker gently as a woman walks by. Her gaze is lifeless. She sits down at an empty table a short distance from us and slumps on the chair.

"You are completely right. Some people are a kind of 'cork.' They have established many green pathways in their brain. They may well be challenged in life, but they are quick to find solutions and get the best out of the situation. Over and over again, they have used the positive paths in their brain in their life, perhaps throughout several lives. The persistent use has made them more resilient. That's why they're better at holding onto the positive attitude toward life." He takes a couple more of my nuts, and now there are many holes in the lines. I push them together so they lie neatly again. "But you are right. Some people are very challenged. They have a hard time seeing a single positive thing in a day."

I look over at the lady at the table. Her big hair looks lifeless. Is she one of those people Thomas is talking about? "It must be hard," I mumble to myself. Thomas hears it and smiles at me.

"It's not fun, but it's also a vicious spiral that just pulls them further down. When things are not going well, and you think it's the fault of others, then nothing changes." He pauses in the flow of words. "There is a concept called 'learned helplessness.' It happens to people who have tried to take responsibility and change their lives but have repeatedly found it useless. Eventually, they give up. They are difficult to help."

"But are they lost?"

He shakes his head so that the long dark blond hair moves easily around his face. "No one is lost completely, but the paths in the brain are so well established that they have a hard time believing that they can change them. They can find the meaning of it all. Or hope. To make a change, we have to do it ourselves. Nobody else can do it for us. But people don't change anything until the pain of what is becomes greater than the fear of the change they are facing."

"The pain of what is becomes greater than the fear of change," I repeat, sitting for a moment and tasting the words. It couldn't be more accurate. The thought of being divorced from Andreas was unmanageable, but only because the fear of being alone was greater. It was not until I could contain that fear and face it that I could act appropriately. But the fear of being alone had even more layers. Beneath was the fear that no one would like me, that I would be all alone. Shame and guilt raised their ugly heads. I had to relate to all of it, observe what it was doing to me, and accept it. Only then could I create the change that turned out to be best for everyone.

We drift toward some very dark clouds, but they dissolve as we approach. The light in the café gets dimmed a bit more. I look discreetly at my watch; it's almost one o'clock at night. Most people have left. A young guy with headphones walks around and cleans up.

I remember when I was at the TV station; some of my colleagues were so negative. No matter what was suggested, they were against it. If it wasn't the work, it was the coffee, the lunch, or the manager. It was impossible to make them happy. They were long-term disappointed. Several of them thought they had the right to complain constantly. But they also got attention while doing it. And sometimes, they even got the more exciting assignments so that the editor didn't have to listen to their complaints. I take a sip of the water and cannot help but wonder how many people are left on the red path because others don't care about them. I also avoided my negative colleagues instead of reaching out and inviting them back onto the green path. I didn't see it as my responsibility, but their behavior affected me.

I look over at Thomas. He is sitting with his eyes closed and breathing calmly. "But you can also take too much responsibility, can't you?"

He opens his eyes slowly. It's as if he can sense how things fall into place inside me like a puzzle, where you suddenly find the pieces that have been missing, and the complete picture begins to take shape. "Sure, but it doesn't have that much to do with the red and green path. It has something to do with the roles we take on."

48

THE DRAMA TRIANGLE

I sit completely still and await Thomas's pearl of wisdom while I drink the last of my chai that has gone cold.

He turns the paper over and draws a triangle. "Everybody has a favorite role that they often take on when they are with other people. It's a role that we have successfully taken throughout our lives. A role where we have fitted into the family we grew up in or the team we work with."

I pull my legs up under me, grab one of the pillows on the couch, and hug it.

"The first role you can take on is the *Fixer*. We can also call it the *Saving role*. It's the same trait. Here, you choose to take responsibility for yourself and others and are energetic. You like to decide and get things done your way, so you take on many tasks and take on a lot more responsibility than is healthy."

Thomas is talking about me. I cannot help but smile.

"But Fixers rarely see themselves taking too much responsibility." He pauses. "They are identified with the role and like the attention and the power position it gives them. They are the ones you come to for help, and they influence the decisions that are made.

They also have control over things and know that things are done their way. They even gain the respect of others." He gives me some time before continuing. "The Fixers often have a little more energy surplus and do not notice if they become exhausted in the same way others do. It's only when the rubber band is stretched to the limit, and it tightens that they react. But they will go to great lengths to make things work." He holds his hands up in front of him, presses his thumb and forefinger together on each hand as if holding a rubber band, and moves the hands further and further apart. "If they are not careful, the rubber breaks, and then they will be stressed." He opens his fingers with one hand and releases the grip on the invisible rubber band. "The fixer, or the rescuer, if you will, will often take over tasks and responsibility. You can count on them; they will help you with anything and find solutions, even for things that have nothing to do with them. If you are not careful, they will even begin to finish your sentences." He smiles.

"But there is nothing wrong with that, is there?" Was that my critical side again, or me trying to defend the Fixer?

"Both yes and no because it's the balance they need to find. When they take too much responsibility, they simultaneously deprive everyone else of the opportunity to take it. When you are used to taking responsibility, it's easy and straightforward. You're not afraid of it, and it feels natural. You know how to deal with things and have control. But there is an imbalance with other people."

I frown and am not sure I'm with him anymore. I mess the nuts on the table up into a pile.

"Why?"

"The balance is only there when we all equally participate with what we can. That doesn't mean we should be able to do the same. We are all different. But we have to take responsibility for what we can, through which the balance arises." Thomas waits to see if I have more questions, but I don't—for now.

"The next role you can take on is *The Prosecutor*. Here you have given yourself the right to shoot at the suggestions of others or the way of doing things. The crucial thing here is that you don't take the responsibility."

"I know these people. They are everywhere on social media and comment for free on other people's posts without giving anything of themselves." I discreetly eat one of the nuts.

"Exactly." Thomas sits perfectly still as he speaks. The words come out of his mouth with the greatest ease. He doesn't need to search or think about what he says. It's like he's picking it up from somewhere else—from a source he drinks from and distributes to others. "The important thing to understand is that the Prosecutor is in a free position. They don't take responsibility or come up with solutions but reserve the right to criticize others. If you try to give them responsibility for a task, they will most likely go straight into the final role, *the Victim*."

"So, there are three roles, the Fixer, the Prosecutor, and the Victim. That's it." I raise my eyebrows, "Only three roles and billions of people. We are not that inventive after all."

Thomas's eyes glow with energy. His inner light is always turned on when he shares his knowledge. "It's a triangle where the Fixer is at the top, and the Prosecutor and the Victim on each side at the bottom. Humans are straightforward to understand when we know the basic emotions and patterns that govern us. It's the way we perform them that sets us apart."

"What about the last one, the Victim? What are that person's strategies?" The great thing about talking to Thomas is that we almost go into a bubble filled with trust where time does not exist. We're just here. There is a loud rumble outside. A giant Boeing 747 passes quite close, and I can see the faces in the windows. They cannot see us.

"The Victim is a person who always has some sort of excuse for not getting things done or for not being able to help or take responsibility. There is always a reason. Everything from time, resources, health, to others being better at the task than themselves." He takes a more prolonged break. "Others are often more skilled because they practice. The victim practices not taking responsibility. Therefore, it becomes unmanageable for many to take responsibility and easier to deliver an excuse. It can be hard to get out of that role." He pauses. "There are many ways to take advantage of the role of being a victim; it can also be powerful." Thomas looks down, "For me, it was a way of living throughout my youth." He looks back up, and I can sense the vulnerability in his eyes. "It was my way of surviving, but it was pure survival. I was not happy." The pain gleams through his eyes, and he doesn't hide it. "I blamed everyone else for losing my parents; I used the role of the Prosecutor. When that didn't work, I switched to the Victim role and felt sorry for myself because I was orphaned." He shakes his head. "None of the roles worked for me or made me happy. They pulled me further and further down and away from myself. But I didn't know how to escape the drama I had created outside and inside myself."

He moves over on the couch next to me, leans back, and looks up at the ceiling. We sit entirely still in our corner of the cafe and breathe into the emotions that emerge to the surface. I can feel Thomas's sense of being lost. Not that I can recognize it from myself, I have always been the fixer type. The feeling of standing with your toes over the abyss without knowing that you can step back and don't have to move forward must be horrible. Not being able to see any other way than the one you are walking on.

We sit for a while without saying anything. He straightens up and takes a deep breath. "We can all switch between the three types and do so often because we are constantly looking for the most appropriate to use in each situation. But as long as we choose one of them, we are stuck in a drama. That is why the triangle is also called the drama triangle. There is often an imbalance in ourselves and with those we are with, so it can be a big or small drama."

"But what can we do?"

He runs his hand through his long hair repeatedly as if trying to stroke some of the pain of the past away. "Give and take responsibility. The fixer must learn to give responsibility and trust others.

Learn that it's not always important that things are done in one particular way, that there are more possibilities, and that less good can also be good enough." He looks directly at me. "Isn't that right?"

I would probably have disagreed six months ago. Back then, I preferred to be as perfect as possible in everything I did and do things my way. *I knew best.* I don't feel like that anymore.

He continues and looks like he knows what I'm thinking. "Prosecutors and Victims must learn to step out of the role of spectator and onto the stage. But it's dangerous for them because out there, others can criticize them, and they must show that they can deliver something, not just come up with empty words. This is the vulnerability we need to address because it's what connects people. Without it, we create distance between us."

My clever brain is running out of capacity. I simply just need all this to sink in. "Thomas, I'm just going to get some more water." He smiles since the carafe on the table is still half full. At the bar, the young man with the headphones is filling up shelves with new colored bottles. He doesn't see me approaching. I stand at the bar and tell myself that now I have to trust him to see me instead of taking responsibility and calling him. That would be the easiest thing in the whole world. I take a deep breath as all of Thomas's words slowly fall into place inside me, like letters finding their proper place in the alphabet. There is no doubt that I have lived as a Fixer. I've never seen it that way before, but now I can see the consequences of my actions. I have always taken responsibility for everything I have come close to—everything from work assignments to the shortcomings of others. I have had my place in the world because I was something for others. But it has also made me forget myself. That's what the In-Between mirror has given me—the opportunity to look inward and see what I need, what I can vouch for, and how I can contribute my inner light.

"What can I do for you?" a male voice tears me back to the present.

"I just needed something to drink."

He pulls the headphones down around his neck. We are waiting for each other to continue. I'm curious; if I don't take responsibility for what I will have to drink, will he take one of the three roles? This is a test for Thomas's theory. I want to see if it sticks. "I don't quite know what I want."

"Shall I make you my favorite drink? Or would you like one of the bottles?"

Bingo, he took charge, and I can just try to test him a little more. "Yes, your favorite drink, please, but it must be good."

He doesn't let himself be pushed by the pressure from my side. "It's my favorite drink. Whether it will also be yours, you must decide for yourself."

He just threw the responsibility back at me and didn't want to enter the drama triangle with me. I can feel small bubbles inside me like a triumph of joy that it all makes sense.

"Voila, mademoiselle, enjoy." A glass filled with ice cubes, mint, and ice blue juice is placed in front of me. Drops run down the glass and make slight stains on the bar counter.

"Would you like a small bottle to go with it?" He smiles at me. "I can recommend this one," he takes one blue bottle, the one that supports clarity.

"Thank you...."

It's one of the most popular places to work here in In-Between. Besides meeting a lot of new souls, they also coach the newcomers —something many use in their process.

"I better get two of both. I completely forgot about Thomas."

I take the glasses and walk back toward Thomas. He sits completely relaxed with his eyes closed and his hands resting on his chest. I place the glasses on the table and sit back on the sofa. The ice cubes splash gently and push against the green leaves on the surface. He opens his eyes.

"I don't know what it is," I say, pushing one glass in front of Thomas. "And I also got these," I place the blue bottles on the table.

He reaches out for the drink and takes a sip. "So, if it doesn't taste good, it's not your fault."

I await the verdict, both over the drink and whether I should be sent into the role of a victim. He gives nothing away. "Are you going to taste it?"

A few droplets run down the side of the glass. I lift it to my mouth while I keep looking at him. The taste is fresh and silky soft with a sweet aftertaste. "I think it's nice." I'm still awaiting his verdict.

"That's the most important thing; what I think is irrelevant."

I must look like a question mark because he continues, "There will always be people who disagree with us and try to get us to fall in line and shut up. When we return to Earth, we will provoke those who want to spread fear. They will do what they can to belittle, ridicule, and sabotage the energy we bring." He takes one more sip of the drink. "It's delicious, no doubt about it." He smiles at me. "While others immediately will be able to feel the energy we bring, suspicion and fear may be greater and more dominant. They will play the role of Prosecutor."

I hold the glass up and roll the ice cubes slightly from side to side.

Thomas shakes his head. "It will by no means be easy, but we will get what we need, both at the level of consciousness and financially, so we can get started. We must not begin to preach or convince anyone of anything. We need to be there and share the new energy. It will do the work for us if our egos do not interfere too much." He takes one more sip and empties the glass so that only ice cubes remain. "In relation to the drama triangle, it is important to be careful not to take on any of the roles because then we lose. None of the roles are appropriate."

"But if I'm not in one of them, where am I then?"

He draws an arrow out of the drama triangle, "You are out here taking responsibility for your life and letting others take responsibility for theirs. Where you have an equal relationship, this is also where the respect between people grows. Respect for differences and for the way we treat each other."

That sounds reasonable. Why can we not just be outside the drama triangle all the time? It seems to be the best place to be. "But how do you get others out there?" My finger runs around the small puddle of drops from the glass.

"You stop fixing and give back the responsibility to the prosecutor and the victim."

That sounds easier said than done. I don't say anything even though the words are lined up and would like to be let out.

"It requires you to become aware of your role and how you act in it. When you see it, you can begin to let it go."

"So, when people take responsibility, aren't they in the drama triangle?" I say, just to be absolutely sure I get it.

"It is about learning the fine balance between letting go and fixing. When to take responsibility and what responsibility to leave to others."

"But, it can have big consequences!" I drink the last drops from my glass, which at the moment is only ice cube water with green leaves and tastes of too thin juice.

Thomas puts a small ice cube in his mouth. "That is why many choose to stay in the drama triangle, to avoid the consequences. But it creates an imbalance in the way we are together. It's going to influence the next many generations of young people. Many don't learn how to take responsibility because they grow up with fixer parents who remove all the obstacles on their path. Helicopter parents. For many people, it's easy to access drugs, online games, and be in shallow relationships." He crunches the remains of the ice cube, and it runs cold down my spine. "Have a look here," he draws two vertical lines next to each other. "Here are two people; they are equal and stand in their light and energy. They both take responsibility for their lives. They work together and support each other." He draws another vertical line and a line that leans up against the vertical line. "Here, you have a person who has 100% energy available and a person who leans on that person. The person who leans uses only 50% of his energy and is dependent on the person standing up vertically not to move because then the person leaning falls. They are co-dependent. The one who stands up is dependent on the attention of the one who is leaning. He needs to be there for others and make them dependent on him to feel a purpose." Thomas places the pen on top of the vertical line and moves it away from the leaning one. "If the one who stands upright moves, the one who leans over will fall. They are dependent on each other in their own way."

I point to the one who stands up, "But what does that person get out of being a rock for the other?"

"A lot; otherwise, they wouldn't be." Thomas smiles at me. "It's all one big psychological game. The one who is a rock enjoys that there is another who needs him. And even if the person sometimes gets enough and moves away, they also like to feel that someone needs them. That's why the addiction is mutual." He draws one more drawing. This time, the two lines lean against each other so that the tops of the lines meet. "Here, they are also co-depending. If one moves, the other falls and vice versa."

I look at it and see if I can find a solution to the deadlocked challenge. But I can't. "What can they do?"

I startle. The guy with headphones has sneaked close to us without me seeing him. He puts two blue drinks on the table, "It looks like you liked it." He winks at me and takes the empty glasses with him.

"If you want out of this constellation," Thomas points to the drawing with the two leaning against each other without being distracted by the guy, "there is only one option: let the other fall. It can be difficult because we will do almost anything to keep each other in unhealthy patterns so that we can survive ourselves." He draws a dotted line to illustrate that one line tries to free itself. It's easy to see how the second line will then overturn.

"In such a situation, a person who doesn't want to get up and start taking responsibility will unconsciously make himself ill as a very extreme consequence. It's hard to leave someone who is sick, so it's the ultimate way to hold onto each other. But many are content to take on the role of victim or accuser. Those roles also work effectively when you want to retain each other."

I shake my head and know he's right, but it's still shocking how primitive we are and what we do to avoid taking responsibility for our lives.

He points to the two vertical lines, "This is where we need to stand. Here, our self-confidence, self-esteem, and courage take responsibility and grow. This is where we rest in ourselves. Cheers." He lifts the filled glass and lets it hit mine. The sweetness with a twist of mint fills my mouth.

When I have been with Daniel, I have felt the temptation to lean on him and just stay there. He has been good at letting go of me and respecting my choices. It has been tempting to ask him to lift the responsibility with me. "So, basically, you're saying it all comes back to us taking responsibility, both in the drama triangle and here." I point to his small lines, representing people.

"Yes, responsibility is the key to our future. But we also need to see what and how we should take responsibility because otherwise, we just end up in the drama triangle and take responsibility from others. It's rare for a victim or prosecutor to rebel and demand responsibility. They slowly lose confidence that they can and resist if you try to give them responsibility." He draws a small arrow pointing downwards under the victim. "The prosecutors suddenly have to show the worth of their accusations if they have something better to bring to the table instead of just shooting at others." The prosecutor also gets a small arrow pointing downwards. "The victim must look at their low self-esteem and beliefs about themselves and others. They will be challenged to use their talent and risk failing or being rejected. Both can be very painful, which often keeps them in their role." He puts two lines under both of them. What is also important to understand is that none of the three roles are healthy. When we are inside the drama triangle, we all lose."

"So, what is it that determines what role we play?"

Thomas leans back. The candles on the table are about to burn down and struggle to stay alive. We're the last two souls in the cafe. "Many people will claim that we can choose freely, but we cannot. Our choices are based on our emotions, and if we don't know them thoroughly, we make choices on an unknown basis." He pauses and puts his hand on his chest. "An emotion is a powerful motivating force that can make us do things that are completely against all common sense. Emotions start wars, create divisions in religion, and destroy relationships."

"It sounds like there's plenty to look into."

"There is a long way to go. This is the path we must walk in the Ring so that we can show others the way later. Soon, we will be able to see the finish line." Thomas looks me in the eye with the most incredible clarity. I lean back. Only once before have I experienced such a clear gaze—the Master's.

A yawn is rising, and I suffocate it by biting my teeth together. "Thomas, I have to go to bed."

All the tables have been cleared and are ready for tomorrow. The light over the bar is off, and it's been a while since the guy with the headphones waved goodbye. We get up.

"There is one last thing I need...." My voice is hesitant. "Do you want to come along and see what Frank is up to?"

Thomas looks at me. "Of course."

"I know we shouldn't deal with him anymore, but I can't let go of him completely. He's haunting my system."

"And don't forget these; you might need them later." He hands me the two blue bottles.

The control room is empty. The blue-green floating steps light up as we enter. We sit down at the same station we were sitting at the day I arrived. I pull up Frank's picture and don't need a keyboard or joystick; that's only for beginners. He is sitting in his expensive suit in a smoky bar. In front of him is a bottle with only a drop at the bottom. His eyes are dark and sunken, his skin ruddy, and his head hangs forward. I zoom in and look over at Thomas.

"Do you think…?"

"That's a good question…."

Frank looks resentful. He takes off his finger ring, throws it in the ashtray, and sets fire to a bundle of matches placed like a bonfire. The fire gets a grip and embraces the ring. In glimpses, we can see a "K" carved into the ring.

49

THE WORLD SEEN FROM ABOVE

The sun's rays land on my cheek and gently tickle me as it slowly warms up the room. It's safe and pleasant to be back. I stretch my arms over my head and feel the joints in my legs give way. No Frank nearby and no cruel choices to be made. Imagine if he's been kicked out of Kingston. Maybe it will open his heart. On the wall hangs all my pictures of Luke, the one I printed when I first came to In-Between, and several more I have printed since—memories that slowly step into the background and allow new ones to emerge. If the pictures did not hang there, I might completely forget the moments; they would gradually be wiped out like paths in the forest that run wild. The door to Luke's room opens slowly, and a small blond tuft of hair appears.

"You are here. It was not a dream." Luke jumps up into the bed and crawls under the duvet. His little body snuggles up next to mine. I hug him close.

"Oh, how I missed you."

He laughs and twists a bit, so I loosen my grip. "What are we going to do today?"

"I don't know. Do you have any plans?" This, right now. It doesn't get better. If life had a pause button, I would press it now.

"I can show you how good I have become at climbing clouds." He turns around so our noses meet. "I'm probably faster than you." He laughs his innocent light laugh that comes right from his stomach.

"Don't be so sure. I will not let you win without a fight." I grab him and tickle him where I know he is most ticklish, right under his arms. He pours out a loud scream and twists.

"Stoooop, stooop."

I hold back and pull him away from the edge of the bed. "Luke, is it okay for you to be here in In-Between?" My voice gets more serious and heavier in tone. I'm trying to catch his eye, but he's in a hurry to wrap himself in the duvet, so I can't tickle him again.

"Yep." He disappears under the duvet to appear at the foot end in the next moment. I can't help but smile to myself. Typically, I want to pull answers out of him and make sure he is fine and feeling good. But he is in the now and doesn't think at all as I do. I have to be careful not to create a problem that doesn't exist inside him based on my own insecurity, which is rooted in fear.

"How about we put on clothes and run out before the sun is up in the sky? Then we can have breakfast afterward."

"Yeeeaaar." Luke jumps out of bed and disappears into his room. It doesn't take many minutes before he stands in the doorway again, wearing jeans and a red T-shirt with Captain America on his chest. "Are you ready?"

That would probably be an exaggeration because I have neither been in the shower nor looked in the mirror. It will have to wait. Quickly, I put on the same clothes as yesterday and gather my hair with an elastic band. Luke grabs my hand and pulls me toward the door. I just manage to cast a glance in the mirror on the way. It's so weird to be Eva again, back in my old body. There is no more gray hair since last time, thankfully. That's one of the benefits of being dead. The door closes behind us with a quiet hiss. It's completely quiet in the hallway. We tiptoe past Thomas's door, past Meera's, and further down where Yoge lives.

"Are you showing the way?" I pull him close and embrace him while walking. He nods eagerly and gets one step ahead of me. We turn right out in the hallway, and further down the hall, there is an exit. The wind rips several strands of hair loose from my ponytail and whirls it up into the air. I look at Luke. He is completely calm and moving on the clouds as if it were the most natural thing in the whole world.

"It's over there," he points to the right at a completely flat area. "There was a mountain yesterday." His little face looks like a big question mark, and he is scratching his hair. "Well, but today it's over there, Mom." On the other side of a cloud bridge, to our left, lies a large cloud mountain. The closer we get to it, the higher it looks. It's been a hundred years since I've climbed on clouds. At least that's how it feels. The sun is just behind the highest peak, and if we hurry, we will be able to reach the top before it does.

"Are you ready?" I release Luke's hand as we cross the bridge.

He looks up at me and gives me a wry smile. "Do you need a head start?"

I rub my hands together and clap lightly. "No, it has to be a straight race."

"Well, 3, 2, 1, ready, go."

In no time, Luke is several steps ahead of me. He jumps up easily on the first part of the cloud, and before I know it, he is gone. I have no idea where he went and have to concentrate on getting up myself. My breathing tightens, and my legs get heavier. There is still a nice stretch to the top and no Luke to be seen. I focus my thoughts on getting up so I don't start worrying about Luke.

"Howdy."

I stop and look up. To the right, Luke sits with crossed legs with a massive smile on his face.

"Do you need a little head start now?" He's one big grin.

Sweat runs down my forehead, and my hair sticks to my face. I bite my teeth together. That cannot be right. Thomas must have taught him how to cheat while I've been away. "No, I'm fine; I just need to warm up." I'm slightly breathless.

"Great, see you at the top." He jumps up, and before I know it, he disappears once again.

I go after him, and the higher I reach, the heavier my legs get. I can almost see the top and sense the sun rising right behind it. The wonderful thing about crawling on clouds is how they form under your feet when you step on them—like a step that receives you and supports you to go further upward; once you have learned, you merge with it. A small foot dangles from the top of the cloud, and when I reach two steps further up, I can see Luke sitting on the cloud as if it were a deck chair with his hands folded behind his neck and his face toward the sun, which is on its way up, right in front of him.

"I came first." He sits with his eyes closed and a triumphant smile on his face.

I must admit that my heavy breathing has probably revealed my arrival. It's hard to argue with his clear victory, though it pains me to have been beaten by a five-year-old.

"You're so cool," I gasp for breath and get enough air for a few more words, "and fast."

Infinite expanses open up before our feet. He moves so I can sit next to him and make the chair a little wider. Down on Earth, there are large green areas, small square houses in rows on the straight roads, and the sea, which reflects the sun's warm golden light; it brings it all to life. As far as my eye can see, the sun sprinkles its light and invites us to a new day with new possibilities. It's like a painting we are slowly hovering over.

"How long are we going to be here in In-Between?" Luke draws a pattern with his finger in the cloud next to him.

I sit still for a moment, searching for the answer in my inner archive, but I can't find it. "I must admit that I've lost track of time." I shake my head, "We'll have to ask Thomas. He knows for sure."

"When are we going to be tested?"

I freeze completely. I don't know that either, and right now, I don't feel ready at all. "I don't know, sweetheart. I will probably find out more today when I go to the Master. Then I can tell you. But you have been tested, haven't you?"

"Yeah, it was just a little test. It wasn't the cool test, Thomas said." He picks up a lump of cloud, shapes it into a ball, and throws it into the air. It floats slowly on its own and dissolves like powder as the wind grabs it.

"I'll probably figure it out and tell you as soon as I know." I put my arm around his shoulders, and he leans into me.

"I don't understand why people can't be good to each other."

I look at Luke and frown, "What do you mean?"

"The guy with the scary eyes, why does he want to hurt me?"

I kiss him on the hair, "Luke, it has nothing to do with you. It has everything to do with him. He had a difficult life and is trying to make others pay for his pain."

"But why, Mom? Why is he doing it by being mean?" Luke pats the cloud beside him so that it becomes round.

I take a deep breath. The air is cool up here. "I don't think he knows what else to do."

"But it isn't hard to help each other?" He throws another cloud ball into the air, which floats effortlessly.

"For some people, it is. They feel like something was taken from them. But you are right. That's the way it should be." I also shape a cloud ball and throw it after Luke's. Together, they float away. Luke still has his naive, childish mind and indomitable belief in the best in all people. When I look at him, I see both the boy and the old soul inside behind the bright blue eyes.

"It's weird. If I share my packed lunch with someone who has forgotten his at Kindergarten, then the two of us will be happy and full." He puts his head on my stomach and looks out over the world.

Occasionally, a cloud drifts past below us and shuts off the view. But it's gone in a hurry, and the landscape with the green fields and tall trees comes into view again. It looks so peaceful and idyllic from up here. But if you zoom closer, you can see the intrigue, the pain, and the conflicts—all the fates that fight. They don't show it but walk with it in the dark and pretend it does not exist. Sometimes, I wonder if it was just me who had a hard time when I was younger because everyone else seemed so happy and clarified. But when I look at it from up here, I know it's not the truth. All people carry their history and tasks that they must solve in this life. But we have become good at hiding it away and pretending that everything is fine. It seeps out between the cracks when we are challenged, and we struggle to close the holes again so everything looks nice on the surface.

There is a loud rumble. Luke starts laughing. It's my stomach that's getting impatient. "Shall we get some food?"

He nods eagerly, gets up in a leap, and stands ready. "What's up, Mom? Can you make it down first?"

I laugh while shaking my head, "Unfortunately, I don't think I can, but I'll try."

"Okay, I'll try to do badly this time." He signals 3, 2, and 1 with his fingers and has already started before I get to my feet. He sat down on his buttocks, pulled his legs up under him, and slid down as if sitting on a toboggan. I sit down and try to do the same, but it reveals both my age and weight. I don't move an inch and have to get up again and walk down the cloud. My legs start running, and I make it down faster than I got up.

Luke stands in front of me with his arms in the air. I run down at high speed, grab him, and swing him up in the air and around with all the power and speed I have gained from the momentum. He is one big smile and spreads his arms out so it looks like he is flying. As the pace slows down, I put him down. "Now, we'd better get some food."

50
THE UNVEILING OF IN-BETWEEN

I immediately see Thomas as we enter the cafe. He sits in our usual corner with the others from the Ring. Heat flares up inside, and I squeeze Luke's hand. The café is full of people, and it strikes me time and time again how many souls make their way through In-Between and how few know that we are here or can remember it when they travel on. We are like a secret entity that helps people on their journey and disappears again without leaving a trace. If it had not been for Frank, no one on Earth would have heard of In-Between. Fortunately, it doesn't seem that his PR stunt in the newspaper had a significant effect. Still, I cannot help but wonder if there are more people here than usual. We pass several tables on the way to the others. One table is occupied by a group of young people who have connected; they laugh and ignore us as we pass. Next to them is the retirement table. The elderly have a fantastic time when they come here. There is no physical pain here, and their bodies feel young again. Their zest for life and laughter flow toward us as we walk past, and one of the older ladies with curly light purple hair waves to Luke. He waves back politely.

"Who was that, Mom?"

I bend down and whisper, "I don't know, but she certainly thinks you look cute."

We approach our fellow travelers, and my body begins to tremble, not in an uncomfortable way, rather with excitement like when you have wanted something for a long time and finally get it. It's been a long time since I've talked to the others in the Ring. It feels like an eternity, even though time is experienced differently here. I suck the air down into my lungs and hold on tight to Luke's hand. He walks with small quick steps next to me and looks curiously at all the people we pass. I don't have time to react before Thomas has seen us and gets up. He opens his arms and gives us a joint hug so that the tension in my body subsides.

"How great to see you both. Have you had fun this morning?"

"YES, I've shown Mom how to climb clouds. And I'm the fastest."

Thomas gives him a high five and laughs, "You're so cool, Luke. Join the others; we're all off duty this morning so that we can gather."

Meera and Yoge sit with their backs to us and haven't seen us coming. Shiva has seen us, and her warm glow shines around her. Her subtle energy vibrates so strongly that it feels like a light breeze slowly enveloping me as she embraces me. She strokes Luke across the cheeks with her lean hands and looks him in the eyes. He smiles at her, jumps up on the couch, and sits down where Thomas sat before. Luke's whole face radiates, and his eyes move curiously from table to table. Meera also gets up and greets me. She has replaced the tracksuit with a slightly loose dress with a flower pattern. "It's great that you are back." Her voice is soft as silk. Her bangs hang straight over her dark blue eyes, and her long gray hair is pulled back in a ponytail.

The Ring is almost assembled. Gabriel is the only one who is not here. I slide onto the bench next to Luke, where Thomas has also sat down. Yoge lights up a big smile when he sees me. The pen sits in its fixed place behind his ear, and in front of him are several sheets of paper with calculations on them.

"It's good to see you, Eva." He mumbles a bit and puts a hand on my shoulder, "You have made a formidable effort. We thank you for that."

My jaw drops, and I try to come up with something clever to answer. I don't know what to say, so I end up saying, "Thank you," with an appreciative nod while I smile in amazement. I've never heard Yoge praise anyone before. What comes out of his mouth is usually strategic and critical.

On the table are plates with fresh fruit, freshly baked buns, small bowls of oatmeal, cereal, cheese, cold meat, chocolate spread, and honey. There are two large carafes, one with light yellow juice and the other with orange juice. Thomas waits until we have sat down and everyone has filled up their plates.

"It's great to see you all. We have each been on our journeys, mostly an inner one, but one of us has also been on an outer one." Thomas looks over at me. "Eva is back, and it is wonderful. Now, we are closer to being able to embark on our final journey that we have been preparing for thousands of years." There is complete silence around the table; even Luke is sitting without saying or doing anything. He has crossed his legs and is resting his hands in his lap. He looks like a little Buddha sitting there with such a gentle and fine energy. Pure and innocent. Everyone's eyes are on Thomas.

"As you know, Eva had a tough run on Earth with Frank. But it should be taken care of for now." He looks at me and nods supportively. I smile back and check to see if Luke responds to Frank's name, but he doesn't. At least not in a way that I can see.

"Frank has been trying to reveal the existence of In-Between and the Ring's mission. He is part of a group that tries to spread fear and devastation on Earth and increase the negative development that is currently spreading worldwide." He takes a deep breath and clears his throat. "It also means that the work of the Ring is more important than ever."

"I have something to add." Yoge grabs his pen and starts tapping it lightly on the table. "I've been keeping an eye on Frank." We all look at him. Nobody says anything. Yoge flips through his notebook. At the top of one of the pages, it says, "Plan C," and there are several lines written below that I cannot read upside down. He rubs his wide nose with the back of his hand and snorts a few times. "Kingston has set the next phase in motion. You know they are a group of very powerful and influential people, and after Frank lost his Skycon…." He looks over at me. "They no longer needed him. They have excluded him from the inner circle."

"WHAT!" I take a big sip of the orange juice in my glass and send an apologizing nod to Yoge. Now, it makes sense that he burned the finger ring. "Did you know?" I lean over to Thomas, whispering. He shakes his head.

"Frank is, as you probably guessed, furious. He has tried to sell his story to several major newspapers. Unsuccessfully. We're keeping an eye on him, but he's not a major threat right now. But he is like a sleeping terror cell. We must not underestimate him."

I lean forward, checking how Luke is reacting. He sits completely still and listens. Thomas puts a hand on my leg, which has started to move quickly up and down under the table.

"Kingston knows very well that it is only a matter of time before the Ring is assembled. Plan C consists of several parts. They have access to print banknotes and can send so much currency into circulation that the world economy will become under pressure. They have even sold out of their shares and bought gold instead." He puts a checkmark next to the first line of his notes. There are two more lines.

It is as if conversations remain at the tables so that they do not disturb others. We have the table to ourselves here at the end of the cafe.

"The next phase is a religious war." Yoge makes an effort to speak so everyone can hear it and looks at us in turn. We all have our eyes fixed on him. "They will play Muslims, Jews, Hindus,

Buddhists, and Christians against each other by bombing churches, mosques, and holy places, including the Temple Mount and the Church of the Holy Sepulcher in Jerusalem, which are important sites for Jews and Christians. Mecca, which will harm the Muslims. The holy river in Allahabad in northern India, where the great pilgrimage occurs every 12 years. It's this year, and it will kill thousands of Hindus. The Mahabodhi Temple is one of four major Buddhist shrines that they also want to bomb." He pauses. Thomas hands him a glass of bright yellow juice. He drinks it without blinking, then puts a checkmark next to the line.

All the muscles in my body start to tense, and I sit completely stiff and listen to Yoge's words. It's as if he is slowly nailing the Ring's coffin shut and burying us before we have begun our work.

"The last part is Social Media. With fake profiles, they will spread videos, propaganda, and attitudes to increase fear and create an even bigger gap between people. They will also spread rumors about In-Between and try to connect the place with religion." He puts a checkmark next to the last line and puts down his pen.

We all sit still and take turns looking at each other. The sun's rays warm me gently from behind, and if it were not for the sun, it would trickle cold down my spine. Luke looks at me with his clear blue eyes. "Are we getting superpowers when we enter the Ring? Because then I think we can win over the dark men."

Our petrified glances get the spark back. I pull Luke close to me. "I believe we do!"

"Cheers to Luke and superpowers," Meera raises her glass, and Luke grabs his. They hit each other so that they rattle, and yellow juice splashes onto the tablecloth. The rest of us join in.

I lean over toward Thomas and whisper, "What will Kingston try to achieve with all that misfortune?"

He looks at me and responds in a low voice. "Power and external wealth." He pauses and swallows before continuing. "They want to rule the world—to conquer more than any other human has, more than Napoleon, Cesar, or even Alexander the Great. It's the masculine in extreme imbalance."

I don't know what to say. In my pocket, I have the two blue bottles from last night. I get them out and offer Thomas one before I drink the other.

He looks around, drinks it, and straightens up. "The Master has asked us to meet with him in an hour. He will tell us about the process from here."

"Do you know how Gabriel is?" Meera leans forward a bit so she can see Thomas better.

"Gabriel is in critical condition. That's the best answer I can give you." Thomas puts down his fork and takes a sip of the orange juice.

Everyone is sitting still and eating, and it seems to me that we have survived the shock of Yoge's gloomy explanation. I guess it's okay to change the subject. "I'm really curious; how far are you in your process?" I look around the table, and the others can't help but laugh. They know I'm always the most curious of us and want answers to everything. I take a bite of watermelon, and it almost melts in my mouth. It tastes like sun and summer and makes my taste buds dance.

"I haven't been tested yet." Thomas takes a bite of watermelon and looks completely calm. I look over at Meera.

"I have not been tested either."

Agitation begins to build, and one leg bounces up and down. I shift my gaze to Yoge, but he just shakes his head. Then only one left is Shiva. We make eye contact. I take a deep breath and wait. She sits just as calmly and looks at me as if she is trying to calm me down, and shakes her head slightly. It tears in my stomach as if a volcano has erupted and a massive meltdown is on its way.

I know Luke has not been tested either. That means none of us knows if we will be ready in time.

"But when are we being tested?"

"When we're ready." Thomas looks at me while smiling.

Sometimes, the answer can be so obvious that it makes the question sound completely silly. And if it weren't for the fact that Thomas never speaks condescendingly or judgmentally, I would probably have felt that way. But here, everything is allowed, and nothing is condemned.

"I'm still hungry." Luke starts to sit uneasily on the chair. He has eaten a portion of cereal.

"So am I," Thomas takes the tray with bread and cold cuts and hands it to Luke. "Can any of this tempt you?" Luke takes a freshly baked bun and a glass of homemade chocolate spread. He tries to cut the bread and ends up with two halves that are very different in thickness.

"More juice?" Thomas holds up the two carafes. The orange one with orange and apple, or the yellow with pineapple and pear.

"The yellow one." He licks his lips.

I also take a bun when the tray is passed around. The food tastes in every way more intense here. It's as if all the nuances of taste become clearer. I reach for a large platter with watermelon, passion fruit, melons in bright red and yellow colors, dark red strawberries, and pineapple in beautiful patterns. There is nothing better than sitting here and listening to Luke's slight smacking sounds combined with excitement when he gets something in his mouth he has not tasted before. It's one of those magical moments worth saving and requires total presence to catch and store.

Around the café, there are so many different souls, each with their own story. They have left family and friends on Earth who must try their best to live on without them. They leave a trail of pain that will take time to heal. In many ways, it's easier to be the one who leaves than the ones who stay behind. They experience the emptiness and longing and don't know that there is a place where the souls can heal before moving on.

Behind us, the clouds float past. I smile to myself and look over at Luke. He has gotten used to In-Between in record time, and it has become entirely natural for him.

Two young guys walk past our table. They look at us with great curiosity and go to a table a little further away, where a group of other young people is sitting. The others at the table turn around and look at us as the two sit down. I lean over to Thomas, "Does anyone else up here know about the Ring?"

Thomas looks at me, wondering, "No, I wouldn't think so."

"I just think the guys over there looked at us as if they knew who we were."

Thomas moves his gaze toward them. They hurry to look away. The two guys are in their twenties and both physically fit. One has a tattoo of a square pattern that encircles an eye in the middle. The other has some narrow leaves on a branch where the sun, moon, and stars are included. The others at the table look a little older. The conversation is lively, and money is put on the table. Thomas gets up and heads straight for their table. A guy with a gold chain says something to the others, and they become silent. I cannot hear what Thomas is saying to them, but they take the money off the table and leave.

Shortly after, he returns and looks at me. "The guys with the tattoos have just arrived and recognized you from the article that Frank sold to the newspaper. They died in a traffic accident on their motorcycles. They had placed a bet with the others at the table. None of the others believed that anyone on Earth knows about In-Between or the Ring. But I could confirm that they were right."

"But," I cut him off, even though I know it's inappropriate. "Is it a problem that they know about the Ring?"

Thomas shakes his head, "Not really, but I have asked them not to tell anyone else. There's no reason to create more attention around us right now as we enter the final stage of our preparation." He looks at his watch. "It's time to pay the Master a visit."

51

THE ENERGY WORK CAN BEGIN

We walk together to the Master's corridor, through the long bright hallways, to the outer part of In-Between, where there are rarely any other people. The walls float diffusely, and the floors are bright white. Outside, the sun hangs majestically in the sky and brings a warm and delightful vibe to the place. Luke is walking between Thomas and me and holds our hands. He jumps in excitement, and I can sense that he is looking forward to seeing the Master. They have spent time together twice a day, every day since I left. What they have talked about or been doing, I don't know. But it's quite clear that Luke has enjoyed it. Imagine how it would be as a child to be allowed to sit with an enlightened human being—just being in the same room as the Master causes my scale of humility to burst. Luke releases my hand and runs ahead. He passes Yoge, Meera, and Shiva, who are walking in front of us like three musketeers.

Thomas looks at me with his clear blue eyes. "How are you, Eva?"

That is an insanely good question that I wish I could answer. But I cannot. I know that Thomas sees through me immediately if I try to disregard the chaos that sometimes rages inside me and which fights against the uncertainty that is a constant companion in my life. "I…" I look at Luke, who has already reached the end of the hallway. "I think it's hard." That's probably the most honest thing I can answer. "I struggle inside myself with the fear that we will not make it. The doubt. The pain of having to continue alone. The loss of Luke. It's all there and turns into a big gray mass inside me, which I tread water not to sink into."

He holds my arm tightly. "See if you can accept the gray mass and let yourself fall through the emotions. Imagine that emotions are like clouds, each containing its own thought and feeling. But they are just clouds, and underneath are new layers. When you are ready to let go and let yourself fall through, you can do it."

We have reached the mirror passage, where there are many representations of us. Luke is waiting for us and makes several funny faces as he jumps toward the invisible door. Yoge, Meera, and Shiva have caught up with him and are trying to outdo his grimaces. Luke knows precisely where to press to make a section of the wall open in front of him. Before we know it, he has slipped through the door and disappeared down the hall. Thomas stops me and lets the others go first.

He squeezes my arm. "Eva, I'm scared too. This is bigger than any of us. It's a deep condition of life for people to exist in a group. That is where we are most likely to survive. But we must paradoxically move forward alone to make a difference in the world together. My fear takes me directly back to past lives, the lives where I, like you, have been persecuted for speaking my truth." He puts his hand on my cheek and looks me in the eye. "But you are strong; people will find you. You will make a difference."

I try to nod, but my head doesn't move. I look Thomas in the eye and hear what he is saying. But that doesn't change the fact that deep within myself, I doubt whether I have anything to share with other people—anything worth listening to.

"There is still time." Thomas places his hand on my cheek. "You will never be alone. We will be connected energetically, even if we go to different parts of the world." He keeps looking at me. I let my face rest against his hand.

"But we don't know how it will be." I struggle to maintain eye contact.

"No, but you are the one best prepared for navigating on Earth. None of us have been back and forth since we came to In-Between. You have, and you know the drill." He blinks slowly.

"Don't you ever get tired of being there for others and sharing your knowledge?"

He answers without time to think. "No, it gives me energy and refuels my soul."

"But how do you know it's not just an escape from…." I stop myself and can feel my fear of losing myself when I have to start telling others what I see and believe.

He stands completely still and looks at me with a warm glow on his face. "Beautiful soul, it's now that you must step into your light, spread your arms out, and shine. Build bridges so other people can connect their heads and hearts, just like you did. When you set your light free, they will come. They will find you."

I stand entirely still and listen to Thomas's words. They hover between us, ready to be captured and embraced. Build bridges. Deep down, I know we all need to find someone who has walked further in their development than ourselves—someone who shows the way you cannot see yourself.

The door to the Master's corridor is open, and the sound of laughter comes toward us at regular intervals.

"Come, let's join the others and hear what the Master has to say." Thomas takes my hand.

We walk down the narrow hallway that leads to the Master's rooms like two people on their way to say "yes" to each other, walking down the aisle and swearing eternal fidelity. Somehow, we are, but we are not the only ones in the relationship. My gaze is locked ahead, and my heart beats markedly. In a way, it feels like we are about to cross the line where there is no way back—the point where the possibilities close like doors around you, and there is only one way to go. We enter the room. The others don't notice us at all. They are so preoccupied with Luke and the Master, who is about to show them a magic trick. The Master can make Luke disappear and suddenly stand somewhere else in the room. I get overwhelmed with love and look at Thomas, who returns a warm smile. He pulls me close as he whispers in my ear. "Look, everything is as it should be. We just have to go with the flow; then it will all work out."

The Master catches sight of us and finishes the trick. Luke is back next to him as if it were the most natural thing in the world. He puts a hand on Luke's head. "Come, let's go to the garden." With levitating steps, he takes the lead. Luke follows by his side. Thomas and I walk at the back. Outside, the sun shines, and the water trickles from a round red marble ball that rotates slowly. It must be new because I have never noticed it before. That's the beautiful thing about In-Between; things are not always as you think.

The white swans walk around freely, enjoying the sun's rays. The bushes bloom with red flowers, and the sky is clear and blue above us. Next to the lake, there's a circle of stools made of clouds shaped like our power animals. My heart skips a beat. Gabriel sits in a chair under an umbrella, which gives him shade. His eyes are closed, his bald head is shining, and his skin is entirely gray. The Master sits in the only chair that is not shaped like an animal. Opposite him sits Luke on a stool shaped like a rearing horse. The Master is, as always, dressed in a long robe. Today, it is black and hangs loosely around his slender body. The warm dark glow in his skin is in stark contrast to the long white beard that flutters in the wind. Luke has pulled his legs up under him and sits with a straight back. He waves to me, and I hurry to wave back. His wave turns to a thumbs-up, and he smiles all over his little face. I find my stool shaped like an eagle. It has big wings that spread out from my shoulders. It's soft and gives in as I sit down. This is the first time we all have been together since we met in the octagonal room. It feels like an eternity. I look over at Luke. Does he know what he is a part of? Thomas, the Master, and I have tried to explain it to him, but he's just a five-year-old boy. I breathe quietly and await the Master.

"Welcome." He speaks with a deep calmness and lets his gaze wander slowly between us. Our gaze meets. His energy is so intense and clear that I get pushed back on the stool. The gaze is like a sword that cuts through the air with the clearest energy. "The time is approaching. In your own way, you have shown great care in your development. You have looked inside and have become wiser about yourself. The last phase you must go through is energy work to support your body. The transformation you need to go through when the Ring is assembled requires that you can handle very powerful energy with a high frequency."

We all sit completely still and listen. Only leaves on the bushes make a sound when the wind plays with them. Even the swans walk around silently. For once, there are no thoughts inside my head that require my attention. I sit in silence and listen to the Master.

"In the days to come, you will all be part of an intense energy training where your body will slowly be able to hold more and more energy. Once you are through the process, we will test you to make sure you are ready for the transition."

The questions begin to line up inside me. What is the energy work about, and what if we don't get ready for the test? Am I the only one who is affected by creeping unrest here? I gently let my gaze wander unnoticed. The others sit completely still and listen.

The Master leans forward. "As you know, Kingston's plans can increase the pressure on In-Between in the near future. Fortunately, some talented people are expanding the capacity up here so that In-Between is not overloaded. Whether that is enough, only time will tell. If In-Between becomes overloaded with new souls, we might not be able to send you back with all the energy that you need." He closes his eyes briefly. When he opens them, he looks directly at me. "Eva, it will be your job to deal with Kingston when you return to Earth. The next time we meet will be in the octagonal room. This is where the manifestation of the Ring will begin."

52

THE FIVE CORNERSTONES

The others have left, but I'm still sitting in the Master's garden. I need some answers to my questions before I can move on. Luke went with Thomas. They decided to check in on my mother and Andreas in the control room. A swan comes toward me. It stands right in front of me and stares at me. I sit completely still and cannot help but laugh. It's so insistent.

"Valdemar. Let Eva be." It's the Master who has stepped out into the garden again. The swan shakes its feathers and goes to join the other swans in the lake. "What can I do for you, Eva?" He pulls his chair in front of me and takes the position of the swan. Insisting.

I sit completely still and am embraced by the clear energy that lights up around him. He looks so thin while exhibiting tremendous strength. "How do we know it's going to go well?"

"We don't." The Master replies with his usual calm, like a mountain that only moves a few inches a year.

I shake my head and narrow my eyes. "But why should I risk my life and Luke's life if we don't know if we will succeed? And how do we know if we can make a difference?"

The Master sits still and looks at me with his insistent gentle gaze. He nods slowly. "I understand your doubt, Eva. I know it. All people have it. It's a faithful companion in us that helps us stay alert. But remember, it's your choice how much power doubt should have, rather than trust." He takes one of his very long pauses, surpassing the pauses between each of his words. A cloud slides in front of the sun, and the wrinkles on his face become less obvious. "There are five cornerstones that we need to master—trust, awareness, gratitude, love, and responsibility. When we fully master them, we are whole human beings. But the world is missing these qualities, and it's only getting worse very fast. These are the five qualities you must bring back to Earth, quite simply."

I'm not sure it's that simple. All five qualities each hold their depth and have many layers. I can clearly feel it inside myself. A big "but" pushes on.

"The five qualities are all rooted in the deepest part of man, in the meaning of life." The Master holds his hand up to his heart. "It's in the meaningful that you will find answers to your questions. This is where you will know if you're on the right track and not here." He points to his head. "Deep inside our soul, we are driven by searching for the meaning of life in everything we do. It's as if something is calling to us—a small voice we must listen to, and when we manage to connect it with trust, love, awareness, gratitude, and responsibility, we are on the right path, remember that."

Thoughts set in motion as if someone had pressed the play button. Meaning of life? The Ring has germinated my seed of deeper meaning. Maybe it's the quiet shiver I've occasionally noticed that has grown and become stronger. Although it's so far from everything I have previously known and believed in, a part of me has not been in doubt that there was more to life. It's only when thoughts are allowed to run free, and fear takes over that doubt sets in.

"You feel it," the Master looks at me. "You feel the meaning in your soul, Eva. It feels like coming home. If in doubt again, look at *why* you are doing things. Your deepest *why* will lead you home and help you light the way for others."

My body quietly hums as if it had been turned on. "Is there anything else I need to know?"

"When people close their hearts, they cannot feel themselves, and then they lose direction. Unfortunately, a lot of people on Earth have done so. They listen to the dissatisfaction, the limitations, and what they are afraid of and only look at what they are missing or what is being taken from them. These are the people who will make the Ring's work challenging." The sun is back and lights up the Master's eyes. The swans have slipped into the lake and are rocking gently. In the giant eucalyptus trees sits a group of noisy Kookaburras. The Master doesn't allow himself to be disturbed. "There is another thing that you also need to be aware of: Speed."

"Speed," it flies out of my mouth even as I try to hold it back.

"Speed," he repeats, chuckling at my reaction, not to ridicule me, but with love and respect. I feel it. "Speed makes all people more superficial, and if at the same time they cannot feel themselves, then it's a dangerous cocktail. The faster things go and the more efficient everything must be, the easier it is for us humans to get lost. We will skate on the surface and live by assumptions instead of getting to grips with how the context is. Quick conclusions and lack of depth will mean that we lose meaning in what we do. When we lose meaning, we lose ourselves."

As a journalist, I know how much time means; it's the whole focus when making news. Everything has to go fast. It stressed me, so I preferred to do more in-depth articles. The pace got too much for me. But it's not just journalists. It's everywhere. There is a focus on results rather than people, streamlining and measuring even the most minor work processes to make it all more profitable.

"Eva, it's not just at work. It's also the way we talk and are together. Presence is lacking. People assert themselves and only feel worthy if they are seen. Many people lose themselves because they try to fit into the notion of how to live in order to be happy." The Master sits entirely still while he speaks and is not in a hurry.

It's like he can read my mind sometimes. I straighten my back and try not to think about anything.

"It's what we say to each other that has become superficial and indifferent. The way we are together with all our electronics. We lose ourselves with each passing day. It's crucial that we stop and find out what is important to us—what gives life meaning. Follow me..." The Master signals for us to go. He extends his arm, and I take it. Together, we walk along the small path around the lake. Valdemar stretches his neck after us.

My hand glides over the leaves of a bush. They are soft and rubbery. I have repeatedly taken it upon myself to make quick silly remarks to others, even though I could see afterward that the other person could be hurt by it, or it just filled empty space. Now, I ask myself for whose sake I say it. Will it enrich the other, or will it bring them down? But the patterns are hard to see since they are buried so deep in the unconscious. It has become a part of who we are, and we don't pay attention to it anymore.

The Master walks with slow steps beside me. His black robe wraps around his slender body. He looks straight ahead where the path winds around the lake. I have had a hard time feeling my emotions and letting others get close; even though I have felt the longing, I didn't know what to do about it before I came here. But I probably have not seen it as a necessity either. Now, I know it is. Without the connection to myself, nothing makes sense. Warmth flows from my heart, and my shoulders are lowering a bit. Maybe I'm on the right track.

I can feel something pecking at my pants. It's Valdemar walking behind me. I try to wave him away with my hand, but he keeps nipping at my pant leg.

"Valdemar, let Eva be." The Master walks on. Valdemar bends his long neck and disappears into the bush next to the path. A little further ahead, he sticks his head out again.

"Do you know where each of us will arrive on Earth?" I try to change the subject. Most of all, I want to have answers to all my questions before we get around the lake.

"No one knows. When you are gathered to manifest the Ring, the ancient energy from a thousand years takes over and sets the process in motion. It requires a huge energy capacity from In-Between to handle the transformation. Even if you all pass the test, it will only become clear if the energy is strong enough when you are gathered." He speaks with remarkable calm. Even though I have my arm under his, his movements are still hovering, and the black robe is shining in the sun.

"Will we be able to remember each other?" I look up at the sky, which is still entirely blue. I see several small koala bears that look slightly burnt in one of the trees. They are eating the leaves from the tree.

The Master smiles at me. His white teeth light up his dark face. "I will leave it to you to find out." Valdemar has gone back to the lake, where he is watching me. We have reached all the way around.

The Master stops, folds his hands in front of his chest, and bows lightly to me. I reciprocate.

"Eva, you have come a long way on your journey. I rarely meet a soul like yours—so persistent and tenacious. You will find your way home, and you will show others the way. There are many things we don't know but that you can be sure of."

53

BEING IN THE NOW

The last ten days have gone by slowly while the energy load on our bodies has been increased gradually. Yoge has developed a system with some of the other IT wizards up here that can inflict very high energy frequencies on the body. They have built a transparent capsule with a high voltage field. Inside it is a floating bench. We have been lying there for several hours each day, with the system measuring our energy and gradually increasing the pressure.

I'm sitting in my room. It's only five o'clock, but I can't sleep anymore. The sun is already hanging out on the horizon, coloring the room orange.

In addition, we have each worked intensively on our development points. I have been challenged on my insecurity and my need for control. Thomas has worked with the fear of failure and opened the door to the source of life energy and creativity. He has danced and painted with Luke, who has had fun with all of us in turns. Meera has been confronted with her anger and ability to keep her heart open. Both Yoge and Shiva have been challenged on their balance between the introverted and extroverted sides. They both prefer to be by themselves, but when the work of the Ring is to begin, they need to stand up among other people and share their knowledge. We have been subjected to exercises that have challenged our confidence, meditated, been distracted to practice presence, and confronted with our childhood in our last life, past lives, and traumas. All for the purpose of practicing the five cornerstones. Trust, awareness, gratitude, love, and responsibility.

Today is the day we are being tested.

Now, it will show if we are ready. My body is full of energy, and I must admit that even though I'm incredibly nervous, I'm also excited about today's task. The door to Luke's room is closed; he's still asleep. On the table next to the bed are all my notes—everything that I want to try to remember: the good learning points and the tools that I can also share with others. Luke is the only one who has completed the big test. When he decided to stay in In-Between, he was scanned to find out if his energy system was ready to let go of life on Earth before the forty-two days was up. The last days in the energy capsule have shown that he was also ready for the last and final test. I've asked him what it was about, but he says he doesn't remember. It's probably the same way our memory is somehow erased when people can't remember In-Between when they leave. We will not be able to recall the test either. Today, it will be revealed if we can gather the Ring and travel back to Earth with new insight and a higher level of consciousness.

The duvet is thrown to the side, and my feet hit the soft floor. I press the button to the closet, and the door slowly slides up. No matter how much I work with myself, I can't deny that my ego loves luxury. I let my hand glide over the jackets, shirts, blouses, and T-shirts. I stop at a turquoise half-length blazer and grab a white shirt with the most delicate pattern embroidered from the collar—the feminine touch. The drawer with watches slides open at the slightest pressure. My favorite watch is the white one with glittering stones around the dial. I clearly remember the first morning in In-Between when I found the closet with all its glories before I went exploring. I always wear the necklace with the strong purple Sugilite. It would be nice if it lived up to its reputation of giving the person who wears it a higher spiritual clarity and helping to protect against negativity. The clothes are laid out on the bed before I go to the bathroom. It may be the last shower in my old body. I don't know if we remain ourselves when we are part of the Ring. It's a bit strange to think about. I had just gotten used to being Eva and Angela. What if I turn into a third person? The challenge is that Luke won't be Luke either, and how will I find him then?

I turn on the hot water and let it caress my body. Steam quickly fills the room. I close my eyes and enjoy the heat from the water penetrating my skin. I'm not sure if I'm ready to let go of Luke one more time. Slowly, I let my hands run through my wet hair. The water tickles my skin. Does my heart have the strength to lose him again? He's just a little boy—my little boy—but an old soul and only on loan. It strikes me—it's not certain he'll come back as a boy. He might as well come back as a girl or as an adult. It depends on what body they manifest for him. I hold onto the shower. My knees give way, and I slide down to the floor. Silently, I sit with my back against the wall. My hand rests on my heart, which is pounding.

I close my eyes—everything is going to be okay. Luke will find his way and be happy. That's the most important thing to me. The water falls on me like a cloudburst, and I let myself be flooded. I'm so close. It feels like my life finally makes sense. My soul can step into a new life and begin what I have longed for through several lives—to enlighten—not preach, not lecture—just enlighten. My path has been winding, and I have been led astray by myself and my ego. But the longing inside me won over my skepticism. Maybe I did not have a choice. That day on the plane. Was it intended? I'm not saying it was my fault we crashed, but I was given a choice.

The easiest thing would have been to choose to go back and continue as before. But the tiny voice from my soul got my attention, and not knowing where it was taking me, I followed. I rub my face with my palms and turn my head so the water runs down my long hair. All souls are on a journey. Thomas has said that. But there is a difference between how conscious we are and how old our soul is. When I get back to Earth, I will try to find the old souls—those who are already interested in personal development. People who are open and curious and who can feel that there is more to life than they can explain. They are probably more open to change, and maybe we can make a difference together.

I turn off the water and run my hand down over my body to remove the last drops of water. My hair drips on the floor. Gently, I step out of the shower and reach for a towel. My feet leave imprints on the marble floor, and I tiptoe into the room. Outside the window, I can glimpse a huge mountain with snow on top. It's filled with small triangular flags fluttering in the wind. The towel falls to the floor, and I go to the window. It's so close that it feels like I can reach out and touch the peaks of the mountains.

Further down are piles of rubbish left by mountaineers. My open heart is contracting, and I can't help but shake my head. Where is the humility of being a guest on this beautiful Earth? Maybe that was precisely what the Master was talking about, the arrogance and "me" culture. That we forget to think of others and that we are too busy to meet our own needs. I step back and reach for my clothes. It's time for breakfast. Luke can have a lie-in. He knows he can always call me on the Skycon.

Carefully, I open the door and leave quietly.

"Hi, Mom, what took you so long?" Luke is sitting next to my door. His hair is messy, and he has turned his red T-shirt inside out.

"LUKE!" I jump a foot and turn around in the hallway.

He gets up from the floor and leaps up into my arms.

"What are you doing out here? Shouldn't you be asleep?" I hug him close.

"Waiting for you," he smiles his sweetest smile, so his slightly crooked teeth become visible. He has put an elastic band in his half-length bangs, so he has a bristly wisp of hair sticking straight up in the air.

"You are the most beautiful boy in the world," I tighten my grip around him, close my eyes, and suck in his sweet, gentle scent.

"Calm down, Mom; you're squeezing all the air out of me." He pokes out his tongue and tries to wriggle free of my grip.

"Sorry, you are just so amazing. Are you hungry?"

"I am dying of hunger; I've been waiting for ages." Outside the large windows opposite the doors are more than a hundred cranes flying by in a wedge formation.

"Wauuu," Luke jumps to the window, puts his palms on the glass, and squeezes his little nose flat against the pane. The flock glides majestically past. The crane symbolizes the enlightened, Thomas once mentioned to me. I squat behind him and put my arms around his waist.

"It's today you have to be tested, isn't it?" Luke looks at me.

"It is. Do you think I will make it?"

"Well, it was nothing special. Of course, you can do it. You are my mother." He leans back toward me. The heat from his body fills me. I have to hold on to moments like this—the moments where we are entirely present and connected. There is something magical about them.

"I hope so." A slight tingling sensation runs through my body. I take a deep breath and inhale Luke's energy.

"Mom, do you know what's going to happen afterward?" He looks up at me and takes the elastic band out of his hair so that his bangs fall and cover the top of his eyes. We start walking and quickly reach the purple corridor. There are more people here. The current flows toward the café.

I pull a smile and shake my head, "Both yes and no. I know that our task is to return to Earth and raise consciousness. How—I don't know."

"What is consciousness?" He shoots the rubber band, so it lands further up the hallway. In a snap, he picks it up again as we pass.

We turn the corner into the hallway where the large control

room is located. I stop and squat in front of Luke. "Consciousness is like a light in the dark; it makes it easier to see the best way to go."

Luke presses his lips together, "That's smart."

"Do you need to see how Dad and Grandma are doing?"

It takes a while before he replies, "No, not now," then he pulls my hand and picks up the pace again. "I'm hungry."

Luke seems clarified—incredibly clarified for a five-year-old. I was not that clever when I was five years old. I decide that he must ask more questions if he needs to know more about the Ring's work. I don't want to push my need upon him and create a need he apparently doesn't have.

"What would you like for breakfast?" We turn to the large opening of the café.

He licks his lips, "While you have not been here, I have had pancakes," he looks up at me and tilts his head slightly. He is undoubtedly aware of the small manipulative traits that can make most parents give in.

"Then we are having pancakes." We head for two high barstools at the counter. Luke climbs up on one as if it is the easiest thing in the world. Before I get around to sitting down, he sits enthroned with a straight back. A young guy with wavy hair and a white T-shirt stands before us.

"What can I do for you this morning?"

Luke quickly glances at me, and when I say nothing, he does. "We would like three servings of pancakes, with syrup, chocolate, and sprinkles next to it. And we would also like freshly squeezed apple juice, and…" he looks at me, and since I am not protesting, he continues. "Then we would like some Danish pastries." His short legs move at high speed back and forth, and every time he orders one more thing, they pick up speed.

"Is that all?" The young man smiles at Luke and looks over at me.

"Yes, that is it." Luke slams the table lightly and looks very complacent.

There are not that many people in the café yet. Although Luke thinks he has been waiting a long time for me, it's only six o'clock.

"You can go and find a table; then, I'll bring it all to you." The young man smiles at us and starts finding apples for our juice. Luke jumps down from the barstool and runs to our usual table at the back of the cafe.

"Eva?" a voice says behind me.

I turn around.

"Allan! You're still here; it's been a long time." Allan from Alabama, who always sat next to me in the control room watching his five daughters and wife, is standing in front of me. He's wearing his red Alabama jersey.

He looks down, "Yes, but not for long." The joy on his face cracks, and the vulnerability shines through his eyes.

"How are your girls?"

"Eva, they are so sad. I didn't know what to do. They miss me so much, and…." He grabs the strings of his sweater and wraps them around his fingers. His lower lip begins to tremble. "I'm sorry."

I put my arm on his shoulder. "What do you mean? Why are you apologizing? There is nothing you can do. You have to move on, and you have been given the opportunity to say goodbye to them properly. I'm sure they'll do well. They know you are with them in your heart, and they will carry you in theirs."

His dark curly hair is filtered together, and his eyes are slightly bloodshot. He looks down and tries to avoid eye contact. "I tried to help them, to make up for me not being there to support them. I didn't know…."

"What are you talking about, Allan? You can't help your girls from here; you know that. They have their process to go through and their own things to learn." I cast a glimpse at Luke. He has settled in and is already eating his first pancake.

He looks up, and our eyes meet briefly. "It was me who took Luke to the departure room. I didn't know." He collapses into crying.

I stand numb.

"I'm so sorry…."

I ought to be upset with Allan, but I feel no anger inside. I pull out a chair, and he sits down. His face is buried in his palms. I take a seat next to him.

"But… why?" I manage to stutter.

He looks up. "They offered to help my girls. My wife has no job and no money to take care of them, and this would also be enough to send them off to college. Without me, no one can support them. I didn't know what they would do to Luke, I swear. They only asked me to bring him along."

"How do you know Luke?" I sit completely still, breathing quietly to keep my heart from shutting down, giving space to my inner warrior, who would attack Allan instantly.

He reaches for a tissue in his pocket. It looks used, but he still wipes the tears away. "I have met him a couple of times at the place where the musicians hang out. But I didn't know he was your son."

"We don't get greater challenges than our soul can handle." I put a hand on his shoulder and squeeze it. "Everything worked out, and Luke is still here."

"What about you, Eva? Why are you still here?"

I smile at him, "There have been some things I needed to learn before I can move on. But I'll be leaving soon too."

"When?" He looks up. Luke waves to me and continues eating the pancakes.

I shake my head slightly, "I have not been told the time, but it's soon."

"I'm leaving today." He swallows again.

"It will be alright." I stand up and open my arms and invite him for a hug. His stocky round body approaches mine, and I put my arms around him. He begins to shake. I let my feminine energy embrace him so that he can give in to his pain. We stand like that for a while, after which he releases me.

"Thank you." He looks at me with his deep brown eyes. "Thank you; you are a good soul, Eva."

"So are you, Allan." I fold my hands in front of my chest, and he does the same. Then he turns around and leaves the café. When I reach our main table, Luke is eating a bun and has chocolate all around his mouth and forehead.

"Do you want company?"

The voice is right behind me. It's Thomas.

"Yes," Luke shouts before I get a chance to answer.

I sit down next to Luke, who is having a morning party with all his food. Outside the large window behind him hovers a large eagle with the most beautiful pattern, but Luke is too preoccupied with the food to see it.

"I allowed myself to order a bit more." Thomas reaches out and strokes Luke's hair. "Did you sleep well?"

Luke nods eagerly. It doesn't seem possible for him to answer with the amount of bun he has in his mouth.

Thomas looks at me. "Are you ready?"

"I hope so. And you?"

"Yes, I have done what I can. The rest must be up to the universe." He lights the small candles on the table.

"Have you heard more about how and when?" I love our place here at the back of the café and must admit that I will miss In-Between. It's very special to be up here in the clouds. In a short while, it has become my second home and the Ring my new family.

Thomas shakes his head. "Let's enjoy the beautiful morning together."

I understand a hint and take a sip of water.

"Here, Mom, do you want a pancake?" Luke hands the dish to me, and I put a steaming pancake onto my plate. "They are good, but not as good as yours. Thomas, have you tasted Mom's pancakes?"

"No, Luke, I didn't know she could make pancakes." He puts one onto his plate and rolls it with his fingers.

“They are the best, I tell you.” Luke prepares for another big bite. Melted chocolate spread runs out onto the plate. He scrapes it up with his finger, rubs it on top of the pancake, and eats.

My pocket shakes. I let my hand slide down after my Skycon. There is a message from an unknown, and I press it. “Please be at Q32 at 10:00.” I look up at Thomas wide-eyed. “Do you think…?”

“Yes.”

54
THE TEST

"Eva." It comes from a slightly piercing female voice with a heavy accent.

I nod because I cannot get any words out of my dry mouth. The sign says Q32, and the time is 10:02 a.m. If I'm not mistaken, we're in the same area as the Master's corridor. Bright lights with a violet glow fill the hallway. There is no one else here besides the lady and me. She is not very tall and has straight black hair. It's razor cut at the sides and longer on the top of her head. She is wearing a white smock, and, on her feet, she has flip-flops. The passage is long, but there are no windows. The only thing that interrupts the floating wall is a door behind her.

"Ready?"

I don't know why I nod because I feel in no way ready.

"Come." She walks through the door, and I keep up. We enter a round room with windows all the way around and a ceiling shaped like a dome. But there is nothing to see outside the windows—no clouds or land. It seems that the glass is frosted. In the middle of the room is a bench made of ebony. The woman points and I hurry to sit on it.

"Questions?" She looks at me a little tightly, not exactly inviting my string of questions.

I clear my throat. "What is going to happen now?"

She nods her head with a firm jerk. "Wait." Then she disappears out a door, which suddenly appears as she approaches the wall. I can't see what is on the other side, even though I stretch my neck. No more than a few minutes go by; then she's back. This time, she is not alone.

"Meera!" I get up, happy when I see her. "How did it go?"

"SHH!" The lady looks at me firmly and signals for me to be quiet. I sit back down. Meera seems wholly calm and just manages to send a reassuring smile to me before she is pulled past me and out the door. I interpret that as her being okay.

Shortly after, the glass section opens again. This time, it's a slightly older lady who comes into view. She is heading straight toward me and extends her hand. "Dr. Schnyder."

I get up, "Eva." Dr. Schnyder has completely white and ultra-short hair. She looks tanned, and her voice is round and soft. She sits down on the bench next to me.

"Welcome, Eva. You have come to be tested, so we can be sure that you can handle the powerful energy you will soon be exposed to. It's not only the amount of energy that is powerful but also the frequencies. These are frequencies that do not exist on Earth and are more powerful than the kundalini energy."

Kundalini energy, I overheard Thomas talking to the Master about it a long time ago. It's an energy that can arise from the lower back and burn up through the nervous system. It sounded like it could do quite a lot of damage if the body were not prepared. Dr. Schnyder brings out a unit she can write on. "I just have some questions before we continue. Is that okay?"

"Y -yes," I stammer and try hard to get my mouth to produce some saliva to get rid of the feeling of Sahara in my mouth.

"When was the last time you were born?"

"1982."

"How many children do you have?"

"One."

"Have you experienced any energy phenomena?"

I nod and remember the day at Daniel's, where I first experienced a window to past lives—in the bathroom where it all suddenly blackened before my eyes.

"Do you know what it was?"

I shake my head. She seems very patient and takes notes every time I answer.

"Well. Before we continue, we must measure and weigh you. Once that is done, we go next door."

I look around; there is no "next door" to be seen. But that must be where Meera came from.

"You will not be able to remember any of what is happening. And if you asked Luke about it, he could not answer."

I smile.

"The energy is so high that it closes your memory storage centers in the brain." She scrolls down on her paper-like device. "I must also tell you that you will be notified as soon as we have run all the results through the program. It takes about forty minutes. You can choose to wait here, but we can also send you a message. It's up to you."

"I'll wait," I say without hesitation. It's noted on the device. "How long does the test take?"

She smiles at me, "It is irrelevant because you will not notice it once we get started. You will fall into a deep sleep and won't wake up until we are done."

I look around; there is nothing but the bench we are sitting on. I clench my fists to camouflage that my hands start to shake a bit. The restlessness runs down my legs, which I would like to move, but I keep them still.

"Well, that was it. All you have to do is follow me, and I'll take care of the rest. Are you ready?"

55

THE CRUCIAL MOMENT

I slowly sit up and support both hands on the couch to keep my balance. My head spins, making it hard to balance. The light feels extremely bright and makes my eyes sting as I open them. The petite black-haired lady is back. She's standing by my side, ready to escort me out. When I step down on the floor, a jolt goes through my entire body as if I have been on the losing team in a rugby match and have been the target for all the tackles. The lady takes a firm grip under my arm and leads me. She's at least two heads shorter than me. My feet follow my body; I can't do anything else.

The door opens in front of us, and now Yoge is sitting on the bench. I make an effort and send him a nod and smile to signal it's okay. He manages to get up and is about to say something, but the lady stops him with her intense "SHH!" We walk past him and out the door where I came in. I thought. But we don't enter the hallway. Instead, we enter a large bright room with huge sofas and armchairs in warm cognac-colored tones. There is also a chaise lounge, and on the table are chocolate, biscuits, and water.

"Sit?" The lady points first at the chair and then at the chaise lounge.

I point to the chaise lounge, and she firmly pulls me there and places me on it. When she has released me, she picks up chocolate, biscuits, and water and puts them on a small floating table next to me.

"Eat."

"Thank you," I stammer and lean back as I close my eyes. A heavy tapping on my shoulder makes me open my eyes again. The lady stares at me.

"Eat." She hands the bowl of chocolates to me, and I don't dare refuse a piece. I produce a forced smile and put the chocolate in my mouth. It tastes like an explosion of sour and sweet flavor nuances, mild and strong.

"Eat." She hands the bowl to me again, and I take another piece of chocolate. "Drink," the water is poured into a tall narrow glass, and she holds it all the way up to my face. I take it and drink it all in a mouthful.

"Wait here." Then she disappears.

My back rests on the chaise lounge, and I look up at the clouds hovering past the large windows in the ceiling. There is not a sound. I'm trying hard to turn back time and find out what happened. But my mind is entirely blank. The last thing I remember is the doctor with the white hair. Then there is nothing else left in my memory. It's like someone deleted a part of my timeline. It feels mysterious and a bit scary. I reach for the chocolate and put two pieces in my mouth. The infinite weight I experience throughout my body lightens up a bit. One thing's for sure… I'm still here. I'm still in In-Between. It can't have been a total failure. But whether I passed, I don't know. I close my eyes again. My inner eye is entirely bright, and it feels like my body is being pushed down toward the chaise lounge. I'm tired without really being tired. It's not like I need to sleep, but I feel used—as if I had run a half marathon without being fit for it.

How long I lie here, I don't know. It's like time passes by like the clouds in the sky without me being able to do anything about it.

There is complete silence inside me, no thoughts, no emotions, no agenda.

It feels very unfamiliar because I usually have several discussions running in my head simultaneously. They're always about the past and the future, but right now, I'm here. There are no worries I can cultivate or topics that my brain can hook onto. I breathe slowly and open my eyes. There are several cracks in the clouds where the sun's light flows through and magically illuminates the room. Even the water in my glass glistens in the rays of the sun. I take a sip and feel how it trickles down into my stomach. In almost slow motion, I sit up and stretch my legs beyond the edge of the chaise lounge. Even though the floor looks cold, it's warm. As I am about to get up, I hear a faint hiss behind me. I turn gently as my body does not allow any rapid movements.

"Eva."

It's the Master. He is either here because it went well or because I didn't pass the test. There are only two options—none in between. And there are no more opportunities to get ready. The Ring must be assembled very soon. I need to stay focused so the fear doesn't take over and run off with assumptions that I did not pass the test and that the Master is the best person to hand me the bad news.

The Master walks with his always slow and almost floating steps toward me. His face is serious. For every step he takes, the fear gradually grows inside me. He approaches and does not give anything away.

"It's time."

My stomach drops, and I straighten my back. *Time.* Does that mean I have to get out of here, or does it mean…?

His clear eyes look directly at me and almost strike sparks at the encounter with my gaze. He still doesn't show anything and stands completely still in front of me.

"In an hour, we will meet in the octagonal room. Then we will know if you all made it."

56

THE COLLAPSE

I'm heading straight for Luke's room. I try to force my legs to move faster, but they drag across the floor. If there's an hour before we meet in the Ring, there may also be only one hour left with Luke. Every little cell screams inside me. There is no time to waste. Before leaving the Master and the illuminated room, I filled my pockets with chocolate and biscuits, hoping they might give me some strength as I force myself down the long hallways back toward our hallway. My gaze is set straight ahead, and even though I pass several people, I only see them as shadows. I try to speed up, but it doesn't work, and even a snail would get stressed by my slow pace.

Finally, I reach our hallway, the door opens in front of me, and I head straight for Luke's door. As I pass Thomas's door, it opens.

"Eva."

I do not respond. Luke's door is right there, six feet in front of me.

"Eva," Thomas calls again.

I still don't respond. I'm letting no one stop me, not even Thomas. My heart is pounding away, and I start sweating and freezing simultaneously. My gaze gets foggy, and even though I'm standing right in front of Luke's door, it's like I can't reach it. Everything turns dark. I land on the floor with a bang.

"Mom," Luke's voice calls in the distance, and I try to get closer, but nothing happens. I can't move.

"Mom?"

It's like I can see him running in front of me. My body twitches when I suddenly feel a hand on my cheek. Luke disappears, and it goes completely dark. I try to open my eyes but only succeed a little bit. The crack is enough for me to see both Luke and Thomas bent over me. They smile at me, and Luke keeps caressing my cheek.

"Mom, are you awake?"

I only manage to think about nodding; my head doesn't move. Thomas grabs behind my back.

"Here, let us help you up. Is that all right?"

I blink to indicate that I can manage. My body doesn't obey a single one of my commands. I can feel it but not make it do as I want. Thomas slowly pulls me up, so I lean against the wall next to Luke's door.

"Here, drink this." He hands me a glass similar to what I had in the bright room. "Did you drink more than one glass after you were tested?"

I get my head to give some small jerks to the sides.

"That explains why you fell over. Your body has been exposed to an enormous amount of high energy that pushes the nervous system beyond the normal. It can cause your whole body to shut down. The water here re-establishes your nervous system where it has been torn or frayed at the edges. Drink as much as you can. One glass is far from enough." His gaze is loving and full of care.

The glass is empty, and Thomas fills it again. Every sip refuels my body with energy.

"Did you eat any chocolate?" Thomas looks at me urgently.

"Four pieces," I stammer.

"You need more. There are some special antioxidants in it. When the chocolate meets the water, they create a very special connection, which helps remove the pain in your body and return your strength."

Why did no one tell me that? I reach into my pocket and dig out the chocolates and biscuits, holding them out in front of me.

Thomas laughs at me, "You are something, Eva. Eat up so you can get on your feet."

"Time?" I try to moisten my lips so I can talk. "How long have I been here?"

"Only a few minutes." Thomas runs his hand across my forehead and moves a long lock of hair that hangs down.

"Did you make it, Mom?" Luke has sat down right in front of me. The hallway is empty, but no one other than the Ring members can access it. Outside the window hangs a vast black cloud; it has shut off the sun's rays.

"Yes…"

Luke throws himself around my neck, and I squeeze him close. Joy and sorrow fight within me like two hereditary enemies. Thomas squats next to us without saying anything. Gently, he puts his hand on my shoulder, and his inner peace flows through me, giving joy space over sorrow. I start laughing, and Luke joins in. He releases his grip and rubs his nose against mine. The black clouds have drifted away and made room for a gigantic rainbow whose colors paint the entire sky outside the windows. We slide into the rainbow, and the colors light up on all the walls around us. Thomas gets up and extends his hand toward me.

"Wow, how cool is that." Luke looks around, jumps up, and reaches for the colors. Together, they get me on my feet, which feels almost normal again.

"Thank you." My heart boils and burns against my skin as if I was branded from within. For a moment, we dance around in the colors, laughing together—present and at one with the energy.

When the sun wipes away the rainbow, I look at them both. "I know it's not time yet, but would you like to come along to the octagonal room so we can be there before the others arrive?"

Thomas looks at Luke, who doesn't protest and then at me. "It sounds like a good idea."

We walk hand in hand—three souls on their way to new adventures, not knowing where they will take us.

57
THE MANIFESTATIONS

The door to the elevator slowly opens. It will take us to the octagonal room. The last time we stood here, it was just Luke and me. Back then, I didn't know if the Ring would be assembled and if Luke was the right one. Today, I don't know if the others have passed the test and if everything I have been through has any significance. My breathing is slow, and my chest gives way when I fill my lungs with air. Luke presses the button. The elevator starts in a sliding motion. The speed increases and makes my stomach prickle. We stand holding hands, and I can't help but smile. It feels like stepping into a part of the world where no one else has been before. Luke's hand gets an extra squeeze, which he reciprocates immediately. This is how the whole trip goes to the octagonal room. I squeeze, and he squeezes back while we laugh, bringing some lightness to a vital moment waiting ahead.

The elevator slows down, and the door opens. In front of us is the octagonal room. The red banners move slightly as the elevator door's air reaches them. In each corner stands a tall candlestick with lit candles. The brightest white light descends from the pyramid window in the ceiling. Down the stairs are the chairs, with the high backs and carvings of each of our power animals. They are placed in a circle on a fiery red carpet. We humbly enter the room. Luke releases my hand and runs ahead. I turn to Thomas. "You have not told me if you passed the test." Our gaze meets.

"I did." He starts walking down the coal-black stairs. "It took you a long time to ask." He winks, and I ignore him.

"What about the others? Do you know if they made it?" I try to stop him, but he moves on. I get up next to him and pull his shirt like a small child wanting an adult's attention. He can't help but laugh at my persistence and turns to me.

"I don't know. We have to wait until they are here."

The small stones on my white watch glitter as I pull my sleeve slightly to see what time it is. There are fifteen minutes until the meeting begins. I look around the room. Only now do I notice that there are several small symbols carved into the armrests of the chairs. Next to me is Yoge's chair with the elephant. There is an eye on one armrest and a yin and yang symbol on the other.

"Thomas." I stop. The words suddenly drown in an overwhelming sense of separation and loneliness—like a depth that opens beneath me and sucks me down.

He pulls me close and holds me tight. "I know. It's time to say goodbye." He looks at me with his very clear eyes. The white ring around his pupils is almost luminescent.

I hug him. "I love you, Thomas," I whisper into his ear. "Thank you so much for all you have shared with me: your help, your patience, and your infinite source of wise words." He hugs me tighter. "Thank you for taking care of Luke. I will never forget you. You will always have a very special place in my heart."

Our bodies melt together in the most subtle energy, and my heart is completely open. All fortifications are lowered, and all defenses are gone. Here is only vulnerability and love.

"Eva, you are the bravest soul I have ever met and also the funniest and coolest." Thomas leans his head back so we make eye contact. "I will miss you, but always carry you in my heart too." He puts his hand on his chest, giving me a gentle kiss on the cheek. It vibrates in every single small cell in my body, and we keep eye contact. I take a deep breath. The feeling of being torn in the middle and suddenly standing alone in the world, with no connection to the mother ship, sneaks up on me. I take a step back. "It will be exciting too."

Thomas holds onto my shoulders, "It definitely will. We must remember to enjoy it."

Luke is trying out all the chairs, and we walk over to him.

"Mom, I like my chair the best." He has sat in the chair with the rearing horse carved on its backrest.

"It's the most beautiful one. Luke.... " I take his hand and pause.

"I know; you need to say no more. The Master told me we must go on each of our journeys. Buuuuuuut I think we'll meet again. I will definitely look for you." He smiles all over his face, "And you too, Thomas." He slaps Thomas on the stomach.

I squat down in front of him. He has pulled his legs up under him, and his hands are resting on the carved armrests. The backrest is twice as high as him and makes him look small. The fringe hangs loosely down and covers the top of his eyes. "I love you infinitely, Luke. You are the most beautiful soul I have ever met. I'm so proud of you. You are not only a good person, but you are also generous and wise."

He sits absolutely still and looks at me with his blue eyes, where a clear ring around the pupil has appeared. Then he jumps up on the chair and embraces me. Tears begin to roll uncontrollably down my cheeks, and I can't do anything to stop them. "I love you too, Mom. You are the best and coolest mother in the world." He holds his small thin arms around my neck, and I hold his little body. We rock quietly from side to side. The tears keep flowing from my eyes. "I will miss you so much. But I know you will do well. And I will look for you too. We will meet again."

"Yes, Mom, you just have to bake your special pancakes, then I will know it's you."

I can't help but laugh. "I promise."

Thomas puts his hand on my shoulder. The others have entered the room without me noticing it. Luke gets an extra-long hug before I release him. My eyes sting and are guaranteed to be doubled in size. But it doesn't matter. Thomas hands me a tissue. I try to wipe most of the tears away. Slowly, Shiva approaches and embraces me with loving energy. There are no words, only her embrace, which ceases too quickly. Luke extends his hand toward me. My feet drag across the red carpet, and I sit down on my chair next to his. Carved on one of my armrests is a cross, and on the other, an elongated "U" with an inverted drop underneath. I don't know the symbol, but it definitely has a meaning.

"It will be all right, Mom, and now we get superpowers too." He pulls his legs up under him. On his armrests, I can glimpse a small carved hand. It's interesting how I suddenly see something that has been there all along without me noticing it.

The energy in the room is exceptional. It's as if there has never been anything here that has disturbed the vibration or polluted it. No quarrels or egos have exploited it—as clean as freshly fallen snow that glistens in the sun and crunches when you step on it.

There are still two empty chairs. Yoge and Gabriel have not arrived. My mouth is dry, and it feels like I have sand in it. There is no water or anything here that can alleviate my drought condition. The elevator door slides open. Yoge steps in. He pushes Gabriel, who hangs over one armrest of the wheelchair. I can't see if he is conscious. Yoge's face is fossilized. He only looks at Gabriel and does not care about the rest of us. Thomas gets up and meets him. Together, they move Gabriel over to his chair, the one with a carved owl on the back. He briefly opens his eyes and collapses over the armrest. His face is all gray, and his hands are almost only bones and raised blood vessels.

I forget to breathe and make an involuntary gasp when my body suddenly needs oxygen—Luke giggles and grimaces at me. I cannot help but laugh back, even though an inner voice tries to tell me that it's very inappropriate. But I ignore it and keep looking at Luke.

Gabriel's bald forehead shines, and there are big bags under his eyes. If I didn't know he was still breathing, I would be convinced he was dead. Yoge has sat down on the chair to the left of Gabriel. He seems tense and a bit petrified, like a mummy, just unwrapped from his linen. Yoge has never been a bubbling bundle of energy or the one who brought the dead to life, but he looks more serious than he usually does. I don't want to jump to any conclusion, even though my brain tries to entice me to interpret; I move my gaze over to Thomas. He looks back at me with his calm gaze. The door slides open again, and a light breeze makes the candles flutter. It's the Master. He walks with almost floating steps down the stairs and toward us.

This is it.

58

HOPE

We sit completely still; no one says anything, and everyone's eyes are fixed on the Master except Gabriel's. He still hangs over the armrest with his eyes closed.

The Master enters the circle of chairs. He turns quietly around and makes eye contact, one by one. Finally, he walks over and puts a hand on Gabriel's head. A loosely hanging robe covers his slender body with a flying swan decorated on his back. His white hair hangs over his shoulders and is almost the same length as the beard that hangs over his chest and ends in a point.

"The time has come."

My body is covered in goosebumps. In one way, I'm bursting with excitement. On the other hand, I don't want to let go of Luke and all the good we have here in In-Between and with the Ring. But nothing lasts forever. I know—another reason to be in the now and be grateful for the star moments we experience. Suddenly, they are gone, and life goes on.

"You have all worked intensely with your personal development. And you have all passed the test." The Master's words hang in the room.

My heart gallops away as if I had just run up the stairs to the tenth floor and down again.

"Your task is simple. Through thousands of years, humans have evolved. Although they have every opportunity to become more conscious and live from the heart, fear, greed, and hatred have taken over. Man's ability to develop technology, systems, and efficiency is dominating and has taken attention away from personal development. Selfishness, lack of understanding for others, closed hearts, and arrogance prevail. It has fatal consequences, not only for humans but also for animals and nature. We are already seeing the first signs that nature is protesting: forest fires, floods, and hurricanes." He speaks with his always calm voice and pauses between each word, emphasizing the importance of what he says. His hands gesture as he speaks, and he slowly turns around so we are all included.

"Development is like an avalanche; it's almost impossible to stop. Everything goes faster, and everything becomes more superficial. And Kingston makes it even worse." He holds back. His index finger smoothly removes a tear in the corner of his eye. I don't think I have ever seen him so focused before. "There is one thing you must remember. You cannot join any religion or go against any religion. The time is not right, and it's not possible to talk about it yet. Many people are so identified with their religion that it is still dangerous to discuss it. It could cost you your life, and that's not the purpose this time." He pauses and turns all around to make sure we've all heard his words. I look him in the eye as he turns to me. "I would ask you to store this message deep in your soul so that you will remember it. You too, Eva."

I straighten up a bit and feel like a school kid caught red-handed looking at the test answers of the person next to me. My head nods earnestly to convince him that I have understood.

"Kingston will continue to pose a danger. They might try to find you when you return. We will continue to do what we can from here to help you. But on Earth, it will only be Eva who will deal with them if necessary. The rest of you must concentrate only on your task. The task for all of you is to raise consciousness on Earth. Trust must become stronger than fear. Love must be more important than hate and gratitude more than greed. Only then will you have succeeded in the Ring's task. It is important that you make yourself visible and let your voices be heard. You must stand in your light. People on Earth need to be able to find you. You have the insight you need, and the energy you get in the transition will also help you." He pauses again before continuing. "You are the main Ring where the energy source is routed. But many people are unaware that they too can be a part of smaller Rings—Rings that are ready to manifest. When you get back, I want you to help others become ready to join the Rings. Some people are ready and will recognize you right away; others need some time and guidance. Many people live in the dark; you will bring the light." He pauses again. "Whether you will be able to remember each other and In-Between, we don't know. The Ring's energy is generated by you gathering here and opens so that we can manifest a new body for you. For those of you who have been in In-Between for a long time, your bodies will be the same, but the trace from your last incarnation is gone. Meera, Luke, and Eva will get new bodies. It applies to all of you that your body will have enough energy to function for the time you need. What you have learned is deeply stored in your soul. It is hard to say if there is anything else you will remember, and it can be very individual. There may be small things that will bring the memories to life. It may also be that some of your past life experiences will come back to you over time. It's been a thousand years since the Ring was last assembled, and there are still many unknown factors." He looks around at us to make sure we are all engaged. "I have a gift for you. He walks toward the center of the circle, where a hatch opens in the floor and a star-shaped display case raises. At each tip hangs a gold ring on a leather cord, with small knots tied at intervals. He takes the ring on the star branch that points toward Luke and holds it so that it hangs loosely down from his hand. It's a small rustic gold ring, where the blows from the tool that has shaped it are obvious. It's about an inch wide, and the hole a little smaller. Luke bends his head slightly forward, and the Master places the leather cord over his head. "It's made of gold, and in the gold is inscribed a mantra for each of you, which was sealed when it was shaped."

Luke picks his up to look at it, and his eyes glow intensely. The Master takes the next gold ring and comes to me with it. Now, I can get a close look at the ring. He puts the leather cord around my neck, and when the ring hits the middle of my chest, it's like I get an electric jolt. I fail to react but feel the powerful vibration the ring sends through me. The gold is wavy and raw. The ring is not just a ring; it's unpolished and authentic, not like a classic polished wedding ring you wear on your finger. The vibration from it is entirely pure and intact from nature. I look over at Luke, who looks proudly back at me.

The Master continues all the way around until everyone has received their ring. The display case disappears into the floor, leaving a gold circle, just like our ring.

"When you need it, your mantra will be shown. Your soul will help you to solve your task. You will each be sent to a part of the world where you will find your way to help enlighten the people. If you will succeed, only time will tell."

I try to clear my throat, and the Master turns to me. "Eva, do you have anything you want to ask?"

"Yes," I hold back and briefly consider whether it's relevant. It is. "Will we have contact with In-Between and each other while we are on Earth?" I try to look calm and relaxed, but inside me, there is a storm that makes my whole body tremble.

"You are alone; there is no help from here. You can't get in contact with In-Between, and you will not bring your Skycon. You will have access to cryptocurrency so you can manage. The account number will appear as a tattoo on your right forearm, and you will use your fingerprint as a code on the phone, which you will have with you too. In case of an emergency, you can seek help from each other, but you must first find each other. And it's only in extreme emergencies that you may do so."

Now, I get excited; the journalist in me comes forward and is uncontrollable. "Do we know where to look?"

The Master smiles at me. "No, Eva, if you want to find the others, you must follow your heart."

The glass pyramid in the ceiling begins to open above us, and the light becomes more powerful.

"Your journey will begin shortly. I wish you all the best and hope for the Earth, nature, animals, and humanity that you succeed in your task." He folds his hands in front of his chest and walks toward the exit. We all sit entirely still. I reach out for Luke's hand; he looks over at me, and our hands meet. "I love you," I whisper. He reciprocates the smile and sits back on the chair.

"Relax and close your eyes." A deep voice sounds in the room, but there is no one to be seen. I look one last time at Thomas. He smiles at me. His mouth mimes, "see you." I smile back and hope he is right. Hopefully, I will manage to find both Luke and Thomas. There must be a reason I have worked as a journalist. I can't help thinking about whether people will look for us if it is rumored that we have returned—those who may have read Frank's story in the newspaper or those who sense that we are there. Would I have been looking for someone in a spiritual ring if I had heard of it? It's like the story of a secret beach, a myth told through generations, but no one knows for sure. The unrest is ravaging and has set fire to the pain, sorrow, and fear. I can hardly be inside my body. I feel like I'm being ripped to pieces. Luke has closed his eyes and looks like an angel with his fine blond hair and gentle expression. I don't know if I'm ready to let him and Thomas go—if I'm prepared to be alone again—and if I'm ready to start all over.

The light from the glass pyramid becomes more intense, and I have to either run away or close my eyes so as not to be dazzled. I stay seated and close my eyes. Everything is bright and becomes more and more white. Luminous. My body is shaking, and I can no longer feel Luke's hand. I don't know whether we have let go, or I just can't feel it. The light feels like a pillar of energy descending from the sky. It's so powerful that I have a hard time getting air into my lungs. The vibration expands the very small particles in my body. A sea of light opens above us. The energy explodes in my body. It bursts into millions of pieces and dissolves. I can't feel my legs or arms, and I can't open my eyes; there is just an infinite light, and I feel like I am floating. In front of me, I suddenly see an old iron gate.

There is a sign on it that is rusted and overgrown with plants and moss. The sign hangs on only one screw and dangles down to the ground. I'm approaching. A light wind sweeps over the sign and removes the moss and leaves from the plants. "HOPE" is written in rusty letters which have long curly ends. The gate opens in front of me, and the overgrown path that leads into the darkness slowly becomes visible. There is more light coming before me. There are huge old, crooked trees all around, but it's as if they straighten up as light creeps forward, like mica shimmer dust being swept out, making a red carpet in front of me. The sky is pitch black, and no sounds are to be heard. I'm led through the gate and along the path as if a big hand is holding me from beneath and guiding me on my way. The darkness fights against the light, and the trail disappears at times but comes back in front of me. I let myself be led. Everything gets dark again, and I float in nothingness. How long, I have no idea; there is nothing, no direction nor time.

Suddenly, there is an opening in front of me. The path is back, and the light is even brighter. But here is not only the little light from before. Here are seven small streaks of light, which come from different directions and gather in an explosion of white light. At that moment, it feels like I am falling—as if I jumped out of a plane and am in free fall. The light is everywhere and embraces me.

Then, suddenly, I can feel my body again. It's freezing cold here, and I'm trying unsuccessfully to move my fingers. They are entirely rigid, and my eyelids don't respond to my command to open. I wait because I know that the manifestation of the body on Earth can take time. I have done it a few times. But something feels different this time. The light around me doesn't disappear, even though I can begin to feel my body. The light keeps embracing me. Now I can feel something hard beneath me. My hand tries to move, and this time it succeeds. I'm lying on something that feels like rocks. Heat roars in my body, but the soil is cold and moist. I lift my arm, which reluctantly listens. It's heavy as a twenty-pound dumbbell. Slowly, I lead it toward my face, and even though the intention is to hit my eyes, my fingers land on my mouth. My hand moves up to my eyes and rubs them a little to see if they will respond. I squeeze them together before I try to open them again. A small piece of cloud appears.

I support myself on my elbows so I can sit. The clouds hang under me. It gives me a jolt. Am I still in In-Between? Didn't the manifestation of the Ring work? I open my eyes a little more and move resolutely back. I'm lying on a slope on a mountainside. Far down at the bottom of the valley, I can glimpse a mountain village under the low-hanging clouds. My head only moves in small jerks, but it's enough to see all the huge mountains around me that stretch up to the sky. The air is thin. It feels like my brain has had a hard reset like a computer. The only thing I can remember right now is the picture of the iron gate with the sign. Everything else is gone. Quietly, I sit and look out over the vast landscape. An eagle is hovering in the distance. It's keeping an eye on me.

"Hope," I say aloud. "Hope." There is a gold ring hanging on a leather cord around my neck. The sun's rays hit it and dazzle me as I hold it in front of me. The refraction of light forms a floating image where seven small rings are connected. *The Ring and In-Between*, I whisper to myself, but it's still blurry. I pick up a small rock and throw it over the slope. As I stretch out my arm, I notice some numbers on the inside of my arm, but I haven't clue what it means or why they are there. Slowly, I twist the gold ring on the string;

maybe it hides the answers I forgot the questions to. I do remember one thing; I'm here to help raise awareness. How I should do it, I don't know. I gently push back a little, away from the edge where a goat spotted me and set off running. Slowly, I get to my feet. My body is stiff and feels several hundred years old. I look down at myself and notice that I am wearing worn-out jeans and hiking boots. My hand moves up toward my head, where I can see that I have long hair. I pull out a strand; it's brown. So far, so good. I take a deep breath.

The work of the Ring can begin.

59

SIX MONTHS LATER...

I'm sitting in the shade under the big tree, which stands next to my clay hut. I'm all alone. No one has found me yet, and I also know it won't be easy. I can't put a sign on the street that says: "Hi, it's me from In-Between. I'm here to raise awareness. Come and have a chat." The ground around me is sunburned, and the air is so hot that it vibrates. The last six months have been challenging. Everything is going slower than I would like. My brain has devised many ways to begin to spread all the amazing things I have learned and become aware of in In-Between—things that have come back to me slowly. I could get my own podcast, start blogging or make videos. But I have done none of it yet. First of all, I've been placed on the outskirts of a big city and have no internet connection. Second, it took time before I could remember it all, or what I think is the whole picture, because I don't know. Small glimpses began to appear in my dreams—the Mission, Luke, and Thomas. And some are more useful than others, like working out what the tattoo on my arm was. I Googled it and realized after many attempts that I have my own cryptocurrency account, allowing me to buy what I need to get started.

The mountain I landed on was isolated from the outside world, and it wasn't possible to leave due to storms, stubborn rain, and strong winds, which would have made the trip life-threatening. I was there for two months and spent the time talking to the locals and preparing for my role here on Earth. Mentally, it's been a long time since I've just had time by myself without really being able to do anything. The locals offered me both shelter and food. My room consisted of a mattress on the floor, a small opening in the wall, like a window with no glass, and a hole in the floor that was the fireplace. The thirty small clay houses where the families lived close together lay in a valley surrounded by high mountains, impassable unless one is native. A young guy from the village offered to lead me over the mountains when the storm had finally released its hold. He was the first person I met when I arrived back on Earth, and he has been following me ever since. Wherever I go, he has been two steps behind me. The way he looks at me makes me think he senses the frequency I brought with me. His deep brown eyes have a longing in them, and at the same time, they are gentle, caring, and compassionate.

The hammock between the tree's thick branches embraces my body as I lie down in it and slowly rock back and forth. It's made of a worn sheet that was once blue, hung up with braided wires in the old, crooked tree. The amount of people and noise in the city is overwhelming. Here, outside the city, there is space between the houses and only stray dogs that bark disturb the peace. I have found a small house with skewed walls where I can live. It almost blends in with the scorched earth and the open expanses. The young guy from the village is still with me. I believe the house belongs to his tribe; he led me here. He sits faithfully outside the fence on an old milk crate. Nabu, I call him. That's the only word he's said to me. Day in and day out, he is by my side, and even though he only reaches up to my shoulders and is so thin that a gust of wind could knock him over, it feels safe to have him around. When darkness falls, he sneaks through the dilapidated gate held together with steel wire and sleeps on a rug in the garden.

I get up and bend my head forward to get through the opening that represents a door. On the wall in my modest, dark living room hangs an old mirror with dark borders at the edge. The shards draw a pattern that tears my mirror image apart. I take a deep breath and see blue eyes, long brown hair, and a pointed nose. I step back and try to look at my body from a distance. Physically fit. It's both pleasant and homey that I have come back in a body that is mostly a combination of Eva and Angela.

Not a day goes by that I do not think about Luke and Thomas or am tempted to start looking for them.

My house looks like something that has stood here for hundreds of years. There is no electricity, so I survive on a pile of power banks that keep my computer alive for the time being. If I want to be updated on the world outside, it requires a trip to the city, where my power banks can be recharged while I am drained by traffic chaos, people everywhere, and what feels like a valve that takes all the energy out of me.

Right now, my focus is on the five areas of learning that the Master has provided us with: trust, awareness, gratitude, love, and responsibility. I have scratched them into the wall next to the mirror and let my fingers run lightly over them. Trust that I will get help to spread my knowledge when the time is right. The awareness that it will not be as easy as I had hoped. Gratitude for being allowed to make a difference. The love for myself and others. Responsibility. This is the one that will make it all succeed. It's my responsibility to choose trust over fear—to practice seeing perspective in challenges by elevating myself above them and not identifying with emotions and interpretations. I must observe my needs and feelings so that they do not control my actions. Remember to focus on all that succeeds and the beauty around me.

I look out through the openings in the wall. Out on the horizon lies the mountains, stretching toward the sky. They are barren on top, completely raw—quiet and stable as they have been for millions of years. I close my eyes and put my hand on my chest. Love, it's essential to be good to myself. *One step at a time*, I say out into the living room to manifest it. My inner doer has long ago figured out how to get an internet connection in the hut, start my own YouTube channel, and get a million followers within a month. The trick is to be patient and flow at the pace that makes the flower grow and blossom when it's ready, not to pull the sprout so that it turns into a long, thin stem that breaks easily at the slightest wind. Yet my impatience makes me wonder if the others have begun their share of the task.

Shiva turns around and looks at a poster hanging on a construction wall. A smiling picture of her with the long black hair that falls around her face is blown up in large format. "Candidate for next city council." She smiles to herself. It's the ultimate challenge for someone like her who prefers to be alone and keep her opinions to herself. But it allows her to practice standing up and clarifying her messages. The poster to the left shows a man in his late forties, chubby and with faded eyebrows. On the poster to her right is a woman with a tight face, staring eyes, and without a single form of facial expression. It was undoubtedly a challenge to stick to her choice of a feminine blouse over a tight blue shirt and avoid the image being photo-shopped beyond recognition.

The traffic rumbles past, and the noise from the machines at the construction site is overwhelming. Her poster reads, "Choose trust over fear. Take responsibility for the future," in capital letters. She walks past several shops where the façade is covered with brown paper on the inside. Self-printed flyers hang outside, side by side with the timetable for the ferry to Staten Island and advertisements for bus trips. Shiva uses all her willpower to smile at the passersby, who look at her as if she is someone they know. She pulls her long, black hair together and puts on a cap, hoping for a bit of privacy. As a truck stops next to her with the exhaust blowing, she can't help but cough. *Time*, she says to herself. Time is both a friend and an opponent. Development is much faster than when she was here last. She stops and stands in front of one of the countless skyscrapers that have turned their backs on the sun. A mother with a pram is immersed in her cell while the child screams. An older man with a cane is pushed by young people on scooters, who are in a rush. Shiva stands still and looks at the tangle of people—like a storm drifting by but never settling. She grabs the ring on the leather cord, which she wears around her neck, and feels a quiet shiver. The trick is to hold on to yourself and not get carried away. The storm has subtle tentacles with tiny, invisible threads that constantly reach out and envelop those not already engulfed. Every day before leaving her apartment, she shakes her body to music for several minutes. It helps her hold onto herself and shake the chaotic energy out of her body—to resist the chaos of resistance and fear that meets her like a tsunami as soon as she leaves her home. She knows the storm will only get stronger. Many see her as a threat to their freedom, even though she wants the exact opposite. When people are unconscious, they only look at what they can lose, not how they can be enriched. She looks at the ring. Occasionally, it lights up as if a candle is burning inside the gold, giving it a very special glow.

The board in front of Yoge is filled with calculations. There is complete silence in the auditorium. Over a hundred young people try to take notes at the same pace as he speaks but have difficulty keeping up. They sit with hungry eyes, looking at the blackboard and absorbing his knowledge—a knowledge they have not been allowed for many years and others around the world take for granted. The speech flow is only interrupted by the necessary air intake. He reaches for a fresh piece of chalk and sends the small piece he is holding in his hand toward the rubbish bin. He finds a small corner of the board that is not already filled with numbers and continues. Sweat runs from his temples, and his thin hair sticks to his narrow face. The light cotton shirt clings to his tall, skinny body. He places the chalk behind his ear and walks back and forth in front of the board with his hands folded on his back while mumbling into the microphone.

"If only everything were numbers, the world would be different." He stops, looks into the eyes, which light up in the darkness around him, and wipes his hands on his trousers, leaving long white streaks. "It's your job to use this knowledge to create incinerators that can convert plastic into green energy. In a month, you will have to hand in your presentations." He folds his hands on his back and tilts his head mechanically from side to side. "That's all for today."

The young people get up and leave the auditorium. A tiny girl stands for a long time in the fifth row before stepping one step down toward him. Her gaze is fixed on the floor, and she frantically pulls down her shirt to make it look freshly ironed. Yoge has seen her but lets her find the courage to come to him. The blue skirt slightly sways as she steps one step closer. Her legs are almost only bones, and on her arms, she has several scars. Slowly, she raises her gaze. Yoge stands still and waits. There may be days, if not weeks, between a student approaching him, although he always points out that they are welcome. The girl looks at him with her deep brown eyes.

"I want to make a difference in the world," she almost whispers. "Will you help me?"

The sun is high in the sky. Thomas looks out over the sparkling water of the lake, which stretches between the high mountainsides covered with freshly fallen snow. Around him sits a group of about thirty young men and women with closed eyes in white robes. Birds are singing around them, and the sun warms their bodies. No wind moves. A footpath is raised above the ground. It's built of wood and winds across the plain toward the place where they sit. He can see several people approaching in the distance. A few weeks ago, he sat all alone by the lake; now, more and more have joined him every day. They arrive in the early morning hours and sit with him until he gets up and walks back toward the city. No one says anything; they sit still in his presence. He runs his hand through the long, dark blond hair and reaches for his black coat, which lies on a rock next to him. Before he gets up, he folds his hands in front of his chest. Every day, he keeps an eye out for signs that he needs to start talking to them. But the time is not right yet; the energy must manifest itself, and perhaps more will come. He doesn't know. With easy steps, he begins to walk along the footpath. The sun's strength diminishes, and he puts up the collar of his jacket. He glances at a passing cloud and feels a stab in his heart when his thought lands on Eva and Luke. He knows they're out there somewhere, but he doesn't know where. Heat flows through his body because he also knows that Eva will probably find him and Luke. The combination of her love for Luke, curiosity, and drive means that it's only a matter of time.

Gabriel's feet drag across the gravel road and make the dust rise. An elephant walks past him. On its back is a young guy in shiny clothes decorated with pearls. The dust sticks to the moisture in the air, leaving several streaks across his bald forehead where his fingers have touched it. The elephant extends its trunk toward Gabriel, who takes an apple from his sack and holds it out. The soft skin from the trunk meets his hand, leaving a touch of saliva. The bag is empty. He folds it and puts it in the pocket of the slightly oversized trousers held up with red suspenders. His body is bent forward, and he leans on a cane, which he always carries with him. He pats the elephant on the stomach and lets it pass. Along the road are several small stalls selling everything from jewelry to vegetables. A small café is nearby, consisting of four tables with flimsy iron stools placed in the shade under an old tree with a huge wooden crown. It has become his haunt. An elderly, wrinkled woman with a single front tooth serves Chai brewed over an open fire. Gabriel sits down in his usual place, right up against the tree's trunk. He reaches down into his pocket and pulls out a notebook. The pages are tattered, and several of the words are smeared. He turns the pages until he finds the page with the names of everyone in the Ring.

Next to each name are several notes written in a convoluted font that only he can read. The pencil, sharpened with a pocketknife, draws a ring around Meera's name. He has spent the last several weeks trying to tune into the energy frequency of the others. He has managed to find out where they are, but not what Meera, Eva, and Luke look like. Only in extreme emergencies must they seek each other out. Those were the words of the Master. He knows that. He also knows that his body is still too weak to handle the task alone. He can channel the wisdom and has some energy, but he needs someone to lean on. Meera is the one closest to him, even though they arrived at either end of the world's largest continent. He takes a sip of Chai and lets the sweet taste of cinnamon and cloves spread in his mouth. A leaf drops from the top of the tree and lands on his bald forehead. He reaches out for it and holds it in front of him. The pattern is chaotic and yet so precise. They will stand stronger together. It's necessary for him for his contribution to the mission to succeed.

The siren from the ambulance stops. The doors are ripped open, and Meera jumps out onto the road to the woman lying in a pool of blood with gunshot wounds to the chest. She looks around fleetingly. The crowd synchronously turns their backs and slips away as a police car drives up next to the ambulance. The woman on the ground gasps for air and loses consciousness. Her blonde hair and shirt, which have been torn to pieces where the bullet hit, are colored red from blood. Meera pulls the stretcher out of the ambulance. Her breath is white. There are several banners and posters on the ground. Another attempt to shout at the government has been shot down.

"Put pressure on the wound and help me get her up on the stretcher." Meera looks over at her colleague, a guy of the same age with small, square glasses.

A buttoned-up officer stands next to the police car with a distant, cold gaze, smiling smugly. Meera tries to ignore him, but his cold energy sneaks up on her and tingles under her skin. The space is empty of people. The showy buildings with colorful domes and golden spires rise around them. Large snowflakes begin to fall from the black clouds above them. They melt at the meeting with her warm skin and continue like tears down her cheek. She grabs a blanket and wraps it around the woman the best she can. Quickly they get her into the ambulance and head for the nearest hospital. Meera puts a finger on her wrist and notices that her pulse is getting weaker. The woman opens her eyes and looks at Meera. "Don't let my struggle be in vain." Her gaze is intense, and her body fragile, but her inner strength is great. The woman is not just anyone. She is the voice of the young generation who speaks against the country's government—a journalist at a small newspaper, which has gained a large following in a short time. Now, she lies on the stretcher and fights in vain for her life. The bullet has hit a main artery. With a light hand, Meera strokes her hair. "Your fight will not be worthless." Her voice trembles a little, and she puts her hand on the woman's cheek.

The woman's pulse stops.

A tall, young guy with clear blue eyes comes cycling around the corner at high speed. The headphones play soft music, which keeps out the worst traffic noise. The sleeves of the tight-fitting shirt are pulled up. On his wrist, he wears a leather bracelet with a silver anchor.

"ALEX!" The voice tears him out of his universe, and he stops. A young woman with long blonde hair runs out through a large, black iron gate. The buildings around here are old, and the walls whisper stories that are almost a thousand years old. The university is like a city unto itself, where you enter another age.

"You forgot this one…." She holds out a book, breathes, and smiles a bit shyly.

"Thank you, what would I do without you?" He runs his hand across his forehead and removes the half-length blond bangs that are on the verge of reaching down over his eyes. "Are you coming on Saturday?"

"Of course, I don't want to miss your twenty-first birthday." She slaps him on the shoulder. "Do you have any wishes?"

If she only knew what he wished for. But he can't tell. Their gaze meets. She has a fresh quick energy around her. Every time he has tried to talk about something a little deeper than their joint study in psychology, it has been like sticking a shovel in the ground and encountering a hard surface that is impossible to get through. It gives a stab in his heart. He longs for the energy of In-Between, the time with the warm care and presence of Thomas and his mother. But he cannot tell her. She will not be able to understand it. He leads his hand up to the ring that hangs on a leather cord around his neck. It burns against his skin.

"What are you thinking about?" Her voice pulls his attention back on the bike, with the narrow bar pressing against his thighs while he keeps his balance. She fidgets in front of him and looks like someone late for the bus.

"Sorry, I was just somewhere else. See you later?" He blows lightly into his bangs, so they move to the side.

"Sure," she hesitantly hands the book to him, "we could also watch a movie together after homework if you like."

Alex nods, puts on the headphones, and sets off. He steps on the pedals with all his strength so that the chain skips a link, and he is about to lose his balance. It's downhill from here, and ten minutes later, he is far away from the university campus and out on the open stretch where he can go as fast as his legs allow. He practices focusing on what he can do something about and not drowning in the longing. When his body was manifested into an older body, his development came along. But the longing is like a bottomless lake, and the memories are like water lilies floating on it. Like a childhood taken from him before he even managed to finish it, he does what he can to get his whole being involved. But the pain has a hook in him and is constantly trying to pull him underwater. It takes all his attention to stay focused—focus on his opportunities and on all the good he has with him. The easiest thing would be to give in and let himself be swallowed by the depths. He steps even harder on the pedals. Deep inside, he knows he will meet both Thomas and his mother again, but not when. It's about holding onto hope. It's those who are persistent who ultimately succeed; he clearly remembers that his mother said that.

He started at the university in the city where he woke up. With greater knowledge and a good title, he will be ready for his further journey. He stops on the hill and looks out over the fields with swaying sunflowers. It's his safe place away from the city and people. Connected with the sun's energy, he can feel himself and nurture contact with the universe. He looks up. The clouds hang over him in several clumps. At that exact moment, the sun breaks through and dazzles him. The rays hit the ring around his neck and throw a floating reflection of seven smaller circles into the air in front of him as if the sun was a kind of projector. He extends his hand. The reflection sends a jolt through his arm, but he does not pull it back. He knows he's on the right track—as long as he listens to himself, remembers to prioritize time by himself, and takes responsibility for his development, the universe will come together and lead him on his way. The Master is with him. It's as if he's getting little hints. The other day, when he was about to lose heart, someone placed a miniature plastic horse on his luggage rack. At university, he got a position even though the faculty was oversubscribed. Not to mention that every time he opens his computer, an icon on the desktop has disappeared, but it always reappears in a different place after a while. He glances up at the clouds and rolls down the hill. When he reaches the bottom, he lays his bike on the side of the road and begins to walk in between the sunflowers, which protrude far above his head. They sway slightly to the side and let him through.

I know it can be a long time before we meet in the Ring. But I believe we will meet again. I get up from the hammock and walk through the old gate, which reluctantly squeaks as I push it—the dry grass crunches under my feet. The heat is thick and embracing. The clouds hang in several layers above me, and the sun is about to set behind the mountains. I reach my arms up over my head and tilt it back. It's necessary to overcome my fear of putting myself in the spotlight. Thomas would have said that I should look deeper into what lies beneath the fear. Even if it's only baby steps, I have to make myself visible. I turn around on my heels and head for the house.

I light one of the countless candles on the table in front of me. Outside, the moon has appeared and is hanging in the now coal-black sky. The clear light finds its way through the small windows and casts sharp shadows on the walls. On the floor, I have laid a large red carpet. I sit in my armchair, which has a high back and ear flaps, just like the Master's chair, and drink in the clear light from the moon.

It's essential to start small because otherwise, I will never succeed. I open the computer. The truth is quite simply that I'm scared. I'm afraid of the reaction of others, of being wrong, and fearful of being ridiculed. I pull my legs up under me and close my eyes.

This time, I will find the courage to stand by myself, set boundaries, and dare to express everything I have learned and not just tell the stories of others. I want to cultivate gratitude and practice the positive paths in the brain. This time, life must be lived in the present out of trust and not out of fear—opportunities rather than limitations. I want to get to know my emotions so they don't control me. Instead of packing them away, I will start accommodating them and greeting them like old friends coming to visit.

I open my eyes and start to write down my thoughts. My fingers dance lightly across the keys as I think on.

I got a second chance, and I will use it to share who I am and the way I see life. Tomorrow, I will head into town and create my social media accounts and my first post. It hisses through my body. It's a start. *Small steps*, I say to myself. The words press on in my chest.

I'm ready.

There is HOPE.

DEDICATION

This book is dedicated to my two amazing boys who fill my life with love and joy. You are the most incredible souls and my light. I love you with all my heart.

And to my mother and father, who have taught me so many essential things in life and always supported me.

A huge thanks to my sister, who has helped me make my dream come true with her brilliant input and sharp editing.

ABOUT THE AUTHOR

Sagar Constantin is a bestselling Scandinavian author with more than seven books. She writes stories that are both captivating but also highly inspirational.

The In-Between series came to Sagar on her way home from a business trip to India, and she instantly knew that this was a story that she had to share with the world.

She has a great ability to make psychological issues easy to understand and comprehend, and through her reading, it is possible to grow inside and at the same time be highly entertained.

Sagar is also an international speaker and lecturer for businesses. Every year, she trains thousands of people in subjects like personal development, change management, EQ, and High-performance teams.

When she is not writing and teaching, she loves to spend time with her family and enjoys nature walks. Sagar lives in Denmark but travels the world with her work.

To be the first to hear about new releases and bargains—from Sagar Constantin—sign up below.

(I promise not to share your email with anyone else, and I won't clutter your inbox.)

To sign up to receive the NewsLetter go here: https://livingbetween.com

---

Follow Sagar Constantin on BookBub here: https://www.bookbub.com/authors/sagar-constantin

Follow Sagar on BookBub

Connect with Sagar online:

https://www.facebook.com/SagarConstantinAuthor
https://www.instagram.com/sagar.constantin.author/
https://twitter.com/ConstantinSagar
https://www.goodreads.com/sagarconstantin
https://www.linkedin.com/in/sagarconstantin/

Website: https://livingbetween.com
Mail to: info@sagarconstantin.com

www.ingramcontent.com/pod-product-compliance
Lightning Source LLC
Chambersburg PA
CBHW030627310726
48979CB00003B/913

9781954938335